MAY I HAVE YOUR ATTENTION PLEASE

DEBBY MELTZER QUICK

ISBN-9798987187401

Cover and interior design by: Jai Design

Author photograph: Milana Gilligan Photography

Printed in the United States of America

For my father, who lived to see the Red Sox reverse the curse.

TABLE OF CONTENTS

iv

"Back Where You Belong"/38 Special
September 4, 1984

It was the day after Labor Day, the first day of junior year at Francis McKinney High. James parked his car in the student lot and walked to the entrance of the school. Before going inside, he took a quick glance at his clothes to make sure nothing was untucked or tucked if wasn't supposed to be. He felt comfortable in his new black leather vest and Levi's, along with the black AC/DC concert T-shirt he had bought at their show at the Boston Garden the previous spring. His wavy blond hair was growing out nicely from his summer cut, and he was aware it looked better a little bit long. He knew he looked passable, and that some of the girls in his class even thought he was cute. He hoped this year one of those girls would be interested in spending some time with him and willing to get to know him better outside of school.

"Hey James," he heard Chris call from the water fountain under the stairwell where they had met up every morning before school the previous year. Carl was leaning on the wall next to him.

He had known Chris Mahoney and Carl Bishop since elementary school, and they hadn't seen each other in forever. He noticed Carl was also wearing a leather vest and T-shirt, but James wasn't going to let that bother him. It was the style, and it was okay for his friends to be in style, too. Besides, Carl had straight brown hair, brown eyes, and a tan skin tone, compared to James's paler features and blue eyes. James was also taller and slimmer than his friend. He was fairly sure no one at school would accuse them of synchronizing their outfits. Chris, who was the tallest of the three and had similar features to his second cousin Carl, was wearing a white baseball shirt with navy sleeves and Levi's, his usual uniform for the school day. His straight brown hair looked suspiciously like it was growing out in a mullet.

"Where were you all summer?" Carl asked. "I thought we'd at least see you down at the lake."

James stood in the hall. There was no room left for him under the stairs. "My parents didn't rent a cabin this year," he told Carl. "The closest I got to the water this summer was getting hit by the lawn sprinkler on the way home from work." He shrugged. "But, you know, my dad was really busy with his new position at work, and there's always stuff going on with my brother and sister."

"How's Howie doing?" Carl inquired about his brother.

"Oh, about the same, you know," James replied with a shrug. "Not much changes with Howie. He basically only comes home to steal food and do his laundry."

Chris was watching the door. James knew he was keeping an eye out for his long-time girlfriend, Rhonda, but he was also checking out the new freshmen girls coming in. The ninth graders looked so small and vulnerable. James didn't remember being that way at that age, but he was sure he probably had been. Eastboro had moved to the middle school model prior to the previous school year, so when he was a freshman, he and his friends were still students at Josiah Randall Junior High School. They'd had the advantage of being the oldest kids in junior high, and they never had to be the youngest kids when they started high school as sophomores.

"Check out the Madonna wannabes," Chris said, tilting his chin toward the door. James looked over and saw several girls clumped together in the hall wearing miniskirts, ribbed black tank tops, off the shoulder tops, and large cross-shaped jewelry around their necks and in their ears. Several of them had blond highlights in their crimped hair, and two of them were wearing black lace tights. "It's definitely gonna be an interesting year," Chris declared.

Carl grinned. "I hope so." He watched the girls for a few more seconds, then held up his class schedule. "Hey, who do you guys have for US history?" he asked. "I have Mr. Gregg, fourth period. I've heard he's not too bad. He has to be better than Miss Clarey."

The boys were checking their schedules to see which classes they were in together when Sally Bachman came through the door. James coincidentally looked up at exactly that moment. It was a moment that, years later, he would remember happening in slow motion. He didn't recognize her at first. She was at least two inches taller than she had been when he'd last seen her at Randall Junior High. And definitely much curvier. Her straight brown hair fell above her shoulders and was softly layered around her face. She wore a button-down pink shirt with ruffled short sleeves, tight blue jeans, and white sneakers with pink stripes. She had her eye makeup done in a way that flattered her pale blue eyes and long lashes. She looked around with wide eyes and seemed unsure of what to do for a moment. She hadn't been a student at McKinney sophomore year, and James remembered she had gone to private school after ninth grade.

She caught his eye and smiled, relief taking the place of all her nervous energy. "Hey, Jamie!" she said, walking toward him. "How are you?" She didn't wait for an answer as she checked out her surroundings. "I'm so glad to see you! It's my first day here and I have absolutely no idea where to go. Can you tell me where the office is? I'm supposed to check in there when I get here."

James smiled back, amused at remembering how talkative she could get. "Hey, Sally," he said, pointing in the correct direction. "Yeah, it's just down the hall past the lockers, to the right."

"Thanks Jamie," she said. She touched his elbow lightly. "Maybe I'll see you later."

"Yeah, see you later," James responded, watching her as she walked toward the office.

James glanced back at his friends, who were both looking at him oddly. "What?" he said to them with a shrug.

"Hey Jay-mie," said Chris mockingly. "Hey, man, pick your jaw up off the floor!"

"Was that Sally Bachman?" Carl asked. "Wow, she's grown up a lot. Like really," he gestured toward his chest. "She must have been a late bloomer!"

James glowered at his friends to hide his embarrassment. "Shut up, you dufuses," he told them. "Look, Chris, there's Rhonda." Carl and Chris became distracted by Chris's girlfriend and her friends coming through the door, and James quickly turned again toward the main office to try to catch another glimpse of Sally walking away.

James realized he had been staring at Sally. He remembered her clearly from classes they had together at Randall. That seemed like a million years ago. She would sit in front of him and his friends and turn her chair around to talk to them before classes, even though they were from completely different worlds. Her world had nice houses that were spaced apart, mail slots in the doors, and newspapers tossed onto shaded porches. He grew up with cramped streets and a higher crime rate. Not that life was bad or anything. His house was comfortable and roomy, and since his brother and sister had moved out, he had his own room. He had great parents and plenty of food to eat.

Sally had always been kind of awkward and shy, lacking confidence. It was obvious to everyone that she'd had a crush on him at one point in ninth grade—as well as Carl, Chris, and their other friend Pete Cooper, who now went to Murphy High—but she'd never done or said anything about it with any of them. James remembered liking Sally. She was friendly, funny, and non-threatening, like an eager little sister.

He wasn't thinking of her as a little sister now. Sally was definitely cute now, well dressed and put together, and as Carl said, she had developed nicely, but that wasn't it. It was . . . something else. He couldn't put his finger on it. They had both gotten older, more mature and less childlike. But that wasn't it either. There was something he couldn't identify.

He was busy wondering if he and Sally had classes together when the bell rang, and students rushed from the hallways into classrooms. James found his way upstairs to his first period algebra class and took a seat next to Chris. They caught up on what they had been up to since July Fourth until the second bell rang to start the class. Junior year had begun for the class of 1986.

James slogged through history and biology before entering English class right before lunch period. He stopped short when he saw Sally Bachman sitting in the second to last row in the center. He realized he had taken too long to get to class, and as the second bell rang, the only seat remaining was at the back of the room, directly behind Sally. He squeezed by the student-filled desks between them and exchanged smiles with her before he fell heavily into the chair-attached-to-desk contraption that would be his home for the next hour. Their teacher, Mrs. Clark, closed the door, and a small breeze passed through the classroom, causing the smell of strawberry to waft from Sally's hair to his nose. He breathed in deeply, enjoying the scent, before realizing what he was doing.

What the hell was that? I'm sniffing a girl's hair?

Before he could put much thought into it, Mrs. Clark started the class. She wrote instructions on the black board for an icebreaker/name-learning exercise. James sighed and slumped lower into his chair. Instead of listening to the other students speak, he stared at the back of Sally's head, and the curve of her shoulder, and let his mind wander until it was Sally's turn to check in and her voice brought him back to reality.

"Hi, I'm Sally Bachman," she announced, jumping out of her seat, "and I'm new to McKinney this year. I went to Gearhart Prep last year, but I went to Randall Junior High before that, so I know a lot of people here. Something interesting about me? Um, I have two Siamese cats, Milo and Ginger, that are almost identical to each other except Ginger has a white spot next to her nose." She pointed to the spot on her own face. James could only see her arm moving. A few of the girls made "aww" sounds. Sally sat down.

Now it was his turn. He remained in his seat. "I'm James Newell," he said, "and I guess something interesting about me is that I've been playing guitar since fourth grade." Okay, he was done, he could relax. The rest of the students introduced themselves, and then the lesson began. James set out to pay attention to what Mrs. Clark was saying about what to expect in class that year, and caught some of it, but he continued to get distracted by the smell of strawberries coming from the hair in front of him.

Lunch time came and James sat with his friends at the same table they sat at the previous year. While they talked about the cars they wanted to get now that they either had their licenses or would be getting one soon, James played with his food and stared out into the distance. He felt his eyes drifting around the cafeteria, and he was startled to realize he was looking for Sally. He immediately knew this was going to be a problem for him. He had woken up that morning without having any weird thoughts and feelings about any specific girl, just a generic hope to meet someone this year. He was amazed things could change so much in four hours. He felt like he had been hit by lightning. If this continued, his concentration on school this year would be shot.

He spotted her, on the other side of the room, sitting with some of her old friends from Randall. They were talking and laughing. He noticed that when she smiled, she almost glowed. He felt his heart rate speed up inexplicably. He hoped she would look his way, but she couldn't feel his gaze from so far away. He felt like a stalker and looked back at his lunch. His square of pizza had gone cold, but he ate it anyway. He drank his chocolate milk, and while his friends continued to talk about cars and music, he did his best to keep up.

He didn't have any more classes with her that day, and he was relieved. He was able to better focus and talk to people he hadn't seen in months. He felt like the old James again, at least for a while. But he still kept an eye out for Sally in the hallways.

As he walked down the hallway to the door that led to the parking lot at the end of the day, James heard Carl calling behind him. "Wait up, man," he said, jogging the last few feet. "Chris and I are heading for Store 24. Pete's gonna meet us there. He got a new skateboard for his birthday and he's gonna let us try it out. You gonna meet us there?"

James gave it a quick thought. Store 24 had been a popular hangout for him and his friends last year. They would stand outside in the parking lot and talk about life for hours. They'd go inside to buy drinks and snacks and sometimes to use the bathroom if they were allowed. The other boys would smoke in the parking lot, but James had only done that a few times; he had finally made up his mind that he wasn't a smoker. Hanging out after school with his friends was something he had needed badly last year when he didn't want to face going home, but he didn't really want to go back to that scene so quickly this year. And he'd already seen Pete's new skateboard. He had been at Pete's house when his parents had given it to him on his birthday.

"Sorry, I can't today," he told Carl. "I've gotta head straight home. I'm working three nights a week now, and I promised my mom I'd keep up with my homework on my days off so I don't get too far behind, like I did last year."

"You're not blowing us off, are you?" Carl asked. "I mean, we barely heard from you all summer, and now with your job . . ."

James felt bad for how his longtime friend reacted to him not hanging out. "No, it's not that," he reassured him. "I just need to get back in the groove for a bit, and then we'll hang out, I promise. Make sure to tell Pete I said hi, okay?"

"I will," Carl said and turned to leave. He waved back at James.

James wanted to go home but not to do his homework. His every thought kept going back to Sally Bachman. He sauntered to his embarrassingly loud car and made the twenty-minute trip home.

He let himself into his house with his key, dropped his book bag on the floor by the door, and headed to the back of the house to his room. His old dog Ringo followed him back, and once he opened the door, the dog jumped onto his bed and arranged himself on the unmade sheets and blanket. James gave the small terrier mix a few belly rubs then grabbed his guitar from its case. He started to play the first chords to "Stairway to Heaven," the first song he had learned when he started guitar lessons. He immediately felt his shoulders relax and his mind clear. He focused on playing his music while the sun slowly moved across the sky and behind the trees in his front yard, and he heard his mother let herself in through the front door.

"James Phillip!" she bellowed from the hallway as he heard the door close. She often called him by his first and middle names to distinguish him from his father, James Daniel, or to let him know he had done something wrong. He was sure this time it was the latter. "How many times do I have to tell you not to leave your book bag in the middle of the hallway? I almost tripped and broke a leg! Now come here and put it away and tell your mother how your first day of school went!"

James shook his head, rolled his eyes, and carefully laid his guitar in its case. He had a soft spot for his mother and would do anything she asked, but he was still a teenager. How could he be expected to remember everything she told him to do? He greeted his mother with a kiss on the cheek, kicked his book bag to the side of the hall, and followed her into the kitchen to help her put away groceries.

"School was okay," he told her as she handed him a sack of flour that needed to go on the highest shelf, beyond her reach. "I got Mr.

Gross again for Spanish, so at least I know what to expect. Everyone else is new to me, though. Music theory seems pretty cool."

"I'm surprised you're not hanging out with the boys right now," Mrs. Newell said, opening the refrigerator and looking through the cheese drawer. "Did you eat all the Swiss cheese, James?" she asked him. "I didn't get any more because I had a full package in here."

"No, Mom," James denied, placing a can of soup in the cupboard. "But you might want to ask your other son the next time you see him. He's been raiding the fridge again."

"Oh, Howie," she sighed and shook her head dejectedly. She quickly changed the subject. "So why didn't you want to hang out with your friends today?"

"I didn't really feel like it," James told her. "I just wanted to come home and play my guitar."

"Playing the guitar is your thinking activity," Mrs. Newell responded, moving food on the refrigerator shelves to make room for a gallon of milk. "Got a lot to think about?"

"Well, I saw an old friend from Randall today. . . ." James started.

"A girl?" his mother ventured, handing him a single-serving bottle of his favorite juice drink.

"Yeah, a girl, but not one I was ever interested in back then. Her name's Sally. We were friendly at Randall, but just, like, superficially." He popped the top off the juice and took a long swig.

"I hope you were nice to her," Mrs. Newell said, catching his eye. "Junior high can be a hard time for girls. I remember what it was like for your sister. She didn't come into her own until high school, and I know kids can be really mean at that age."

"We were all nice to her when we saw her in class," James said thoughtfully. "But then she left for a year and now she's back. I wonder what her story is."

"You should ask her," his mother encouraged. "If she's new to McKinney, I'm sure she'll need people to talk to, or eat lunch with. Maybe you could be her friend again."

"One more thing, though," James admitted. "She's kind of cute now."

"Oh," his mother said, turning to look at him. "Well, that sure makes things much more interesting."

"Since You've Been Gone"/Rainbow
September 4, 1984

Sally was prone to panic when she was feeling stressed out. Her stomach felt like it was full of butterflies, and her hands were shaking as she got dressed. She was afraid she would poke a hole through the delicate fabric of her pink puffy shirt or stab herself in the eye with her black eyeliner. Eventually she was able to pull it all together and emerged from her room, gold hoop earrings dangling from her ear lobes, to go downstairs for breakfast. She almost tripped on her empty book bag, which had dropped off the banister onto the floor in front of the steps.

Great, she thought, *I'll spend the first day of school in the emergency room and come in tomorrow with a black eye. Great way to make a first impression.* She picked up the bag and hung it back on the railing.

She started toward the kitchen through the dining room. "Don't cut through the dining room, Sally!" her mother yelled out. Sally stopped herself, grimaced, and tiptoed back to the stairs. Cutting through the dining room had become against the rules this summer when her mother had the dining room carpet replaced, but it was hard to remember after being a habit for most of Sally's life. She made her way through the back hallway, past the laundry machines and bathroom, and plunked down in her usual chair at the kitchen table.

"I'm not hungry," she announced to her mother. "If I eat anything, I'll throw up."

Mrs. Bachman smiled supportively at her daughter as she bustled around the kitchen. "Well, try to get to the bathroom first if you're going to vomit. And you have to at least eat an English muffin. I am not sending you to school on an empty stomach." She slid the butter-coated purveyor of nooks and crannies onto the small plate in front of Sally and poured orange juice into the tiny glass behind her plate. "Drink up," her mother commanded. "You'll need the energy to walk to school."

Sally threw her head back in mock distress. "Mother, I don't understand why I have to walk to school! You always drove me last year!"

"Sally Ann, Gearhart Prep was seven miles away," Mrs. Bachman replied, straightening her nylons and strapping on her shoes. "And two towns over on all side streets. School would've been over before you were able to walk there!" She kissed Sally on the top of her head. "You'll be fine. You'll find your old friends, you'll make new friends, and you will not keel over on your walk. Plus, I need to leave for work right now." She pulled her dark brown hair back in a ponytail and applied ChapStick to her lips.

"Fiiiiine," Sally whined in response. "I'll walk to school."

"Good girl," said her mom, walking toward the hallway while putting on her blazer. "Have a great first day. I'll see you around seven tonight." She plucked her overstuffed pocketbook off the top of the washing machine and walked out the back door toward her car.

Sally took two bites of her English muffin and threw the rest in the trash after her mother was safely out the door. She chugged down her orange juice in two gulps and closed her eyes. "It'll be ok, Milo," she said aloud to her brown and tan cat as he weaved around her ankles. "I wanted this. I wanted this. This is what I wanted."

She ran back upstairs to her room and found the pile of Beatles pictures she had cut out of fan magazines. She secured them in a manilla folder so they wouldn't get wrinkled, brought the folder downstairs, and put it gently into her book bag with a roll of tape. "Ginger," she said to her other Siamese cat, "John, Paul, George, and Ringo will make it all okay, right? I hope people still decorate their locker doors in high school!" Gearhart Prep had tiny cubicles instead of lockers, and there was no place for decoration, no room for a personal touch.

She was about to walk out the door when she remembered her house key. It was always embarrassing in junior high when she had to knock on the neighbors' door to borrow their spare key to get into her own house. She once had to wait for two hours in the screened-in porch behind her house until her father got home and let her in. It would be better now, though. She was more focused, more motivated. She could do this.

As she approached the end of her road and turned left onto the busy street she would need to stay on for a little less than a mile to get to her new school, she started to see other students walking in the same direction. They were all ages and sizes. Some she vaguely recognized; others were strangers. They were mostly in pairs or threes. She felt kind of alone.

When she got to McKinney High School, Sally approached the door and took a deep breath. Then she walked through. Much to her relief, the first face she saw was friendly and familiar. Jamie Newell from Randall Junior High. He was standing in the hall with his friends. She felt herself smile. He was always nice to her in the past. She made the quick decision to approach him to say hello and ask directions to the main office. He smiled at her and pointed her down the hall, which appeared to be about a mile long, the last door on the right. She was pleased he had recognized her and called her by name.

Having secured her schedule and school map from the office, Sally made her way to history, her first class. She sighed in relief when she saw Michelle Gorman, her petite red-headed bespectacled friend from Randall, waving to her from the far side of the room. She made her way over and slid into the desk next to her. She had told Michelle she was coming back to public school and was glad she had been on the lookout for her.

They compared schedules and were thrilled to see they had four classes together: history, art, biology, and French III. "You'll really like Monsieur Jones," Michelle told her. "He's hysterical. And he kind of looks like John Taylor from Duran Duran!" They both giggled. They had discovered new age music together in the seventh grade, listening to Flock of Seagulls and Dexy's Midnight Runners while doing projects in art class.

The second bell rang, and Mr. Gregg started to write historical date ranges on the black board. Class had begun.

Right before lunch was English class, and Sally looked forward to it, as she loved to read and discuss plots and write stories and poems.

She hoped for a good teacher who really liked the subject and got the class to like it, too.

Right as the second bell rang to start class, she saw Jamie Newell walk into the room. He saw her and they smiled at each other for the second time that day. He awkwardly squeezed by and sat down at the desk behind her. The classroom was so full, she could feel his breath lightly tickle the back of her neck. Luckily, she couldn't smell his breath.

When lunch finally came around, Sally was starving, having thrown away most of her breakfast. She met up with Michelle in line in the cafeteria, and once they had their steaming hot square pizzas secured on their trays, they made their way to a table where three other girls were already sitting. She knew Kim Drake and Darlene Feinman from Randall and was introduced to Traci Walsh, who had gone to Fremont Junior High. It was an easy group to talk to, and soon Sally was feeling at ease as she laughed and ate. She continued to feel conspicuous in her new surroundings, however, and at times felt people were looking at her. When she looked up and around, she realized her fears were unfounded. Everyone else was focused on their food and their friends, and they were not concerned about the new girl. She let herself relax and concentrate on the conversation.

After the last bell of the day rang, Michelle and Sally met outside the front door of the school and walked to Sally's house. They chatted about their classes, and Sally agreed that Monsieur Jones did look a lot like John Taylor, only with much tamer hair. She was pleased she had retained most of her French from the previous two years. She also told Michelle she was going to enjoy English class and reading the modern classics, *The Great Gatsby* and *Lord of the Flies*. When they got to Sally's house and settled in her bedroom, they talked about boys.

"I'll point out Freddy Pierce to you tomorrow," Michelle said, lowering her voice slightly although no one else was home except the cats. "You probably won't even recognize him. He's gotten super tall. He's still really hot, though. Remember that time in seventh grade when we followed him after school to see where he lived, and he just kept on walking, for like two miles?"

Sally laughed. "Oh my God, how could I ever forget that! We finally had to give up and take the bus home. I always wondered if he realized what we were doing. He must be a senior now!"

"Yes," Michelle replied. "He's the captain of the basketball team. And he's dating Marla Rossi. She's on the cheer squad. I always thought she would end up on the cheer squad dating someone on one of the sports teams. It fits her personality. She was always so rah-rah about everything."

"That's so true!!" Sally exclaimed. "Hey, I saw my favorite band of bad boys from junior high this morning right when I came into school: Chris, Carl, and Jamie. They all still look kind of cute. I can't believe how much older they look! Are they still getting into trouble all the time?"

"No, not so much anymore," Michelle told her. "They still hang out together, but Chris has been going out with Rhonda Jenkins since last year, and he's calmed down a lot. And the other two kind of take his lead. They're a smaller group, too, since Pete went to Murphy, so they can't really cause too much trouble anymore. I think Carl still thinks of himself as a bad boy, though, which is pretty funny, because he was always the least bad of them all!"

They spent the next hour talking and catching up, then Sally put a Journey album on the stereo turntable and they did their homework. By the time Sally's father got home at five thirty, Michelle was ready to go home. Sally and Mr. Bachman gave her a ride. On the way back, Sally filled her dad in on the details of her day.

"It sounds like it went really well," he said. "Are you glad you made the change?"

"Well, I definitely don't miss the uniform!" Sally replied, smiling. "And I like most of my classes and teachers so far. And it's nice to see my old friends. And since my old friends have made new friends, it's like the new friends are already my friends!"

"You can never have too many friends!" Mr. Bachman said, laughing. He made friends easily. He was an avid tennis player and always had partners available when he wanted to play. "Maybe you can get a doubles match together!"

"I don't think so, Dad," Sally said, shaking her head. "One tennis fanatic in the family is enough. I think I'll settle for going out for ice cream at Friendly's or listening to albums in someone's room."

"Speaking of Friendly's," her dad started, "Mom wanted us to fix our own dinner tonight since she won't be done with work until late. Since we're already out, let's go to Friendly's instead. We can have hot fudge sundaes for dessert."

"Obsession"/Animotion
September 6, 1984

James knew the second day of school was always easier. You had met your teachers. You had gotten an idea of what they expected. You knew right away if you would like them, or if they would make your life a living hell for the next nine months. You pretty much sat in the same seats you'd sat in on the day before. There was no school rule about this; it was a universal rule.

Fourth period came around again, and again there was the enticing aroma of strawberry hair in English class. James felt as if it had saturated his clothes, as he could swear he could smell it during lunch.

"Do you guys smell strawberries?" he asked his friends.

"Yeah," Carl replied, swallowing a bite of the sandwich he'd brought from home. "My mom made me peanut butter and jelly with strawberry jam."

"Oh, right."

This time he caught Sally's eye during lunch and gave a small wave. She waved and smiled, then went back to talking to her friends.

It was a different experience, James looking for attention from Sally and feeling like he would take whatever she gave him. It must have been how she'd felt in ninth grade. Now he started to wish he could go back in time and give her more of the attention she sought from him and his friends.

"James. Earth to James," Chris said, waving a hand in front of his face. "Where are you, man? It's like you haven't come back to school yet this year."

"Yeah, I guess I'm just distracted," James admitted. "I've got a lot on my mind."

"You've never had much in your mind, good thing you have something on it!" Carl joked, and Chris laughed. James smiled. Carl's comedic timing was usually off, but this time, he was pretty funny.

"I was trying to say," Chris went on, "that my cousin Vince might be able to hook you up with a new muffler. Your car sounds like a motorboat."

"Vince Bishop?" Carl asked. "Uncle Frank's son? I thought he moved to Framingham this summer."

Chris shook his head. "No, Vince Farmer, Uncle Benny's oldest son. He's the one who was expelled from Murphy a few years ago for trashing a teacher's car when he failed his class."

"I hope his mufflers didn't fall off the back of a truck or anything," James said skeptically. Chris and Carl always had a cousin or two who were up to something, and it was not always on the correct side of the law.

"No, nothing like that," Chris assured him. "He's on the level. He works at a muffler repair shop. He could probably work on your car after school and give you the family discount if I ask him. Do you want me to give him a call tonight?"

"Yeah, that would be great," James said. "The sooner the better. Do you think he could fix my heater fan, too? I need a new blower motor. It's gonna get really cold really fast in there this winter, and I can't afford to bring it to a real mechanic."

"I don't think so," Chris said. "I think he's just got mufflers. But you should definitely get that thing fixed. Can't you ask your parents to pay for it?"

"Nah, my mom told me if I wanted to use my sister's car, I'd have to take care of any repairs on my own," James explained. "But I'm trying to save all my work money to spend on a new car, not on a rusted out old station wagon. If the Cruiser breaks down, I'm gonna have to start taking the bus again."

"I don't even think anyone would have parts for a 1974 Vista Cruiser," Carl said, "and no one's gonna want to ride in that major eyesore with you this winter when it gets freezing outside."

"Yeah," James agreed, his gaze inexplicably drifting to Sally's lunch table again. "That's exactly what I'm worried about."

"Wild Boys"/Duran Duran

Sally recognized most of the boys she'd had crushes on during her three years at Randall, and they still seemed to hang out in the same packs. Some were seniors and some were juniors. Many were the bad boys of her younger days. Back then, she'd had a thing for bad boys. They were different from the other boys she'd grown up with. They would get bad grades and get sent to the principal's office for disrupting class, mouthing off to teachers, and sometimes for smoking in the boys' room. But they didn't seem to care about getting in trouble. Sally was attracted to that attitude, although she tended to care too much about what other people thought. She dreamed of not caring and being able to let loose and do what she wanted. Most of the old bad boys were still cute, and some she would even call handsome now. They had all gotten taller, their shoulders broader, their faces more mature, and generally, they appeared to have mellowed out over time.

Her eyes drifted from boy to boy, taking in the sights. If she made eye contact with a boy, she smiled. And she got a wave from Jamie Newell. She waved back. He had always nice to her. He and Chris, Carl, and Pete had made life easier for her during her awkward early teen years by talking to her, and one time, one of them snapped her bra. She couldn't remember which one. She knew she should have been horrified, but to her, it had been the ultimate 1982 compliment. A bra snapping meant a boy was acknowledging that you existed and had boobs. It felt good to see these boys. The boys at Gearhart had not been quite so welcoming; in fact, they had been the opposite of welcoming, and it hadn't gotten much better as the year went on.

She pushed her food around her plate and made gray gravy rivers in her mashed potatoes. Michelle watched her creating her food landscape. "You could use the carrot rounds to make roads," she suggested. "Or maybe eat your food, one or the other."

Sally laughed. "Yeah, it's pretty gross," she admitted, "but I'm too lazy to get up early and make my lunch." She pushed the food around some more, making mountains and valleys along the sectioned tray. "Michelle, there are so many kids here," she finally said. "I don't know if I can get used to all this chaos. How did you get used to it?"

Michelle shrugged. "I don't know," she answered. "I guess after a while, I just did. But when I came here, we were all new, so we were kind of in it together. It helped to be in classes with other kids from Randall. I guess it was kind of exciting to start high school. You were probably excited when you started Gearhart, right?"

"Yeah," Sally said. "I was excited about getting all dressed up in my uniform for school, and the guys in ties. And some of the teachers were young and cute, like right out of college, so they were fun to look at. Boring though. But then it got cold and icy, and I had to walk outside to get from class to class. I used to use my high heels like an ice pick on the sidewalks! My mom got pissed off because she would have to go get my shoes reheeled!"

Michelle laughed. "Getting shoes reheeled? I didn't even know that was a thing! I guess private school is really different."

Sally nodded and ran her fork along the gravy river. "Yeah, you have no idea," she agreed. "In so many ways. Some I never would have guessed before I went there."

"Along Comes a Woman"/Chicago
September 6, 1984

Thursday was cloudy and nippy with a chance of rain. Sally felt chilled from her walk to school and tried to snuggle into her favorite black and red Boston University sweatshirt as much as she could through her first few classes. She was looking forward to a nice warm lunch for comfort but ended up with a cold tuna sandwich and a Red Delicious apple. When she finished, she brought her tray to the return window and leaned against the wall near the garbage cans, digging through her purse to find a piece of gum or hard candy to combat her tuna breath.

James was sitting with his friends, halfway through his tuna sandwich, when he noticed Sally standing alone by the trash cans. He saw his chance. Without thinking about it further, he pushed his chair back.

"Where are you going?" Carl asked around a bite of his daily peanut butter and jelly.

"I'm gonna go talk to her," he responded, standing up and pushing his chair under the table.

"To who?" Carl followed his gaze. "Sally Bachman?" he asked, looking surprised. "That chatty girl that always tried so hard to be one of the guys? I mean, she definitely looks much hotter these days, but she might still be a total spaz."

"I think she's pretty cute," Chris said. "I might even consider going after her if I didn't have a girlfriend. You should go snag her before someone else does."

"Helpful advice, guys," James responded. "I'll see you later. I'm going in."

"What're you gonna to say to her?" Carl asked. "You can barely even talk to your own self in the mirror!"

James grabbed the tray containing his half-eaten tuna sandwich and an apple with two bites missing and started to walk away. "I'll figure that out once I get there," he called back.

Sally looked up as James approached. "Hey Jamie," she said, her hand still reaching around inside her purse.

"Hey Sally," he said, feeling a slight quiver in his voice, although he wanted to sound confident and flirty. He dumped his trash in the can and stowed his tray in the return area. "How's it going?"

Sally pulled her hand out of her purse, holding a pack of Trident bubble gum with two pieces left.

"Want a piece?" she offered, holding it out to him. "You know, tuna for lunch."

"Thanks," he said, accepting the gum. "So," he said, shoving the gum in his mouth. "Did it hurt?"

Sally looked perplexed. "Did what hurt?"

James cracked an amused smile. "When you fell from heaven."

Sally burst out laughing. "What? Oh my God," she said, glancing at his lunch table and noticing Chris and Carl looking directly at them. The boys immediately turned away. Sally looked at James. "Did Chris and Carl dare you to come over here to give me a corny pick-up line?"

James shoved his hands in the front pockets of his jeans and grinned. "No," he admitted, "I just wanted to talk to you, but I wasn't sure what to say, so I thought I'd say something to make you laugh. That always worked in junior high."

"Well, it worked now, too," Sally told him with a friendly smile. "You've got my attention."

James wavered momentarily, but when he looked at Sally's face, he gained confidence. "So things didn't work out for you at Gearhart?"

Sally nodded. "Yeah, it just wasn't the right place for me. I didn't ever really fit in there. I never knew how to act, or what to say, or how to be myself. So, I asked my parents if I could come back to public school and they said yes, thank God."

"Wow," James sympathized. "I don't think I could've handled feeling like that either. But you seem to be doing okay at McKinney so far, and you've found all your old friends. I'm glad you came back."

"Thanks," Sally replied, looking at James carefully and trying to interpret where this conversation was going. She liked that it was taking place at all. She was glad she ran into him. Jamie was a good guy. Maybe they could be friends again, like they were at Randall. She would really like that. . . .

"So, Sally, do you think you might ever be interested in going out with me?" James blurted out before his common sense could tell him to stop. *She's gonna say no*, he thought immediately. *She hardly knows me anymore. This is gonna be awkward.* But still he continued. "Like on a date?"

Sally quickly looked James in his eyes. And she was shocked to see something there she had not noticed only moments before. She could see he was looking at her differently than he ever had before. And suddenly, without warning, Sally knew she wanted nothing more in the world than to go out on a date with Jamie Newell. "Yeah, that would be great!" she answered quickly and impulsively before she could think of something different or clever to say. "I'd like that."

And then, in that moment, both of their worlds were irrevocably changed forever.

James looked visibly shocked. "Cool," he responded, trying to look and sound cool and feeling like he was failing. But she did say yes. So that was cool. "Maybe this weekend?"

"Okay," Sally said, feeling like she was being compelled by some inner force to speak. She pulled an old, wrinkled receipt from the GAP and a pen out of her purse. She wrote against the wall and then handed the receipt to him. "Here's my number. You can call me, and we can plan something."

James smiled, making his blue eyes twinkle. "Okay, great. I'll call you. Thanks." Miraculously the bell rang to end lunch, right as James ran out of things to say. He wanted to talk to her more, to learn more about who she was now, to watch her looking at him, but not in the middle of the school cafeteria.

"Okay. See you later, Sally."

"See you later."

As James walked out of the cafeteria, he tried to figure out if he had thanked Sally for giving him her number or for agreeing to go out with him in the first place. Either way, he did feel thankful.

"Swept Away"/Diana Ross

When fifth period started, Sally dropped a folded note on Michelle's desk as she made her way to her own desk. It read "Walk home from school with me. Need to talk. Strangest thing happened." Before Michelle could respond, the second bell rang, and Monsieur Jones started speaking to them in French.

They met at the doors after the last period. "What happened?" Michelle asked, grabbing at her arm.

"Wait until we get further away," Sally murmured, pulling her friend along with her until they crossed the street.

"You won't believe who asked me out," she said as they walked along.

"Someone asked you out?" Michelle asked, turning to look at her friend. "On the third day of school? I have no idea. Who was it?"

"Jamie Newell!" Sally exclaimed. "Just out of the blue! It never occurred to me that he might like me!" She took her scrunchie off her wrist and pulled her hair into a high ponytail.

Michelle put her palm to her face. "Jamie Newell? You're kidding! Sally, no one's called him Jamie since ninth grade. I meant to tell you the other day. He goes by James now. He asked you out? What did you say?"

Sally stared at her friend. "No one calls him Jamie? Oh my God! Now I feel like a total idiot. I wonder why he didn't tell me!"

Michelle grinned. "Maybe he thinks you're special or something," she teased. "Please. Tell me you said yes!"

"I said yes!" Sally responded, "He asked me, and I looked at him, and I just knew I had to say yes. I knew I wanted to be alone with him outside of school. I knew I wanted to know every little thing about him. I've never felt anything like that before, and it was so weird, because like five minutes earlier, I wasn't even thinking about him at all! I was sitting at lunch with you, talking about French class!"

"Oh my God, Sally," Michelle stated, shaking her head. "You and James? That's so amazing! You would have just died two years ago if he had asked you out. It's like destiny or something!"

Sally smiled, relieved to have such a positive response from Michelle. "So, he's okay, then? I'm not gonna become a social pariah or anything if I go out with him?"

Michelle laughed. "No, James is still a super nice guy. People like him. And I don't think he's gotten in any trouble since Randall, so that's not an issue anymore. I mean, he's a bit quiet for my tastes, but he's perfect for you."

"Well, that's good to hear." They walked across a busy intersection before Sally spoke again. "Michelle, I need to know, has he dated anyone else since ninth grade? Has he had a girlfriend?"

Michelle thought about it for a minute. "Well, a lot of girls would probably like to go out with him since he's so cute, but I don't think he's been interested in anyone. Wait, he did go out with Cyndi Wells a couple of times last year, but that didn't last too long. It wasn't serious."

"Cyndi? Cyndi with the y in the middle? Didn't she dot the i at the end with a tiny little heart?"

Michelle nodded. "Except she doesn't do the heart thing anymore. And she also dated Carl. And Pete. But not Chris. Well, only because Chris had started going out with Rhonda."

"She sounds like she's gotten kind of trampy," Sally mumbled thoughtfully.

"Sally! Don't be so judgmental!" Michelle said. Then she leaned in closer. "Well, okay, she is kind of trampy. She makes the rounds. But you don't have anything to be jealous of."

"I'm not jealous!" Sally retorted defensively. "I didn't even think of Jamie in that way until about three hours ago. But since then, it's like he's all I can think about!"

"Big Brother"/David Bowie

"So you just asked her out, out of the blue?" Howie asked while pouring laundry detergent directly from the bottle into the washing machine in the basement and turning it on. "And she said yes?"

"Yup," James said as he threw himself down on the floor atop an old, ripped couch cushion, pushing aside a pile of clean sheets and towels. "It's not like I was meeting her for the first time. I've known her since seventh grade." He paused and reflected. "She calls me Jamie."

"Oh no, my brother's got it wicked bad!" Howie chuckled, joining James on the floor. "'She calls me Jamie,'" he mocked in a falsetto.

James picked up a throw pillow from the basement floor and tossed it at his brother's face. "Shut up, jerk. It's not like you've got girls lining up at your door. Your sixteen-year-old brother is doing better with the ladies than you are!"

"Okay, that's true," Howie admitted. "But that's all gonna change. I can't have my kid brother showing me up. I'm gonna go down to the high school and pick up girls, like you. Look out, teenage girls. Maybe I'll find someone who'll call me Howard!"

"Howie, you're a disgusting pervert. You'll just get yourself arrested." James paused again, then asked, "Should I call her tonight?" This was basically a rhetorical question since he had already decided that he would.

"Don't be too desperate, bro. Let her wait a bit. Keep her guessing what you're up to."

James didn't want to wait. He wanted to talk to Sally, even if it did make him seem desperate. Keeping Howie's bad luck with women in mind, he decided to proceed with his original plan of calling her that night.

"Call Me"/Blondie

"Sally! Phone's for you!" her mom yelled from the bottom of the stairs. Then she quickly ran up the stairs and poked her head into Sally's room. "It's a boy," she said in an exaggerated whisper.

Sally's heart skipped a beat. It had to be Jamie. James. She hadn't been expecting a call so soon. She picked up the extension on her nightstand and said, "Hello?" She heard the click of her mother hanging up downstairs.

"Hey Sally, it's Jamie."

"Hey Jamie! James! Oh my God, Michelle told me no one calls you Jamie anymore. I'm sorry, I didn't know. It's like I traveled forward in time, and everyone's different but me!"

"No, Sally, it's okay," he insisted. "I like it when you call me Jamie. Please don't stop."

Sally could feel herself blushing and was glad Jamie couldn't see her. "Oh. Okay, I will then. Jamie."

"And that time traveling thing?" he asked her. "You were affected by it, too. You've changed a lot. In a totally good way."

"Thanks, Jamie," she said, feeling the conversation had headed into uncharted waters.

"So are you still up for going out this weekend?" James asked hopefully.

"Yes, of course. I haven't changed my mind. What do you wanna do?"

"We could go get something to eat on Saturday night, maybe?" he suggested. He thought this would be better than a movie, where he wouldn't be able to look at her and talk to her. "We can always do something else after if we want to."

"I have to work on Saturday from twelve to seven," Sally informed him, "but maybe after that?"

"Yeah, that would be fine. Where do you work?" James asked.

"Over at the Main Street Mall, at a cookie place. It's actually called The Cookie Place. Maybe you've heard of it?" she teased.

"Everyone's heard of The Cookie Place," James stated. "They make the best double chocolate chip cookies. But I've never seen you working there."

"I started there in August, right after my birthday," Sally admitted. "So only about a month."

"So you're just barely sixteen," James said. "Have you gotten your learner's permit yet?"

"Yep. My birthday was on a Sunday, and I went down to the Registry on Monday to get it. But I only started driving lessons last week, so I really don't know what I'm doing yet. Do you have yours?"

"I got my license in July," James boasted. "I turned sixteen in January. Passed the test the first time. So I can come and pick you up at the mall on Saturday."

"Do you have a car?" Sally asked.

"Don't laugh at me," James started, "but I have a 1974 Vista Cruiser station wagon. My sister got it used back in 1979. It has like 225,000 miles on it. It's a total embarrassment!"

Sally laughed. "I'm not laughing at your car; I'm laughing because the embarrassment is having to have your parents drive you around on dates! Having a car is great!"

"That is true," James admitted. "It also beats the bus. I had to take it to school all last year."

"I know the bus well," Sally replied. "I used to take it home from Gearhart. I would have to get two transfers. I am so glad to be done with that!"

"Yeah, I bet," James sympathized. Sally could hear a woman's voice in the background. "Sally, my mom just told me she needs to use the phone, so I have to go in a minute, but let's plan to meet at the mall entrance on Jefferson Street at seven on Saturday?"

"Make it quarter after seven. Give me time to change out of my white polo shirt and tan pants work uniform before we go out. Any ideas where we'll go to eat?"

"What's your favorite type of food?"

"I love Italian," Sally revealed.

"Oh, great, I know a fantastic fancy Italian restaurant we can go to. It's called Papa Gino's." He referred to a local cheap pizza chain that made mediocre food.

"Ah yes, Papa Gino's," Sally played along. "Fancy. And they have that ritzy buffet de salade, with all you can eat slices. You have officially wooed me!"

James laughed. "I'm really looking forward to it. I can't wait to hear what you've been up to since ninth grade."

"Same here."

There was a slight awkward pause as James tried to figure out how to end the call. "So, I guess I'll see you in English class tomorrow. Oh, I know what I wanted to ask you. Why does your hair smell like strawberries? Our desks are so close, I can smell it all through class."

Sally had to stop herself from snorting with laughter, knowing Jamie could smell her hair while she was feeling his breath on her neck. "It's Herbal Essences," she told him. "Strawberry shampoo and conditioner. I hope it's not too overpowering."

"No, it smells really good on you," he admitted. "I like it. Okay, my mom is about to grab the phone out of my hand. I'll see you tomorrow. Have a good night, Sally."

"Good night, Jamie."

"Bye."

"I Can't Fight This Feeling"/REO Speedwagon
September 7, 1984

The next day, when Sally sat down at her desk in English class, she felt her heart start to thump in anticipation. One minute later, James walked toward her. He smiled, and she smiled back.

"Hey," he said, stopping in front of her.

"Hey," she said, feeling like that might be the only word she was capable of speaking at the moment. Looking at him, she felt the stirrings of a new, or maybe a reawakening, attraction. She felt giddy and lightheaded, and her hands were a little shaky. This was different from how she had felt about any of her crushes before, including the one she'd had on James in junior high. She blamed hormones, and the R-rated romance movies she'd seen in the past two years. She was seeing James very differently.

"I wish we had more time before class to talk like we used to," he said, putting his books down on his desk.

"It seemed like we always had more time back then," Sally said.

"And a much smaller school," James said.

Mrs. Clark closed the door as the bell rang. They smiled at each other again before James slid into his seat and they had to turn their attention to the class.

At nine o'clock, James called her again. "I'm at work," he told her, "taking a quick break. I wanted to check in one more time to make sure you still haven't changed your mind. We're still on for 7:15 tomorrow?"

Sally knew by the tone of his voice that he was teasing her about changing her mind. "Yes, my mind is totally made up," she told him. "I'm looking forward to it."

"Okay, great! Me too. I've gotta go. I'm not supposed to be using this phone. So I'll see you tomorrow," James said.

"Bye Jamie." Sally hung up and caught her breath. Two calls in two days. There was something really scary or wonderful or both going on, and she liked it.

At work, James was also catching his breath. He had wanted to call Sally, if only to hear her voice. He had never felt this way before, so immersed in his feelings about a girl. He tried to distract himself with his work but found it wasn't possible. Sally was the distraction now.

"Steppin' Out"/Joe Jackson
September 8, 1984

On Saturday, Sally got up earlier than usual and took a long hot shower. She took extra care with her curling iron and gave her hair a generous spray of Mink hairspray. She packed her makeup to bring with her to work so she would be able to look fresh when Jamie saw her. She woke up Michelle by phone in a panic about what to wear.

"Sally, relax," Michelle encouraged her. "James has seen you in your regular clothes and he still asked you out, so I'm guessing he won't care what you wear. But you can never go wrong with a miniskirt and some cleavage."

Finally settled on an outfit, Sally promised to tell Michelle all the details of her date the next day, ended the call, and got dressed in her work uniform. She grabbed her backpack and called goodbye to her parents as she headed to the bus stop.

"Don't forget your midnight curfew," her mom called after her as the front door closed. "And have a good time, sweetie!"

James had spent most of the day cleaning and detailing his car. Then he ran it through the car wash and prayed it didn't rain. Then he ran himself through the shower and got dressed. He called goodbye to his parents, let them know he would be home late, and was on his way.

James parked his car at a metered spot on Jefferson Street, dropped a dime in the slot, and walked to the entrance of the Main Street Mall five minutes early. Sally was five minutes late, but the wait was worth it. She walked out the door carrying a backpack, looking like she had stepped out of a teen fashion magazine. She was wearing a short sleeve navy blue mini dress that exposed summer tanned legs and muscular calves over her white Keds and matching navy blue socks. A wide navy belt cinched her waist, giving it an hourglass appearance. The neck of the dress was low cut but not too revealing, and she carried a denim jacket over her forearm. She wore a thin gold chain around her neck and large gold hoop earrings to match. Her ears were double pierced, and she wore studs with green stones in her second holes. Her blue eyes seemed to glimmer with her black eyeliner and mascara. There were sparkles next to her eyes and in her hair, and they caught the last rays of the mid-evening sun. She smiled and James nearly tripped over his own feet. He knew he looked decent in his clean Levi's and a button-down, long sleeve, freshly ironed light-blue shirt that matched his eyes, but now looking at how beautiful she looked, he wondered if he was under dressed. She didn't seem to notice. She greeted him and brushed her hand gently against his arm like she had at school. After saying hello, they walked the short distance to the car in a companionable silence.

"Nice car," Sally said as they approached the Cruiser. "It almost looks brand new!"

"Thanks." James smiled. "It takes a bit of maintenance to keep it that way." He silently thanked Chris's cousin Vince for hooking him up with a new muffler so quickly. He opened the passenger side door for Sally, and she slid inside. He waited until she was safely seated before shutting the door and walking around to the driver's side. He could see Sally leaning across the seat to unlock his door.

As he backed out of the space and pulled into the flow of traffic, James told her, "I hope you know I was kidding about Papa Gino's. I really do know a nice Italian place. The place where I work, Luigi's. They have Italian food made by a real Italian chef. I made us a reservation last night. It's not super fancy, but it's good, and the owner and staff there are nice."

"Sounds great," Sally agreed. "Is the owner really named Luigi?"

"He is," James affirmed. "Like the guy in Mario Brothers. But the restaurant was originally opened by his father, who's also named Luigi. My Luigi goes by Lou. And he has a son named . . . guess what?"

"Luigi the third?" Sally ventured.

"You win the big prize," James told her. "Except they call him Trey. That means three in Italian."

"Good thing they're not French or they would call him Trois," Sally said, pronouncing it *twah,* "and that just sounds weird."

James laughed and pushed a cassette into the tape player on the dashboard. The stereo filled with the sounds of Def Leppard's *Pyromania.* "Is this okay?" he asked.

Sally said yes. "Joe Elliot and I actually have the same birthday. And also, Jerry Garcia and Tim Bachman from Bachman Turner Overdrive, who, by the way, is not related to me. I saw Def Leppard at the Centrum last year. They were really good."

"I was at that show, too," James said. "I was in the nosebleed seats, but I think my ears are still ringing from the sound!"

Sally laughed. "I have a grandmother who's been deaf since she was a little kid. She gets upset when I tell her I'm going to concerts. She thinks we're gonna be a whole generation of middle-aged adults with hearing loss! She's probably right. And don't get her started on the evils of headphones!"

They rode on, talking about concerts they had seen, and discovered they had similar taste in music. They were both getting into the Irish band U2, who would be touring the United States the next year, and they both hoped to get tickets for a show when they came to town.

After about fifteen minutes, James pulled the Cruiser into the parking lot of a small restaurant with an Italian flag on the sign.

"I've been here before!" Sally exclaimed. "I think it was for my sister's birthday a couple of years ago. They've got great chocolate cake here."

"It is really good. Sometimes I get leftovers. We could share a piece after dinner if you want," James suggested.

"No thanks," Sally objected quickly. "If you're gonna hang out with me, you'll need to learn that I'm pretty selfish when it comes to dessert, especially chocolate! We'll each have to have our own piece."

James laughed as he parked and then came around quickly and opened Sally's door before she had a chance to do it herself.

They crossed the parking lot and entered through the open front door. A pretty hostess in her twenties with long brown hair and large brown eyes looked up and smiled when she saw them.

"Ciao, James!" she said in Italian with an American accent. "I've got a table ready for you. Welcome." She looked at Sally warmly.

They were led past other diners to a small table by the window. A flickering tea light candle glowed from inside a clear glass globe at the center of the table, and a single red rose in a bud vase stood to the side. They were given a basket of warm rolls and butter along with their menus, and the hostess returned immediately to fill their water glasses. Sally saw the hostess give James a friendly wink as she walked away.

"She seems nice," she told him.

"She is," James agreed. "I've worked with Estella for a long time. She's Lou's niece. When I told her I was coming in tonight with a date, she told me she would make sure to save us the best table in the place. I've never actually brought a date here before," he admitted. "It pays to have connections."

The waiter, who also greeted James warmly, soon came over, first to take drink orders and then again for their dinner orders; eggplant parm, garden salad with honey mustard dressing on the side, and a Slice for Sally, and spaghetti with meatballs, garlic bread, and a Coke for James. Menus removed from the table, they now turned their attention to each other.

"You were telling me about Gearhart Prep the other day. What was it like there?" James wondered.

"I mean, I guess the school itself is okay," Sally started. "It's a beautiful campus with old buildings and a nice green quad, and mostly everyone is friendly to your face."

"Only to your face? That doesn't sound too great," James sympathized.

"No, it wasn't. I would hear that people I thought were my friends were talking about me behind my back, about things I said, how I did my hair, the cars my parents drove . . . all sorts of stupid things. I thought having a school uniform would help level the playing field, but it didn't. It wasn't only me. They all talked about each other, too. Some of the kids in my class tried to get me to join in, but I couldn't get into that."

"Sounds nasty."

"It was," Sally agreed. "It was impossible to be one of the new kids, and try to fit in. A lot of the girls had their own horses that they showed. And a lot of the boys had sports cars. They all went to the same country club. Well, not all of them. I mean, there were some other kids with scholarships like me, but I didn't have much in common with them, either. They were just trying to blend in with the other kids. I always seemed to be putting my foot in my mouth when I tried to start conversations with kids in my classes."

"I know that feeling," James related. "Sometimes, I keep my mouth shut, because I'm afraid I'm gonna say something stupid."

"Well, you don't need to worry about that with me," Sally reassured him. "If you said something stupid, I would probably say something even stupider back to you."

"Why did you go there in the first place?" James asked.

"Well," Sally recounted, "my older brother, Nathan, was bullied a lot at Randall. My parents thought he'd do better in a private school with smaller classes where he could focus on academics instead of survival, and it turned out to be good for him. When it was time for me to go to high school, they asked me if I wanted to go there, and I thought it would be nice to have a fresh start. So, when I did well on the scholarship test, I decided to give it a try."

"Makes sense," James agreed.

"Yeah. But it turns out it wasn't better for me. Either socially or academically. I didn't get particularly good grades, and I ended up losing my scholarship." She stopped for a moment and looked him in the eyes. "Please don't tell anyone. It's pretty embarrassing." James made the motion of zipping his lips. "My parents asked if I wanted to still go there, and they would find a way to pay for it, but I just couldn't do that to them. They probably would have had to put a second mortgage on our house or something. Plus, I missed being a normal kid in a normal school, and not sticking out like a sore thumb."

James nodded. "I think you made the right choice."

Sally smiled. "I do, too. What about you? Weren't you supposed to go to Murphy High last year? How did you end up at McKinney?"

"My story's pretty much the opposite of yours," James told her. "My older brother, Howie, was probably one of the kids that bullied your brother at Randall. He was getting in trouble all the time. He was always getting suspended for some type of stupid thing. I think they only gave him a diploma in the end so he'd leave. My mom thought it would be hard for me to go to Murphy after him, and always be known as the brother of the bad kid. Which is weird, because my sister Erin's a senior at Brown University, and she was a really good student. All the teachers loved her. You know, I might have been one of the bad boys at Randall, but compared to Howie, I was a boy scout. I mean, I was a bad student and hung out with troublemakers. But Howie was bad enough to ruin our family name. My mom works for the school district, so she was able to figure out a way to get me a transfer. It's a long drive, but I'm glad I got to go to McKinney, because it turns out I kind of like it there."

"Well, I'm glad you transferred," Sally revealed. "It would be weird to see Carl and Chris around school without you. And I don't know what I would have done on Tuesday if I didn't see you right off. I probably would've wandered the halls like an idiot trying to find where to go. I might still be there now!"

"Yeah," James agreed with a grin, "and if I hadn't transferred, I never would have asked you out by the garbage cans!"

They laughed together. "Yeah, that was a bit of a shocker," Sally said. "I was not expecting that."

"To be honest, Sally, neither was I," James admitted. "I didn't plan to ask you out. I just wanted to talk to you. But when you were digging for the gum in your purse and talking about tuna breath, I couldn't help myself. I wanted to talk to you more, to hear what else you had to say." There was a moment of silence neither dared to fill. Then James said, "I wish we had more classes together. It would be like the old days at Randall. Making fun of teachers before class, and generally just goofing around."

"Yeah, that was fun," Sally agreed, looking off in the distance with her memories. "Remember when we were in shop class together in eighth grade?" she asked.

"Yes!" James responded. "I loved that class. We made metal bird houses and did silk screening on shirts."

"Remember the shirt I silk screened with that complicated picture from the J. Geils album cover?"

"Oh, yeah, I remember that! It took you weeks to finish that thing. It turned out pretty good. How come you don't wear that anymore?"

Sally shot him a look. "I was thirteen years old. I kind of grew out of it."

"I guess you did," James said with a smile.

In the short silence that followed, James had an epiphany.

"I figured it out," he said.

"What?" Sally asked.

"I know why things were so weird for me on the first day of school," he told her.

"They were?"

"Yeah," said James more confidently. "When I first saw you coming in the door that day, I was completely caught off guard. I wasn't expecting it. I had, what do you call it . . . a visceral reaction or something. It was kind of weird."

"I'm sorry," Sally said genuinely.

"No," James reassured her. "It's not your fault. But I couldn't make sense of it. Now I kind of can."

"What is it?" Sally insisted.

"I missed you," he revealed. "Without ever knowing it, I missed you last year."

"What?"

"Okay," James started, "just remember I have no filter between my brain and my mouth, so bear with me. Sometimes I blurt things out without thinking them through first."

Sally grinned. "Yes, we've established that we both do this. So go on, you missed me?" she urged him to continue.

"Yeah, and I didn't know it until I saw you again. I liked having you around at Randall, talking to you before class and joking around with you. You made me laugh. Like a lot. And the fact that you never missed a beat with me and my friends was pretty cool. Even though it was obvious you had crushes on us."

"I did not!" Sally objected strongly. She sighed and slumped a little in her seat. "Okay, well maybe I did, but they weren't serious, and it was just one of you at a time. I probably would have died on the spot if any of you had actually asked me out. Hanging out with you guys helped me to get through the long, boring afternoons of junior high."

"It was a small service we provided," James said, showing her a smile. "And I guess one I liked, too. I'm thinking maybe you had more of an effect on me than I ever knew. It's hard to imagine what those classes would have been like without you. And last year was a rough year for me. There was a lot of stuff going on at home. It would have been nice to have some things to laugh about. I guess maybe I realize now that things would have been a lot nicer if you had been around." He collected his thoughts for a moment. "I don't know why it took me three days to work up my nerve to talk to you. I mean, we never had trouble talking to each other before. But I finally did. And it was the smartest thing I've ever done at school. Well, that, and then asking you out. I'm glad I did that, too." He stopped talking and looked at her for several seconds. "I don't think I told you, but you look great tonight."

"Thank you," Sally responded. "You clean up nicely, too," she said, borrowing a phrase she'd heard her father say.

She didn't know what else to say. She had never had anyone feel anything but friendship or familial love toward her. She had dated, but never had a real boyfriend or anyone she was as interested in talking to, or being with, and it was all happening so fast. She felt she and Jamie had known each other for years, and talking to him was so easy, but then he would say something that would render her silent. They both stayed quiet for what felt like minutes, but was probably less than one minute, looking at each other.

Finally, James reached out and touched Sally's cheek lightly. "I like those sparkles on your face," he said softly. "Do you think if I kissed you later, I would get sparkles on my face, too?"

Sally felt the blush rising from her neck and her face tingled beneath his touch. Her heart started to pound. She answered, "Yes, for sure, you will get sparkles on your face."

They both paused for a moment to contemplate what they had said to each other then resumed their conversation as if they hadn't said it, knowing they had.

They ate their food slowly, taking care not to spray tomato sauce on each other, taking long pauses to chew. When they finished and their plates were cleared away, they talked more about their families, their pets, and things they liked to do.

The waiter came back out with two servings of chocolate cake they had ordered. "These are on the house, James," he stated. "Lou knows how much you make here!"

James took a forkful of his cake and watched Sally do the same. "I don't know, Sally," he said, smiling, "it might have been more fun to have one plate and two forks!"

After James paid the bill, he suggested they go for a walk at Twin Bridges Park. It was on the way to Sally's house, and it was a nice evening to be outside. She agreed to this plan, and they returned to James's car.

"Can't Take My Eyes Off You"/Frankie Valli and the Four Seasons

They parked on Wichita Street and walked slowly through the park toward the pond. By silent consensus, they made their way to the taller of the two bridges and started to climb to the top. James stepped behind Sally and playfully helped push her up the steep incline, feeling happy to be able to touch her in any way. When they got to the top, they leaned against the safety rail, looking out toward the water, and silently watched the ducks and swans swimming out from under the bridge by the light of the streetlamp. Both noticed an increase in their heart rate, and James discretely wiped his sweaty palms on the legs of his jeans.

They turned to each other to speak, but before either of them got a word out, they found themselves kissing, neither of them sure who initiated it. Sally felt her knees start to buckle. She had kissed boys before, on dates, at dances, and at youth group events, but never anyone with whom she had such an intense attraction. She felt electricity through her lips, traveling down her spine and throughout her body, and somehow knew James felt it, too. She sensed his arms circling her waist, and she let hers rise up and encircle his neck. She felt them pull closer to each other until their bodies were touching completely. The kiss continued, even as they pulled away briefly to make almost too intense eye contact then came back together. It felt like time was standing still. Their connection felt both old and new.

They heard the sounds of faint footsteps behind them, and Sally felt a cold dog nose poking at her calf. They came apart to see an older couple walking up one side of the bridge with their Pomeranian on a long leash. The couple looked at them, not with judgment, but with what Sally thought were wise and wistful eyes. They smiled at the younger couple and then continued down the other side.

James took Sally's hand and said, "C'mon, let's go down by the pond and sit on one of the benches."

James could hardly feel his feet beneath him as they walked down the opposite slope toward the benches. They sat down quietly for a moment, and then, with no words exchanged, they were kissing again. Now they didn't need to worry about losing their balance and accidentally falling down the side of the bridge, and they were not so conspicuous out of the direct streetlight.

After some time, they stopped, out of breath, and sat with James's arm around Sally's shoulder, her head resting on his chest. They talked intimately about everything and nothing for a long time.

"So, you missed me?" she asked him, entwining her fingers with his.

"I guess I did," he admitted.

"I wonder if it would have been the same if I had never left."

"I don't know, but let's pretend it would be."

"I'm glad I came back."

"I am, too. Very glad."

"Jamie, you have sparkles on your face."

"Just leave them there, Sally,"

"I have to go home before I turn into a pumpkin."

James hadn't realized how much time had passed. It was 11:15, and they had been at the park for nearly two hours. Sally had a midnight curfew. They sat up, and then he reached over, put his arms around her, and kissed her deeply and thoroughly one last time. After another five minutes, they walked hand in hand to his car.

"West End Girls"/Pet Shop Boys

Sally directed James back to her neighborhood. He hadn't envisioned what her house would look like, but he wasn't expecting what he saw when he pulled into her driveway. In his mind, Lincoln kids were all well-off, although Sally had made some comments that made him think that might not be the case with her family. The house Sally lived in was a two-story blue colonial but not much bigger than the ranch he lived in with his family. It had a medium-sized nicely manicured front yard with ornamental trees, just like the lawn at his house. In his headlights, he could see a maroon Honda Accord sedan, and a blue Ford Escort station wagon parked at the foot of the driveway. It occurred to him Sally might be growing up in a family kind of like his own: comfortable, but not rich, with parents that chose practicality over excess. He was going to have to stop making assumptions about people based on what elementary school they'd gone to.

"Nice house," he told her honestly.

She smiled. "Thanks! I love it. My parents bought it when I was four. We used to live on two floors of a three-decker over by East Firehouse, but I don't remember living there too well. It's my grandparent's house, and I had to share a room with my older sister." She pointed to the right corner window upstairs. "That's my room," she told him. "The house was tiny when we moved in, but my parents had an addition put on to add the den and to redo the bedrooms upstairs so we could all have our own rooms."

"You live pretty close to Lincoln," James realized.

"Five blocks away," Sally informed him. "Three blocks down, two blocks to the right. I had to walk there and back for seven years. I've counted all the houses between here and there many times. Twenty-three."

"That's a lot of walking back and forth," James said. "I used to have to walk around Carson Lake to get to and from Randall. That was a drag." He turned to face her. "Sally," he said, "you're gonna go out with me again, right?"

Sally smiled. "Obviously," she said, "But you're gonna have to ask me out on another date."

James grinned at her. "I'll think of something great for us to do."

They stayed in the car kissing for another ten minutes, and then he offered to walk her to the door.

"Kiss me one more time here," she said softly, her arms resting atop his shoulders. "I can almost guarantee that one of my parents will hear us when we walk up and open the door."

They waited until as close to midnight as they could manage, and then he walked her to the door. True to prediction, the door creaked open, and Sally's mother peeked out. "I thought I heard something out here," she declared innocently.

"Mom," Sally said, "this is James Newell. Jamie, this is my mom, Phyllis Bachman."

"Nice to meet you, James," Mrs. Bachman said, smiling at him. "I'd ask you to come in, but it's getting late. Maybe next time?"

"That'd be great," James replied. "It was nice meeting you. Sally, I'll talk to you soon."

Her mother stepped inside, and Sally quickly reached over to give James a good night kiss. "I'll talk to you soon, Jamie. Thanks so much for dinner. Bye!"

"Bye, Sally."

James watched as the door closed, then walked quickly back to his car. He was already thinking about what he would ask her to do on their second date. He didn't want to think about the fact that their first date had already ended. He sat in his car and exhaled deeply. He had heard the word before but never thought it would apply to him. He already knew he liked her, but after spending time with her that night, and the electricity he felt when kissing her, he knew that he was totally smitten with Sally.

"The Other Guy"/The Little River Band
September 9, 1984

James awoke at eleven and decided to get up instead of staring at the ceiling for another hour. He put on pajama pants and a T-shirt and walked out to the den, scratching the cowlick on the back of his head. He hadn't noticed when he came in the night before that Howie was sleeping on the couch. Howie stirred a bit and opened one eye.

"Hey, bonehead," he groaned, as Ringo, who had been curled up at his feet, barked and jumped off the couch to the floor. "Did you finally get some action in the Cruiser last night?"

"Mind your own business," James replied, walking toward the kitchen, opening the fridge, and taking out the milk. He retrieved a bowl and spoon for cereal.

"C'mon, man, throw me a bone," Howie said, sitting up and dropping the blanket that covered his mostly naked body onto the floor. Shirtless and tighty whities. More than James wanted to see before breakfast. "At least tell me you did some tongue wrestling."

"You're disgusting," James yelled from the pantry. He did want to talk about it, but first he needed to get past their brotherly banter. "And you ate all of my Apple Jacks." He stowed his bowl back in the cupboard. "And if you must know, yes, we did kiss a little. Or maybe a lot." He grabbed a box of strawberry Pop Tarts, tore open the foil packet, and put two pastries in the toaster.

"Way to go, bro," Howie responded. "Not bad for a first date."

"Can you please put some pants on?" James pleaded. "Your hairy legs are gonna make me hurl."

Howie picked up his jeans from the floor and pulled them on. "So, she was into it?" he asked, fastening his belt.

"She seemed pretty into it," James said thoughtfully. "I mean, yeah, she was totally into it."

"Did you ask her out again?" Howie inquired as he put his dirty socks on one by one.

"We talked about going out again," James answered. "I'm gonna call her in a little while."

"Bro, you should wait. Don't seem too desperate," Howie instructed him. "Leave her guessing and wanting more."

James smirked at his brother. "Oh, is that what you're doing now? Leaving some mystery girl guessing and wanting more?"

"Very funny, moron," Howie responded while digging through the couch cushions to find his T-shirt. "But you should at least wait until you see her at school tomorrow."

"Yeah, I'm not gonna do that. I guess I don't have the social skills you do, Howard. But luckily Sally doesn't seem to care about that." His breakfast popped up in the toaster. He lifted the pastries out with a paper towel, grabbed his glass of milk, and started toward his bedroom.

"Good luck with that," Howie said, sounding sincere as he threw himself back on the couch again, this time fully dressed, and closed his eyes.

"Sweet Dreams (Are Made of This)"/Eurythmics

Sally answered the phone on the second ring after yelling out "I got it!" through her closed door.

"Hey Sally," James's voice said over the line.

"Hey Jamie!" She felt like her heart leapt into her throat. She stopped dressing and flopped down on her bed in her bra and underwear. "I was hoping you'd call."

James gave himself a silent pat on the back for not listening to Howie. "I wanted to see how you slept last night," he improvised.

"At first I couldn't sleep at all," she told him, "so I stayed up reading. But then I slept like a baby for like ten hours. I felt great when I woke up."

"Yeah, I'm feeling pretty good myself," James stated truthfully.

"I had a really good time last night," Sally said. "Thanks so much for dinner. And, like, everything."

"You're welcome," he replied. "I had a great time too. Any big plans today?"

"My sister, Andie, and my niece, Josie, are coming over soon, then we're going to my grandparents' house for dinner. How about you?"

"I'm heading out to work in a couple hours. But I wanted to call you first, to say hi."

"I'm glad you did."

They talked for a little longer and promised to meet up by the front entrance at school the next day before classes started. After they hung up, Sally stayed on her bed for a while longer, thinking she would rather skip everything else and go off with Jamie for the afternoon.

Not long after she hung up, Sally answered the phone again. It was Michelle.

"So, how did the big date go?" she demanded.

"It was okay," Sally teased.

"Just okay??"

"No," Sally admitted. "It was a-may-zing!" She fell onto her bed again.

She gave her friend all the details and Michelle asked clarifying questions. When she finished, Michelle knew as much about their date as she did.

"So, I assume you're going out again?" she inquired.

"You assume right," Sally answered. "I told him he has to ask me on a real date again, but we're meeting up before school tomorrow."

"Wow, Sally," Michelle responded. "Only last week we were talking about you transferring to McKinney! You were so worried it was gonna be awful, and one week later, you're already in a relationship with a totally nice guy! That's so radical!"

Sally smiled. "I don't know if I would call it a relationship yet . . . but I do hope it becomes one. He's so awesome. I have never met a guy like him. I mean, I met him before, but you know what I mean. He says whatever he's thinking. It's kind of nice to not have to guess. And oh, he's an amazing kisser! It's like we were meant to kiss each other! I hope I don't do anything to mess it all up."

"Listen," said Michelle sternly, "you're not gonna mess anything up. If anything, it'll be James doing some bonehead thing to piss you off. Just keep being yourself. He's lucky you agreed to go out with him in the first place!"

"I'll try to believe that," Sally said. "I just need some time to recover from the Gearhart horror show, and then I'll feel much better."

"It won't be a horror show at McKinney," Michelle assured her. "You already have friends, and no matter what happens, you have me. Remember, not only James is glad you're back. I am too. I missed you last year."

Sally sat up on her bed, feeling a sensation of relief flow through her. She finally felt like things were starting to come together for her. She figured it was about time.

"Got a Hold On Me"/Christine McVie
September 10, 1984

Monday brought with it an early fall wind, and the first giant red, orange, and yellow maple leaves flurried to the ground in Sally's path as she walked to school. She shivered through her windbreaker and regretted not wearing a heavier jacket as her mother had suggested. She deluded herself into believing she was rushing to get to school only to get out of the cold. She walked up the stairs that led to the front entrance and was not surprised to see James wasn't waiting outside. She stepped into the warm hallway, and there he was. He broke out into a big smile when he saw her, and she reciprocated. He snuck in a quick kiss as a greeting and took her hand as they walked down the hall toward the juniors' lockers. Sally felt conspicuous.

"I think everyone's looking at us," she whispered.

"Good. They should," James whispered back, still grinning, his confidence putting her at ease.

When they reached her locker, she put in her combination and opened the door. She hung her jacket on a hook, careful not to disrupt her Beatles picture display.

"Nice," James said. "I like your pictures. I remember you were into the Beatles." He took her textbooks from her and added them to his pile as she closed and locked her locker, and they started to walk toward the stairs. "Y'know, when I got to work yesterday, everyone had nice things to say about you," he told her. "Our waiter, Jack, said you were pretty and seemed nice, and Estella said we looked cute together. I told them both I totally agreed."

They started to climb the stairs, and Sally kept her eyes on her feet so she didn't trip. "That's so sweet," she replied, silently cursing her tendency to blush. "Thanks for telling me that, Jamie."

"So, listen," he said as they stopped in front of Sally's history classroom, "I know you're new here, and you probably want to hang out with your friends and stuff, but I would really like it if you would eat lunch with me today. I'd love to have more time to talk to you, and maybe they'll have those special fake mashed potato flakes I'm sure you love, the ones with the gray gravy?"

Sally laughed. "Yes, I'll have lunch with you, Jamie," she said. "But you have to promise to save me from the potatoes!" The first bell rang, and James handed her textbooks to her, and they parted until English class with another small kiss.

"Fools"/Van Halen

After English class, they headed to the cafeteria together and stood in line. They got their mixed vegetables and Salisbury steaks with gray gravy, picked up two chocolate milks, and handed their punch cards to the lunch lady. They found an empty table on the far side of the room, in the corner by the window. It wasn't a table for two in a candlelit restaurant, but it was still private time together to talk.

"What do you think of *The Great Gatsby* so far?" Sally asked, glancing at the novel as she set it down next to her tray.

"It starts off a bit slow," James admitted. "I've never been much of a reader, so I hope it picks up the pace soon."

"That's one thing I've always been," Sally responded. "A reader. I have always loved to read fiction. I get in the zone, and sometimes hours go by before I know it. Like on Saturday night. I read before bed, and next thing I knew, it was almost two in the morning!"

"That's exactly what it's like for me when I play my guitar," James said. "*In the zone* is a good way to describe it. When I learn a new song, or a new chord, I stay on it for a long time, until I get it just right. My parents know not to knock on my door when they hear me playing in my room."

"I can't wait to hear you play," Sally said. "I wish I could play an instrument. I tried to play the flute when I was younger, but I never practiced. I wanted to, but I couldn't seem to figure out how to get started. I'd be watching TV and get anxious that I wasn't practicing, but I still wouldn't do it. My mom finally told me that if I didn't get with it, she'd stop paying for lessons, so that's pretty much what happened."

"I was like that with karate in third grade," James disclosed. "My friends were all doing it. I liked the idea of doing it, but at each class, it was obvious to the teacher I hadn't practiced since the last class. He told me practice was a discipline I had to develop, but in the end, I decided not to. It was too hard for me to stay focused."

"It's so weird we both do that," Sally said, shaking her head. "Some things we can totally focus on for hours without anything stopping us, and others, we can't even start. I wonder what that's all about?"

Before James could respond, a tray came to rest on the table next to him, and Carl sat down in front of it. "Hey man," he said. "How come you're sitting all the way over here?" Chris made his way over and sat down next to Sally.

"Hey, dude," he said, tilting his chin toward the window, "nice view of the street over here."

James felt his heart fall but tried to act natural. "Hey guys, you remember Sally from Randall, right?"

"Hey Sally," Carl said, dumping his sandwich from his brown lunch bag onto his tray with his chocolate milk and cookie. "Yeah, of course. We used to all hang out before class in ninth grade. We're in the same math class now. How do you like Mrs. Russo so far?"

Sally made quick eye contact with James, and they both knew their private moment was over. Sally shrugged. "She seems okay," she responded. "I like algebra a lot more than geometry. It makes so much more sense to me."

"You still live over on Justice Drive?" Chris asked, cutting into his steak patty with his plastic fork. "My gram lives on Farnum, right near there. I remember seeing you once in the yard of the blue house with the white shutters when we were driving to her house."

"Yeah, we still live there," Sally confirmed. "Farnum is really close."

The conversation turned to people and places Carl and Chris knew in Sally's neighborhood and then to what they did that past weekend. Every now and then, one of them asked Sally a question, and she answered, but James remained mostly quiet, picking at his food.

Toward the end of lunch period, Sally excused herself. "I need to go meet Michelle before French class," she told them. "Nice having lunch with you guys. Jamie, I'll talk to you later." James gave her an apologetic smile and said goodbye as she stood and walked away with her tray.

Chris and Carl watched Sally as she rounded the corner. "She really is kind of cute," Chris said, turning to look at James. "I can totally see why you'd be into her."

"Yeah," James said, trying to keep the irritation out of his voice. "We were sitting over here because we were trying to have lunch alone. Just the two of us."

Carl furrowed his brow in surprise. "Oh, I'm sorry. Did we interrupt something? I had no idea you two were an item all the sudden."

James gave him a stern look "Well we are, okay? I wanted to have some time with her. Next time, just stay at the usual table."

"Did you actually go out with her?" Chris asked. "I mean, we've been in school for less than a week. You were working up your nerve to go talk to her a few days ago. That was fast work, man."

"Yeah, we went out Saturday night," James divulged. "I didn't tell you guys yet because I kind of wanted to see how things went first. It went well, and I really like her. Listen, all I'm asking for is like one day a week to have lunch alone with her."

"Maybe you two should go have lunch in the Vista Cruiser if you want to be 'alone,'" Chris said, making air quotes on the last word. Carl laughed.

"Don't be idiots, you guys, okay?" James pleaded. "So I like someone. When was the last time I liked someone? Just give me a break, okay?"

"Okay, okay," Carl said. "But you need to give us details. Did you get anywhere with her?"

"I am NOT gonna tell you that," James said, shaking his head. "Listen, you guys are my oldest friends, so I'm gonna give you a break this time, but cut me some slack, okay? Sally's not some random girl I just met. We've known each other for years. I don't want to blow this. And please try to be nice to her. She's still the new kid at McKinney, even if she did go to Randall."

Chris held up three fingers on his right hand in the boy scout salute. "I solemnly swear to be nice to Sally," he promised. "And so does Carl, right?" Carl nodded. "She remembers us from back then. We were always nice to her. I would even say we were all kind of friends with her at Randall. You know, we all goof around when we're together, but I think we're pretty respectful when we need to be.' You can ask Rhonda."

"True," Carl agreed. "Someday I'll have a girl in my life, and you can ask her, too."

"Okay," James said, sitting back in his chair and letting himself relax. "I know you guys won't do anything stupid. You're my best friends, so don't make me regret trusting you." He picked up his fork and turned his attention to his lukewarm lunch.

"Those morons," Michelle said, shaking her head. "They saw you there eating together, and they came and sat with you?"

"I think they're just clueless," Sally said, grabbing her books from her locker for the second half of her day. "Things happened so fast with me and Jamie. I don't think they knew we went out."

"Well, just to let you know," Michelle told her, "I heard something earlier about you and James making out by the front entrance before school this morning."

"What?" Sally exclaimed. "That's just not true! He gave me a couple of little pecks on the lips, and we held hands! That's hardly making out! I've had more romantic kisses with my grandmother!"

"Calm down, Sally," Michelle encouraged her. "I only heard it from Traci, who heard it from Jason Bennett, who has a locker near yours, so I don't think it's the hottest news in the school. I mean, if Chris and Carl hadn't heard anything by lunchtime, you're probably safe. I'm guessing Jason saw one of your kisses and thought he was on to something. Everyone likes to know a bit of gossip, and if they've got nothing, they'll just make it up."

"I just don't want to start off my first days at a new school with a reputation," Sally said. "I like Jamie a lot, and I want to be able to show it, but Gearhart was really bad with gossip, and I wanna be able to be myself here."

Michelle grasped her elbow and squeezed. "Don't worry, Sally," she said softly. "I won't let that happen. I know these kids. I'll set them straight. I've got your back. Just have fun with James. And don't worry about Carl and Chris. They've got James's back, too. They've all known each other since we were in kindergarten. They may give him a hard time because he's sensitive, but they won't do anything to hurt him. Deep down, they're good guys. They only act tough. They care about their reputations, too."

Sally sighed. "I know. Remember, they were always nice to me at Randall, but that seems so long ago. I know I'm completely different now. I'm not some clingy little girl desperate for attention from some boys who are willing to talk to me. I have to give them a chance to get to know me again. And I need to get to know them again. But what I really want is a whole lot of time to get to know Jamie, like right now."

"Break My Stride"/Matthew Wilder
September 14, 1984

As much as Sally wanted to spend more time getting reacquainted with James away from the prying eyes of her classmates, it was not going to happen the following weekend. She caught a nasty cold from her infant niece, Josie. By Thursday night, she was sneezing and coughing, had a throbbing headache, and had started to run a fever. She was excused from school on Friday and stayed in bed all day with a box of tissues and bowls of steaming Lipton noodle soup made by her mother, who had stayed home from work to care for her.

When the phone rang at four o'clock, she knew it would be James.

"Are you okay?" he asked. "I got worried when I didn't see you this morning. No one knew where you were."

"I'm sorry I made you worry, Jamie, but I'm really sick," Sally told him, embarrassed that his name sounded more like "Jaymbie" with her stuffy nose. "I have a bad cold. I was up most of the night sneezing and coughing. And I'm a huge mess. I feel like I'm trying to breathe underwater." She tried to blow her nose discreetly away from the phone.

"I'm sorry you're not feeling well," James empathized. "But I think you sound kind of sexy."

"Obviously, there is something wrong with your ears!" she replied.

James laughed. "That's a bummer that you're sick," he sympathized. "I was gonna ask you if you wanted to go roller skating tomorrow night. It's Carl's birthday, and he thought it would be fun to go to the roller rink with a bunch of friends just to goof around. Do you think it's possible you'll be feeling better by tomorrow?"

Sally sighed. "I don't think so," she responded, "although it sounds like a lot of fun. I haven't been roller skating for a long time. But I haven't been out of bed all day. My throat hurts, and last time I checked, I had a fever, too. I don't think my mom would let me out of the house even if I felt up for it."

"Do you want me to come over and hang out with you instead?" James offered.

"That's really sweet, Jamie," Sally said, "but there's no use in both of us getting sick. You should go roller skating. Maybe if I'm feeling better Sunday, we can hang out or something."

"I guess going alone would be better than staying home alone," James said, "but it'd be much more fun if you were there with me."

"I know. I wish I could go, too. But I'm sure there'll be other times, and I don't think this cold will last forever. At least I hope not. But thank you for asking me to come with you."

"I promised I would ask you out on a real second date," James responded, "and I always keep my promises. I'll call you when I get home tomorrow to check on you, okay?"

Without thinking, Sally smiled and cracked her lip. "Okay. Have a good night at work tonight, Jamie. I'll talk to you tomorrow." She touched her tongue to her sore lip and tasted metal.

"Bye, Sally. I hope you feel better."

"Bye Jamie."

Sally banged the phone down in frustration. She wiped her lip with a tissue, and it came off red with blood. "Aaaarrrggg," she bellowed, which upset her throat and set off a flurry of coughing. Soon, her mother appeared at her door with a bottle of Formula 44, a spoon, and a lot of sympathy.

"Skateaway"/Dire Straits
September 15, 1984

James made an effort to look decent on Saturday night, but his heart wasn't really in it. He felt it wasn't fair that he didn't get to have his second date with Sally. He wouldn't have minded catching her cold if it meant he could be with her while she was sneezing. Still, he decided to make the most of the night and have a good time with his friends. It was a good distraction. They were a fun group, and no one could stay mopey while gliding around on two sets of four wheels.

He parked in the large lot outside the Rollaway Rink and Arcade and went inside. He dodged some small kids rolling directly toward him and stood in line to get his rental skates. With skates in hand, he went to the locker area, where he found Carl, Chris, Rhonda, Pete, and Pete's girlfriend, Carolyn. They laced up their skates and hit the floor, skating to "Rock You Like a Hurricane," "Round and Round," "Get Down Tonight," and "Another One Bites the Dust." James felt silly but amused going around in circles with his friends, watching the adults in disco outfits in the middle of the floor doing their roller dance moves and twirls. He saw tiny children who couldn't have been more than five or six grasping the wall of the rink, trying not to fall. He saw one small girl end up on the floor in what must have been an especially uncomfortable split position. A couple of sophomore girls he had seen around school rolled past him. One waved and said, "Hi James!" He smiled politely and waved back. She had been in one of his elective classes the previous year, but he couldn't remember her name. He couldn't figure out if she was flirting with him or not. Two weeks ago, he would have been sure. Now he hardly cared.

After a few more songs, the DJ announced a couples only skate, and Carl and James cleared the floor. They stood outside the wall of the rink watching the happy couples skating around together and chatting loudly over the sounds of Steve Perry belting out "Open Arms." The sophomore girl who had waved earlier skated up to James on the carpet and asked him to skate with her. He thanked her and said no.

"I notice she didn't want me for a consolation prize," Carl said, shaking his head.

"You're not much consolation!" James joked, and then they shoved each other good naturedly, just enough so they didn't lose their balance and fall over.

"Too bad Sally couldn't come," Carl lamented once they'd settled down. "She could have brought some of her friends. Traci's pretty cute. Maybe she would've skated with me. It is my birthday, after all."

"You only like the girls who don't know you yet," James chastised. "Michelle and Darlene are cute, too. And Kim's got major potential. You've just known them too long."

"That would be like dating my own sister," Carl said. "We can't all have our long-lost loves show up again after a year like you did."

"Sally's not a lost love," James told him. "You know that. She was just a friend before, barely a friend. But maybe I should've thought of her as something more. You never know how someone's gonna turn out. And she made us all laugh back then. You have to admit, she had guts to try to fit in with us."

"Yeah, we were pretty badass in junior high," Carl asserted. "Some of us still are."

James grinned and shrugged. "I don't know about that," he stated. "You don't look too badass right now in that Cookie Monster T-shirt and roller skates!"

Carl looked down at his yellow T-shirt with the iron-on decal of the blue *Sesame Street* character chomping on a chocolate chip cookie. "Dude, have some respect," he retorted. "My gram got me this for my birthday."

The couples' skate ended. Carl started back toward the rink to skate, and Pete headed over to the side and stood with James.

James had known Pete most of his life, and he was his closest friend. The Coopers lived three houses down from the Newells on Greenhill Road, and the boys had played together since they were toddlers. They'd gone to elementary school and junior high together and were only separated in high school by James's transfer to McKinney. Pete was the only friend James had made any effort to see over the summer; they'd hung around each other's houses and watched TV or played video games on Pete's Atari system.

They watched their friends skate as Pete updated James on what was going on with their childhood friends and other news from Murphy High. Then he questioned James about his life.

"Chris told me earlier that you're going out with Sally Bachman," he said. "I can't believe I haven't heard about this until now!"

James smiled. "Yeah, well, I am," he told his friend. "We've actually only been on one official date. I wasn't keeping it a secret, but I haven't seen you since I asked her out. She would have been here tonight but she's home sick. It is kind of weird that I saw you right before school started, and since then, it's like my whole life has changed. Strange how things turn out, huh? I mean, at Randall, I never would have thought of Sally as someone I wanted to be with, but now, I can't think of her in any other way. You should see her, Pete. You'd barely recognize her anymore. And it's not just her looks. She's . . . well, she's still herself, but then she's also different, you know?"

Pete opened his mouth to speak then stopped. Then he started again. "You know, J, I'm not sure I should tell you this," he said guardedly, "but I will anyway. Well, now I kind of have to. I actually had a huge crush on Sally when we were in ninth grade. So yeah, I can kind of see what you're saying."

James almost pulled a muscle in his neck as he turned to look at Pete. "What? Really? I didn't know that." He had always thought Pete was the best-looking member of their friend group, as girls would often do double takes to get a good look at him as he walked by. He was the most fashionably dressed and groomed of them all, with light brown hair, brown eyes, straight teeth, and dimples. He had an athletic build and was approaching six feet tall at age sixteen. James couldn't imagine him having an unrequited crush.

"Yeah, well, probably because I never said anything," Pete said, looking down at his skates. "That was a long time ago. I thought she was funny and cute in an awkward kind of way. But I never would have done anything about it. I mean, we were like fourteen. I barely knew how to talk to girls. But I used to do things to try to get her attention. Nothing major, but you know, throwing wadded up paper at her during class, teasing her, and one time I even snapped her bra. I don't know what the hell I was thinking!" He laughed at the memory. "But it definitely got her attention! I'm surprised she didn't square up and hit me in the jaw!"

James laughed, too. "I kind of remember that," he said. "I thought you were just goofing around, like we always did." He stopped for a moment and his face became serious. "But you're not into her anymore, right?"

"No," Pete responded quickly, looking right at James and shaking his head. "No, not at all. I got over that before we left Randall. I haven't seen her since the last day of school at Randall. I thought I saw her once this summer at the cookie place in the mall, but I don't think it could have been her. And I'm totally into Carolyn now. She's great, and her dad has a '79 Mustang convertible that he let me drive once. But I'll admit, I'm glad one of us ended up with Sally, though. Now we'll all get to be friends with her again, and that's pretty cool."

James nodded, relief overcoming him. "Yeah," he agreed. "It is pretty cool."

Their friends skated over to them, and the group went to the snack bar to get some drinks and popcorn. James let himself relax in the presence of the people he grew up with and found he was having a good time. They laughed and traded stories of their younger days and recent antics. James skated for another half hour and then told his friends he was going to head home.

"We're gonna go hang out at Burger King after this," Chris announced. "You don't wanna come with us?"

"Naw, I have to work tomorrow so I need to get to bed early," he replied.

"It's only nine o'clock," Chris said. "It's okay to say you want to go home and call your sick girlfriend instead."

James started to say "She's not my girlfriend," but then stopped himself. He realized Sally was kind of his girlfriend, even if they had only been on one official date. Since then, they had met up before school every morning until she got sick and talked on the phone at least briefly each night. So instead, he smiled and said, "I'll tell her you all said hi." He wished Carl a happy birthday again and then went to change back into his street shoes.

"Call Your Name"/The Beatles

"Did you have fun?" Sally asked James when he called. She was feeling dopey from nighttime cold medicine but had wanted to stay up long enough to have a conversation with him before trying to sleep.

"Yeah, it was fun to hang out with my old friends," James admitted. "They make me laugh. But they don't kiss nearly as well as you do."

"You flatter me. Hold on a sec." Sally pulled the phone away from her face and sneezed twice. She wiped her nose. "Ugh," she said into the receiver. "Sorry, I'm so repulsive!"

"You are not repulsive," James insisted. "Everyone gets colds. You sound awful, though. I mean like you feel awful."

"Yeah," Sally said, letting her head fall on the pillow. "I really do. I don't think I'll be able to do anything tomorrow either."

"Yeah, I wouldn't think so," James agreed. "You need to focus on getting better so you can be back at school next week. It'll give us both a reason to look forward to school, anyway!"

"But you'll call me tomorrow, right?" Sally pleaded. "I may be sick, but I'm also so bored and lonely. And there's only so much I can take of my mother trying to cheer me up."

"Yeah, I'll call you," James promised. "I'll let you sleep in and then I'll call. And then I'll call you again later before work. And then when I get home. You'll get sick of me calling you."

"Never," Sally responded fondly. "You'll keep me sane. You and my Madeleine L'Engle book series."

They said their goodbyes, James realizing he had made the choice not to tell Sally about Pete's junior high crush. He wanted her to be friends with his friends, and although he knew she would be flattered by the information, the last thing he wanted was for either of them to feel uncomfortable with the other. And if he was honest with himself, he also didn't want to have to worry about himself being uncomfortable when they were all together.

"Doctor Doctor"/Thompson Twins
September 18, 1984

Sally was still home sick on Monday but was able to make it to school on Tuesday. James met her outside the door, took her book bag, and walked her into school. She looked worn out but was still a sight for his sore eyes. At her locker, she blew her nose and grabbed her books. She declined James's hand when he reached out to her, citing germs.

"I'm here," she told him, "but I really shouldn't be. I could use a couple more days at home. And a whole lot of NyQuil."

"I wish you were feeling better," James said, slipping his arm around her back as they walked up the stairs. "I wish there was something I could do for you. Like bring you tea in history class or something."

"Tea sounds nice," Sally agreed. "With lots of honey. And my pillow."

"I'll drive you home from school," James offered.

"I'm not good company," Sally warned him.

"That's okay," he told her. "I'll just get you home and let you go rest. So you can be better and we can go out or something this weekend."

Sally sighed. "I'd like that," she responded. "I can't believe we've only been on one date. I wish I could kiss you, but I'm still worried about getting you sick."

James reached over and kissed her on the top of the head. "Mmm, strawberries," he said, taking a deep whiff.

Sally laughed and then coughed. They had reached the door of her classroom, so they parted until English class.

Sally was feeling a bit better on Wednesday and more like herself on Thursday. Still, her mother wanted her to take it easy and have a low-key weekend. She agreed she could see James if there wasn't too much excitement. So when James called and informed her that his parents had splurged and bought a VCR and invited her over to watch their first video with them on Saturday night, she jumped at the opportunity. Her mother agreed, as long as she was home by ten o'clock.

"I Can't Wait to See You"/The Impressions
September 22, 1984

Sally took a long, hot shower, marinating her hair in her strawberry conditioner. She blow-dried her hair and applied a conservative amount of makeup. She put on her warm oversized Boston University sweatshirt, her loose cozy jeans, slouch socks, and sneakers. She cuddled quietly on the couch with her mother as she read her work trade magazine and stroked her hair. Mr. Bachman had gone to Andie's house to help her put up some shelves, and with Nathan off at college, the house was peaceful and quiet. Sally considered it was sometimes nice to be the only child living at home with her parents.

She got up at five to fluff and hair spray her hair and waited for James to pick her up. She saw the Cruiser pull into the driveway and grabbed her light jacket. When the doorbell rang, Mrs. Bachman answered, and Sally followed her to the door.

"Hello again, James," Mrs. Bachman greeted him. "You look nice tonight."

Sally saw James was wearing a vertically striped button-down shirt over crisp-looking blue jeans and bright white sneakers with green stripes. He had combed his hair neatly, and his smile carved a dimple in his left cheek. "Thanks, Mrs. Bachman," James said. "Thanks for letting Sally come over. My parents are looking forward to meeting her."

"Take good care of her," Mrs. Bachman instructed. "She may be better now, but we don't want a recurrence."

"I will. I'll have her back by ten."

"I know you will." Mrs. Bachman gave Sally a hug. "Be good, sweetie," she said.

"I will, Mom, thanks," Sally said.

As the front door closed, James announced, "Your mom is so nice."

Sally shrugged. "Yeah, I guess so," she said. "But she's my mom, you know?"

"Yeah, I know," James replied. "I have one, too."

"Our House"/Madness

They drove to James's house on Greenhill Road. Sally noticed the road was brown and flat. "Why is it called Greenhill Road if it's not a hill?" she asked.

James shrugged. "My dad says that often they name neighborhoods and streets after what they tore down to build them," he explained. "Like Pine Grove Apartments? They ripped out a grove of pines to clear a space for it. Weird, huh?"

"Yeah," Sally agreed. James's mention of his father reminded her she was about to meet his parents. She felt nervous butterflies rising in her stomach up to her throat.

"That's Pete's house," James said, pointing to a brown split-level ranch on the left and slowing down. "And here's my house." He pulled into the driveway of the yellow ranch house where he lived with his family.

"I didn't realize you and Pete were neighbors!" Sally said. "It's so weird that you don't go to the same school anymore."

"I know," James agreed. "But we still see each other all the time. Oh, I forgot to tell you, my brother Howie's here to see my parents' new VCR, too." He put the car in park and turned off the engine. "Don't worry about how he looks," he went on. "He's really harmless."

That statement seemed strange to Sally, as if James was describing a stray dog. She shrugged it off. They approached the front door of the house, and James let them in. His parents were sitting on the couch in front of the TV in the den, which was at the end of the short hallway from the door. They stood and walked over, smiling, when the teens approached.

"Hello!" James's mother said enthusiastically when she saw Sally. "You must be Sally!" She grasped Sally's right hand with both of her warm hands. "I'm Julia Newell, James's mom, and this is my husband, who's also James, but we call him J.D."

"Hi, Sally," Mr. Newell said, shaking her hand.

"Hi, Mr. and Mrs. Newell," Sally responded. "It's nice to meet you. I've known James for a few years, and it's nice to finally meet his family!"

Mr. and Mrs. Newell glanced at each other approvingly, as though they appreciated Sally's manners.

"James, why don't you get Sally something to drink?" Mrs. Newell suggested.

"Tea with honey?" James asked knowingly.

Sally smiled. "I would love that, Jamie, thanks."

As James went through the door into the kitchen, another door opened in the hallway toward the back of the house, and Sally got a view of what she guessed must be James's brother, Howie. He was James's height, about five-foot-nine, but that was where the resemblance seemed to end. He had long, greasy-looking dark brown hair with bangs that grew past his eyes. He brushed them away with his hand as he walked toward the den. He was wearing a black Aerosmith concert shirt that appeared to have been washed and worn way too many times. The shirt rested directly on his collar bones, giving the effect that it was hung on a scarecrow. His jeans were so loose on him that he had to keep pulling them up, even though he was wearing a belt. The most striking feature, however, was his eyes. They were framed with dark circles and appeared to be sunk into his head, making him look a bit like a barred owl. His cheeks and chin were coated with patchy dark stubble. The whole picture was difficult to look at. When he noticed Sally standing in the den, he looked at her and smiled, transforming his face. Sally could sense there was still a glimmer of intelligent light burning somewhere inside of Howie.

"Hey there," he said, walking into the room. "You must be the famous Sally I've heard so much about. I'm Howard, but you can call me Howie. Everyone does." He reached out to shake her hand. He did look relatively harmless, so Sally took his hand. "So, you've been hanging out with our Jamie. I hope he hasn't done anything so far to sully our good family name!"

"Oh, no," Sally replied. "He's been great!"

James returned from the kitchen with Sally's tea to see his brother holding onto her hand. "I see you met my brother," he said, approaching them.

"Yes," she said. "Nice to meet you, Howie." She shook his hand firmly and let it go.

"Mom," James asked, "would it be okay if I showed Sally around before we start the movie?"

"Sure, dear," Mrs. Newell answered. "Don't show her our bedroom, though. It's a mess."

James put Sally's tea on the coffee table and took her hand. He led her though the kitchen, the dining area, and the back hallway past the bathroom and the bedrooms. Sally glanced at the family pictures on the walls as they walked by, focused on the tow-headed youngest child flanked by his older brother and sister in yearly portraits. She thought Jamie was an adorable baby. He showed her his room, and she noticed twin beds. He told her he had shared a room with Howie from the time they were small children until Howie moved out last year. He showed her his guitar and his albums and introduced her to Ringo, who was sleeping on his bed. Sally pet the small lap dog, and he wagged his tail. James pulled back his shade and showed her the backyard.

"My dad built the tree house when Erin was in kindergarten," he told her, pointing up into a tall oak tree. "I think my parents are keeping it for when we all have kids. We had one of those old metal swing sets next to the shed, but it rusted and fell apart by the time I was in fifth grade. We used to play wiffle ball and use that rock over there for home plate. The trees were the bases. They weren't really the right distance apart, but we didn't care."

Sally smiled at how excited James was getting at showing her his house, his room, and his treasured belongings and telling her about things from his childhood. She wanted to hear it all, but there would be lots of time for that. James put the shade back in place, and they returned to the den to start the movie.

"Howie," Mrs. Newell said to her older son, "why don't you take a seat on the beanbag chair, dear. J.D. and I will sit in the recliners, and Sally, you and James can take the couch. I've put on a casserole for dinner, and it'll be ready in about an hour, so we can take an intermission to eat when it's done."

"Do you like tuna casserole, Sally?" Mr. Newell asked.

"I do," she answered. "I like anything with tuna or noodles, and both of those together are the best."

"Then you'll love Julia's casserole," Mr. Newell told her. "It's an old Italian recipe, one that includes a secret ingredient passed down from generation to generation that gives it its bold and vibrant flavor."

"What is it?" Sally asked, curious how tuna casserole could come from an old Italian recipe.

"If I told you, it wouldn't be a secret," he answered, winking at her.

"It's Campbell's Cream of Mushroom soup," Mrs. Newell said, shaking her head at her husband. "The recipe's on the can. And don't call me an old Italian. It's insulting!"

Sally laughed. Mr. Newell shrugged and gave her a conspiratory smile.

James shook his head. "My parents do that old Italian bit for everyone who comes in the house," he told Sally, rolling his eyes but smiling. "They think they're amusing."

"Hey, we try to have a little fun over here," his father said. "So sue me."

Sally sat next to James on the couch with ample space between them since she didn't know how close to sit with his parents there. He clarified by moving so close that their sides were touching and putting his arm around her shoulder. Her head naturally nested between his arm and chest. None of the Newells appeared scandalized, so she kicked off her sneakers and pulled her feet up next to her so she could snuggle even closer. She could feel both of their hearts beating, and she tried not to let it lull her into a contented post-cold slumber.

Soon the previews were playing, and everyone ooh-ed and aah-ed over the ability to watch recent movies right from their own TV instead of paying to go to the theater.

"We only have to watch 250 more videos before this thing pays for itself," Mr. Newell lamented.

"Or until you have to buy the next new thing," Howie quipped. "The way I see it, in a few years, the price of VCRs will go way down, and then suddenly there'll be some new and exciting way to watch movies at home. They'll keep making them smaller and smaller until you can hold it in the palm of your hand. And the smaller it is, the more expensive it'll be."

Sally looked at James, who shrugged at her. She would have to remember to ask James about Howie sometime when they were alone. For now, they watched the movie, *Eddie and the Cruisers*, and Sally liked the story. It was similar to that of Jim Morrison and the Doors, and Michael Pare made an excellent Eddie. Sally remembered him from the show *The Greatest American Hero*.

The timer buzzed in the kitchen, marking the completion of dinner. Sally felt her stomach rumble. She had been living mostly on tea, toast, and soup for the past week. Real, flavorful food sounded, and smelled, good. James figured out how to pause the movie, and they all went to the kitchen to eat.

Sally was seated next to James, with Howie facing them, and James's parents were on each end of the table. She looked around discreetly at the group. She had noticed the similarities in the eye color of James and Howie, but now she searched for him in the faces of his parents. The eyes came from his father, who appeared to know that wearing a blue shirt made the color pop. The Newell men had a strange handsomeness about them, a careless handsomeness, as if they had discovered it by mistake. Mr. Newell had a full head of white hair, and Sally wondered if he had once been blond like James. Sally had picked up that Mrs. Newell was Italian. She had thick, dark brown eyebrows above hazel eyes and an olive complexion. James was paler, and his features slightly smaller and more symmetrical than his mother's, but he shared her smile. Mrs. Newell wore her dark hair in a neat medium bob with bangs, used minimal makeup, and wore simple gold post earrings as her only adornment. She had a slim build and was dressed casually in blue jeans and a pullover collared sweatshirt.

Mr. and Mrs. Newell fussed over Sally, making sure there was enough food on her plate and joking about making her eat more because she needed her strength after being sick. Sally did have seconds and enjoyed every bite, even though it was an old Campbell family recipe rather than a Mrs. Newell one.

"I didn't have a chance to make dessert today," Mrs. Newell said apologetically. "Saturdays are always so busy with running errands and going to the market. The boys can tell you I make a mean cannoli. That really is from an old Italian recipe! But I did pick up an Entenmann's chocolate cake, with marshmallow frosting."

"Do you like chocolate cake, Sally?" Mr. Newell asked. "Because if not, I'd be happy to eat your piece. We wouldn't want it to go to waste."

Sally laughed. "No, I'm a big fan of chocolate cake. Jamie can tell you. That chocolate cake especially. My dad gets one every now and then, and sometimes we eat the whole thing in one night!"

"Better give her a big piece, Jules," Mr. Newell told his wife. "You really scored big with the cake."

Sally looked at James, and he raised his eyebrows with a smile. His family seemed to like to joke around, especially his father, and his mother just played along. James didn't seem embarrassed, and Sally was thoroughly enjoying them.

"I'm going to warm up some water in the microwave for Sanka," Mrs. Newell stated as she passed out dessert plates and then served the cake. "Sally, do you have a microwave at your house? I think more people are getting them now that the prices are going down."

"Oh, yeah," Sally replied. "My parents went out and bought a huge microwave a few months ago. My mom wanted one that was big enough to defrost a Thanksgiving turkey. My dad still thinks it's radiating our food, but I don't think that's true."

"Microwaves are totally safe," Howie announced. "People are so afraid of change. I mean, a machine that can take a frozen lasagna and cook it in ten minutes, rather than having to wait an hour for the regular oven . . . seems like a culinary miracle to me."

"Well, I mostly stick to my conventional stove and oven," Mrs. Newell said as she cut another piece of cake and put it on Sally's empty plate. "But for heating up water, or leftover coffee, the microwave has no match. Would you like some coffee, Sally?"

"Oh, thank you, but I'll stick to my tea for now." James picked up her teacup and brought it to the counter for a refill. He was generous with the honey. He handed it to Sally then stood behind her with his hands on her shoulders as she sipped it and finished her cake.

"You have enough to eat, James?" his mother asked.

"Yeah, Mom. Thanks. Dinner was great. I'll help clean up."

"Oh, no, dear, you and Sally go back to the den and visit. Howie, Dad, and I will take care of everything. You two relax." Mrs. Newell started to clear the table, and Mr. Newell started to rinse the dishes. Howie stood and grabbed a dish towel.

Returning to the den, Sally and James sat facing each other cross-legged on the couch, grinning. Sally cradled her warm tea in her hands. She said, "Jamie, your family is awesome. I thought I would feel uncomfortable hanging out with them, but I don't at all. Are they always like this?"

James nodded. "Yeah, pretty much. I think they like you and they're showing off, especially Howie. He usually sits quietly and mopes. My dad can be so goofy sometimes. I'm glad you picked up on his humor. He must really like you, too, or he wouldn't have started in on you so quickly."

"I like them," she responded. "Howie's interesting. You'll need to tell me more about him sometime."

"I will," James promised. "Believe me, there is no way you're not gonna be hearing more about Howie."

"I never would have guessed you were half Italian," she told him. "You don't look it at all!"

James laughed. "I have some cousins in Maine who are one hundred percent Italian and have blond hair and blue eyes," he told her. "But yeah, I definitely look more like my father's side of the family."

"Why does your dad go by J.D?" Sally asked, wanting all her questions answered at once.

"His name is James Daniel and mine is James Phillip," James explained. "He was always James, and I guess they planned on calling me Jimmy. But apparently, I didn't look like a Jimmy at all when I was born, so they called me Jamie instead, and, as you know, when I started high school, I told people to call me James. It started to get too confusing. Some of Dad's coworkers called him J.D. anyway, so he just went with it. He says it makes him sound more managerial. He calls me J.P. sometimes too, to be funny. Only Howie ever calls me Jimmy. He does it to bug me."

Sally smiled. "And only I get to call you Jamie," she said fondly.

James felt his stomach flip as a result of Sally's affectionate statement. He took her tea from her and placed it on the coffee table. He decided he had time to pull her closer for a kiss. They hadn't been alone since their first date, two weeks earlier. He felt an increase of intensity as he had her in his arms and longed to let himself give in to his impulses. But he knew he had to keep himself contained. He didn't want Sally to be embarrassed if his parents walked in. They pulled apart and resumed their movie-watching positions. Sally picked up her tea and sipped it slowly, leaning against James's shoulder. Ringo jumped onto the couch, sniffed both of their laps, and decided on James's, the lap he knew. He circled three times and settled on top of his thighs. Sally reached out to pat him.

The Newells came back, and Howie restarted the video. When the movie ended, they discussed it. "I thought Eddie was dead," Mr. Newell said, "just like Jim Morrison. People try to say Jim Morrison lives, but it's only because that's poetic justice. He's timeless. But when you're dead, you're dead. There's no coming back. So I don't know."

"But he was there at the end, in the reflection in the window, J.D.," Mrs. Newell insisted. "I believe it was the same actor but with a beard. I don't think it's any mystery. I mean, they led us to believe he was alive, but then tricked us, but then, there he was."

"I liked the music," James put in. "John Cafferty and the Beaver Brown Band have a good sound."

"I liked the story and the soundtrack," Sally contributed. "Words and music, man. I hope they make a sequel so we can find out more."

"What did you think, Howie?" asked his father.

Howie appeared to be dozing off on the beanbag chair. "What?" he said. "Oh, yeah, it was a good movie. I liked it. Hey, can I sleep on the couch tonight? It's getting too late to take the bus to Jeff's place, and I'm pretty beat."

Mr. and Mrs. Newell looked at each other, and Mrs. Newell nodded.

"Okay, Howie, you can stay tonight," Mr. Newell told him. "But we're going to have to have a talk about guidelines again in the morning, understand?"

"Yeah, I get it, Dad. We'll talk, I promise."

Sally excused herself to use the bathroom, and when she came out, James was waiting for her in the hallway.

"I think that was our cue to leave," he said softly. "Howie needs the couch, and pretty soon the snoring's gonna start. We still have time until you need to be home, though. Are you feeling up for going somewhere we can be alone for a while?" Sally smiled and nodded, and James went to retrieve their jackets.

"Oh, are you leaving?" Mrs. Newell asked. "I hope you come again, Sally. It's so nice to have James bring a friend over."

"Mom," James corrected. "Sally's my girlfriend, not just my friend."

"Oh, okay, sorry. Girlfriend. Well, I'm glad to hear that. I didn't want to assume. This is the first time James has brought a girlfriend home, so we're very happy to have met you."

"I'm happy to have met you, too, Mr. and Mrs. Newell. Thanks so much for dinner. Your tuna recipe was amazing!"

They all said goodbye, and James walked outside after Sally, closing the front door.

James shook his head as they walked toward the driveway. "My mom is so weird sometimes, but you were a good sport with them. What? Why are you looking at me like that?"

"Jamie!" Sally exclaimed. "You just told your mother I'm your girlfriend!"

"Oh, I'm sorry. Was that bad? I guess we should have talked about it first, but . . ."

She put her arms around his neck and kissed him before he could continue. When they pulled away, she said, "Okay, so if I'm your girlfriend, that makes you my boyfriend. We are girlfriend and boyfriend."

James chuckled. "That's right, you weren't there last weekend when Chris called you my girlfriend at the roller rink and I didn't correct him. I liked the way it sounded. So it's okay with you, then, if I introduce you to people as my girlfriend?"

"Yes, my boyfriend," she said, smiling, "I'm good with us being boyfriend and girlfriend." She practically skipped toward the car.

"Well, that's totally awesome," James stated.

"And I promise, boyfriend," Sally told him, "I will stop with the girlfriend and boyfriend thing in a few minutes. Right now, I just want to enjoy it for a bit."

James looked at Sally and grinned. She was doing that thing she did, being perfect. Even though her nose was still red from her cold last week, he thought she was perfect. She'd come into his home, and his parents had taken right to her like they had known her for years. She had met Howie and didn't run out of the house screaming. Now she was going nuts over the idea of them being boyfriend and girlfriend. Not only was she perfect, but she was adorable, too. And he knew under the puffy cold face and baggy clothes, she was also sexy as hell.

"You Can't Hurry Love"/Phil Collins

They got into the car and James drove to the Episcopal Church parking lot on the next block, which was shaded on all sides by tall hedges. For the next half hour, James did everything he could above her clothes to make Sally feel special and to let her know something amazing was happening between them. He knew he would have to wait as long as needed until they were both ready for more than that, even if his body was telling him otherwise. They hadn't been together long. He was willing to wait. She was worth it. He wanted to make things just right for her. He would wait as long as it took. But it was going to be a struggle.

"I don't understand why we didn't start doing this back at Randall," James said as they started the drive to Sally's house. "Why didn't I ask you out back then? I mean, we could have been dating for two years by now. Why didn't I open my eyes and see you there in front of me?"

"I was so awkward back then," Sally said. "I don't think I was someone anyone would've wanted to date. And I was so shy about things like that."

"I was shy, too, Sally," James admitted. "But I wish we could have started a real friendship, something outside of school. I wish I could have that time back and do it again."

"I know," Sally agreed. "It would be nice to have a lot of things back. But if I had never left, and we were in classes together last year, you never would have had the chance to miss me, and you never would have realized you liked me. That would be horrible."

"That's true," James said. "I guess we could spend the rest of our lives second guessing our choices. We need to make the most of what we have now."

Sally smiled contentedly and reached for his hand across the seat. "Jamie, I like what we have now. I'm glad everything went exactly the way it did."

James smiled back and squeezed her hand as he drove. She was proving to him again how perfect she was.

"I Can Dream About You"/Dan Hartman

When Sally got home, she filled her parents in on her night with the Newells.

"What do they do for a living?" Mr. Bachman asked. He was always interested in what people did, even characters on TV shows. Sally would tell him it didn't relate to the plot of the show, but he would still want to know.

"She's an elementary school special ed aide, and he's some sort of department manager over at Aries Corp. I really didn't understand when he explained it to me. Kind of like I can never explain to anyone what it is that Mom does. But they're smart and funny, and the food was good."

"I wish you would have brought me home some of that chocolate cake, Sally," Mr. Bachman lamented. "Phyllis, when you go to the market tomorrow, can you pick one up?"

Mrs. Bachman smiled. "Or you could come with me and pick one up yourself," she suggested. "I'm teasing. I'll get one for you. I don't want to disturb you and Sally and your weekly football date."

"Thanks, Phyl," Mr. Bachman said, picking up his early edition Sunday newspaper and looked for the sports section.

Sally yawned. "Sweetie," her mother urged, "why don't you go to bed now. You look tired and you need your rest."

"Okay, Mom." She gave her mother a kiss then leaned over to kiss her father.

"You should invite James over here sometime," her father said. "Does he like sports?"

"Yeah," Sally told him. "And thank God he likes the Red Sox and Patriots. Otherwise, we'd have a huge problem!"

"Well, I really should meet the young man my daughter is running around with," he stated. "I would have wanted to even if he didn't like sports. But it's better that he does!"

"Dad, we're not 'running around'!" Sally objected. "We're dating. There's a difference. I think. But I would like to ask him over to meet you. I think you two have a lot in common."

"Well, if he likes you, then we already have that in common!" he teased.

Sally rolled her eyes. "Good night, Dad," she said as she turned away from him.

"By the way," her mother called out as Sally walked down the hall toward the stairs, "you can just tell people I work with computers if they ask. Everyone understands that!"

Sally went upstairs, changed into her pajamas, and got ready for bed. She was tired but happy. She got into bed with *A Wind in the Door*, the second book in the Wrinkle in Time series, her fourth time through. But she found she couldn't concentrate. She was feeling distracted by her night, by how well it went, and how nicely she thought she fit in with James's family. She thought about James, and it brought chills throughout her body. She thought of his lips on hers, and his hands on her body. She turned off her lights, lay down, and let the thoughts flow through her. She knew he was going to be her first, but she didn't know when or how it would happen. She hoped it would be really special. She knew he was thinking about it too. She could tell from the urgency of his kisses, and his breathlessness when they pulled apart. She also knew that he felt other things for her, tender and sweet things, like wanting her to meet his parents, see his room and his guitar, and eat a meal with him and his family. And he would rather spend a Saturday night at home with her than go out with his friends or to a party. That was huge. She never would have imagined in junior high that James was like this outside of school. It didn't mesh with his former bad boy image.

She felt tender and sweet things for him, too. She wanted him to spend time with her parents, and her grandparents, to instruct him how to speak slowly to her grandmother so she could read his lips. To listen to her father talk about his job and the Boston sports he loved so much.

For James to get down on the floor to play with Josie. She wanted Andie to like him, and to tell her how great he was. She grew drowsy with these thoughts, and let sleep take over. She hoped that when she finally drifted off, she would dream about James so she could think about him again the moment she woke up.

"We Are Family"/Sister Sledge
September 27, 1984

One of Sally's bedtime wishes came true that week. She received a call from her sister Andie, who announced that her husband Derrek was home on a brief leave from the army. He was stationed at Fort Benning in Columbus, Georgia, and only made it home to visit periodically. While he was there, he wanted to take Sally and her new boyfriend out to dinner and spend some time with them since he considered Sally his "favorite sister-in-law."

"Uh, I'm his only sister-in-law," Sally said.

"That's not relevant," Andie answered. "We want to go to the Fishmongers, and we need to make a reservation and make sure Mom and Dad can babysit, so are you in?"

"I'm in for sure," Sally told her. "You know Derrek was my first crush when I was, like, ten, so of course I want to see him. But is it wise to bring Jamie? I mean, wouldn't Derrek get jealous?"

"Haha, very funny," Andie responded. "I wasn't threatened by your crush when you were ten, and I'm not threatened now. I'll go ahead and make a reservation for four and assume Mom will babysit. Let me know if Jamie can't come for some reason."

"Okay," Sally replied. "But you have to call him James. I'm the only one who can call him Jamie."

"Wow!" Andie exclaimed. "Special rules just for you! Sounds like young love to me."

"Yeah, that would be okay with me," Sally responded hopefully.

Sally called James to invite him to dinner. He told her he did want to go, and that the Fishmonger was one of his favorite restaurants.

"It's expensive, though," he said, thinking he wouldn't get paid until the next Friday. While he didn't want to pull any money out of his car savings, he would if he had to. "I've only ever been there on super fancy occasions, like my sister Erin's high school graduation. And that was only because she was valedictorian!"

"Don't worry about that," Sally assured him. "Derrek and Andie invited us. They'll treat. They want to meet you and make sure you're good enough for me, and you totally are, so you don't need to worry about anything."

"I'll try to prove myself to them," James promised. "I will earn every bite of my shrimp scampi for sure."

"My Eyes Adored You"/Frankie Valli
September 29, 1984

Sally breathed in the aroma of the Fishmonger as they walked in the door. The mingling of the shellfish and lemon scent made her mouth water. She and James were led to the table where Andie and Derrek were already seated. They stood up, and Derrek gave Sally a bear hug. He was six-foot-two and had a muscular build, so Sally virtually disappeared in his arms.

"Look at you, Tiny Mouse!" Derrek said to her, holding her at arm's length. "You look great! I think you've grown another inch since I last saw you!"

Sally blushed. "I have not," she objected. "I think I stopped growing over a year ago. But you look like you've been spending all your free time at the gym!"

Derrek laughed. "Free time? No way, Mouse, it's all part of training. Free weights and aerobic. Five-mile runs every morning. I would let you punch me in my stomach, but my abs might break your hand!"

Sally laughed. Then she introduced James to her sister and brother-in-law. They shook hands and exchanged pleasantries, then sat down. The waitress came and took their drink orders.

"Why do you call Sally 'Mouse'?" James asked Derrek after the waitress walked away.

"Sally was a little girl when Andie and I met," Derrek started.

"I was not a little girl," Sally protested, "I was ten. I was just small for my age!"

"I was seventeen and you were a mere baby," Derrek responded, grinning. "When she got excited about something, she would make this high-pitched squeaking sound, like a mouse. It was pretty cute. I told her she sounded like a mouse, and she got mad, so of course I kept doing it! I don't have any brothers or sisters, so I had to have some fun with her. But we became friends pretty quickly, and I've called her Tiny Mouse ever since. Even though she's all grown up now."

James smiled. "That's kind of sweet," he said, glancing at Sally, whose cheeks were still pink. It was obvious she was among her favorite people.

They reviewed the menus. When the waitress returned with their drinks, they were ready to order. Everyone ordered shellfish and salad. When the salads arrived, they paused momentarily from their conversation to dig in. Then James turned to Andie.

"So, Andie," he said, dabbing the corner of his mouth with his napkin then putting the napkin on his lap like his mother had taught him to do in fancy restaurants. "I met Sally in junior high. We were both totally awkward back then. No offense, Sally."

"Oh, none taken," Sally said enthusiastically. "I completely agree. I was totally awkward back then. Well, until like a month ago!"

James smiled fondly at Sally and turned back to Andie. "So, what was she like as a little kid?" he asked. "I bet she was a cute baby."

"Oh, she was!" Andie agreed. "I was seven when she was born, so she was my little baby doll. She had these springy curls and round pink cheeks that always looked like they needed to be pinched! Mom was still pretty busy with our brother, Nathan, who was two when she was born, so I would entertain Sally with my stories and songs and puppet shows. She had such a laugh, so I was always trying to do things to make her laugh. She had a short attention span, so I had to come up with new things to do to make her happy all the time. If I didn't, she would cry."

"Is she like that with you, James?" Derrek joked.

"I've never seen her cry," James admitted.

"Take her to a sappy movie," Derrek advised him. "But bring Kleenex. And bring Andie too. She could use a good happy cry."

Andie nodded. "It's true," she confided. "I really could."

"Sally may have been awkward at school," Derrek said, "but at home, she was always the life of the party." He looked at Sally.

"Remember? You were always singing, dancing around, trying to get everyone's attention."

Sally blushed. "Oh God, that was such a long time ago!"

He turned back to James. "And she loved to bake with her mom and grandma."

"Yeah," Sally said, "so you always had cookies and brownies to eat."

Derrick grinned. "Can you still bribe her with chocolate?"

James raised an eyebrow. "What?"

Andie laughed. "We learned that if we gave her a chocolate bar or a cookie, she would let us watch whatever we wanted on TV."

"Or give us some alone time when we needed it," Derrick added.

Sally gave a little shrug. "Well, I guess I still respond pretty well to chocolate."

James caught her eye and smiled. "Good to know." He remembered the shy version of Sally at Randall who was separated from her friends in class and relied on him and his friends for some friendly interaction each day. He thought about how easy it would have been for them to ignore her and how grateful he was now that they hadn't. She must have brought out the best in them, even back then.

"Sally has been a godsend for Andie, too," Derrek continued, "I was deployed in Germany for a year before I was assigned to Fort Benning, so Andie really needed her family. And when Josie was born, Sally was really there for her. She's more like a second mom to Josie than an aunt. Sally, even if Andie had another sister, you would still be my favorite sister-in-law."

James looked at Sally and noticed her wiping a tear off of her cheek with the back of her hand. On the other side of the table, Andie sniffed. He was struck by how similar Sally and her sister looked, with their brown hair and sparkling pale blue eyes. They had similar facial expressions, and both appeared to wear their emotions right on the surface.

"Well," Derrek said, reaching out to take Sally's hand, "now you've seen her crying." They smiled at each other affectionately.

The entrees were served, and they all composed themselves to eat.

James took a bite of shrimp, and it melted like butter in his mouth. Everyone else was quiet as silverware clinked on plates.

The plates were cleared when they were done, and there was nothing left for doggy bags. They ordered coffee, tea, and dessert, and continued to talk and get to know each other. Soon, they noticed a troupe of waitstaff heading toward them with plates, one of them containing a piece of chocolate cake with a lit candle. They all looked confused, except for Derrek, who was smiling. The staff sang the happy birthday song to Andie and then walked away, leaving the desserts behind on the table.

"Derrek!" Andie exclaimed. "My birthday isn't until the end of October!"

"I know," Derrek responded. "But I won't be here to take you out to celebrate, so I took the opportunity." He leaned toward her and gave her a kiss. Andie was radiant. She blew out the candle and hugged her husband.

Soon the dessert plates were empty, and Andie announced she needed to get back to the baby and go home. Derrek paid, and they all hugged their goodbyes. Sally and James walked to the parking lot and toward the Cruiser.

Sally turned to James and asked, "Would you ever consider joining the military?"

He shook his head. "Hell no," he told her. "I have no desire to join the military. I don't want to shoot anyone or be shot at. And I definitely don't want to drop any bombs on innocent people. But I guess I have a certain amount of respect for people who do join up, if it's what they want to do."

"You still have to register for the draft when you're eighteen, though," Sally said solemnly. "We have to hope there's never another war like Vietnam. I don't remember it, but Andie and Nathan do. I can't imagine all the moms and dads that had to say goodbye to their sons, not knowing if they would ever see them again. A lot of them didn't."

James nodded. "We were pretty young then. We were watching *Sesame Street* while the news about the war was on the other channels. I guess we've been really sheltered. It must have been an incredibly scary time."

Sally took his hand. "War or not, I don't know how Andie does it. I think being a military wife must be so hard. I'm glad the military isn't in your plans. I'm not as strong as she is."

James knew this was true. Although Sally was a strong person, she needed her support people around her. She would not be likely to go out to find new people. He knew this about her, and he knew it about himself, as well. He squeezed her hand.

"Next time I go to your house," he told her as he unlocked and opened the passenger side door, "I'm gonna ask your mom to show me your baby pictures."

"What she'll probably end up showing you is a ton of pictures of baby Andie, a handful of pictures of four-year-old Andie with baby Nathan, and maybe one blurry picture of the back of my head. With Nathan and Andie." Sally laughed. "You're a third child, too, Jamie," she said. "You must understand."

He understood exactly. But he was happy they had changed the subject and that he was able to hear her laugh.

"What do you want to do now?" James asked as he started the car. "We still have a couple of hours before you have to be home."

"What are your friends up to tonight?" Sally asked.

"I don't know where they started," James told her, "but they usually end up at the Burger King parking lot when they're done."

"Let's head over there and see if they're there," Sally suggested. "Carl has been making a huge effort to talk to me in math class lately, which has been awkward, but nice. It would be fun to see those guys outside of school. And it would be great to see Pete again."

James nodded. "Yeah, that might be fun," he agreed. "Just to warn you, though, there's not much action over there. Usually, the most exciting thing is when someone in a hopped-up classic car peels out of the parking lot."

Sally laughed. "We can rate their performance," she proposed. "It might be more entertaining than a movie!"

"Let's Hear it For the Boy"/Deniece Williams
September 30, 1984

"Well, it's about time you got up, Salamander," Andie said over the phone when Sally returned her call at noon. "I've been up with Josie since five thirty. I actually fell asleep on the playroom floor while she was rolling around."

"I'm sorry," Sally said, "but I don't have to be home until midnight, and I'm not going to get home one minute earlier if I don't have to. I have a boyfriend now, Andie." She shrieked. "I have a boyfriend, Andie!"

Andie laughed. "It's okay, one day you'll be the one with the baby, and payback will be sweet. So yes, you have a boyfriend! And we like him! Derrek thought you were practically glowing, Sally. And James. Wow! He is so cute, and he is so nice! And my God, Sally, he likes you so much! He may even love you!"

"What makes you say that?" Sally asked, her heart thumping from hearing those words.

"Sally," she said, "he looks at you the way Derrek looks at me. The way Derrek looked at me when we first fell in love. He is so into you. And he kept asking questions about you. I was supposed to be the one grilling him, but all he wanted to talk about was you! He is so special. He's a keeper."

Sally closed her eyes and sighed. "I feel the same about him," she said. "I think about him all the time. Sometimes I stop thinking about him just so I can think of a different thing about him."

"Is it getting in the way of your being able to do other things?" Andie asked.

"No."

"Have you stopped seeing your other friends because you don't want to be with anyone but him?"

"No."

"That's a really good sign, Sal," Andie told her. "It means you're developing a healthy relationship. Enjoy it and take it slow if you can. I remember falling in love with Derrek, and it was so hard, but if you do, it will be worth it. Keep getting to know each other, everything you can about each other. There will always be new things to learn about him, so you'll never get bored."

"Andie," Sally asked, "can I ask you something personal?"

"You can ask me anything, sweetie," Andie assured her.

Sally hesitated. "How old were you, your first time?"

Andie laughed. "You don't have to be embarrassed to ask me, Sally," she responded. "We're sisters! It was my senior year. I was seventeen. So, I was a bit older than you. It was after senior prom. I'll tell you, though, I would not recommend prom for your first time. Way too much pressure. Everyone thinks doing it on prom night is so romantic, but it's not. You're all stressed out, and tired, and it feels so rushed. Sally, for your first time, do it when you and James both feel it's right and you're both ready."

"I will," Sally said. "I know I want it to be special. I want it to be special for both of us."

"It will be," Andie assured her.

"You really liked him, huh?" Sally asked.

She could hear Andie smile. "Yes, I really did. I do. And Derrek, well, he approves. James has the Derrek Fischer stamp of approval, and I know how much that means to you."

"It means a lot. Did he seem jealous?"

"Oh, you!" Andie chastised her sister. "You have your own man now. Hands off mine!"

"I hope Dad likes Jamie. What if he doesn't?"

"Sally, Dad will like him," Andie reassured her. "What's not to like? Dad must see how happy you are since you've been going out with James. It's so obvious to everyone."

Sally sighed. "I hope so. I can picture the three of us going to a Red Sox game together this summer. But that will only be fun if they like each other!"

"Sally, if Dad doesn't like James, I will eat my own shoe," Andie promised. "Oh, Derrek just got back from his mom's house. I gotta go. Talk to you soon, Sal. I love you."

"I love you, too, Andie."

Sally hung up the phone feeling slightly torn between the need to have her father like James and her desire to see her sister eat a shoe.

October

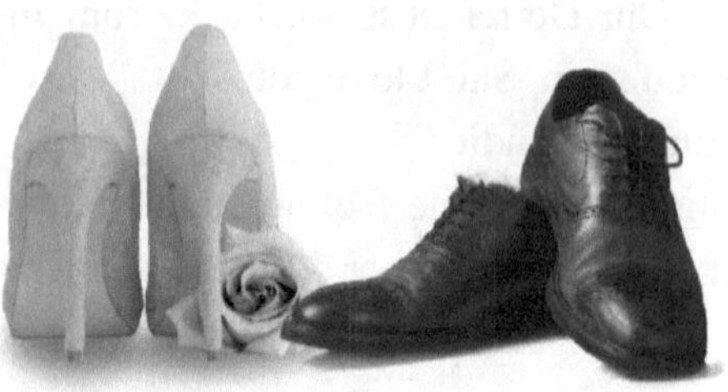

"People are People"/Depeche Mode
October 3, 1984

The McKinney High School Homecoming was the next weekend. The festivities would start with a pep rally in the gym on Friday during school, then a football game on Saturday, and a dance on Saturday night. The dance would be James and Sally's first public appearance as a couple. They made plans to meet up with some of their friends for dinner after the game and before the dance, and James officially asked Sally to be his date at the semi-formal evening event. She excitedly agreed.

Michelle and Darlene talked Sally into volunteering for the decorating committee with them. They were on it the previous year, which is where they had met Traci. They had fun and thought Sally would enjoy it, too. It would give her a chance to make some new friends at the same time.

After school, the committee met in the gym to work on the decorations for the pep rally. In addition to Sally and her two friends, there were several other girls from all four grades and two freshman boys. Sally recognized a couple of girls she had known from Randall. One of the juniors was in English class with her and James.

They spread four lengths of banner paper on the floor and talked about what to write and draw. Their school mascot was a tiger, so they tried to think up funny or inspirational quotes including this theme. One girl shouted out "Go Get 'em, Tiger!" and everyone laughed. They broke up into four groups to work on the different signs. Sally was with her friends, one of the freshman boys, and Kathy Marie D'Angelo, a girl that Sally had known from Lincoln Elementary and Randall Junior High. The groups were given markers and poster paint, stencils, and rulers.

They discussed their vision for the banner and decided to write out "Grab 'em By the Tail, Tigers!" Michelle informed the group that Darlene was good with printing and nominated her to complete the lettering. While Darlene worked on this, the other group members sorted and poured the poster paint into Styrofoam bowls. The freshman boy accidentally kicked over one of the flimsy bowls, and red paint spilled on the basketball court, creating a crimson stream. Panicking, the girls started to dab at the paint with paper towels. That just smeared the paint on the floor.

"We won't be able to get all of this up with dry paper towels," Kathy Marie stated with authority. "We need to go get some wet ones. And maybe a mop bucket from the janitor closet. Sally, will you come help me get them?"

Sally shrugged at her friends and headed toward the hall with Kathy Marie. As they neared the janitor's closet, Kathy Marie turned to face Sally. "So," she said, conversationally. "I hear you're going out with James Newell."

Sally smiled at her. "Yeah, we started going out a few weeks ago. It's going really well."

"Oh, cool," Kathy Marie said. "I remember when we were at Randall, he was kind of a bad boy. Is he still like that?"

"Well, no, I don't think I would call him a bad boy anymore," Sally answered. "He's just trying to figure everything out, like the rest of us."

"I always had the impression back then that he was, I don't know, but like, maybe a little slow on the uptake," Kathy Marie said with a trace of what sounded like pity in her voice.

"Slow on the uptake?" Sally repeated, feeling her blood turn cold. "What do you mean by that? You think he wasn't very smart? Why? Because he wasn't in honors classes like you? You know, I wasn't in honors classes either. But being super smart in school isn't everything, Kathy Marie."

"Yeah, maybe," Kathy Marie said thoughtfully. "But he always seemed to be behind, you know? Like he couldn't keep up with everyone else. He didn't say much, and he always looked so intense." She opened the janitor's closet and rolled the mop bucket out to the hall. "And you know, I've heard some stuff about his brother. He was always getting in trouble over at Murphy High. I hear he was even kicked out of his own house. Not even his own family wanted him around. Apparently, everyone thinks he's a loser."

"What?" Sally exclaimed coldly. "Where on Earth did you hear that?" Sally had never heard a negative word about James or his family from anyone, and having met them, it was making her feel sick to her stomach.

"I don't know. It's common knowledge, I guess," Kathy Marie answered innocently. "I guess because James is so quiet, and has always hung out with, like, a group of thugs, I just put two and two together and assumed maybe James was heading in the same direction as his brother. I've been concerned about you, Sally, and, you know, your reputation. Especially since you've been hanging out with those girls that went to DeMarco Elementary since you've been back. People might be getting the wrong idea about you."

They had been heading toward the girls' room to get some more paper towels, but Sally stopped in her tracks. "Oh," she said. "I see. So now there's something wrong with the DeMarco girls, too? Because I thought we were all McKinney girls now."

Kathy Marie laughed. "Oh, come on, Sally. You went to Gearhart Prep. You know there's a difference. The girls from our neighborhood have been raised to go to college and have careers and good lives with successful husbands. Those girls don't think about those things. They just want to get done with high school and go to community college until they meet some poor jerk who will take care of them. Or they want to have a bunch of kids and stay home painting their nails and collecting welfare."

Sally felt stunned. "Wow, Kathy Marie," she said, trying to gather thoughts, which were flying through her brain at record speeds. "Just wow. What the hell happened to you? You seemed so nice when we were kids, but you're not anymore. You've become a spiteful and mean person. There's no difference between us and the kids who went to

DeMarco. As a matter of fact, I'm learning right this minute that I have much more in common with them than I do with you. And James, well, James is the best thing that ever happened to me, and I'm not gonna stand here and listen to you say one more bad thing about him or his family. So just shut your stupid preppy mouth and get out of my way!"

Sally pushed the mop bucket aside and heard it roll into the wall as she stomped angrily toward the gym. She hoped it tipped over and soaked Kathy Marie. Michelle caught her eye as she came through the door and immediately knew something was wrong. She ran to her side to see what happened. She followed Sally out of the building through a side door. Sally started to feel lightheaded. She approached the brick wall that sided the school, turned her back to it, and let herself slide down until she was sitting on the cold ground. She pulled her knees to her chest and began to sob.

"What happened?" Michelle asked, kneeling in front of her.

Sally tried to speak, but she couldn't catch her breath. Michelle sat against the wall and put her arm around her shoulders. She sat with her like that until Sally's chest stopped heaving. Sally took a few deep breaths and recounted the whole story to Michelle.

"Oh, my God," Michelle said, shocked. "I had no idea Kathy Marie was such an incredible snobby bitch! I mean, I know lots of kids from Lincoln, and I've never heard any of them say anything like that. Do people really think that way?"

"It's like I was telling you before," Sally said, tears still running down her face. "It was just like last year at Gearhart. That attitude of being better than everyone else. I don't get it. How can anyone say such awful things about Jamie? Or you and the other girls, for that matter? So we come from different neighborhoods, but are we really all that different?"

Michelle took a wrinkled, clean tissue from her purse and handed it to Sally. Sally blew her nose hard.

"Well," Michelle started, "I know there are some obvious differences. I mean, my mom is a stay-at-home mom, so we don't make as much money as kids whose parents have two incomes, and we rent our house, and we only have one car. And there are more kids in my neighborhood whose parents are divorced, and they live in apartments and stuff, but nothing we can't overcome. Everyone I know works so hard. Darlene lives near me, and she gets all A's and is planning to be a biologist someday. And what did she mean about having lots of babies and painting nails? Have you ever heard of anyone doing that around here?"

"No!" Sally exclaimed. "It was like she was saying a line from a movie or something! I mean, has she even taken the time to get to know anyone from DeMarco? I have so much more respect for people who come from a place where they have to work hard to get what they have, not people who expect to have it handed to them. And my family isn't rich, even if I did go to Lincoln. My parents saved for years to buy our house! We had to live with my grandparents in a three decker and my mom had to carry groceries up two flights of stairs to the kitchen! And oh my God, Michelle," Sally sniffed, "the way she talked about Howie! This is exactly why Jamie said he didn't go to Murphy."

"I know," Michelle said. "But you know what? You know James is a decent person. You've heard it from so many people! And you know he's not stupid. He must know what some people think about his brother. But I don't think he cares. Or if he does, he hides it well. Sally, don't waste any energy on stupid Kathy Marie. She means nothing. She is nothing. Don't let her ruin homecoming for you and James."

"What do I say to Jamie?" Sally sniffed.

"Don't say anything," Michelle advised. "You've heard that living well is the best revenge, right?" Sally nodded. "Well, you know Kathy Marie will be at the dance on Saturday. You just show up at the dance with James, and you have the best time possible. Don't even think about her. I bet she's jealous of you because you came here after being gone for a year and had a boyfriend in literally three days. My mom says girls like her act that way because they're jealous."

"You think?" Sally asked.

"I do," Michelle answered, "but don't you dare tell my mom I said she was right. I'll never live it down. And I want you to remember," she added, squinting her eyes in her best expression of toughness, "the DeMarco girls, who by the way will go to the grave for you, will look out for you. If anyone gives you a hard time again, we'll have our uncles or older brothers mess them up!"

Sally laughed. "Michelle, I know your families aren't in the mafia!" She wiped her eyes and blew her nose again. "I think I'll be okay now," she said. "But I can't believe I stood up to her like that. I've never done anything like that before in my life. Now that I'm thinking of it, I'm actually in disbelief. I think I'm getting a delayed reaction. I think I might throw up."

"It's okay," Michelle said soothingly. "You're gonna be ok." They sat quietly for a few minutes. Then Michelle spoke. "Do you want to go back to the gym to get your stuff, or do you want me to go get it for you?"

"Can you go get it for me?" Sally pleaded. "I can't go back in there. I'm shaking. I might be cold, but I don't think that's what it is." She held out her hand to show Michelle her trembling fingers.

"Okay," Michelle said, standing up. "I'll go get your stuff. And then I'll walk you home. I'll have Darlene pick me up when she's done with the banner."

"Your Mother Should Know"/The Beatles

They walked to Sally's house quietly, once in a while one of them remembering something to tell the other or pointing out a cool leaf they saw on the sidewalk. In front of her house, Sally fished her house key out of her purse and let them in. They went to Sally's room and did Mad Libs until they were both rolling on the floor with laughter. Darlene arrived an hour later and joined them to listen to records and to gossip. Sally filled her in on all the latest with James, and she told Sally about Charlie, the boy she had been flirting with in her English class. Then they raided the kitchen and ate graham crackers with peanut butter. Sally felt like she was ten again. When her mother came home at six thirty, the girls jumped up from the table as if they were doing something wrong, which they weren't. Sally introduced Darlene to her mother, who asked both girls to stay for dinner. The girls said they needed to get home to their own mothers, said goodbye, and left.

"I've always liked Michelle," Mrs. Bachman admitted. "And Darlene seems nice." She sat at the table and patted the chair next to her. Sally obediently took a seat. "Now, sweetie, you've been crying. I can always tell. Did something happen at school today?"

Sally immediately felt the tears spring back up. She told her mother every detail of what Kathy Marie had said and about Michelle's advice.

Mrs. Bachman put her hand on top of Sally's hand. "Sally, I'm so sorry that happened to you," she told her. "Michelle is so wise. I might have said something similar. Don't let this girl ruin your plans. James has made you happy, and there is nothing wrong with the kids from DeMarco. D'Angelo you said?" Sally nodded. "I know her mother,

Sylvia D'Angelo. We were in the PTA together when you girls were at Lincoln. Ugh, horrible woman. I never liked her."

Sally was flabbergasted. "Mom!"

Her mother shrugged. "Sally, there's no rule that says we have to like everyone, but there is one that says we need to remain civil to each other. And apparently Sylvia didn't teach that rule to her daughter." She shook her head. "I don't know what the D'Angelos have to be so snotty about anyway. They may have a nice house and good jobs, but they came from the same background as the rest of us. I just can't tolerate people who think that way."

"I don't get it, Mom," Sally said with a sigh. "I mean, just because one person's dad is a lawyer, and another person's dad works in a factory, it doesn't mean one is better than the other. And just because Michelle's mom stays at home and doesn't work in an office, it doesn't mean Michelle won't do great things with her life. Or even end up sending her kids to private school someday. Kathy Marie sounded so stupid, saying the things she said. Especially about Jamie. I wish I never had to see her again."

"I know sweetie," Mrs. Bachman said softly. "It would make things easier. But you can't avoid people and things that make you feel uncomfortable forever. Think of all the things you'd miss. Sally, I agree with Michelle. You go to your homecoming events. Get all pepped up at the pep rally. Root for the home team at the game. Then, get all excited with your friends about getting ready and going to the dance. And you and James will have a wonderful time. You'll dance and spend time with the people you really care about, and who care about you. Ignore this Kathy Marie. She's not worth the space she's taking up in your brain right now."

"I know, Mom," Sally agreed. "And I know I can't transfer schools every time someone makes me feel uncomfortable. And if I did, there'd be no more Jamie, and that would be the worst."

Mrs. Bachman nodded and pushed her chair back from the table. "Yes, that would be the worst," she agreed, standing up. "I was going to ask you to help me make dinner, but instead, I think I'm gonna put you in charge of dessert tonight. Why don't you make us a chocolate pudding cake?"

Sally recognized her mother's attempt to cheer her up by having her make her favorite dessert. It worked, and they stood side by side in the kitchen, preparing their food.

The pudding cake helped, as did watching funny sitcoms with her parents after dinner. Sally answered the ringing phone in the kitchen to find Michelle on the other end. She stretched the long cord from the wall-mounted kitchen phone to the cellar steps, sat at the top step, and closed the door for privacy.

"I talked to Marianne Foley," Michelle said, "and told her what happened today, and she said no one from Lincoln really likes Kathy Marie anymore. She's gotten totally intolerable and snobby, and the other girls don't even wanna be around her. Remember that thing you asked me about being a social pariah a while back? Yeah, that's what she's become. So, the bottom line is, don't listen to a word she says, and if she says everyone feels the same way as her, they don't."

"I wonder what happened to make her so mean?" Sally wondered.

"Well, this may just be a rumor, but Marianne said she thinks her parents may be splitting up."

"Oh no!" Sally exclaimed. "I almost feel sorry for her. Or I would if she wasn't such a horrible person."

"Right," Michelle agreed. "I wouldn't wish divorce on anyone, but it's not an excuse to be mean."

"No, it's not." Sally paused. "Michelle, for the thousandth time already this year, thanks so much for being my friend. You were really there for me. I am so lucky to have you. I hope I can repay the favor one day."

"You're welcome, Sally, and yes, I am sure the favor will be paid back in full the next time I come crying to you about some guy that doesn't respond to all my earthly charms."

"Any guy that doesn't see the benefits of being with you doesn't deserve you," Sally said honestly. "Gotta go do some homework now. But I'm guessing you know I'm not going back to the decorating committee unless Kathy Marie doesn't come back."

"Oh, she came right back alright, apparently right after we left, like nothing ever happened, and Darlene says she started criticizing everyone's work. She won't be wanted on any committees if she's gonna act like that."

"Too bad," Sally said. "I would have enjoyed getting to know some new girls and doing some painting. I thought it would be fun. Maybe next time."

"Next time for sure," Michelle agreed. "And if there are ever any more accidents, I'll go with you to get the mop. Only until we know for sure who we're dealing with."

Sally got to her room before the phone rang again. "Hey Sally, it's just me."

"Just you?" Sally responded fondly. "Jamie, I would say you are a sight for sore eyes, but we're on the phone, so I don't know the equivalent."

"Is everything okay?" James asked with concern.

"Oh, there was some catty girl stuff earlier today at school. But my girls were there to help me, and I think we turned it around pretty well, so it's all good now."

"Oh. Well, I guess that's good. I like that you call them your girls."

"Well," Sally said, "there are five of us all together, and even though I can only handle a couple at a time, I like them all."

"Yeah, it gets too noisy with too many at once," James agreed. "So, are you getting excited about the dance?"

"Yeah," Sally answered in the most enthusiastic voice she could muster. She was looking forward to the dance, but now she was feeling like she was at the end of her energy. Talking to James helped. "How formal is the dance supposed to be?"

"Girls in dresses, boys in ties," James said. "But you don't have to buy new clothes. You can wear something you already have."

Sally smiled. "But Jamie," she protested, "shopping for a brand-new dress is half the fun of it!"

"I'd be happy if you wore the dress you wore on our first date," James admitted. "I know I told you that you looked great, but honestly you looked smokin' hot. My feet almost melted to the sidewalk!"

"Well, imagine how surprised you'll be when you see me in a hot new outfit," Sally teased. "You'll become a puddle of goo on the floor."

"Ah, yes, a goo puddle," James said. "That really gives me something to look forward to. I can't wait to see you."

"I can't wait to see you tomorrow," Sally said. "I'm gonna give you the biggest kiss, and the biggest hug. . . . I might knock you over!"

"Alright!" James responded. "I like your enthusiasm. Do you want me to pick you up in the morning, like, at eight?"

"I can do eight," Sally agreed. "And we can sit in the car for a while before we go in."

"My new favorite morning activity," James told her.

"I have to go now. I haven't had a chance to get to any homework yet, and I don't want to start getting behind. So I'll see you at eight?"

"Wild horses couldn't keep me away."

"Good. Well, goodnight, Jamie."

"Goodnight, Sally."

"Legs"/ZZ Top
October 4, 1984

Sally felt more confidence after her morning rendezvous with James, but walking in the halls between classes, she felt her pulse rise at the thought of seeing Kathy Marie. To her great relief, that didn't occur until after fourth period, when she was walking to lunch with James, holding his hand. They made eye contact, and Sally gave her the death stare. Being with James made her feel stronger. Kathy Marie turned away. Kathy Marie knew better than to mess with her again. It felt like a small victory.

James felt a slight spring in his step all morning after being able to share kisses with Sally before school in his car. His classes flew by, and he was in his element sitting behind Sally in English class. Mrs. Clark broke the class up by rows into groups to discuss three chapters of *The Great Gatsby*, and since James was in a group with Sally, he felt more comfortable making some contributions to the conversation. On the way to lunch, he continued the conversation with her, and he enjoyed it. At one point, he saw her look toward another girl he vaguely recognized in the hallway, and the girl quickly turned away. He felt Sally's hand tighten around his, and he wondered if this had anything to do with what had happened on Wednesday. She kept talking about the book, though, so he didn't say anything. If she wanted to talk to him about it, he figured she would, and he would be there to listen.

James dropped Sally off at the table where her friends were sitting and gave her a quick kiss before going off to his own table. Sally sat with the girls, and they made plans to go to the mall after school to find dresses for the dance.

Kim drove them all to the Main Street Mall in her father's old Chevy Chevette. It was a tight fit for all five girls, but luckily it was a short ride. They went to a small boutique that specialized in formal wear for teens.

The girls looked through the selection and picked out prospective dresses to bring to the fitting room. Sally grabbed a maroon, sleeveless, belted dress that went below her knees and a black long-sleeved dress that fell three inches above her knees and had a scoop neckline.

When she came out with the black dress on, her friends responded favorably.

"Wow, Sally," Kim said, "I didn't realize you had legs under those jeans you always wear. You need to buy that dress. And wear a miniskirt to school every now and then."

"Yeah," Traci said, looking her up and down. "You won't be leaving only James's eyes bugging out if you wear that. You'll also be making all the other guys drool!"

Sally blushed. "You really think so, you guys?" she said, feeling embarrassed to be gawked at by her group of friends. "I'll need to get some nylons and new shoes, and for sure some new jewelry."

"We'd better get a move on," said Michelle, who had already found a beautiful knee-length kelly green dress that went with her red hair and flattered her petite figure. "We've got a lot of stores to hit."

After all the girls had chosen and paid for their dresses, Sally stopped at a payphone to call her mother at work to see if she could use her emergency credit card to buy accessories. Her mother told her that since she had been responsible with her money lately, she would give her the okay.

After the last shop, they stopped at The Cookie Place, and Sally's coworker snuck her a big bag of double chocolate chip cookies that had been deemed not fresh enough to sell after being in the display for over an hour. They were delicious. She shared them with her friends.

While their friends snacked, Michelle pulled Sally aside to go to the ladies' room. "I heard something else from Marianne," Michelle told her, closing the door to a stall behind her and raising her voice to be heard. "She heard that the D'Angelos are for sure splitting up, because Mr. D'Angelo had an affair with someone at his office. Marianne heard it from her brother Rich, who's friends with Tom Harrity, who lives down the street from Kathy Marie, and he heard it from his mother. So it looks like Mrs. D'Angelo's gonna have to sell the house and move, and I would guess they're gonna have to downsize."

"Yikes," Sally responded, looking under the other stall doors to make sure there was no one else in the bathroom to overhear them gossiping. "That's awful."

"Yeah, but it explains a lot. But she should watch herself if she doesn't want to end up alone forever," Michelle said. "I mean, your friends are what get you through this kind of stuff."

"What she needs is a good therapist," Sally stated.

Michelle came out of the stall, washed her hands, and took out her eyeliner for a touch up. "Yeah, well, for what it's worth, I hope she gets one."

They returned to their friends, who had finished the cookies, and they headed to Kim's car for the drive home.

Later, Sally modeled the whole outfit for her parents and Andie. "Wow," Andie said. "All that walking you've been doing has paid off. You've got great legs!"

"Thanks," Sally said, smiling brightly.

"You do look beautiful, sweetie," her mother agreed. "We'll need to get some pictures of you and James before the dance."

Mr. Bachman approached his daughter and put his hands on her shoulders. "You're really growing up, honey," he said, and she thought she may have heard his voice crack a bit. "But slow it down a little bit, okay? You're my last little girl." He embraced her.

"I will, Dad," she said affectionately, glancing at Andie, who smiled at her.

"Rebel Yell"/Billy Idol
October 5, 1984

The Pep Rally was at noon on Friday. School would be let out right after so the facilities could be set up for an alumni reception that night. The end-of-fourth-period bell rang, and instead of rushing to the cafeteria as usual, students proceeded to the gym for the mandatory event. The banners had been placed high on the walls, and streamers waved along with the air currents from the movement of the students finding a place to sit in the bleachers. James and Sally found seats together among the mass of students and held hands as they waited for the festivities to begin.

Soon, the marching band tramped in from the hallway, dressed in uniforms consisting of the green and black school colors, playing "Eye of the Tiger." They stopped, facing the audience, and marched in place as they completed the song. Everyone applauded, and some of the rowdier students yelled out compliments or jeers. The band started up again, playing a Sousa march. Sally secretly liked this type of music but would never tell her mother, who wanted to listen to it in the car instead of the rock stations Sally preferred.

The band marched out of the gym, playing "Semper Fidelis," and soon, Tim Lambert, senior class president and a running back on the football team, came out to give a rally speech. He was met with cheering and shouts of approval, especially from the senior class. He praised the team, which was now 4-0, and named some of the players who had been most instrumental in this winning record. Cheerleaders held up signs lettered with messages such as "Go, Tim!" and "Ryan the Rocket" to massive applause. At the end of his speech, Tim' grabbed the microphone, pounded his fist in the air, and yelled, "Go, Tigers!"

And the crowd followed suit in unison, "Go, Tigers!" with right fists pumping in the air.

The Prince song "Let's Go Crazy" came on over the speakers, and the cheerleaders took the floor and engaged in a choreographed dance routine. Sally was impressed, as the cheer squad at Gearhart included only three girls who could barely synchronize their pompoms. They didn't get much practice since Gearhart only had lacrosse and tennis in their sports program. The McKinney girls looked ready for competition. When the dance ended, the cheerleaders led responsive cheers, and the crowd joined in. This went on for about ten minutes, and when the crowd was duly pepped, the principal, a jovial middle-aged woman named Mrs. Catalano, came to the microphone. There was some applause, and then she thanked the band, the cheerleaders, and the students for their participation and encouraged them all to attend the game and the dance the next day. She reminded the students to bring their IDs to the game and ended with a rousing, "Go, Tigers!" All four grade levels echoed it back.

Sally felt her blood pulsing through her as they got up to leave. The energy was contagious. She and James stopped at his locker first to get his jacket and weekend homework and then went to Sally's for the same. They ran into Chris and Rhonda in the parking lot and decided to all go out for lunch together. James had to work that night, but he and Sally still wanted to enjoy their afternoon off. They decided on Saydie's Diner and split up to take their own cars and meet there.

"How'd you like the pep rally?" James asked in the car. "You looked like you were getting into the spirit."

Sally smiled brightly. "I finally feel like I have something to get into the spirit about!" she exclaimed. "There wasn't too much of that at Gearhart. People weren't all that into sports there outside of golf and dressage. This is my first big high school event, if you don't count museum field trips and chemistry lab fires. It was fun to see everyone get into it!"

James smiled back. "Yeah, it was pretty good. It was more fun with you than it was last year."

"Did you go to the dance last year?" Sally asked.

"I did, but not with a date," James recalled. "I went with Carl and Chris. It was before Chris and Rhonda hooked up. It was okay, but it's gonna be a lot better with you. I assume you'll say yes if I ask you to dance. I wasn't as confident about that with the girls last year."

Sally was always amazed that James didn't realize how much the girls at school found him attractive. "When did you date Cyndi?" she asked, not out of jealousy but more from curiosity.

"Oh, you know about that, huh?" James chuckled. "I don't know if I would call that dating so much as desperation. It was around Christmas. I went to a party with Chris and Carl. Cyndi was there with her friends, and somehow, we ended up making out under the mistletoe like idiots. She tasted like cigarettes and beer, but I was a fifteen-year-old boy, so I wasn't objecting. I asked her out the next weekend, and we went to the movies, but she wasn't really that into it, so it fizzled out quickly."

"Wow," Sally responded. "You're right, not much to that."

"Yeah, and then she went out with two of my best friends. It was weird. It's like we had this weird thing in common. Not something you want to have in common with your friends. Kind of awkward, to say the least. Anyways, she has a boyfriend now, so maybe she's settled down."

"That's good," Sally said. She felt a tiny twinge of jealousy when Jamie mentioned the way another girl tasted, but nothing to make her feel insecure. She didn't know much of James's romantic history, but she was hoping he was just as inexperienced as she was. It would make things easier in the future, she hoped. But she didn't dare to ask him, not just yet.

"Black Coffee in Bed"/Squeeze

They pulled up to the small parking lot behind Saydie's Diner situated under a highway overpass. It was one of the famous original diners in Eastboro, built to serve factory workers early in the twentieth century. This twenty-four-hour diner had been refurbished with shiny new booths and personal jukeboxes at each table. The lunch rush had ended, and they were able to get one of the large, roomy booths by the window. Sally slid in toward the window, and James sat next to her. Within minutes, Chris and Rhonda came up the steps, entered the dining car, and joined them. Rhonda slid in across from Sally, and Chris after her. Some of the booths were occupied, and there were a few men sitting on stools at the counter, sipping coffee, reading newspapers, or chatting with the waitress. She broke away from her conversation, came around the counter, and approached the teens at the booth, carrying a pot of coffee and a pitcher of water.

"Coffee for you guys?" she asked. Rhonda accepted a cup, and everyone else asked for water.

"Lunch menus are on the table," the waitress said, gesturing toward the loose, wrinkled, unlaminated blue papers on the windowsill. "Breakfast is served all day." She pointed to a list of breakfast options on a blackboard attached to the wall. "Give me a wave when you're ready to order." She walked back to the counter, put the coffee pot on the burner, and resumed talking to a man who had a large golf umbrella perched against his stool even though there wasn't a cloud in the sky.

"Nothing like an old diner for a little bit of local culture," Chris said, picking up the menus and passing them out. "You can't beat the food, but it's really the atmosphere, and lack of any kind of service, that you come in for."

"I don't know, babe, she seemed nice," Rhonda said sarcastically, looking up from her coffee cup at the blue-uniformed, white-aproned server. She sipped her coffee.

"I don't know how you can drink that stuff," Sally said. "I get all jittery and can't sleep at night if I even smell coffee."

"I've never had a problem with it," Rhonda responded. "Sometimes it makes me sleepy. I'm the same way with cold medicine."

"Did you know they give speed to kids with attention problems?" Chris informed them. "Yeah. But it's supposed to calm them down instead of making them hyper like it does to other people. Weird shit."

"That is weird," Sally agreed. "I wonder how they figure that stuff out. Like, one day a scientist says, 'hey, let's give this kid some speed and see how it helps his attention.'"

They all laughed. "Yeah," James said. "Kind of like the first circus performer who decided to put his head in a lion's mouth."

Chris added, "Or the first person who thought it was a good idea to hook a bungee cord to their feet and jump off a bridge."

"Oh, that's a horrifying thought," Sally said, getting the chills. "Maybe they weren't the first. Maybe someone else went first and bashed their skull, so the next person who came along just made their bungee shorter."

"There could have been a whole string of bungee jumping deaths before someone got it right," Rhonda agreed.

Chris leaned in toward James. "And these girls don't like to go to horror movies," he said. "They could probably write one."

James laughed. It was the first time he and Sally had double dated, and it had gotten off to a good start. He was worried Sally and Rhonda might not have much in common, but they seemed to be comfortable together.

The girls looked over the songs on the jukebox, turning the knob to see all the titles. "Oh, they have Styx!" Sally exclaimed. "Jamie, do you have a quarter? It's three plays for a quarter."

James found a coin in his jacket pocket and handed it to her. She and Rhonda discussed their choices, and in the end, they picked "Snow

Blind" and "Lady," and "Jump" by Van Halen. Sally had seen them in concert two years earlier.

"David Lee Roth was wearing these funky leather pants with the butt cheeks cut out," she confided. "And I was like this naive little fourteen-year-old who had never been to a concert before, and I didn't know what that weird smell was from the cigarettes people were smoking around me!"

"I remember you from back then," Rhonda said. "You used to always wear Chic jeans and black concert T-shirts. And you had really long hair that was parted in the middle."

Sally chuckled. "Yep, that was me. In ninth grade, I went and got a Dorothy Hamill haircut. I wasn't exactly at the front end of the fashion line when they handed out taste, but I'd like to think maybe I've gotten a little better over time. I still have those T-shirts, though. They might be worth something someday!"

They signaled the waitress, and they all ordered sandwiches that came with chips and a drink. The waitress yelled their orders to the kitchen, even though she had written them down on a ticket. Then she walked away.

"So, are you guys psyched about the dance tomorrow?" Rhonda asked. "It should be good. This is the first time it's going until midnight, and they got a good DJ. I wonder if people will stick around until the end."

"Last year, they caught a couple in one of the science labs and the guy had his pants down around his ankles," Chris said. "They're gonna be extra careful to make sure the classroom doors are locked this year."

"They should just let 'em do what they want," Rhonda insisted. "I mean, isn't it better to let kids drink and have sex in a safe place rather than doing it out on the streets?"

"That's kind of a good point," Sally said. "My parents always offer to let me have some of their drinks at home so it's not such a mystery to me, but I don't really like the taste of alcohol, so it's no big deal."

"I don't like the taste much either, but I like the way it makes me feel," Rhonda admitted. "It makes me feel like I can do anything. At least for a little while. I mean, it's not like I drink all the time, but I've had my moments."

The waitress came back with their food. The music had stopped, and Chris and Rhonda were trying to decide what to play next. James and Sally looked at each other and smiled. Sally felt like James's smile went through to her soul and they shared some kind of secret. She just couldn't remember what it was.

Rhonda dropped a quarter in the slot and selected "Pinball Wizard" and "Baba O'Riley" by the Who and "Lucky Star" by Madonna. Sally was surprised that Rhonda liked Madonna, as she seemed to be mostly into rock, but a lot of people seemed to be getting more into Madonna these days.

They ate their sandwiches, and Sally gave her chips to James. They chatted about their classes, their classmates, and *The Muppet Movie*, which had been on TV the previous weekend. They all thought it was hilarious.

They finished eating and ordered two slices of apple pie to share. Sally wasn't as particular about sharing pie as she was with cake. They got four forks and two dishes of vanilla ice cream. James ate most of their pie, and Sally, most of the ice cream.

They got the bill and paid it, and then both couples left the diner, holding hands.

"So we'll see you at the game tomorrow?" Chris asked.

James raised his hand along with Sally's. "We will be there," he said. "We'll try to get there early and save seats, but it might get pretty crowded."

"Well, if we can't sit together, we'll see you for sure at dinner before the dance," Rhonda said. "I can't wait to see your dress, Sally. It sounds fancy."

"Yours too," Sally responded.

"See you guys," Chris said as he let Rhonda into the car and then drove away.

"That was fun," Sally said as they approached James's car. "When do you have to be at work?"

James checked his watch. "In about an hour," he said, unlocking Sally's door with his key.

"Oh," Sally said, disappointed. "I was hoping we would have more time this afternoon."

"I wish we did, too," James agreed, slipping his arms around her waist. He kissed her then opened her door.

As they drove toward Sally's house, they listened to Tom Petty and the Heartbreakers' *Damn the Torpedoes* on cassette. They sang along to the songs they liked, and James especially emphasized the lines he related to in "Here Comes My Girl." He knew every word and nuance by heart. Sally just knew he had been listening to that song a lot lately.

They pulled into her driveway. Her parents weren't home yet, so they didn't worry about anyone spying on them in the car. James turned down the music.

"Tomorrow it will be four weeks since our first date," Sally said with a sly smile.

James smiled. "Happy anniversary, Sally." He leaned toward her and kissed her softly.

"Happy anniversary, Jamie," she responded and reached out to kiss him more. This continued for five more minutes, until James had no choice but to leave for work. He reminded her that he would pick her up on Saturday for the game at twelve thirty so they would have time to get seats.

"Be sure to dress warm," he told her. "The temperature's supposed to drop overnight. The bleachers are metal, so they get really cold. It makes it hard to sit there for a long time. But they sell cider and hot chocolate at the game, so that helps."

"Okay," Sally said. "I'll see you tomorrow." She sat there for a few more seconds then placed one hand on his cheek and kissed him once more. "Okay," she said, opening the car door, "bye."

"Bye," James said. The door shut, and his car was quiet. He turned up the music, rewound the tape back to "Here Comes My Girl," and started off toward Luigi's.

"We Are the Champions"/Queen
October 6, 1984

The day of the game dawned bright but frigidly cold. Sally stepped out to the front stoop of her house to feel the air and saw her breath out in front of her. She went to her room and considered what to wear. She settled on her jeans, topped with a pastel pink and gray striped wool sweater over a white turtleneck. She laid her clothes on her bed, went downstairs in her pajamas to have breakfast with her parents, and then took a shower. She figured she would need another one later before the dance. She wouldn't bother making her hair fancy for the game, since she would be wearing a winter hat and scarf. She hoped it would warm up some before the dance, but the forecast was not looking promising. At least the sun was shining.

She dressed carefully then put a pair of knit knee socks and a pair of leg warmers over the cuffs of her jeans. She went down to the front hall, grabbed her sneakers, and brought them to the den. Her father was watching college football. She wasn't familiar with either team. She sat down next to her father and laced up her shoes.

It was eleven thirty, and in her enthusiasm, she was ready an hour early.

"Will you be here to meet Jamie when he comes to get me at twelve thirty?" she asked her father.

"I'm sorry, Sal," he responded regretfully, "but I have an indoor tournament at the tennis club that starts at one. I'm leaving at noon. And Mom and I are going out to dinner with Uncle Bill and Aunt Betty tonight." He saw the disappointment on her face. "But I will meet James soon, I know it," he assured her.

"I hope so," Sally said.

She watched the game with her father until he got up to get ready to go. She wished him luck, then changed the channel and watched *The Superfriends*, which she hadn't watched since she was twelve. Strangely enough, she was pretty sure it was the exact same episode she had seen last time she tuned in. Her mother came down and told her she wouldn't be there to take pictures that night, which Sally already knew, but she was going to have Andie come by and take them for her. Sally was glad not to lose the opportunity for pictures of herself with James, especially all dressed up.

Twelve thirty finally arrived, and at 12:32, James pulled up in front of the house. He jumped out of his car and walked up the walkway. Sally opened the door before he rang the bell. "Is that James?" her mother called from upstairs.

James kissed Sally quickly. "Hi, Mrs. Bachman!" he called up.

She came to the top of the stairs, trailing a long phone cord behind her. "I'm sorry, I'm on the phone with my sister in Canada," she said, "but I wanted to tell you two to have fun at the game and the dance. Mr. Bachman and I will be out when you leave, but Sally, I'll see you when you get home."

"Twelve thirty, right?" Sally asked, to confirm their earlier agreement.

"Yes. James, have her home at twelve thirty. Just for tonight. Special occasion. Okay, have a good time!" She went back into her room.

Sally took her long jacket out of the closet and put it on. She wrapped her scarf around her neck and fixed her hat atop her head in front of the hallway mirror. She put her purse over shoulder, grabbed her gloves, turned to James, and stated. "Okay. I think I'm ready." She felt like she was hauling luggage.

"It's freezing out," James declared, pulling his own hat down further over his ears.

"I know! It's always like this when it's sunny this time of year. Some sort of atmospheric thing." She had seen this on the news once.

"I brought a couple of blankets," James said, "and we'll have to sit really close to each other. You know, to conserve heat." He smiled at her.

"Of course," Sally agreed, grinning back. "We wouldn't want to waste any heat!"

The McKinney High School parking lot was full of cars from students, alumni, and parents. James skillfully parallel parked the Cruiser on a side street, and he and Sally made their way to the field behind the school. They could hear the band playing and announcements over the public address system as they approached. Sally could smell popcorn in the air, and as they got closer, she picked up the scent of apple from the hot cider. She had gone to a Renaissance Faire once with her family when she was younger, and the aroma and atmosphere at the school made her recall that day. They both showed their student IDs at the gate and were let in for free.

As they walked toward the bleachers, Sally spotted Michelle waving to her. She was seated near the back beside her parents, who were McKinney alumni. Sally and James climbed the steep metal stairs and managed to find some space between Michelle and another Tigers fan dressed in the school green and black. Everyone shifted to make room, and James laid one of blankets over the metal bench for him and Sally to sit on. They greeted Mr. and Mrs. Gorman, Michelle's parents, who they both had met several times before, and then confirmed visually that there was no way they could have saved any seats for Chris and Rhonda. They would have to fend for themselves in the crowd.

The band wrapped up their arrangement of "25 or 6 to 4" by Chicago and then marched off the field. Principal Catalano approached the podium and welcomed honored alumni, students, and guests. She thanked everyone for coming out on such a cold day, reminded them to purchase hot drinks, and she left the field. The players ran out to rousing applause and music from the band on the sidelines. The cheerleaders began to cheer, and soon the referee whistled the start of the game. McKinney kicked off, and they were underway.

By halftime, McKinney led 14-3, and Sally couldn't feel her fingers or her toes. James went to the snack bar with Mr. Gorman, and they came back with trays with cider, hot chocolate, and bags of popcorn to share. Sally held her hot chocolate in both gloved hands and let the heat permeate to her fingers. She burrowed further under the blanket she and James were sharing, and her jaw began to chatter. She sipped on her hot drink and felt the sweet liquid warm her insides. She knew the effect wouldn't last long, but she savored the feeling. Somehow, James didn't seem as cold, but he was much more stoic than her regarding many things, at least in public.

The cheerleaders danced onto the field, and Sally felt for them in their short skirts without jackets or hats. They were bad ass, even though they probably wouldn't give her the time of day at school. AC/DC's "You Shook Me All Night Long" started playing over the public address system. The girls started to dance vigorously. Sally started to sing aloud. She could hear Michelle singing, too. She looked at James. He was mouthing the words. He looked at her, and they sang together. Then they both laughed.

They all finished their snacks, and James slipped his arm around Sally's shoulder. She huddled into him as much as she could, finding some warmth. She felt a glow, though, as she reveled in the chance for them to be so close for so long. Then, James reached over and gave her a long kiss. Sally smiled at him. It was their first kiss in public. The cold seemed to fade away for a moment.

James was also enjoying the chance to be so close to Sally in public. He would have put up banners in the gym with the homecoming signs to announce their relationship if he could. He was proud to be seen with her and couldn't wait to take her to the dance that night so everyone there could see him with what he thought was the prettiest girl in school. The more time he spent with her, the prettier she got. And she had agreed to be there with him. He still couldn't believe his good luck. He wondered if they'd be able to get away with making out under the bleachers. He decided that they probably would not.

The game ended in McKinney's favor, 21-6, the opposing team having scored no touchdowns. The crowd was ecstatic. Sally was relieved after saying goodbye to Michelle and her parents to step into James's car, even if the heating fan was faulty. She had enjoyed the game, the camaraderie, and the cuddling, but she was anxious to get home to get ready for the dance. And she needed a long hot bath.

"People Get Ready"/Curtis Mayfield and the Impression

When James got home, he was still freezing. He cursed the broken blower motor in his car and went quickly into his warm house. His mother greeted him and helped him peel off his jacket and scarf. He was shivering, so she sent him to the shower to warm up and made him tea. James was not a big fan of tea, but he was a fan of his mother, so he drank it gratefully, glad for the warmth.

James was planning on going for a haircut before the dance, but his mother wouldn't hear of him going out in the cold again so soon. She had gone to beauty school after high school but never ended up working as a hairstylist. She liked to keep up her skills practicing on her family members when they let her. She sat him down on a kitchen chair, laid a towel on the floor, and gave him a trim while they talked about the game and the upcoming dance. James checked out the cut in the mirror when she was done and nodded his approval. She was just as good as any barber, and cheaper to boot.

"So," his mother asked him as she swept blond hair into a pile on the floor. "Have you seen Howie lately?"

James thought about it. "No, it's been a couple of weeks. Last time I saw him, it was when we were all watching *Eddie and the Cruisers* together. Why? Is stuff missing again?"

His mother shrugged. "Oh, no, nothing like that. It's just getting cold outside, and I want to make sure he's got warm clothes. I'm a bit worried about him." James sometimes forgot his brother was also his mother's son, and although he had not been allowed to live in their home since he was caught stealing the previous year, she still worried about his safety.

"I'm sure he's okay," James reassured her. "He usually is. But if you want, the next time he comes by in the afternoon, I'll talk him into staying for dinner."

Mrs. Newell smiled gratefully. "I would appreciate that, James. Thank you."

James gave her a kiss on the cheek and went to his room to get ready for the dance. He set up the ironing board and pressed his khaki pants and dress shirt. He went into his parents' room to borrow a tie and asked his father to help him choose one to match his shirt.

"So, this is your first dance with a date," Mr. Newell stated. "Are you ready?"

James shrugged. "I have my clothes ready," he said.

"Good," his father said, nodding. "Just remember to be a gentleman. Hold the doors for her. Offer to get her some punch. Dance with her to her favorite songs."

James nodded. "Yeah, I can do that," he said. "I'll dance with her all night if that's what she wants."

Mr. Newell laughed. "Make sure to sit down every now and then," he suggested. "But I think you two will have a good time tonight. You're a good couple." James chose between the two ties his father offered. "Here, you can borrow this, too." His father handed him his bottle of aftershave. "Don't use too much. A little goes a long way." James thanked him for his help and went back to his room.

He put on his clothes, sprayed a small amount of his father's aftershave into the air around him, and went out to the living room to wait until it was time to go. He was going to pick up Sally early so her sister could take some pictures and then meet three other couples for dinner at Benihana. He had never been there before and heard it was a fun place for groups. He was also starving after eating only shared popcorn all afternoon.

"All She Wants to Do is Dance"/Don Henley

At five thirty, James left, yelling goodbye to his parents and letting them know he would be home by one.

He felt nervous approaching Sally's house. His palms were sweaty despite the cold, and he could feel his heart fluttering. He went to the door and rang the bell. Andie answered, holding an infant. "Hi, James!" she said. "This is Josie."

He smiled at the baby, who surprisingly volunteered a wet, toothless smile back at him. "Hi, Josie," he said, thinking it would be nice to hold her, but deciding he didn't want to risk getting his dance clothes dirty with her drool. "I'm assuming Sally's here?"

"I'm right here," said Sally, making an entrance from the dining room.

James looked at Sally, and his eyes widened. The person who stood before him was a beautiful young woman in a sophisticated dress and stylish hair and makeup. Her legs seemed to go on for miles, and she was wearing high-heeled shoes that made her calves seem even more sculpted than usual. She wore a gold necklace with a sparkling green stone charm, gold hoops in her ears, and the same green stone in studs in her second piercings. He stood there feeling like an idiot, not saying a word. Finally, he managed to swallow.

"Wow, Sally. You are so beautiful," he told her softly. He wanted to say more, but he was stupefied.

Sally smiled brightly, and Andie put her hand over her heart. "Thank you," Sally said. "Let me see you."

James took off his jacket, and Sally stepped back to get a better look. "Jamie," she said with a smile, "you look amazing. I mean, I always thought you were super cute, but you are so handsome. And you got your haircut! You look great!" She stepped closer to him, carefully put her hands on his cheeks, and kissed him.

Andie cleared her throat. "Oh, my, you two," she said. "You both look so great! You most certainly don't look like a couple of sixteen-year-olds going to a homecoming dance. Do you think we could go outside really quick so I can get a few pictures before it gets too dark? The lighting is perfect right now. I know it's cold, but we can take a few more inside before you go, too." She grabbed her mother's camera in one hand and shifted the baby into position on her hip with her other.

They agreed to go outside briefly, and Sally started to hand her point-and-shoot camera to her sister. "I just put new film in here," she said. "So take as many as you want."

"Hold on," Andie said, walking into the living room and placing Josie in her portable playpen with her toys. "Let me get my bearings really quick. Once we step outside, Josie will get separation anxiety and start to cry, but I don't want to have to bundle her up for like five minutes outside." She grabbed Sally's camera from her hand, and they hurried outside. They had to close the door so the cats wouldn't escape, so they worked quickly. James put his arm around Sally's shoulder, but when Andie snapped the first picture, he was looking at Sally instead of the camera. They tried again and took several pictures with both cameras. Finally, they went inside, and Andie picked up and consoled a crying Josie.

They posed for several more shots inside the house, and Sally had Andie take some of both her and James alone, then one with her and Josie. Eventually, both cameras were out of film.

"That was fun!" Andie said. "We'll have to do this again for prom this spring." Sally and James quickly turned to face each other and then turned away. They hadn't even thought about prom yet, since it was only October, and they had only been dating for a month.

"Whoops," Andie said quickly, taking the baby from Sally. "Okay, well, I'll take my foot out of my mouth now. You two should head out for dinner."

"Yeah, we have a reservation," James agreed. "Thanks for taking pictures, Andie. And say hi to Derrek for me when you talk to him."

"Of course, James! Now you two kids go out and have fun."

"Thanks, Andie," Sally said as she and James put on their jackets. "I'll see you soon." She gave her sister a hug and her niece a kiss, and they left the house.

Once in the car, James turned to Sally. "Sally, I'm totally planning on asking you to the prom. There's no question."

"I know, Jamie," she answered, smiling at him reassuringly. "It's much too early to think about prom. You don't have to worry about it. I know you'll ask me later."

James smiled back. He was glad Sally was so easygoing. Nothing he said or did seemed to faze her in a negative way. He hoped he could keep up the trend. He also knew if he couldn't, she would probably be receptive to a chocolate apology.

Benihana was fun, and James and Sally enjoyed watching the food being made at their table. They were seated in a half circle with Chris and Rhonda, Carl and Michelle, and Darlene and Charlie. The conversation flowed between them and their friends without effort. The food was good, and they all agreed they were sufficiently full when they were done.

It was finally time to go to the dance. The couples, and Michelle with Carl as her platonic date, all went their separate ways to drive to the school. Sally felt her stomach flip-flop in anticipation and was glad James took her hand as they walked through the familiar halls of the school and into the gym. The overhead lights were dimmed, and disco lights hung from the ceiling. Small spotlights shone on the globes to make a strange effect of rainbow beams crossing back and forth across the room. There were a few dozen students already there, and some were dancing in an area set aside for that purpose. There were fruit and vegetable plates with dips set out on some lunch tables pushed together by the wall and a punchbowl guarded by a chaperone. A DJ was in one of the corners, surrounded by a large sound system and wearing a headset. He was bobbing his head to the music as some students queued up to make requests.

Sally quickly found Michelle and Carl, and together they all watched people dancing and listened to music as they chatted. Soon, their other friends filed in, and in no time, the gym was full of noise and dancing bodies. Sally and Michelle tugged their dates out to the dance floor, and they all moved awkwardly to the music, enjoying the feeling of letting loose. The place was too crowded for anyone to observe and judge their dancing, and they took full advantage of it.

James noticed a few of the senior boys checking out Sally, and he stayed close by her side. When a slow song came on, he grabbed her hand and then held her close as they swayed to the music. They would instinctively reach for kisses and then return to their embrace. The chaperones weren't monitoring anyone for physical activity on the dance floor, so they didn't monitor themselves.

Sally was exuberant. She could sense other eyes on her body, but she was focused on James. He was attentive and sweet and made her feel even more beautiful than he told her she looked. She noticed her friends were also having fun with their dates, and she knew the night was a success.

She had almost forgotten her fears from earlier in the week about seeing Kathy Marie until she saw her on the dance floor, dancing with her date, Chad, a boy that Sally recognized from Gearhart Prep. Sally knew Chad lived outside of town in an exclusive area and had probably never set foot in a public school before that night. Sally thought about Kathy Marie for a moment, and then realized she didn't want to waste any more time thinking about her. She was having the most perfect day, and no one could ruin it for her.

They danced to a few more songs and then took a break to catch their breath and have some punch. Sally sat with Michelle and Darlene on the wooden bleachers while the boys went to get the drinks. They all exchanged compliments on their dresses and how nice their dates looked that night. The boys cleaned up well and were on their best behavior.

The night went by quickly, too quickly for Sally's taste, and soon it was eleven thirty. James made eye contact with her and motioned his head toward the door. She nodded. She told her friends they were heading out, and they all knew that leaving early meant only one thing: making out in the Cruiser.

James helped Sally put on her jacket then put on his own. He took her hand in his, and they walked into the hallway toward the exit. James noticed Chris was right; the teachers were milling around the entrance to the stairways and long hallways, watching for stray couples looking for privacy. Sally smiled at her French teacher, and he smiled at her, and she and James walked outside into the chill.

As they walked together toward the car, James noticed a police car inching slowly down the street and another parked on the side street near the Cruiser. He noticed an officer on foot shining a flashlight into a car window.

"See those cops?" he said to Sally, pointing. "I think they're looking for kids making out in their cars. The neighbors probably complained."

Sally shook her head. "Party poopers," she said. "Jamie, I think I know a place we can go, where no one will find us and there are no police."

"Really? Where is this magical place?" he wanted to know.

"Just head toward my house and I'll tell you where to turn."

"I Think We're Alone Now"/Tommy James and the Shondells

James started the Cruiser, shifted into drive, and pulled onto the street. He turned onto the main road and then took a right toward Sally's neighborhood. He took another right onto her street, and then she directed him to drive past her house and take another right. They drove around the dark back streets, around curves and over potholes, until Sally directed him to turn onto a dead-end street.

"Go to the end," she instructed him. "You'll see where we are."

James came to the end of the street, pulled to the side, and stopped. He looked to his left and saw a large field. No, it was a playground. He realized they were at the backside of Sally's grade school, Lincoln Elementary. There were no houses this far down the dead-end street, and on the right was the back end of the parking lot for a large church. They were behind the Sunday School.

"Wow, Sally, you weren't kidding. No one would ever find us here," James admitted, impressed.

Sally giggled. "Kind of sounds like the start of some depraved horror movie!" she stated. "But it's not. It's totally safe here."

They figured it was safer to turn off the engine, so James grabbed the blankets from the game. He handed one to Sally, and then he reached over and kissed her, first gently, then harder. Their hands found comfortable places to rest, and they continued in this manner for some time. James felt his heart pounding and felt himself holding Sally closer and tighter. He knew they had limited time, so he did his best to keep his control and to be respectful of Sally's control. At 12:15, they stopped, breathless, and agreed it was time to head to Sally's house.

First, Sally fixed any makeup that was smudged, and then they drove to her house.

James walked her to the door, and they lingered for a bit, hoping Mrs. Bachman wouldn't open it to check on them. By some act of God, she didn't.

"I had the best time tonight, Jamie," Sally told him, resting her head on his chest. "I couldn't have asked for a better night."

"Me too," James responded, kissing the top of her head.

They held each other for a few more moments, and then they kissed goodnight, promising to talk to each other the next day.

Sally walked into her house like she imagined she would walk on a cloud. She felt like the lovestruck protagonist in a cheesy movie, like Molly Ringwald in *Sixteen Candles* when she finally gets to kiss Jake Ryan in front of her birthday cake. She loved that scene. Now she got to kiss her own Jake Ryan, but he was Jamie Newell, and he was much better.

"Mothers Talk"/Tears for Fears
October 7, 1984

Sally woke up, pulled her Boston University sweatshirt over her pajamas, and put her hair in a scrunchie bun. She thumped downstairs and stopped herself before she cut through the dining room. She slid on her oversized socks across the linoleum-floored hallway and into the kitchen. Her mother was sitting at the table, reading the Living section of the Sunday paper and sipping her coffee. An empty lunch plate rested on the table in front of her.

"Good morning, sleepyhead," Mrs. Bachman said when she looked up at Sally. "Actually, it's good afternoon. Glad you finally got up. I'm going to drop the film from yesterday off at Fotomat this afternoon. Do you want me to get doubles for James?"

"That would be so great," Sally said, falling hard onto her kitchen chair and putting her head on her hands on the table. "Where's Dad?"

"He went to Dunkin Donuts to get snacks for the two of you for your Patriots game date," her mother told her. "He should be back soon. Would you like me to make you some oatmeal with brown sugar?"

"Yeah, that would be really nice, thanks." Sally sat while her mother got up and started to gather the oats and milk for her breakfast.

"I could see your light was still on last night when we went to bed," Mrs. Bachman said, as she poured the milk into the saucepan. "How late did you stay up reading?"

Sally lifted her head slightly. "I don't know, two maybe? I was too hyper to go to sleep."

Mrs. Bachman put the cover on the pan then sat down. "I remember homecoming always being a lot of fun in high school. You had a really good time last night, huh?"

"Mom, it was totally awesome," Sally told her. "I wish every weekend could be homecoming, but then it wouldn't have been so special."

Mrs. Bachman smiled. "There'll be lots of other dances, sweetie." She paused and wrinkled her forehead in concentration. "Sally, you know," she started, "now that you have your first boyfriend, I'm wondering if we should have a talk, you know, about things."

"Like what things?" Sally asked cautiously, knowing full well what her mother was about to say but hoping she was totally wrong.

"Well, you're growing up, and I'm sure you're having some feelings, you know, when you're with James, and I want to make sure you know you can talk to me about it."

"I know, Mom. I'll talk to you if there is anything I need to talk about," Sally assured her.

"Do you have any questions for me now?" Mrs. Bachman asked, trying to look supportive but instead appearing uncomfortable.

"I'm good, Mom, but thanks," Sally told her. "I can also talk to Andie about things, you know? I mean if it's easier for you."

"Oh, sweetie, you don't need to worry about making things easier for me. This is about you. You know, when I was your age, Grandpa Irving would never have talked to me about this type of thing, and I told myself if I had a daughter, I would talk to her about anything." She put her hand over Sally's. "I want you to know I support you, and I know you're capable of making good decisions. I want to make sure you think things through before making those decisions. And if you can't talk to me for some reason, Andie is fine. Or someone else you trust."

Sally smiled at her sleepily. "Mom, I do appreciate it. I've always been able to come to you with my problems. If there's anything I need, I'll ask either you or Andie. I promise."

The oatmeal started bubbling and raising the lid on the pan. Mrs. Bachman hurried out of her chair to the stove, lifted the lid with an oven mitt, stirred, and removed the pan from the burner. Sally exhaled hard, glad the talk was over so quickly.

The lock on the front door turned, and Mr. Bachman came in. Sally could see him take a step into the dining room, and then step back and turn toward the hall. He came into the kitchen just as Mrs. Bachman was spooning the brown sugar into Sally's bowl. "Sal Gal, you're up!"

he exclaimed, putting a pink and orange box on the table, opening it, and taking out a chocolate frosted donut. "I got us donuts. You like the chocolate cream filled, right?" Sally nodded as she blew on a hot spoonful of oatmeal before putting it in her mouth. "Okay, honey, I'm going to warm up the TV. The game will be on soon. Come join me when you're done."

"Okay, Dad," Sally agreed.

She scooped up spoonful after spoonful of the sweet, warm oatmeal, hoping it would give her the energy not to fall back to sleep while watching the Patriots with her father. She finished, and her mother told her to soak the bowl in the sink and to put it in the dishwasher later.

Sally shuffled into the den and plopped down on the couch next to her father. She leaned heavily on his arm and put her feet up on the coffee table. He spread an afghan over her and together they watched the pregame show. Tony Eason was going to be the starting quarterback. Sally liked their regular quarterback, Steve Grogan, but he was having a bad year and had been injured several times. The game started, and it was a frustrating first half. Sally found herself waking up more and yelling at the TV along with her father when they saw a bad call. The half ended with the Browns leading 9-3, and Sally and her father were livid.

"They have got to start passing if they want to score a touchdown," Sally insisted.

"That's right," her father agreed. "I would love to be a fly on the wall in the locker room to see what Ron Meyer is telling them. I don't think they can stand another loss. I doubt they'll make the playoffs as it is, at this rate."

Sally smiled. She loved these conversations with her father. He had taught her about sports when it was clear her brother, Nathan, wasn't going to have any interest in going into the backyard to play catch or going to see games with him. Now Sally knew almost as much as her father about football, baseball, basketball, and hockey, and he knew it. He never questioned her knowledge because she was a girl, was never condescending, and never called her cute when she talked about sports. That had been her experience with boys around her own age ever since she had gotten into sports. Sometimes they gave her an amused smile and turned away, and other times, they would verbally push her out of the conversation by ignoring her all together. It was infuriating. They lived in a state with excellent sports teams, so there was a lot to talk about. Most of her girlfriends weren't interested in sports. This is where she and her father bonded.

The second half started poorly for the Patriots, and Sally felt her anxiety increase. She took it personally when her teams lost. But then Tony Eason made a beautiful forty-two-yard pass, and the Patriots scored their first touchdown. Sally and her father made whooping noises and gave each other high fives.

The phone rang, and Mrs. Bachman answered. "Sally," she yelled across the kitchen. "James is on the phone."

Sally hesitated. The fourth quarter was about to start, and this was her special time with her father. "Mom, can you tell him I'm watching the game, and I'll call him after it's over?"

"Okay, sweetie," her mother said.

Sally glanced sideways at her father, and she could see a smile on his face. She had made the right choice.

She was glad she stayed to watch. The Patriots scored one more touchdown and ended up winning the game, 17-16. Sally and her father had a donut to celebrate—her second, his third.

"That was a really good game," Sally stated, wiping chocolate cream from her cheek. "At the half, I didn't think they would pull it off!"

"It was a good comeback," Mr. Bachman agreed. He paused for a moment, looking at her. "So, Sally," he started.

Oh no, Sally thought, *not the talk from him, too.*

"Yeah, Dad?"

"It seems like things are really coming together for you this year," he said. "I'm glad. You're keeping up with your schoolwork even with having a part time job. You've made some friends, and you have a boyfriend. Not too shabby."

"No, it's not," Sally agreed, still not sure where this was leading.

"I will meet James," he promised. "It's been a busy time at work, and I have to take every job now that I'm working for myself."

"I know, Dad. It's okay, you don't have to explain," Sally told him.

"No, it's just that I want you to know I can see it's important to you. It's like I told you the other day, you're my last little girl. I want to be there for you. Things will slow down in the new year, and I'll be around more."

"I know, Dad," Sally repeated. "You've always been there for me. I'm not worried. And we still have a year and a half until I go to college, so we'll watch lots of games together, and maybe go to some games?"

"For sure," Mr. Bachman said. "But things do change as you get older, and especially with a boyfriend. Just don't forget about me, okay?"

Sally felt her heart might melt in her chest. "Of course, Dad. You're a major priority for me. I won't stop watching games with you, or going to Friendly's with you, or even going to watch you play tennis."

Mr. Bachman put an arm around Sally's shoulder and gave a squeeze. "You're a good daughter," he said. "And a good sport-watching companion."

"Thanks, Dad. And you know," Sally said, "I'm not your last little girl. There's still Josie. We could start training her to watch all the games with us now. That way, when I'm in college, she can come over and watch with you, so you don't have to watch alone."

Mr. Bachman rubbed his chin thoughtfully. "That's not a half bad idea," he admitted. "I don't think Mom would be willing to make that sacrifice. I'll talk to Andie about it. Now go call James. I'll see you at dinner if you didn't ruin your appetite with all those donuts."

"Thanks, Dad," Sally said sincerely, and she gave him a hug before sliding back through the kitchen and heading to her room.

Her bed was just as inviting as it had been when she had left it. She pulled the covers up over her lap and grabbed her pink princess phone. She pushed in James's number then laid back on her pillow. His father answered, then put James on the phone.

"Hey, Sally," he said. "Did you see the end of the game?"

"It was a great game!" Sally said excitedly. "Did you watch? I can't believe they pulled it off."

"Yeah, I was watching with my parents. It was a great comeback. They might have to keep Eason on as the starter if he keeps this up. That one pass was incredible. So what are you up to now?"

Sally rolled her eyes. "Well, both of my parents for some reason felt like they needed to have some real-life conversations with me today."

"Really?" James inquired. "What are those like?"

"Well, my dad wants to make sure I don't leave him behind now that I have a boyfriend, and my mom wants to make sure I know the facts of life, I guess."

"For real?" James asked, sounding amused. "Did she, like, give you the details?"

"No," Sally told him. "She handed me a book about all that when I was eleven. She wanted to make sure I know I can talk to her if I need to. It was kind of sweet, I guess, but I would actually die before I would ask her any questions about that kind of stuff."

"I think your parents finally figured out you're in a serious relationship," James suggested.

"Yeah, I guess," Sally agreed. *Serious relationship.* She wondered if her parents had been thinking the same thing as she had. She and James were getting closer as the weeks went by. It was only a matter of time before they became even more serious. She was pretty confident James was thinking about it, too. They hadn't talked about it, and Sally had no idea how to bring it up. She didn't have the right words yet.

"I have to go to work soon," James said. "I'm kind of beat today, though. I'm glad it's not a full shift. What're you doing tonight?"

"Pretty much nothing," Sally admitted, "which is nice after such a busy week. I'll probably watch TV with my parents. Maybe there will be a Wonderful World of Disney movie on."

"Fun," James said. "I used to love those Witch Mountain movies when I was a kid. The special effects seemed so cool back then before Star Wars came out."

"Jamie, please don't judge me," Sally pleaded, "but I've never actually seen any of the Star Wars movies."

"What?" James exclaimed. "Oh, come on, Sally, how could that possibly be?"

"Well," Sally explained with a sigh, "my parents didn't have time to take me to see Star Wars, and Andie had already gone with her friends. Nathan refused to see it because that's just what he's like. I was nine, so I couldn't go by myself. When the second and third movies came out, I didn't want to see them since I didn't see the first one and I wasn't sure I would be able to follow the story."

"We really need to fix this, Sally," James said solemnly. "We have to rent all three movies and watch them. Maybe next Saturday afternoon? You can come over here and we can get some pizza."

Sally smiled. She loved that idea. "That sounds great!" she told him. "So, I get to see all the movies and spend the whole day with you. Sounds like a good deal!"

"I'll ask my parents if I can move the portable TV from their room into my room, and I can hook up the VCR. It'll be much more comfortable than the den, and we won't have to deal with my parents. I'm sure my mom would make us keep the door open, though."

"That's okay," Sally said. "I think if your parents are home, I would prefer the door to be open anyway. I don't want to think of them thinking what might be going on in there."

"Yeah, I'd probably end up getting the talk like you did," James agreed. "Okay, I've gotta go get ready for work. Have a good time with your parents tonight."

"I will. Have a good time at work. I hope it's a slow night."

"I can't wait to see you tomorrow at school."

"Me, too."

"Bye, Sally."

"Hey, Jamie?"

"Yeah?"

"When I come over next week, will you play your guitar for me?"

"Uh, yeah, I think I could do that."

"Really? Okay then. Bye, Jamie."

"Celluloid Heroes"/The Kinks
October 13, 1984

Jamie picked up Sally on Saturday after he picked up the three Star Wars movies he reserved from the rental store. Sally held the cases in her hands and turned them over and from side to side as if they would reveal the story within.

At James's house, they made Jiffy Pop popcorn on the burner on the stove and managed to only burn a few kernels. As James had promised, he had moved his parents' portable TV from their room to his, and he had already hooked up the VCR. His parents were watching TV in the den, so James started the previews with the volume low so as not to disturb them. Soon, he and Sally realized they would miss half the experience of the movies without turning up the volume to get the full effects. The first movie started, and music started to play. Then there were the sounds of lasers and ships, and loud voices. It took less than ten minutes for Mr. Newell to come back and ask to close James's bedroom door, which he did. James and Sally grinned at each other, then lay on his bed and watched the movie while spooning, their first time being horizontal together. They turned off the light, ostensibly to make the movie appear more theater-like. They were able to watch enough of the movie between their other activities that Sally felt she could watch and understand *The Empire Strikes Back*. This time, she and James stayed focused on the TV aside from some random ear kisses and neck nuzzles.

After the second movie, they were hungry and ready to order pizza. They consulted with Mr. and Mrs. Newell and decided to get two large pizzas. James and Sally chose to have one of the pizzas with half pepperoni, half vegetarian, as Sally didn't like meat on her pizza. They also ordered two family-sized garden salads and four cans of soda. Sally offered James's parents some money for her share, but they adamantly refused, stating she was their guest. They left to pick up the pizza, and James and Sally waited in the den for them to come back.

"What do you think so far?" James asked.

"I'm glad I didn't go to see *Empire Strikes Back* before I saw *Star Wars*," Sally admitted. "*Star Wars* stands alone, but the second one, well, it has a cliffhanger ending and you can't watch *Return of the Jedi* without seeing it. I'm curious to see how it all turns out. I love Harrison Ford. Indiana Jones is awesome. Well, only *Raiders of the Lost Ark*. *Temple of Doom* wasn't nearly as good. It had a stupid story and bad acting. I think someone wasn't paying attention when they made that one."

"That's true," James agreed. "It was bad. I hope they make more Indiana Jones movies though, and maybe they'll get better. *Blade Runner* was a good movie. Harrison Ford was really good in it."

"I can't wait to see *Return of the Jedi*," Sally said, excitedly. "I wanna know how it all ends. Can we eat the pizza in your room?"

"Let's just bring it in, and see if my parents say anything," James responded.

Soon his parents were home with the pizza. James took one pie, one salad, and two cans of soda, plus several napkins, and they went into his room. His parents didn't object. He closed the door. He started the movie, and they ate sitting on the floor. He could tell Sally was entranced by the story, since she was staring at the TV and not saying a word. James got on the bed, sat behind Sally, and started to rub her shoulders. She pushed her back into his hands. When the movie ended, Sally smiled.

"Alright," she said, slapping her hands on her thighs. "That was good. It all resolved itself, and I feel satisfied. Usually at the end of movies, I have questions about what just happened. I have no questions right now."

James laughed. "Well, that's good," he said. "So, are you a Star Wars fan now?"

She nodded. "Yes, I am. I also like Star Trek, but I think you can like both. I might be turning into a sci-fi geek. I hope that's okay with you, Jamie."

"You can be any kind of geek you want to be," he said, grinning.

"Um . . . okay?" Sally said, and she laughed.

"Come up here to me," James urged her, patting the bed beside him. Sally joined him, and they lay on the bed, side by side. Sally feared her breath smelled like onions, but she also sensed James didn't care. As James leaned in for a kiss, there was a knock on the door.

"James and Sally?" Mrs. Newell said through the door. "It sounds like your movie's over. I'm going to open your door."

James and Sally bolted up and sat on the edge of the bed. Mrs. Newell opened the door and smiled at her son and his girlfriend. "It's not that I don't trust you two," she said. "I just want you to be able to trust yourselves." With that, she walked away.

"Ugh, busted by my mom." James said. "Now what?"

"Play me something on your guitar?" Sally asked.

James paused. "Okay, I told you I would." He got the guitar out of its case and quickly checked for tuning. "What do you want to hear?"

Sally smiled. "I bet you know 'Stairway to Heaven.'"

James laughed. "First song I ever learned. It's a classic." He sat up straight, braced himself, and started to play. He was nervous at first to have an audience, but soon, his skill took over and he was playing boldly. Sally watched with a smile on her face while he played and applauded when he was done.

"Wow, Jamie, that was awesome!" she said. "Do you know any Beatles' songs?"

"I do," James replied. He plucked the strings a few times to get the right feel, then played the first chords of "Blackbird" while tapping his foot on the floor. He could see the recognition immediately on Sally's face. She loved Paul McCartney; he was her favorite Beatle.

"That was so good!" Sally exclaimed. "Can you do another one?"

"Okay, one more. I know you like this song." He began to play "I'm Not the One" by the Cars and Sally loved it. She closed her eyes as he played, and James could see her swaying slightly and mouthing the chorus. The song had key changes, which changed the feel and added depth and emotion. James had recently learned the song to impress her, but he didn't let her know this.

Sally was impressed. She looked at him with admiration. "I had no idea you played so well, Jamie. You're really good. You can tell you totally love to play."

James didn't blush like Sally, but he could imagine at that moment how that might feel. "Thanks," he said self-consciously while stowing the guitar in its case. "What do you wanna do now?"

"Wanna play a game?" Sally suggested. "I mean, one we can play with the door open? How about *Yahtzee*?"

They spent the rest of their time at James's house playing *Yahtzee* facing each other cross-legged on his bed and listening to albums. When it was time to leave, they took the long way home, stopping at the dead-end street by Lincoln and picking up where they left off in the Cruiser. Sally couldn't imagine a better end to their long evening together.

"Love is a Battlefield"/Pat Benatar
October 17, 1984

James worked on Wednesday night, and Sally took advantage of the time to work on the homework she had fallen behind on. She isolated herself in her room and put the Genesis album *That's All* on her stereo, the volume on low. She propped herself up against the headboard of her twin bed, opened *The Great Gatsby* to chapter 8, and removed the cap from her pink highlighter pen. As she started to read the final two chapters of the book, Ginger jumped on to the bed and settled on her lap, purring.

As she started the second page of chapter 9, the phone started ringing. Sally glanced at her clock radio and saw it was eight thirty. James wouldn't get home until after ten, and Michelle was babysitting for her neighbor, so figuring it wasn't for her, she ignored the call and continued reading. Less than a minute later, her mother was at her door.

"Sally, the phone's for you. I think it might be James?" she said unsurely.

"Thanks," Sally said as she reached for the receiver. "Hey, did you get out of work early?" she said into the mouthpiece.

"Um no, I don't have a job," a vaguely familiar male voice answered back.

Sally fumbled the phone but quickly caught it and put it back to her ear. "Wait, who is this?" she asked, confused.

"This is Chad, Sally. Chad Whitman. You know, we went to Gearhart Prep together?"

"Chad?" Sally said, disappointed this wasn't somehow Jamie.

"Yeah," Chad said. "I saw you at the homecoming dance last week at McKinney, and I found your number in last year's Gearhart directory."

"Oh, okay. Hi, Chad," Sally responded. "What's going on?"

"You know," Chad replied. "Same old stuff. I have Mr. Chang again for English this year, and he's just as boring as he was last year. So, I finally got to see McKinney. That place looks like an absolute nightmare. I can't believe you go there. Are you ready to come back to Gearhart yet?"

"No," Sally told him. "I'm not going back there. I like McKinney much better. I've made friends there, and I really like my teachers."

"It doesn't sound like you've made friends with Kathy Marie," Chad said. "She said you two got in some kind of argument a few weeks ago."

"Yeah, I guess we did," Sally admitted uncomfortably, not wanting to rehash the event, especially with Chad, who had gone with Kathy Marie to the dance. "I didn't know you knew her before I saw you at homecoming. How do you know her?"

"Her family belongs to the City Club," Chad said. "My family have been members for three generations. We're having the Gearhart prom there this spring."

"I've heard of the City Club," Sally said. "I know a lot of Gearhart families belong there. I've never been there." She was wishing Chad would get to the point of his call. She was friendly with him briefly at Gearhart early in their sophomore year when they had been in a few classes together. At one point, she had agreed with one of her classmates that he was one of the cuter boys in their class, even if he did use too much gel in his hair. But they had drifted apart as the year went on. She had felt he was too into himself and his social status, and sometimes he would be rude to her if there were people around that he thought were more at his level. Sally had moved on to different friends and hadn't given Chad a single thought since her last day at Gearhart.

"Yeah, that's kind of why I was calling," Chad told her. "Remember Amanda Blake? She was in our geometry class. She's having her sweet sixteen birthday party next Saturday night at the club, and I wanted to see if you would come with me, as my date. It should be a good time, and you would get to see what it's like there."

"Chad," Sally said, "I have a boyfriend. I was with him at the homecoming dance. His name is James. You must have seen me with him. We were together the whole night."

"Yeah, I saw you cozying up with some blond guy at the dance," Chad said. "I mean, it's no big deal, you can still go to the party with me. I mean, I'm not asking you to marry me or anything. It's just a party. And some of your old friends from school will be there."

Sally paused briefly to pull her words together. "No, Chad, I'm sorry, but things with James are serious. I'm not interested in going out with anyone else. I appreciate the invitation, but no thanks. Why don't you ask Kathy Marie? You two seemed like you were getting along well at homecoming."

"Yeah, we've been kind of seeing each other on and off," Chad admitted, "but I thought it might be nice for us to mix things up a little bit. I mean, we're sixteen. Why do we need to be tied down to one person?"

"Is that how Kathy Marie felt when you told her you were calling me?" Sally said sarcastically. Ginger, sensing the change in Sally's mood, stopped purring, jumped down from the bed, and scurried out of her room.

"I didn't tell her I was calling you," Chad replied. "It's really not that big a deal."

"Well, I think it would be for her," Sally said, not sure why she was defending a person who had so recently been so mean to her, but also keeping in mind what she'd heard about Kathy Marie's father having an affair.

"Well, I'm not planning on finding out," Chad said dismissively. "So Sally, are you saying if this James guy wasn't in the picture, you might be interested in going out with me? I mean, you're going to college in a couple of years. It's not like anyone stays with their high school boyfriend after they go to college."

Now Sally was starting to get mad. "Chad, I am not even willing to talk to you about this. I already told you I'm not interested. I'm with James, and I'm happy with James, and I think it's time to end this call. I have to finish my homework."

"Fine," Chad snapped. "Whatever. Like I said, it's no big deal."

"Goodbye, Chad." Sally slammed the phone on to the receiver, fuming.

Mrs. Bachman came to the door and looked in on Sally. "Are you okay, sweetie?" she asked. "It sounded like you were getting upset. That wasn't James, was it?"

Sally sighed. "No, Mom. It was Chad Whitman from Gearhart, calling to ask me out. And not wanting to take no for an answer. Wow, what a jerk. I am so glad I don't go there anymore."

Mrs. Bachman sat on the edge of the bed. "Sally," she said, "I'm sorry you had such a bad experience at that place. Maybe it would have been the best if we had sent you to McKinney in the first place. I guess hindsight is twenty-twenty."

Sally felt a wave of guilt pass through her stomach. "No, Mom," she said, "you asked me what I wanted. I wanted to go there back then. It was my choice. There's no way we could have known it wasn't the right place for me. But you let me leave, and that's the important thing."

Her mother smiled. "I'm glad it's all working out for you. I'm glad you were able to stand your ground with Chad. Sometimes people just don't get the message. But keep standing your ground."

"I will, Mom," Sally promised. She held up *The Great Gatsby*. "I need to finish this book."

"Okay," Mrs. Bachman said, standing. "Come say goodnight before you go to bed."

At ten, Sally put her books away and changed into her pajamas. At quarter after ten, the phone rang. Sally answered it, confident it would be James this time.

"Jamie, I am so glad it's you," she said without thinking.

"Who else would it be?" he asked.

"Oh, I had a weird experience tonight," Sally told him. "This guy Chad I used to know at Gearhart called me and asked me out. Of course, I told him no, but he was really pushy. I had to pretty much hang up on him."

James was silent for a moment. "Some guy from Gearhart just called you out of the blue to ask you out?" he asked.

Sally instantly regretted beginning this line of conversation. "Well, it wasn't out of the blue," she told him. "He was at homecoming with Kathy Marie D'Angelo last week. They go to the same country club. You remember Kathy Marie? She's tall and skinny and has dirty blonde hair? She always wears a headband? She was in Mr. Sanders's class with us in ninth grade."

"Wait a sec," James said, "I remember who she is now. I couldn't remember her name. Is she the one you were having problems with a few weeks ago?"

"How did you know that?" Sally asked. "I didn't tell you who it was. Did Michelle tell you?"

"No," James answered. "We passed her in the hall the next day. I could tell there was something up with the two of you. I don't think you realize, but I can usually tell when something's going on with you. I figured you would talk to me about it if you wanted to. Was your fight about this Chad guy?"

"No!" Sally said defensively. "Our fight was because she was being a colossal snob! She was saying terrible things about my friends, and I finally snapped and told her off!"

"But now her boyfriend is asking you out?" James asked.

"No!" Sally protested. "I mean, yeah. This is getting all confusing. Kathy Marie and I had a fight during the decorating committee after a freshman spilled some paint, and then she went to homecoming with Chad. I recognized him from school. We were friends for a bit, but then we grew apart. I didn't know he would be there. And I definitely didn't think he would end up calling me!"

"So, you were friends with him at Gearhart?" James asked, not sure why his voice was feeling strained. "Did you like him?"

"No!" Sally said. "We were just friends. I mean, all of my friends thought he was cute, but I didn't consider him more than a friend, and that was only for like a month."

"So what did you say to him when he called?"

Sally exhaled hard. She wanted this interrogation to end so they could move on to something more pleasant. "I told him I have a boyfriend and I wasn't interested. Then he asked me if I would go out with him if I didn't have a boyfriend, and I pretty much told him I wasn't going to discuss that with him, and then told him I was done talking to him. He had a lot of nerve. I hope he doesn't try to call me again."

"Yeah," James responded. "Maybe if he does, this time you can tell him that you wouldn't go out with him no matter what."

"Jamie," Sally said carefully, "I think I handled it pretty well. I don't think it matters whether or not I would date him if I didn't have a boyfriend. I do have a boyfriend, and that's all that matters. But for the record, I wouldn't date him."

"I guess that's good to know," James said.

"Jamie," Sally told him, "I am not interested in any other guys. You have nothing to be worried about."

"I'm not worried," James said. "I don't know what I think. I don't know why this is bothering me, but it is. Some guy you used to know last year calls and asks you out. It's weird. I don't know. Let me think about it. Can we talk about it at school tomorrow? I had kind of a stressful day at work, and I need to go chill out before I go to bed. I think I'm gonna go play my guitar."

"Oh," Sally said, feeling dejected. "Okay. I guess. So, I guess I'll see you tomorrow morning?"

"Okay," James responded. He wanted to say more, but he didn't know what. "I'll see you in the morning. Bye, Sally."

"Bye, Jamie," Sally said softly. She hung up the phone and then stared at the receiver, expecting at any moment that it would ring again and James would be calling back to explain what the hell just happened.

James hung up the phone and sat for a minute with his hand on it. He was not sure what had just happened, but he knew he was feeling sick to his stomach. His work shift had been busy, and Lou was in a bad mood. When Lou was in a bad mood, working in the kitchen could be unpleasant. James sat on his bed and took a deep breath. He reached for his guitar and mechanically started playing chords.

He let his mind drift and hoped it landed on an explanation. Sally was his first real girlfriend. She was the first girl he ever thought about when she wasn't in the room with him, at least thoughts he could speak aloud about. And also, those he couldn't. All he wanted was to be with her, to talk to her, to hold her. He wanted to call her now and apologize for the way he had spoken to her, but he couldn't, because he didn't even know why he'd done it. He would sleep on it and then talk to her in the morning. It would be okay. He just hoped she was still his girlfriend in the morning after they talked.

He played his guitar for a while longer, playing harder and harder chords, trying to take his focus away from his thoughts. Then he put his guitar gently in its case and got ready for bed. He lay there in the dark, trying to go to sleep, but he found he couldn't rest. He got up at midnight and went into the den. He turned on the TV and turned the volume low and watched late-night shows for the next hour while his parents slept in their bedroom. Finally, he went back to bed and felt himself drift fitfully to sleep.

"Love is Unkind"/Donna Summer
October 18, 1984

In the morning, Sally got to school as early as her feet could bring her and found James waiting for her, leaning against the wall by the door. She started to smile but didn't get the response she was hoping for. James gave her a half smile back.

"Are you okay?" she asked him.

He shrugged. "I had trouble falling asleep last night. I'm tired. And work was really busy. I didn't get a chance to finish *The Great Gatsby* yet."

"I just barely finished it last night," she told him. "Is everything else okay? I mean, I don't think our phone call ended all that well, Jamie. Are we okay?"

"Yeah, I guess," he answered. He still wanted to talk, to reassure her, but instead he stayed quiet.

"Oh, okay," Sally said, not knowing what to say to him to make this all go away.

They made their way to her locker, and she took out her books. Jamie unconsciously reached out and took them. They started toward the stairs. "Do you want to have lunch today?" Sally asked. "Maybe we can talk about what's bothering you."

"I don't know," James answered. "I need to finish my Spanish homework. I thought I'd do it during lunch. And I need to catch up on the homework I didn't finish last night after school."

"So you're saying we're not gonna hang out after school?" Sally asked. She felt a lump restricting her throat. "Jamie, I'm not sure what I did that upset you. Can't you just tell me, and we can talk about it?"

"Sally, I don't know," he told her. "Just give me a little time. I'll talk to you later, I promise. Right now, I need to think, okay?"

Sally swallowed. "Okay," she agreed. "You let me know when you're ready to talk." She reached up and kissed him on the cheek, took her books from his hands, and walked into history class before the first tear fell down her cheek.

After school, James drove straight home. He pulled into his driveway, and he could see Pete walking from his driveway to his door as he got out of the car. Pete abruptly changed direction and started toward the Newells' house.

"Hey, James," he called out as he approached. "I never see you after school anymore. You're usually at work or hanging out with Sally or something." They walked to the door, and they both went inside.

"Yeah, I think Sally and I had our first fight," James told him.

"You think?" Pete asked, heading straight for the refrigerator and getting juice bottles out for him and James. "Isn't that something you kind of know when it happens?"

They both sat at the table and opened their drinks. "I don't know, man," James admitted. "I was talking to her last night, and she told me about this guy she went to private school with who called and asked her out. It's kind of freaking me out."

"Why? Did she say she'd go out with him?" Pete inquired.

"No! Of course not. She told him she had a boyfriend, and she wasn't interested, but for some reason, it hit me the wrong way. I don't know why, but it upset me."

Pete looked at him, confused. "So, what did she do wrong?" he asked. "Did she do something to make this guy think she was interested in him or something?"

"No," James said, not feeling too sure of himself. "She ended up basically hanging up on him."

"And then she told you about it?" Pete asked, raising his eyebrows.

"Yeah, she did. She told me all about it."

"So, dude, what did she do wrong?" Pete asked again.

"Nothing! She didn't do anything wrong. I don't know why it upset me. I guess it made me think about the year we weren't in school together. I don't know what went on last year. I don't know any of those kids she went to school with. I mean, these are prep school kids. I know she hated it there, and wanted to come back to public school, but still. I mean, she was there for a whole year. Those kids, well, they've got money. And nice cars. With heat that works. And they belong to country clubs. And they apparently don't care if girls have boyfriends!"

"Sounds like she cares, though," Pete said. "She told him to get lost. She did exactly what you would want her to do, right? And then she told you about it. I mean, I get being jealous and insecure, especially since she's your first girlfriend, and she's Sally Bachman, but to be honest, J, I think it sounds like this is your problem, not hers."

James opened his mouth to speak but exhaled heavily instead. "I'm such an idiot," he said. "She has no idea why I'm upset, but I think the reason I'm upset is because I don't wanna lose her, but if I keep acting like this, I'm gonna lose her anyway. How do I fix this?"

"You apologize to her," Pete stated. "It sounds easy, but it's not. You tell her you're sorry and you tell her why. She'll know if you don't mean it. Girls can tell if you're not being sincere. Trust me, I've been there. I've learned from my mistakes. Tell her you're an idiot. She'll like that."

James cracked a smile for the first time that day. "Yeah, well, I would deserve that. I'll call her tonight. I'll talk to her. I'll apologize."

Pete nodded. "And if I were you," he told his friend, "I would bring her something tomorrow. Something she likes."

"I know exactly what that would be," James said confidently.

"Talk To Me"/Stevie Nicks

At ten o'clock, he called her. Her mother answered and went to let her know he was on the phone. Sally almost refused the call, but she couldn't. She needed to hear his voice, even if it was angry. At least he would be talking to her.

"Hello?" she said tentatively as she put the phone to her ear.

"I'm a total idiot," James said.

Sally allowed herself to smile. She could sense an apology coming. "Yeah?" she said. "Well, tell me something I don't already know."

"Sally, I'm so sorry," he told her. "I'm just not any good with this stuff. I mean, you're the first and only girl I've ever felt this way about."

"What way?" Sally prodded.

"Sally, you're the only one I want to be with, and I want to be with you all the time. I think about you all the time. I wanna do things to make you happy. I wanna see you looking happy. And the way I acted today? Exactly the opposite of happy, I know. But please, bear with me. I'm learning. I'm insecure, but I trust you. I have every reason to trust you, and I want you to be able to trust me, too. I know you have no control over some guy calling you to ask you out. Hell, if I wasn't your boyfriend and I saw you at a dance, I'd want to ask you out too. But you did exactly what I'd want you to do in that situation. And you told me about it. I bet you regret that now."

Sally laughed. "Yeah, I kind of regretted it as soon as I said it," she admitted. "But I'm glad I told you. And about Kathy Marie. Jamie, she said some awful things. You have to understand, last year was so bad. I told you about the way those kids were. I would think they were nice, and then I'd find out the truth. Kathy Marie might not go to Gearhart, but she might as well for the way she acted. But you know what? Weird enough, I started defending her to Chad on the phone. Because no one should be treated that way, even the mean people."

"You told me all about it, on our first date," James remembered, "and still, I acted the way I did. I hope you can forgive me."

"I've already forgiven you, Jamie," she told him. "Just promise me if something's bothering you, you tell me, and we'll talk about it. I don't want to be with anyone but you. You're my boyfriend and it's gonna stay that way."

"Sally, I promise. And I always keep my promises."

"Jamie, you have so far. I have no reason to believe you won't."

"I wish I was with you right now."

"Me too, Jamie. I can't wait to see you."

"Can I pick you up for school in the morning?"

"I'll be at the door at eight."

"Sweet Baby James"/James Taylor
October 19, 1984

The Cruiser rolled up in front of her house at 7:59, and Sally came out the front door, locked the deadbolt, and walked quickly to the car. She was prepared to throw her arms around James, but when she opened the door, there was something on the seat. It was a giant Hershey's bar with a gift bow stuck to the front. She picked it up.

"Jamie!" she said, smiling and getting into the car. "Thank you! You didn't have to give me something. I already forgave you. But the chocolate is a nice touch."

James smiled and then reached out to embrace her. He held her tight, stroking the back of her head. "I remembered what Derrek had said about bribing you with chocolate," he told her after inhaling her strawberry scent. "I didn't wanna take any chances."

They kissed and held each other in front of the house for several minutes. Then James pulled away.

"There's something else I need to tell you," he said, "that I should've told you before. Nothing bad, I promise."

"What is it?" Sally asked.

"Remember when I went roller skating with my friends when you were sick?" Sally nodded. "Well, that night, I was talking to Pete about you, that we had gotten together, and he told me when we were at Randall, he had a major crush on you."

Sally looked at him in disbelief. "What? Pete? Really? When was that?"

"I'm not sure exactly," James admitted. "He said he did things to get your attention. One time he snapped your bra."

Sally laughed. "Oh my God, that was Pete?" she said. "I couldn't remember who that was. I thought maybe it was Carl. It seems like something he would have done. Wow. I had no idea. I wonder if that was around the same time I had a crush on him. Why didn't you tell me?"

James shrugged. "I don't know. I guess I didn't want to make anything uncomfortable for any of us. But he assured me that by the time we went to high school, he was over it, and I believe him. And I know I can trust you, so I think it's better that I told you."

Sally nodded. "I agree. I would hate for it to come out some other way, and then we would all be uncomfortable. But you know you have nothing to worry about. And I like Pete, as a friend. I mean, you know I had crushes on all of you back then. But that's history. But I do need to let you know something that I don't think you know."

Now James was curious. "What?" he asked.

"Well," Sally started, "pretty much every girl in the junior class has a crush on you."

"No, they don't," James objected.

"Oh, yes they do," Sally protested. "I don't know how you don't see it. Everyone thinks you're cute. I think last year, a lot of them would have gone out with you, but you never asked them."

"Well, I wasn't interested in any of them," he admitted. "How do you know this? Do people say things to you about it?"

Sally shook her head. "They don't have to," she said. "I can see the way the girls look at you when we're walking down the hall holding hands. And they look at me, too. Not always nicely. They would switch places with me in a second! But I don't let it get to me. I think of it like I won the lottery, and they're just jealous!"

James laughed. "Well, I still don't know about that, but I mean, I believe you. At the dance, a bunch of the senior guys were checking you out in your hot dress."

Sally nodded. "Yeah, I know," she told him. "But I didn't care. That dress was for you, and for you only."

They stopped talking and spent their last few minutes alone kissing and caressing. James was glad they still had to drive to school, because he needed a few minutes to cool down before going inside.

After they stopped at their lockers, James walked Sally to her first-period classroom. "Do you want to have lunch together today?" he asked.

"Yes," she answered. "I would like that. Especially since you have to work tonight."

"I could call in sick," he offered.

"No, don't do that," Sally said. "We might need to save that trick for another time. But there's still tomorrow. And I'm not on the work schedule until Sunday."

James clenched his books in his hand and put his arms around her. "Tomorrow's gonna be a great night. I'm gonna take you out to dinner, and then we'll go to a movie. Your choice." He kissed her.

"Mmm, that would be fun," Sally said. "The new Paul McCartney movie isn't coming out until next week, but I think the Steve Martin movie's out now. *All of Me*."

"I'll see where it's playing," James said. "I'd better get to class. I'll see you in English."

"Bye," Sally said after one last kiss.

She walked into the classroom and sat down next to Michelle.

"So he apologized, huh?" Michelle asked.

"Yes," Sally said. "And it was a good apology. And he gave me a big Hershey's bar."

"Good choice," Michelle said.

Sally nodded. "You know, Michelle," she said, "Chad said something to me the other night that bothered me. He said no one stays with their high school boyfriend once they go to college. It's got me worried. What if that happens to me and Jamie?"

Michelle furrowed her brow. "That's just not true," she stated. "My parents stayed together after high school, and they're still together. And Andie and Derrek. They started dating in high school, and they're still going strong. I don't think Chad knows what he's talking about."

"I guess so," Sally responded. "I mean, I get it that a lot of people might break up, but I'm not in this relationship just to get hurt when things change. I don't want this to only be a high school romance. I want the whole nine yards."

"And you might get it," Michelle told her. "You have no way of knowing what things are gonna be like in two years, so there's no point in worrying about it now. If it's meant to be, it will happen."

Sally sighed. "I hope you're right," she replied. "It really feels like it's meant to be."

"I Want Candy"/Bow Wow Wow
October 31, 1984

James walked to the front door and rang the bell. He heard Sally yelling loudly "I'll get it!" and her footsteps running to the door. It flew open, and James said, "Trick or treat!"

"Meow," she said, pretending to paw at him.

James stepped back and checked out her homemade costume. She was wearing a tight black shirt, a short black miniskirt, black tights, brown slip-on shoes, a brown tail pinned to the bottom of her back, and brown cat ears. She had a pink spot on the tip of her nose, black whiskers on her cheeks, pink lips, and a white spot drawn on by her nose. She had her shoulder-length hair in pigtails on either side of her head and her bangs, usually feathered, were combed down over her forehead. She was holding her wriggling pet cat under her right arm. "Wow," James said.

Sally smiled. "I'm Ginger," she said, letting the cat down and pulling James inside by the hand.

"Well, you sure as hell ain't Maryann," he replied. "You look *good.*"

"Thank you," Sally responded. She had a lot of Halloween energy. James assumed she had already hit the candy hard. "And look at you! You look totally repulsive!"

"Thanks," James answered proudly. He was dressed as Freddy Krueger from *A Nightmare on Elm Street*. He was wearing his father's gray fedora, a red-and-black striped rugby shirt, black pants, and gloves studded with long, sharp-looking nails. He had bought a mask from the mall Halloween store so he wouldn't have to deal with makeup. On his way to Sally's house, he had seen at least three other Freddy Kruegers out trick-or-treating. It was definitely the Halloween trend of the year. The movie had come out in September, but Sally had no desire to see it with him. He had gone with Chris and Pete instead. It was gruesome. They all loved it.

Mrs. Bachman bustled into the front foyer, looking for her keys. "Hi, James," she said, rifling through the mail on the table and finding what she was looking for. "I'm glad you were able to come over to help Sally give out candy. I was always the one to do it while the kids went trick-or-treating with their dad. I'm looking forward to going out with Andie and Josie tonight."

James pulled off his mask and wiped plastic powder residue from his cheeks. "It'll be fun," he told her. "Oh, you got Reese's Peanut Butter cups," he said, picking one out of the bowl.

Mrs. Bachman smiled. "Yes, they're my favorites, so if I'm buying the candy, that's what I'm going to get." She grabbed one from the bowl and put it in her purse. "We'll probably get some trick-or-treating, but, you know, just in case."

Sally rolled her eyes. "Mom, you're such a dork," she said.

"Yes, I'm a total dork," her mother agreed. "And be glad I am, or else all of your friends would want to spend time with me instead of you!!"

James laughed. He knew the only ones who were embarrassed by a mom were that mom's own kids. And so far he liked Sally's mom. "Where's Mr. Bachman tonight?" he asked.

"He's in Hartford. He has to go out of state several times a year to help coordinate printing newspaper flyers," Mrs. Bachman explained. "They might get their turn with the press at any time of day or night, so he has to stay until the job's done. It's grueling work, but he says he loves it. He's certainly good at what he does."

"I'm sorry I missed him again," James told her. He had yet to meet her father two months into their relationship. He knew Sally wasn't happy with that.

"Yeah," Sally said. "I know he wants to meet you, too. You'll like him. He's funny."

"Yes, and he's fun," Mrs. Bachman agreed. "He's the one who takes Sally out for ice cream all the time. I give her apricots from a can!" She secured her purse over her shoulder. "Okay, I'm off to the races. I'll be back in less than two hours, I think. The baby will probably fall asleep in the stroller after a bit, so we'll probably walk around visiting neighbors. I'll be back in plenty of time for you two to go to your party."

"Have fun, Mom," Sally said, biting into a peanut butter cup.

After she left, James put his arms around Sally and gave her a long kiss. "Mmm, peanut butter," he said. "Are you sure you're up for this party later?"

Sally nodded. "Yeah, I've never been to a high school house party before. I'm curious. We can go for a while, and if it's no good, we can leave whenever we want."

"That's what I was thinking," James agreed. "If it's too crowded, or if everyone's drunk and stupid, we can just go."

The doorbell rang. Sally disentangled herself from James's arms and opened the door.

"Trick or treat!" three elementary school-aged children yelled.

Sally got a handful of candy and put one in each pillowcase held out in front of her. "Oh look," she said to James, who came to stand next to her. "Another Freddy Krueger."

The little Freddy raised his long-nailed hand and growled. James resisted the temptation to growl back. He knew that probably wouldn't go over well with the parents waiting at the sidewalk.

"Do you wanna see my room?" Sally asked James after she closed the door.

"Okay," James agreed, and they went up the stairs. There were four doors off the upstairs hallway, and two of them were closed.

"That's my mom and dad's room," Sally said, pointing to the open door to the left. "Andie was in the room next to them. My dad uses it as a home office now. That room over there," she pointed to the right, "is Nathan's old room. It's kind of my mom's office, too. And this," she said, walking into the open door on the right and switching on the light, "is my room."

James stepped inside and looked around. It was a large room. The two windows were surrounded by hot pink curtains. The walls were pale pink and covered with posters of Boston sports teams and players. There was a poster of a white kitten with a daisy and reproductions of photos of Sting and Robert Plant, both in action on stage. There was a tall bookcase filled with hardcover and paperback books, which overflowed into piles on the floor. There were books piled on the nightstand, and more stacked and sprawled on the floor between the beds. She had twin beds, one of them in the corner, neatly made and covered with throw pillows and stuffed animals, and the other, closer to the door, was made but wrinkled, with pajamas strewn over the top.

"Who sleeps over there?" James asked, pointing to the neater bed in the corner.

"No one usually," Sally told him. "It's for friends sleeping over. Sometimes Andie stays over, and she stays with me. All of this is mine." She pointed to a large brown varnished dresser with a huge hutch mirror on top. "My parents got that for me for my bat mitzvah," she told him. "I picked it out at the furniture store, but I had no idea then it was part of a waterbed set!" She laughed. "And look." She picked up a framed picture from a shelf on the hutch. "Here we are before the homecoming dance."

James took the frame from her and looked. She had chosen to enlarge and frame the picture where he wasn't looking at the camera but at her face. "Why did you frame this one?" he asked. "I was actually looking at the camera in all the other pictures."

"Yes," Sally said, taking the frame and perching it back on the mirror. "But in this one, you were looking at me. And look how you're smiling."

James grinned. That was such a Sally thing to do. She never ceased to amaze him. The doorbell rang. Sally turned off the light, and they both ran down the stairs to give out candy to the kids.

When Mrs. Bachman got back, the candy bowl was almost empty, and the doorbell had not rung for at least fifteen minutes. It was still early for the party, so the three of them watched the remainder of *The Rocky Horror Picture Show*, which James and Sally had been watching between handing out candy and kissing on the couch, and together they finished the bowl of chocolates.

"I Didn't Mean to Turn You On"/Robert Palmer

At nine, Sally and James left for the party. It was hosted by Dean Bianco, a boy who was in some of James and Sally's classes. Dean lived closer to James's house, so they arrived at his house, parked, and went inside at about nine thirty. The party was in full swing. Halloween music was blasting, and there was a fog machine blowing spooky-looking smoke throughout the living room. Sally saw Kim and Darlene, and she and James made their way to where they were standing near the food table. They all complimented each other's costumes. Kim was Raggedy Ann, and Darlene was a sexy vampire. Chris, in a cowboy hat, boots, and a large Texas belt buckle, found them along with Rhonda, who was also a cat, Carl in a Freddy Krueger costume, and a girl Sally had never met before, named Vicki, in a sexy nurse costume. Vicki had gone to elementary school with the boys and was there as Carl's date.

"Are Dean's parents home?" Sally asked Kim.

"They're upstairs in their bedroom," Kim answered after taking a sip from her clear plastic cup. It was filled with a pinkish red fluid. "Dean said they promised they wouldn't come down unless they heard police sirens outside the house."

"What are you drinking?" Sally asked her.

"It's punch," Kim told her, holding it to her face. "Try it."

"No thanks," Sally said, waving it away. She could smell the alcohol permeating from the cup as it came near her. "Is it spiked?"

Kim shook her head. "Not the punch bowl," she explained. "Darlene stole a bottle of rum from her father's liquor cabinet. We've been spiking as we go along!" She giggled and took another sip.

"Don't worry," Vicki confided to Sally, seeing concern on her face. "I'm not drinking and I'm driving these clowns home later. They'll be fine. As long as they don't barf in my back seat!"

"I'm not a clown, Vicki." Kim objected, glaring at her. Then she giggled. "I'm a doll!"

James appeared by Sally's side and handed her a full cup of punch. She sniffed it. It was fine. She took some sips from the cup then helped herself to some chips and candy. They chatted with their friends for a while and then made the rounds to see who else was there. They caught up with some of their classmates, and some of James's old friends who went to Murphy. Then they went back to their current friends, who were laughing too hard, and appearing to be wavering on their feet.

After a few minutes, James leaned over and spoke loudly into Sally's ear. "Sally, these guys are getting wasted. Maybe we should head out soon."

"We can go now," Sally agreed. James nodded to her, took another handful of candy, and they started toward the door, calling a hasty goodbye to their friends.

"Well, was it everything you thought it would be?" James asked her as they settled into the car and fastened their seatbelts.

"Uh," she started, "the candy was good, but it was loud in there. And hot. And everyone was acting like idiots. Do people really enjoy this type of thing?"

"Maybe," James replied. "I can't imagine they'll be feeling too good when they wake up tomorrow morning. I like doing things where there are a lot less people and you can talk without straining your vocal cords. Next time, let's go to a movie or something else."

"I'm glad Michelle had to stay at home to babysit her brothers," Sally stated. "I don't think this would have been her scene at all."

James drove up the on-ramp to the divided highway. "It's still pretty early," he said. "Do you want to, like, go hang out at the place by the school for a while?"

"Yes," Sally agreed, smiling. "The only thing I like better than being alone, is being alone with you!"

They arrived at the spot behind Lincoln Elementary and hungrily reached for each other. As they began to kiss more eagerly, James found his hand wandering up from Sally's waist, to under her shirt, to over her bra, and he began to explore with more confidence when she didn't make a move to stop him. He could hear sounds coming from the back of her throat that told him she liked what he was doing. Her hands began to move under his shirt, and he kissed the delicate skin beneath her ears. He slowly began to explore lower when he felt her move away slightly. He stopped in his tracks. "Sorry," he whispered.

"No, it's okay," Sally breathed. "I'm just . . ." She paused.

"What?" he asked gently.

She sat up straight and smoothed her shirt and took a deep breath. "It's just, well, I know I want us to be, you know, *together*, and I can tell you want that, too, but it'll be, like, my first time, Jamie, and I definitely don't want my first time to be in a car. No offense to your car."

"No offense taken," James said. "For my car. But I understand, Sally, I really do. It'll be my first time, too." After he said this, he could sense her relief. He was feeling it, too, now that they were finally talking about it. "I don't want it to be in a car either," he said. He stopped his impulse to say *but I still would do it in the car in a second if you wanted to.* "We'll need to figure something out. We need to come up with a plan."

"Well, I think our plan for tonight should be for you to take me home," Sally said, "because I know what I told you I want, but I also know what I really want and you really want, too, and we need to leave now if we're going to be true to what we really really want."

James thought about what she said for a moment. "Got it," he said.

"Really?" Sally asked. "Because I'm not so sure I get it!" She laughed. "Yes, we need a plan. And we need a good plan." She paused. "And soon."

"Finding a plan will be my full-time job until I figure it out," James promised solemnly.

"Jamie," Sally stated and giggled. "I'm sorry to laugh, but it's hard to take all this serious talk seriously with my cat makeup smeared on your face."

November

"Think About It"/Stevie Nicks
November 4, 1984

"And I have no plan," James told Howie after he explained his dilemma during halftime of the Patriots game that Sunday.

"That's tough, Jimmy," Howie responded. "I don't remember my first time. I guess it would've been nice if it had been, like, special." He poured the remainder of the chip crumbs from the Lays bag directly into his mouth, leaving residue on his facial stubble, his grease-stained T-shirt, and the couch.

"Yeah, well, this has to be special," James insisted. "She's special. You've met her. She's not like anyone else I've ever met. She's willing to let me be her first, and I don't want her to remember it the rest of her life as being in a stinking station wagon with the engine running so we don't get frostbite. And I don't want to have to wait until summer. I might die first!"

Howie chuckled. "You're funny, James. You won't die. It'll just feel like dying. You can always lock yourself in the bathroom with one of Dad's *Playboy* magazines to ease your pain!"

"Gross," James replied, although he knew his brother was probably right.

"Let me think about it, bro," Howie said, handing James the empty bag of chips. "I'll come up with some sort of idea. That's what big bros are for."

"Oh, really? I thought they were for eating all of our chips and leaving grease stains on the couch," James said as he deposited the empty bag on the coffee table.

"Watch it, Jimbo," Howie warned. "Don't forget, you're putting your life in my hands. Wait. That didn't sound right. Forget I said that."

"Can we just watch the game?" James pleaded. "Halftime's over and Dad will be back with the pizza any second. I don't want to be talking about this when he gets home."

"You don't think Dad knows about sex?" Howie retorted, making James squirm even more. "Where do you think you, Erin, and me came from, the stork? And if you ever think of it, do the math from when Mom and Dad got married, and Erin was born. You might be surprised."

"Oh," James responded. He had never really considered his parents' sex life, and he was glad they were out so they couldn't hear this conversation. "Oh, by the way, Howie," he remembered to say, "stick around until Mom gets home, okay? It's been a long time since you've been here. She's been worried about you."

Howie turned sharply and looked at him in surprise. "She has? Oh, okay. Cool."

"You Tell Me"/Tom Petty
November 5, 1984

Sally walked out the exit door of the movie theater into the cool night with Kim, Darlene, Traci, and Michelle. She was feeling mortified.

"Wow!" Traci exclaimed. "If I ever meet anyone named Sarah Conner, I'm totally gonna run the other way!"

Darlene laughed. "'On your feet soldier!'" she quoted. "Man, that Kyle Reese guy was totally cute. I would totally do it with a hot soldier from the future if he turned up in my bedroom. Even if it meant I had to have his weird future baby. That would be awesome."

"What is it with you and military guys?" Traci asked, rolling her eyes. "I had to practically drag you away from that Junior ROTC drill on the football field last week. You'd better hope if you bag one of those guys, we don't end up in some sort of World War Three. Or a nuclear disaster."

"Nice, guys," Michelle said. "Now I'm gonna have nightmares for weeks. And they'll all have Arnold Schwarzenegger in them! I thought we were done with all this scary crap after *The Day After*." They all groaned at the mention of the nuclear disaster movie that had been aired on national TV when they were in ninth grade.

"Ugh, that movie terrified me!" Sally exclaimed. "I remember I checked the newspaper every morning for months for the headline 'President Warns Soviets' like they had in that stupid movie. I was so sure we were all gonna die in a nuclear winter."

"Let's talk about something else," Kim insisted. "So, Sally," she said, turning to face her, "how have things been going with James lately?"

Sally was glad they had changed the subject, but she wasn't thrilled about the one Kim had chosen. She did not want to be grilled for intimate details. She liked these girls, but she wasn't ready to talk to them about her sex life, or lack thereof. "Things are going really well," she said with enthusiasm. "We get along great, and we have so much in common. We never fight, and we talk about everything."

"Talk?" Kim responded. "That's boring, Sally. You can talk to anyone! What I want to know is, have you guys gone all the way yet?"

"Kim!" Michelle broke in, glaring at her. "That's wicked rude!"

"Just sayin'," Kim said, shrugging. "I mean, you two have been together since, like, the first day of school and last week was Halloween. You guys need to get some action going! I mean, at least tell me you've gotten to third base."

Michelle grabbed Sally's arm. "C'mon, Sally," she said, pulling her toward her car. "Let's get going. You don't have to answer those kinds of questions!"

They all said good night and promised they would see each other in school the next day. Sally was going to sleep over Michelle's house and take the bus to school with her in the morning.

They climbed into Michelle's parents' Datsun. "I'm sorry Kim was so rude to you," Michelle said. "That was totally uncalled for." They closed the doors, and she turned the engine. "So," she started, "have you decided when the big night is gonna be?"

Sally laughed. "So, you just want the scoop all to yourself, don't you? But thanks, I really didn't want Kim blasting my business to the whole school!"

"Well, I figure by now, your business is my business, and believe me, if I had any business going on, I would share it with you!"

Sally giggled but then got serious. "I'm pretty sure I'm ready," she told Michelle. "But I told him I don't want to do it in a car. I really don't, but I also don't think I can keep up the good girl act for much longer if we don't do it!" She giggled again when she heard the words come out of her mouth.

"Wow," Michelle said. "If only you could make your parents go out of town for a night or something."

"I wish," Sally said, rolling her eyes. "They still make me stay at my sister's house when they go away. It's like they don't trust me." She paused and thought about that. "Maybe they're right not trust me!"

"It's not like you would trash your house or anything," Michelle said. "I mean, I couldn't see you having any wild parties. You don't even like to drink. And you definitely don't like wild parties!"

"True," Sally agreed. "But if Jamie and I did go all the way in their house, I would always know it, and wonder if they somehow knew, and that would freak me out. We need to come up with another plan. Maybe his parents will go away."

"Then you'd probably be stuck with Howie on the couch, shuffling back and forth to the bathroom all night."

"Ew," Sally responded. "I mean, Howie is not all that bad when you get to know him, but still, grodie . . ."

"To the max!" they finished together and then laughed.

"Hey, Michelle?" Sally asked once they were quiet again. "Can you remind me what third base is again? Because I honestly don't know if we've actually gone there!"

"While You See a Chance"/Steve Winwood
November 10, 1984

The next Saturday, late afternoon, James was sitting on the couch, watching Looney Tunes cartoons and eating Smart Food from the bag while his parents were running errands. The front door opened, and he saw his brother loping down the hall.

"Think fast, bro," Howie yelled as James looked up and saw something metallic whizzing toward his face. His hand shot out and he caught it before it embedded itself in his skull. It was a key on a small key ring.

"Hey Jimmy, nice catch," Howie said, looking impressed. "You should go out for the baseball team if you're gonna be catching line drives like that!"

"What is this?" James asked, looking at the key.

Howie smiled. "It's a key, genius. To room 126 at the Breakaway Motel on Route 18. Call your girl and change your plans for the night. The room's yours until 11am tomorrow."

James met his brother's eyes. "You're kidding, right? Really? You got me a room at a motel so I can have sex for the first time with my girlfriend? Howie, that's so incredibly cool! I don't get paid until Friday, but I swear I can pay you back then. Or we can go to the bank right now and take it out of my car savings."

"Don't worry about it," Howie said. "I know some low people in high places. This isn't the Ritz, I assure you. It's all taken care of."

"Oh, okay. Wow, thanks! I'm not sure what else to say."

"Well, you know, I can't really be seen walking around town much longer having a sixteen-year-old virgin for a brother." Howie came nearer to him, leaned in close, and said into his left ear, "And here is a little moola for your night. Make sure to bring me any change." He handed him three condoms.

"Okay, wow, thanks, man," James said again, feeling blown away by his brother's gesture. "I'll go call Sally right now!" James took his wallet out of his back pocket and put the little packages into the billfold. He realized how lucky he had suddenly become in the brother department. "Tell mom I'll be home late!"

"Wait! Slow down a second, Romeo," Howie said, following him to his room. "I would be remiss if I let you go without telling you a few things before you, you know, do it. You know, some brotherly pointers."

"Really? I mean, won't we just know what to do?" James asked innocently.

"Yeah, some things do come naturally," Howie admitted, "but there are some things you, like, probably wouldn't think of on your own that will make your lady very happy and satisfied. And make things go a lot more smoothly, if you know what I mean. Nah, you don't know what I mean, but hopefully you will after tonight."

"Oh, okay, I'm listening." James sat on the bed and listened carefully and with slight embarrassment to what his brother told him. For once in his life, he was able to pay attention in class without getting distracted and even managed to ask a few questions.

James's fingers were sweaty as he dialed Sally's number a half hour later, his brain an arsenal of knowledge on how to please a woman in bed. Or standing up. Or on a table. He wasn't sure what he would say when she answered. When her father answered, he felt like his throat was going to close. He asked for Sally and waited on the line until she came on.

"Hey Sally, are you in your room?" he asked when he heard the click of her father's phone hanging up.

"Yeah, why?" she asked.

"Because I don't think I would be able to say what I'm gonna say if I knew your mom and dad were there," he admitted.

"Okay?" Sally questioned.

"My brother just handed me the key to room 126 at the Breakaway Motel," he told her, "and if you're up for it, it's ours for the night. I mean, until I have to bring you home at midnight."

There was a pause. "So, Jamie," Sally finally said, "you're saying, instead of the movies tonight, we're going to go to some motel?"

"Well only if you—"

"No, Jamie, I know!" Sally broke in. "Remember? I say stupid things, especially when I'm excited. No movie! I like your plans better. The best part of it is that it doesn't involve the back seat of a 1974 rust colored Vista Cruiser. How soon can you come to get me?"

James looked at his watch. "I can be there in forty-five minutes. And just so you don't worry about it, Howie gave me some, you know," he lowered his voice, "protection."

"Oh, okay, yeah, that's great. Okay, I'll be ready when you get here," Sally promised.

"I'm already ready," James admitted.

"You're My First, My Last, My Everything"/ Barry White

It was dark when they arrived at room 126 and unlocked the door with Howie's magic key. They let themselves in, turned on the light, and took in the surroundings.

"Whaddaya think?" James asked, looking around at the dark brown curtains and threadbare bedspread on the queen-sized bed.

"It's . . . well, it's not your car," Sally said. "At least it looks clean."

"Clean is good," James agreed.

They removed their jackets and put them on the back of the chair at the small writing table. They stood two feet apart, not touching and not speaking.

"So, what do we do now?" James finally asked.

"I don't know," Sally admitted shyly. "I was hoping you'd know."

James thought quickly. "Okay, let's do this. We'll keep it slow, okay? We'll sit on the bed, fully dressed, and pretend we're in my car. Except it's not freezing cold in here. And we can just do what we always do, only this time, we don't have to stop. At all. Unless you want to for any reason."

Sally agreed. Feeling a bit shaky, she walked to the bed and sat down. James followed her and sat beside her. They made eye contact and then started to kiss tentatively, and over the next few minutes, they gained confidence. Soon they found their hands moving and exploring each other's bodies over their clothes. When James started in where they had stopped the last time, he felt Sally stiffen for a second and he stopped.

"Are you okay?" he asked.

"I'm fine," Sally reassured him.

"Are you scared?" he asked her softly.

Sally shrugged. "A little. Are you?"

"A little nervous," He looked at her closely. "If you want, we can wait. I want it to feel totally right for you."

"No," she reassured him, "it's okay, really. I'm ready. Let's keep going. Please."

Soon they were kissing breathlessly, and James kissed Sally's neck. She pulled away and started to untuck her shirt. James helped her to pull it over her head and she did the same for him. Then he fumbled to remove her bra and spent some time staring at her naked chest.

They felt and kissed their way around each other's torsos for a while, until Sally courageously reached down to unfasten James's belt. Per Howie's instructions, he hadn't worn the 501 button-down jeans he had put on that morning, as he knew that would make undressing much more difficult. Slowly, they helped each other out of the rest of their clothes. They took in each other's naked bodies with wide eyes and curious hands and then resumed kissing. They fell onto the bed together.

James felt compelled to begin the act immediately, but again, remembered his brother's advice. With his right hand, he began caressing her breasts, then her stomach, and kept going lower. Sally reacted by arching her back slightly and verbalizing her approval. He responded to what she responded to and altered his course according to her requests. After several minutes, she looked at him, then closed her eyes, and let out a loud moan, arching her back and raising her hips. This went on for several seconds until James felt he couldn't take much more. When she began to wind down, he grabbed for his jeans, found his wallet, and removed one of the tin foil packets within. He ripped it open with his teeth and from there, they both instinctively knew what to do.

They started slowly, unsurely, and clumsily, but became more confident as they felt their stride. As James felt he was reaching climax, he lowered his head, and Sally said, "no, look at me. I want to look at your eyes." He made eye contact and lost all restraint.

After a few moments, he collapsed on top of Sally, his face in the space between her head and her shoulder, as they both caught their breath. Soon, Sally said, "Jamie, I think you're crushing me."

He laughed, said "Oh, sorry," and rolled off of her. They lay next to each other, still breathing hard and holding hands for some time.

Finally, Sally spoke. "Well, that was pretty awesome."

James agreed, "Yeah, that went a lot better than I thought it would."

"I didn't expect to enjoy my first time so much. Are you sure that was your first time?" Sally teased. "You sure knew what to do."

"Positive," James affirmed. "Very first. I was a certified card-carrying virgin until about ten minutes ago."

"Well," Sally said, turning her head to look at him, "rip up the card. We're definitely not virgins anymore."

"Yes," James agreed. "And thank you for that."

Sally laughed. "No, Jamie, thank *you*!"

"Sally," James said softly, "I am glad you are my first. And only."

"Me too," Sally agreed, feeling a rush of affection toward James.

"Did it hurt?" he asked gently.

"When I fell from heaven?" She giggled. "Well, to be honest, it was kind of uncomfortable at first," she admitted, "but then it was okay. I think what you did at the beginning really helped."

Again, they lay in silence for some time. Then James spoke up. "So, what do you want to do now? It's only like seven o'clock!"

Sally started to sit up, self-consciously pulling the bed spread up over her chest. "Well, I am kind of hungry," she said. "We haven't had dinner yet."

"We can go get something to eat then," James agreed. "What are you hungry for?"

"I could go for a Grand Slam breakfast."

After a few more minutes to let their heart rates return to normal, they got out of bed, cleaned up in the bathroom, and put their clothes on. They looked around to make sure they weren't forgetting anything then stepped out of the motel room and locked the door. Then they headed to Denny's.

"Hungry Like the Wolf"/Duran Duran

They got a booth by the window overlooking the parking lot. They held hands across the table and talked, looking into each other's eyes, until they ordered, and then talked until their food arrived. Suddenly they found themselves willing to share things about their lives that had previously felt a bit too intimate.

"You never talk much about your brother Nate," James said. "Why is that?"

"Oh, Nate," Sally responded. "He was okay when we were little kids, but I think the years of bullying wore him down. I mean, he's really smart and gets good grades in college, but he doesn't know how to act around people. Maybe he's always been that way and I didn't realize it since I'm two and a half years younger than him. Sometimes it can be embarrassing, but mostly it's just sad and uncomfortable. My sister and I are totally different than him. It's like we grew up in different families or something. He's in his second year of a pre-med program at Wesleyan in Connecticut. Andie thinks it would probably be best if he became a pathologist and didn't have to work with other people, just lab samples in some hospital sub-basement. It sounds lonely, but to be honest, I would not want to be in an emergency room and have him come in as my doctor and be all awkward and have no bedside manner. He always says the wrong thing."

"That's too bad," James agreed. "I kind of feel sorry for him that he had such a hard time with bullies. I wonder sometimes if I hadn't had the friends I had, if I would have been bullied, too, since I was a scrawny little kid in seventh grade. Y'know, it's weird that you and I both have an older sister and then a middle brother who has major issues."

"Yeah, there's always that thing about the middle child. What's Howie's deal, anyway?" Sally wondered. "I mean, I know he had problems in high school, but what happened that made your parents kick him out?"

"Well," James stated, "it's basically drugs. He's been doing them for years. I don't know what he uses, at least pot, probably coke and other stuff. It keeps him from being able to do anything useful. When he was eighteen, he stole some of my mother's jewelry and money from her purse. He pawned the jewelry for drug money. I mean, it wasn't fancy stuff, so he couldn't have gotten much. He took a jar of change I had in our room. There was probably about fifteen dollars in it. My parents were so mad, and everyone was yelling all the time. They threatened to call the police on him at one point, but my mom couldn't go through with it. Finally, they told him he needed to leave. I think the last straw was when they found out he stole from me. I tried to stay away when it was all going on and hung out with my friends at the Store 24 or the Burger King parking lot. Howie was never much of a big brother to me anyway. He was more like this creepy guy that lived in our house. I guess it's been a little bit better in the last couple of months. I'm not sure why, but he's been nicer to me. Maybe it's because I don't see him as often or something. I mean, he did get us the room, and he sat me down before I came to get you to give me pointers on what to do tonight."

"Oh, wow," Sally said quietly, putting her hand over his. "I had no idea all of that happened. No wonder you're always saying last year wasn't a good year for you. Is that why you don't drink or smoke pot?"

"Well, I don't have a perfect record on the pot," James admitted somewhat reluctantly. "To be honest, there was a time in junior high when my friends and I were smoking joints over by the lake during school and then going to class high. I don't remember how it started, but it went on for a couple months. Remember that time that Chris, Pete, and I got suspended and we wouldn't tell you why? What happened was, we got caught by Mrs. Fox while we were sneaking out the emergency door in the stairwell during lunch period, and we got sent to the principal's office. Chris was the one holding the joint, and he ended up getting suspended for three weeks. He probably could have been expelled, but it was his first offense. Pete and I didn't have anything on us, but we got suspended for three days. All our parents had to come in for a big conference, and it was not pretty. Apparently getting caught with drugs at school is kind of a big deal. That night, my father lectured me about how my poor mother was having to deal with Howie and all his problems, and how could I hurt her like he did, and they expected better from me. He told me he was disappointed in me. I can tell you, Sally, there's nothing worse than your parents telling you they're disappointed in you. Or comparing you to your loser brother. It was awful. I never wanted to go through something like that again. So I stopped using pot. It's not worth it."

"Oh my God, Jamie," Sally said, shaking her head. "I kept trying to figure out what you guys had done to get in trouble, but I never guessed it was that serious. And I can't believe how naive I was that I never once noticed you guys were high in class! It must have been so hard for your parents to think about having another one of their kids using drugs."

"Yeah, well, since I'm telling you all of our nasty family secrets, there's also the fact that my dad's father was a raging alcoholic," James confided. "He was not a nice guy. My dad has preached to me since I was a little kid that drinking can make you into a total loser. I don't know. I think the guy was probably a loser first anyway, and the alcohol made it worse. My dad had to grow up with it. He told me once that it was the happiest day of his life when his mom finally took him and his sister and left him. I never met him, and he died from liver failure when I was about three."

"Wow, that's super intense," Sally said. "I assumed you didn't drink when we went out because I don't, or because you're always driving, but I get it now. I'm glad you don't drink or use drugs. I'd hate to see you end up with a problem like your brother or your grandfather. My mom always warns me about peer pressure, and even though I tell her that I wouldn't give in to it, it still worries me. I mean, I've never liked the taste of alcohol, so I don't want to drink it. Then I see everyone else acting so weird when they drink, and I don't want to be like that. It's never been a moral thing or anything. But I still think about fitting in with everyone else, and I get scared I could give in and drink just to fit in, you know? And I just know I'm the type of person who would totally overdo it. At least if we both don't drink, we can be squares together."

James smiled. "Sally, there's no one else I would want to be a square with," he said. "Or any other shape for that matter. I'm glad you don't drink though. It makes things a lot easier to explain."

"Well," Sally said, "it's kind of weird that Howie knows what we were doing tonight, but it was really nice of him to get the room for us. And to give you 'the talk.'" She made air quotes. "That part's kind of weird, but it turned out pretty awesome."

"Yeah," James agreed. "Kind of awkward for sure, but it was a wicked nice thing for him to do."

Their food came, and they both dug in like they had never eaten before. James was amazed to watch Sally consume an entire Grand Slam breakfast and then ask for a bite of his French toast.

When they finished eating, they sat for a while, digesting their food. Then James looked at his watch. "It's 8:25," he announced. "What do you want to do now?"

Sally looked at him sheepishly. "You know what I think?" she asked. "I think we should go back to the motel. I mean, we have nothing else to do, and we still have the key, and there are a couple of other things I might be interested in trying, now that we're both, y'know, all experienced and everything!"

James had considered the idea of going back to the motel, but he hadn't wanted to appear overly eager. He hadn't been sure if it would be too much for their first time. But he liked where she was going with this. "Like what?" he asked, leaning closer and watching her face.

"Well, for one," Sally said, lowering her voice so only he could hear, "I would be curious to see what it feels like to be on top. And I don't know, maybe some other things I've heard about? I mean, I don't know if I'll get up the nerve, so I'm not gonna say yet, but I might give something a try."

James didn't need to hear any more. "Let's go," he said. He took out his wallet and left a wad of money on the table to pay the bill, leaving a generous tip. Then, hand in hand, they headed to the car. It wasn't until later that he missed one of the two remaining condoms, which he had left on the table along with the money.

"All I Need"/Jack Wagner

Once they were in the motel and appropriately naked, Sally began to slowly explore James's body with hands and kisses, starting at his neck, moving to his chest, and concentrating on his nipples. When she reached the area around his navel, he thought she would stop there, but she kept going. He had never felt anything like this before, nor did he know he could, and he wanted to make it last as long as possible. He asked her to do certain things, and she complied. She spent time exploring and asking him what felt good. After a while, he said, "I think you need to get on top now if you still want to try," and she crawled on top of him. The second tin foil packet was extracted from his wallet.

They were awkward at first, and had a few false starts, but finally got a rhythm going. James felt much more in control this time, knowing better what to expect, and it went on longer. He reveled in watching Sally move, and he grabbed her hips to guide her. She leaned over to kiss him and then rose back up like a cowgirl. He lost control watching her move, and after letting her go for a little bit longer, he stopped her with his hands, and laid still with his eyes closed.

"Oh, my God," he finally said, opening his eyes and looking at her in awe. "You are fucking amazing, Sally. And I mean that literally."

"James Newell!" Sally feigned astonishment, still in position above him. "I don't think I have ever heard you use the f-word!"

"Some occasions warrant the use of the f-word," James explained. "And this is definitely one of them. How on Earth did you know how to do that?"

Sally smiled smugly. "I have an older sibling, too. And she has lots of women's magazines at her house. You wouldn't believe the articles they're allowed to print in there. They're like instruction manuals! Plus, once I got the hang of what I was doing, it was pretty great to see how it made you react, and I wanted to keep doing it to make you feel good."

"Sally Bachman," James said softly, "you are the bravest, and the most daring person I have ever met. You could really teach me some things." He reached up and affectionately brushed her long bangs away from her eyes and behind her ear.

They separated their bodies and lay down again on the bed in each other's arms. They were both feeling sleepy after eating a large meal and making love twice. Sally pulled the sheets and blankets up over them. James worried they would fall asleep and then miss Sally's curfew, but despite his concern, he felt himself drift off.

"Jamie," he heard Sally whisper in his ear. "Wake up. It's eleven o'clock. I want to take a quick shower before we leave for my curfew. Would you maybe want to come with me?"

James realized he had been asleep for about an hour. He shook his head to rouse himself and went to join Sally in the bathroom. She turned on the tap and felt for the water to turn warm. She stepped in, and he followed her. She unwrapped the tiny motel soap and started to lather herself. He took the soap from her and began to wash her back. He wanted to repay her for what she had done earlier. He thought she was courageous to try so many things during their first night together. He began to touch her wet body and caress her most sensitive area. She leaned against him, anchoring her arms around his neck, and raised one foot up on the side of the tub. Once she was satisfied, she turned her attention to him. Then they stood embracing under the warm flowing water. James would have loved to have made love again, in the shower, but by then he had realized he had somehow lost the third condom. He also had no idea if condoms would work in the water. They would have to save that experience for another time. He smiled to himself thinking they would do this again. And again. Soon, they knew it was time to get out and get ready to go home.

They dried their tell-tale wet hair with the motel blow-dryer. Sally fixed up her makeup enough to not look suspicious to her parents. They both put on their clothes, shoes, and jackets and then headed out.

They pulled into Sally's driveway right before midnight. They sat in the car quietly for a few minutes, not knowing how to end a night they would remember forever.

"Well, it seems kind of an understatement to say I had a good time tonight," Sally finally said. "I guess I could say I had a wicked awesome time!"

James laughed. "You sound like a Valley girl. I had a wicked awesome time, too. I mean it, Sally, you are amazing."

"So are you, Jamie," Sally replied. "You made this really easy and wonderful."

"I can see your mom looking out through the window upstairs," James said, looking up to the left. "I guess you should go before she comes out here."

Sally paused. "You know I'm probably gonna tell Michelle about tonight, right?" she admitted to him. "And by probably, I mean definitely. But I won't tell her everything."

James nodded. "And I'm probably gonna tell Pete, who I am sure will be knocking on my door tomorrow morning! But yeah, not everything. I know he won't say anything to anyone."

They kissed, and it felt more intimate to both of them than any other kiss they had ever shared. Then James said, "I have to work tomorrow, but I'll call you when I can," and Sally replied, "You'd better," kissed him again quickly, and got out of the car. James watched her walk to the door, turn around to wave, and then go inside.

"I Want To Know What Love Is"/Foreigner

After she hung up her jacket, Sally walked up the stairs. Her mother called her into the master bedroom. She entered to find her mother not at the window, but now in her bed with the covers pulled up to her waist with an open book in her hand, like she had never been spying on them. Her father was propped up on his pillows next to her doing a crossword puzzle.

"Hey, Sal Gal," Mr. Bachman said with a smile. "Did you have a good time with James tonight?"

Sally felt flushed and embarrassed knowing what she knew about her night and like she was keeping a major secret from her parents. At that exact moment, Milo walked across the bed to her and tried to sniff her crotch. He meowed loudly. Sally knew immediately that Milo knew every detail of her night. She scratched him between his dark brown ears.

"Yeah, Dad," Sally answered as nonchalantly as she could. "We had a great time. We went to Denny's for dinner, and I had a Grand Slam. It was so good, even with their fake maple syrup."

"Sounds great, sweetie," Mrs. Bachman said. "I got some of the Chips Ahoy chocolate chip cookies you like at the market today, if you want a snack before bed."

"Thanks, Mom," Sally said affectionately, "but I'm really tired. I think I'm just gonna brush my teeth and go to bed. Good night." She bent down and she and her mom kissed each other's cheek. "Good night, Dad," she said, and they blew each other kisses.

Sally brushed her teeth, took off her makeup, put on her warm pajamas, and climbed into bed without her book. She reached up and switched off the light. She grabbed her childhood teddy bear from her night stand and grasped it in her arms. She spent some time reviewing the amazing events of the night before drifting to sleep, Ginger curled up reassuringly at her feet.

James opened the door and went inside his house. *I left this house a virgin,* he thought, and then laughed at himself for thinking that. He hung up his jacket and tried to walk quietly through the den. He noticed the lights on in the kitchen and went in to see who was up. He found his mom sitting at the table finishing up a game of *Scrabble* with Howie.

"Hi, James. Did you have a nice time with Sally?" she asked.

James smiled at her. "Yeah, Mom, we had a really good night," he told her honestly.

"Hey, Jimmy," Howie said, grinning at him mischievously. "Got any change for me?"

"Nope, not a cent," James told him, throwing a smug grin back at him.

"Oh, how nice," his mother said, looking back and forth at her sons. "Your brother loaned you some money for your date? That was so nice of you, Howie!"

"Yeah, Howie. I appreciate the loan," James said, trying not to crack up. "I'll have to return the favor someday."

"You know it, bro."

"I'm gonna go get ready for bed. Good night, Mom. Love you." James leaned down and let her kiss his cheek.

"Good night, dear."

"Good night, Casanova," Howie called after him.

He could hear his mother ask Howie, "What did you mean by that?" but he didn't stop to hear how Howie answered.

James walked toward his room just as his father came out of the bathroom in his pajama pants and a T-shirt.

"Hey J.P., did you have a good time on your date?" Mr. Newell asked him.

James nodded. "Yeah, Dad," he answered. "I did." He stood still by the bathroom door.

His dad looked at him quizzically. "You got something on your mind, junior?"

"Dad . . ." He hesitated.

"Out with it, son, it's late."

"How do you know when you love someone?" he forced out. "A girl, I mean. Do you just know?"

Mr. Newell smiled. "I wasn't expecting such a big question so late at night." He paused to put his thoughts together. "I wish I had more time to think about it so I could say something eloquent and wise that you'd never forget. But I think you do just know. It all comes together for you and makes sense. That's how it felt with your mom, anyway. We were together for months before I told her I loved her, but I think I knew it a long time before that."

"Why didn't you just tell her?" James wondered.

"Well, because I needed to be sure. I needed to know it was love, and not only physical attraction. Lust and love may seem like they're similar, but they aren't. Lust is something that happens in the heat of the moment. Love is in all the little details of your daily life. Like what to have for dinner, and who's gonna take out the trash. It's also about a physical relationship, but I'd say that when you're in love, the physical part takes on a whole new dimension. There's a lot riding on love, James. It's not just romance and heart-shaped candy on Valentine's Day. If you tell a girl you love her, you'd better make darn sure you're ready for the consequences of those words. Do you get what I mean?"

James nodded thoughtfully. "Yeah. I think so."

"One more thing, though," Mr. Newell continued. "I'm guessing it's probably not a good idea to tell your girl you love her for the first time right now."

"Why is that?"

"Because," his dad started, "she's gonna have a hard time telling where it's coming from." He put his hand over James's heart. "Right here, or from some other part of your body. Give things a chance to settle down for a day or two. Show her you're still there. Then tell her anything you want." He patted James on the shoulder. "Now go to bed. You need a good night's sleep."

"Okay. Good night, Dad. And thanks."

"Anytime, slugger," his dad responded as he walked toward the room he shared with James's mom. Then he stopped and turned around to face James, who still hadn't moved. "Oh, and one more thing," he said. "I might be the cool dad you can talk to about anything, but don't say anything about this to your mother, okay? She still thinks of you as her sweet innocent little boy. Let's keep it that way for just a bit longer."

"Okay, Dad. I will."

James went into his room and sat on his bed. He went over what his dad had told him in his head and tried to match it up with the feelings he was having about Sally. And then it suddenly occurred to him that he had no idea how his father had known he was no longer his mother's sweet innocent boy.

"Wouldn't it Be Nice"/Beach Boys
November 11, 1984

He called her the next morning to make sure she was okay and didn't have any regrets.

"I'm good, Jamie, really," Sally reassured him. "No regrets. It was a great night. You made it something I'll never forget."

Jamie resisted the urge to tell her everything he felt, as he decided his father was right. There was still time. "I'll always remember it, too. But that being said, I want to remember us doing it many more times."

Sally laughed. "I think we can count on it. I think we're both hooked. Jamie . . ."

"Yeah?"

"I'm really glad it was with you."

"Me too," James responded. He knew he always wanted it to be with her.

"What are you doing now?" Sally asked.

"I'm lying in bed. I'm feeling pretty lazy. I haven't gotten up yet."

"Me neither. I wish I could stay in bed all day."

"I wish we could have spent the whole night together."

"If only we could do that," Sally sighed. "I would love to cuddle up with you all night and wake up with you in the morning."

"We will. One of these days we'll have one of our houses to ourselves, and we'll play house for the night."

"I'd like that," Sally agreed.

"Me too," James replied.

They said goodbye, promising to speak again before the end of the night.

James hung up the receiver lightly and held the phone in his hands as he lay on his side under his covers. He thought about Sally lying in her bed, sleeping, her hair mussed and no makeup on her face. He wished he could be there with her in her room, with her Larry Bird posters and pink curtains.

Sally rolled over to her side in the fetal position and hugged her teddy bear. She was tired but felt restless and relaxed at the same time. She also felt sore, inside and out. She hadn't expected that. She felt it was a good sore, and she knew it would remind her of last night throughout the day. She felt like a different person, like she had passed some sort of entrance exam. She felt tingly in all her nerves. She felt vulnerable and secure, which was conflicting and confusing. She felt relieved that James had called her. She tried not to think of the stories she had read and heard about where the guy gets what he wants from the girl and then loses interest in her. She couldn't see that happening with her and James, but she thought about it just the same. Being with James made her want more. Lots more. But not just the sex part. She wanted all of him. She wanted him to reassure her, to let her know this was real, that they were something to believe in. She didn't know exactly what it was she wanted, but she knew she wanted James.

The phone rang again, and she let her mother answer. She heard a light knock at the door, and her mother opened it slowly. "Sal? Are you awake?" she said softly. "Michelle's on the phone."

Sally rolled over to face her mom. "Yeah, mom, I'm awake, but I'm not ready to get up yet. Can you just tell her I'll call her back later?"

"Sure thing, sweetie," her mom answered, and she closed her door gently.

Sally did want to talk to Michelle, but first she had to have time to herself, and she wanted to keep her thoughts and the details to herself for a little bit longer. She would call her after she got up, showered, and got ready for work.

James wanted to do something for Sally, something to show her he wanted to be with her, he wouldn't hurt her, and that he wanted everything with her. He spent the afternoon scouring pots and pans at Luigi's, up to his elbows in dish soap, thinking about the night before and how he could show her how he felt before he told her.

He called her at 10:15 when he got home.

"Been slinging cookies all afternoon?" he asked her.

"Yup, slinging cookies and sneaking cookie dough. I can't believe how hungry I was today!"

"Me too. I snuck a lot of leftover breadsticks at work." He stopped to change the subject. "Hey, Sally . . ."

"Yeah, Jamie?"

"Will you go to the prom with me?" he asked.

Sally laughed. "Jamie! Prom isn't until spring! It's only November! Are you sure you want to think that far ahead?"

"Yes, Sally, I'm positive. I want to take you to the prom. It would mean everything to me to be your prom date. Please say yes."

In an instant, Sally saw what James was doing. He was planning for the future. He was letting her know their connection was not just about last night's sex, that he was going be in her life for a long time.

"Yes, Jamie Newell," she answered. "I will go to prom with you. I would love to. But you need to ask me again officially when we actually know when the prom is. Okay?"

"Okay, Sally Bachman."

"Jamie?"

"Yes?"

"You are a very sweet person."

"I am literally made of sugar. Just ask my mom. Sally?"

"Yeah, Jamie?"

"What do you wear to bed at night?"

"Oh, okay, well, in the warm weather I wear an oversized T-shirt, but when it gets cold, like now, I wear flannel pajamas. What about you?"

"Usually boxers. I sleep hot. But my grandma gives me pajamas every Christmas, so sometimes I wear them around the house."

"This is good information to know."

"Sally, I want to know everything about you."

"Jamie, I want to tell you everything about me, too."

"Sally, I think I have feelings for you I just can't put into words yet. Give me a few days, and I'll try not to say anything stupid."

"Jamie, I get it. I have some wordless feelings for you, too."

"I need to read a chapter for history class."

"I need to get ready for bed."

"Sally, when you put on your flannel pajamas and crawl into bed tonight, spend some time thinking about me before you go to sleep."

"I always do, Jamie. Now I'll think about you in your boxer shorts. Think about me in my pajamas."

"I will. Good night, Sally. I can't wait to see you tomorrow."

"Good night, Jamie."

Sally sauntered out of her room into the bathroom, squeezed toothpaste on her brush, and began to clean her teeth. Her mother rapped lightly on the open bathroom door and stepped inside.

"Hey, Sal," she said, sitting down on the edge of the bathtub. "Is everything okay?"

Sally could see concern on her mom's face. "Yeah, Mom," she assured her after rinsing out her mouth. "I'm good. Why do you ask?"

"You've been awfully quiet today. You've barely said a thing to me or Dad since you got home from work. And not wanting to talk to Michelle when she called this morning? That's just not like you. I wanted to make sure you were alright. Is everything okay with James?"

Sally gave her mother her best reassuring smile. "Yeah, Mom, everything's good. Everything's great actually. I just have a lot on my mind. But it's good stuff, I promise. Really, I'm good."

Her mother didn't look entirely convinced. "Remember what I told you a few weeks ago. If you ever need to talk to me about anything, and I mean anything, I'm here for you. You know that, right?"

Sally nodded. "I know, Mom. I will if I need to. Thanks."

Mrs. Bachman stood up. "Okay, sweetie, well good night then. I'm going to go watch the news. Oh, and Andie and Josie are coming by tomorrow afternoon and staying for dinner, so make sure you're home right after school. And don't forget your house key."

"I won't, Mom. Good night." She kissed her mother on the cheek and went to her room. She put on her pajamas, climbed into bed, and turned out the light, again without reading. She knew her sister would be coming over the next day because her mother was worried about her and wanted them to talk. This wouldn't be the first time. But this time she welcomed it. She wanted to talk to her sister. She closed her eyes and thought about James in his boxers, with his smooth bare chest, and eventually drifted to sleep.

"Like a Virgin"/Madonna
November 12, 1984

Monday morning, when they saw each other by the door, they both felt their stomachs flip. James wasn't expecting this, since they had been dating for two months now, and most of the intense fluttering he had been having upon seeing her had faded to a low roar. Sally still looked like herself, but she also looked like a new person to him. Someone only he knew.

Sally knew right away the school day would be wasted on her. She saw James and her brain went numb, like she had taken a drug. They fell into step together, holding hands, like every other day, but this day was different.

"Y'know," Sally said softly when they were partially obscured by her locker door, "I had a friend at Gearhart Prep who said she could tell who was and wasn't a virgin by the way they walked. Do you think that's true?"

James laughed. "Well, only if it means you're walking taller and look like the cat that ate the canary!" he replied. "I don't know where people come up with crap like that. She was probably only trying to impress you with all her sexual knowledge."

"Probably," Sally said into her locker. She turned to him. "Jamie, can you come over tomorrow after school to do homework with me? We have that English essay due on Friday, and I don't think I'll be able to concentrate. Maybe we can help each other. And my dad will be there. I really want you to meet him."

"Okay," James replied. "You don't think it will be too distracting for us to work together?" He leaned in closer and lowered his voice. "You know, I've seen you naked now. It might be hard not to think about that while we're doing homework." He smiled at her and put his arms around her waist, pulling her closer.

"Jamie!" Sally exclaimed in mock horror, leaning into his embrace. "You'll just have to figure it out! We'll sit at the dining room table. We'll have to stay focused. You can have dinner with us."

"Okay," James responded apprehensively. "As long as no one tells your dad that I'm the dude that deflowered his little girl, I'm okay with that."

Sally looked mortified. "Trust me, Jamie, my dad will never know that kind of information about me. Ever."

Sally daydreamed through her first three classes and Michelle promised to share her class notes with her later. Thankfully, none of her teachers called on her while she tried to remain invisible.

Fourth period was English class. James had arrived first and was sitting at his desk. The bell was about to ring, so Sally came into the classroom hurriedly and slipped into her seat breathing hard from exertion. She could feel James's breath on her neck, and then she felt his hands on her shoulders as he gave them a quick massage. Mrs. Clark entered the room.

"Mr. Newell," she called out, "hands to yourself, please."

Everyone turned to look at them, and Sally sank slightly in her seat. It was no secret among the students at McKinney High that she and James were a couple. She was used to the looks when they walked through the halls holding hands. But she still felt uncomfortable with the attention.

"Sorry," James whispered.

"Not your fault," she whispered back.

When the bell rang to end the period, Sally and James headed for the door with their classmates.

Mrs. Clark called to Sally, "Ms. Bachman, do you have a moment, please?"

James and Sally made eye contact. "Sure," she said. She handed her books to James and said, "I'll meet you by my locker in five minutes."

James shot her a concerned look and she nodded. He walked out slowly, looking back at her before disappearing down the hall. Sally walked over to Mrs. Clark's desk.

"Sit down for a sec, Sally," she instructed, and Sally sat in the chair next to the teacher's desk.

"I wanted to check in with you really quick. I know we have tight quarters here, and I was concerned that Mr. Newell sitting behind you in the back of the room might be causing you some problems?"

Sally's heart sped up. "No," she replied. "No, Mrs. Clark, there's no problem. Jamie's my boyfriend. We've been together since the second week of school. He knew that I was stressed about almost being late for class, and he was just trying to help me relax. He's really a great guy."

Mrs. Clark's eyebrows rose. "Oh," she said, "I had no idea you two were a couple. That's a bit of gossip that surprisingly hasn't made its way to the teacher's lounge yet." Seeing the look on Sally's face, she continued. "Don't worry, Sally, they won't hear it from me."

"Thank you," Sally replied, gratefully.

"Well," Mrs. Clark said, "I apologize if I embarrassed the two of you earlier. In the future, though, keep it out in the hallways, okay?"

"Okay, we will," Sally told her.

Mrs. Clark still looked concerned. "Are you sure everything's okay, Sally? Nothing else going on with you that you might want to talk about? You look a little . . . on edge today."

Sally tried to smile reassuringly once more. It wasn't easy. "No, really, everything's fine. But thanks for asking."

Mrs. Clark nodded and smiled at Sally. "Okay, why don't you go off to lunch then. But if you ever do want to talk about anything, I'm here."

"Thanks, Mrs. Clark."

Sally left the room and felt her heart continue to palpitate. She went down the stairs and found James leaning on her locker. "What was that all about?" he asked. "Are we in trouble?"

"No," Sally said as she unlocked her locker. "But we have to 'keep it out in the hallways' from now on." She turned to him sharply. "Jamie, why does everyone keep asking me if I'm okay?" she asked him, feeling slightly annoyed. "Do I not look okay or something?"

"They do?" he asked. He looked carefully at her face. "I don't know. You look good to me, but maybe you seem a bit distracted, or stressed out."

"I'm always distracted," she snapped at him. "You know that about me! Nothing's different! I'm fine. Let's just drop it and go to lunch."

James was baffled by Sally's abrupt reaction but nodded and took her hand as they walked down the hall. He wondered if he had done or said something wrong but couldn't think of what it could be.

They walked to the cafeteria and got in line for their lunch. Sally had been encouraging Michelle to come eat lunch with her at the boys' table, and when they reached the normal spot, she was already sitting there with Carl and Chris. Traci came over to join them. Rhonda sat down next to Chris. Sally took a seat next to James, who immediately placed his hand on her knee under the table. She put her hand over his and squeezed. They began to eat their dry hamburgers with ketchup, mixed fruit in heavy syrup, and pudding cups.

"Where are Kim and Darlene?" Sally asked, secretly glad Kim wasn't there to ask her any awkward questions.

Michelle swallowed her bite of burger and washed it down with some milk. "Darlene's out sick, and Kim has lunch detention for smoking outside on school property."

"She needs to learn how to not get caught!" Rhonda stated, shaking her head then scooping up a spoonful of chocolate pudding.

"Or just not smoke," Michelle replied, giving Rhonda the evil eye. Michelle had known these girls since kindergarten and could say things like this off-handedly. Sally still didn't feel comfortable enough with them to be that blunt even though they had gone to junior high together. They had all changed so much in one year.

Carl cleared his throat to change the subject. "So, did anyone do anything interesting over the weekend?"

James and Sally both tried not to choke on their food. Michelle, who had been filled in by Sally the day before about their big news, caught on quickly. "I went to see *Terminator* again with my little brothers and their friends," she said. "My dad made me take them. It's actually better the second time you see it and you know when the gory scenes are coming. The little kids loved it! Especially the Arnold Schwarzenegger character."

Chris made a face meant to look intimidating. "I'll be back," he mimicked in what was intended to sound like an Austrian accent. Carl and Traci laughed.

Rhonda shoved him on the arm. "Arnie doesn't sound anything like that," she told him. "You need at least five years on steroids before you can sound like him!"

The conversation turned to movies, and Sally smiled her thanks at Michelle.

It was raining at three thirty, and James offered to drive Sally home. She took him up on his offer.

When they pulled into her driveway, Andie's car was already parked on the street in front of the house.

Sally turned to James. "Jamie, I'm so sorry I snapped at you earlier," she said. "I think I must be tired. It wasn't about you, I promise. But really, I'm okay."

James gave her a kind smile. "Don't worry about it. I know you're okay," he said softly. He leaned over and kissed her gently on the lips. "Go inside and have a good time with Andie and Josie, and I'll call you when I get home from work."

"Thanks for the ride, Jamie," Sally said as she opened the door. "And don't forget, you're coming over here after school tomorrow. For homework. And for dinner."

She closed the door, waved through the car window, and walked toward the house.

"Two Sisters"/The Kinks

Sally could hear Josie babbling through the door even before she turned the key and let herself in.

"Is that you, Salamander?" Andie called from the den.

"Hey, Andrea Doria," Sally called back. She cut through the dining room toward the den, and Andie gave her a stern look.

"Sally Ann Bachman!" Andie exclaimed. "You know you aren't supposed to cut through the dining room. Mom will blame you personally when her new carpet wears out and needs to be replaced!" They grinned, then gave each other a quick hug and kiss on the cheek. Josie looked up at Sally from the floor, cooed, and lifted her arms to be picked up. Sally picked her up and took a deep inhale of her baby head smell.

"If people weren't meant to walk through the dining room," she asked Andie, "then why was it put right here conveniently in the middle of all the other rooms?" She didn't wait for an answer. "So, I take it Mom asked you to come over here to talk to me," Sally said as she placed the baby on her blanket with her toys and sat on the floor to join her and Andie.

"Of course she did," Andie replied, rolling her eyes. "What good is an older sister if she can't be there when she's needed?"

"Not that I don't adore you, Andie Rooney, but why exactly does Mom think I need you?"

"She thinks you look sad, or distracted, or something," Andie answered while helping Josie pull up to stand.

"I'm not sad or distracted . . ." Sally started.

"But . . ." Andie said. "But something. I can tell. Did something happen with James?"

Sally crossed her legs, put her elbows on her knees, and lowered her head to her hands. "Well, to be honest, Andie, *everything* happened with James," she revealed.

"Oh," Andie replied. Then she looked up at Sally. "Oh!" she said again. "Oh, that makes sense. Wow, Sally. Just wow. That's big news. When? Where? Was it okay? Did you enjoy it?"

"Saturday night," Sally answered, looking up. "At a motel room his older brother got for him. And of course I enjoyed it! It was amazing." She rolled over lazily on her back, and Josie climbed on her belly. "Jamie is the best. He was patient, and caring, and he asked me questions and checked in with me the whole time. All three times, actually. And he called me the next morning to make sure I was okay. He even asked me to the prom! He is the perfect first person for me."

"Well, then what's wrong?" Andie asked softly.

"I . . . well . . . I don't know . . . it's just . . . it's just such a big freaking deal!" Sally felt tears spring to her eyes and roll down into her ears, and it felt good to let them out. Andie sat her up and put her arms around her as she cried.

After a minute, Andie spoke. "It is a big freaking deal, sweetie, a huge deal. Life changing." She smoothed Sally's hair with her palm.

"That's just it," Sally admitted, pulling away. "I feel like I'm supposed to be a different person now. Like I need to be all grown up. I need to be mature. It's like I feel that having sex makes me into something I'm not ready to be yet!"

"That's a lot of feelings to process." Andie was two semesters into her master's degree in psychology and often made statements like this, much to Sally's dismay.

"Yes, I am having feelings, Andie," she said sarcastically. "I'm a teenager. I have drastic mood swings."

"That's it exactly, Sally," Andie said. "You *are* a teenager. You're sixteen years old. You're not an adult. Sex is an adult concept. So when you're as young as you, even when you're ready, and even when you're in a loving and kind relationship, it's gonna feel weird and alien to you."

"I did feel ready. I still do. I want to do it again, like right now. Seriously, Andie, I pretty much want to kick you and Josie out and call Jamie to tell him to come over here and take off his clothes! But at the same time, I still want to be who I was three days ago. But I never can be, can I?"

Andie shook her head. "No, you can't go back, but would you really want to? This is what growing up is all about. Having new, exciting, and scary experiences and feelings, and learning to integrate them into who you already are. You're still my Salamander, and Derrek's tiny mouse, and Dad's little girl, and you're still the same sweet, wonderful girl you were three days ago. But now you've been let in on the big secret adults think they own. Sex feels good. It feels good to be with someone you really care about. And it can be fun! No matter how old you are. And it's still okay to be playful and immature in your everyday life."

"And sleep with a teddy bear?" Sally asked timidly.

Andie smiled kindly. "Yes," she said. "You can still sleep with a teddy bear."

Sally sniffed and wiped her sleeve across her nose. "But what if we have an accident and I get pregnant?" she asked.

"Yeah, that's definitely something to think about," Andie agreed. "Did you use protection?"

Sally nodded. "He had condoms."

Andie nodded. "Good man," she said. "But I have an idea. Why don't we get you an appointment at Planned Parenthood next week? I can take you there and we'll get you started on the pill."

"Really?" Sally asked, grasping Josie's donut-shaped rattling toy in her fist like a baby life preserver. "We can do that? Don't we have to get permission from Mom?"

"No, don't worry about it, Sal," Andie reassured her. "I'll take care of everything. Mom doesn't have to know a thing. I have it on good authority that Mom doesn't want to know a thing. So you don't have to tell her. Unless you want to."

Sally grimaced. "Are you out of your mind? No thank you. She acts like she'll talk to me about anything, but I know she would die of embarrassment if she knew that I . . ." She leaned closer and whispered, "went all the way with a boy."

Andie giggled. "I'm guessing she suspects," she said, "but she really doesn't want to know. That's probably why I'm here today. Dad's no better. As a matter of fact, he's worse. I think he's convinced himself that I became pregnant with Josie by immaculate conception or something, even though I was married! We have to face it, Sally. Our parents are prudes!"

"Lucky us," Sally said.

"Are you feeling any better now?" Andie asked, grabbing hold of Sally's foot and squeezing.

"Yeah, I am," Sally admitted. "I think I'm gonna be okay. I just needed to talk about it. Maybe it would help if everyone stopped asking me if I'm okay. First Mom, then my English teacher. But Jamie was good. He said he believed I was fine when I told him I was, and he held my hand. Then he told me to go inside and have a good time with you. He gave me space. And I was so mean to him today at school. I almost bit his head off before lunch."

"James is a good guy," Andie stated. "He'll forgive you. He cares about you a lot. And he'll do right by you, I know it. He's a lot like Derrek."

"He is," Sally agreed, "except for the part where he is shorter, blond, and has blue eyes. And he would rather die than join the military. And he's not an only child, and he doesn't work out . . ."

"Okay, okay, well at least they share the good guy status." Andie stood up. "I want to try to get Josie down for a nap for a couple of hours before dinner. I could really use the break. Maybe I can study while you do your homework. Come with me upstairs. You can usually bore her to sleep pretty easily."

Sally shook her head. The psychology student had left the room and her older sister had returned. She was glad. She was tired of not being okay. They collected the baby and her belongings and headed upstairs.

"Mom got some Chips Ahoy chocolate chip cookies," she told Andie. "After Josie's asleep, let's come back down before we start our homework and ruin our appetites for dinner."

"I'd like that," Andie replied. Then she turned to face Sally. "Did you say James's brother got him a motel room?"

"Yeah."

"Oh," Andie replied. "I never would have thought of having someone do that when I was your age. Damn! That would have been a totally awesome idea!" She paused. "Wait . . . did you say all three times?"

James called Sally that night. "Did you have a good time with Andie and Josie?" he asked, which was code for "are you okay?"

"Yes," Sally reassured him, which was code for "I am now." "We had a nice afternoon, and the baby just keeps getting cuter. I could swear she said 'Lala,' which I think is short for 'Aunt Sally.'"

"Most likely," James agreed.

"Jamie, I am so sorry I freaked out on you today before lunch," Sally felt compelled to say. "I know I apologized already, but that was unfair. I was having a hard time, but I'm good now."

"I know," James responded. "It's okay to freak out every now and then. It's nice to know we don't have to be perfectly behaved around each other all the time. You forgave me when I lost my head that one time, and I am sure there are gonna be other times you think I'm acting like a giant ass hat. I apologize in advance."

"Ass hat," Sally laughed. "Thanks. I needed to hear that."

"How about douche canoe?" Jamie teased.

Sally laughed harder.

"Dingleberry?"

"Okay, enough Jamie! You're making my side hurt!"

"Fine. We'll talk about something else. What topic did you choose for your English paper?"

They returned to talking about more mature subjects then said goodbye when Sally's mother told her it was getting late and she needed to get off the phone and go to bed.

"The Old Man Down the Road"/John Fogarty
November 13, 1984

Sally enjoyed the crispness of the morning on her walk to school the next day. Most of the leaves had fallen from the trees, and many of the neighbors had raked the ones in their yard into tall piles along the street for the city to pick up. The wind was low but biting, whipping some of the leaves into the air and back into the cleared yards. Sally felt warm in her winter jacket, gloves, hat, and scarf. She knew pretty soon the temperature would drop below freezing in the mornings, and she was planning to beg her mother to start driving her to school, even if it meant she had to leave earlier.

She got to school and removed her hat to fluff her hair before going inside. She stuffed the hat and her gloves in her bookbag and opened the door. The wind blew in through the door, making loose papers rise up from the floor and settle back in other locations once the door was closed. Everything seemed fleeting.

But not James. He was the one thing she could depend on the most. He was waiting patiently for her by the warm radiator. She approached him and he took her in his arms in a warming embrace. They shared one slow kiss before moving away from the heat and to her locker. Sally took off her coat, hung it up, and shoved her bookbag on the floor of her locker.

"Sally," James said, "would it be okay with you if I started picking you up in the morning? It's getting too cold outside for you to walk so far. I don't want you to get another nasty cold." He touched the tip of her nose, which was pink from the chill.

Sally felt relief that she wouldn't have to broach the subject with her mother. And James made it sound like she would be doing him a favor by letting him pick her up. "That would be so great!" she admitted.

"It means you'll have to get up earlier," he reminded her. "But it also means we can stay warm together in my car for a bit before we go inside." James knew she knew his car didn't get warm, but he also knew she knew that was not what he was implying.

They shared a conspiring smile. Their mornings together were too short now. Sally secretly wished she could wake up with James each morning and they could get ready and come into school together. Then she reminded herself she was only sixteen years old, and she shouldn't get ahead of herself.

When the first bell rang, they hurried up the stairs to the second floor and parted ways until fourth period.

After school, they headed for James's car and drove the mile plus to Sally's house. It was still midafternoon, and they thought they might have the house to themselves for a little while. But when they went inside, they found that Sally's brother, Nathan, in the kitchen eating a bowl of cereal.

"Hey, Nate," Sally said, cutting through the dining room to the kitchen, James trailing close behind. "What are you doing here?"

Nathan stood quickly when he saw Sally wasn't alone, and his spoon fell to the floor. He quickly picked it up and wiped it on his polo shirt, leaving a small wet spot. "Hey, Sal," he said. "I have an anatomy project I'm working on, and I had to come home to get my old papers and research manuals. They're much better than any of the stuff I can find in the school library. Is this James?" he asked.

"Oh yeah," Sally responded, stepping aside to let James come into the kitchen. "Sorry. James, this is my brother, Nathan. Nate, this is James Newell."

"How're you doing?" Nate asked, reaching out to shake James's hand. "You're Howard's brother, right?"

James stiffened briefly. "That's right," he answered. "I guess you must've gone to Randall with him?"

"Yeah, I did," Nate said, sitting back down. "He was okay. He was kind of the security force for those of us who were not, let's say, athletically inclined. I may have done some of his math homework for him, and he might have kept some of the more, well, vile bullies away from me."

"Oh!" James exclaimed. "Well, that's not what I expected to hear. Howie had some, well, troubles in school. Well, in life really. But I think he's starting to turn things around a little bit. At least I hope so."

"Good to hear," Nate responded, turning away abruptly and going back to his bowl of cereal.

"Well," Sally said, inching backward toward the dining room. "Jamie and I are gonna be in here working on our homework. Are you staying for dinner?"

"Yup," Nate answered with cereal still in his mouth. He swallowed. "I'm staying over tonight and Dad's giving me a ride to Hartford in the morning. I'm taking the bus to Middletown from there."

"Okay," Sally said. She pointed James toward the dining room.

"Nice to meet you," James yelled over his shoulder.

"Same," Nate yelled back.

"So that's the famous Nate, huh?" James whispered as Sally took his jacket and hung it over hers on the banister in the front hall.

"Yes," Sally whispered back. "He will definitely lend a bit of color to the dinner conversation tonight."

"He's a lot taller than I pictured," James revealed. "I thought he would be short and scrawny."

"He was," Sally told him, "but then he had a growth spurt. He was a late bloomer. We all were."

They took out their English notes and books and started to work quietly at the dining room table. Sally felt a bit deflated that they weren't alone but tried to take it in stride. When they finished the first drafts of their essays, they proofread each other's work and gave some feedback. After making corrections, they wrote out their final drafts in their neatest handwriting and stowed them safely in their bookbags. Then they pulled out their history books and quizzed each other on American battle dates. When they were up to the War of 1812, they heard the front door lock turning, and Sally's father entered the house.

"Hey, Sal. Is Nate here, too?" He came over and gave Sally a kiss on her forehead.

"He went upstairs about an hour ago," Sally replied. She stood up, and James stood with her. "Dad, I'd like you to meet James Newell. Jamie, this is my dad, Jacob Bachman." Her father had taught her the fine art of introduction when she was in fifth grade, and now she was showing it off for him.

Sally's father smiled at James warmly and procured his hand for a shake. "Nice to finally meet you, James. I've heard a lot about you from Sally and my wife. All good, I assure you. You can call me Jake, or Mr. Bachman, whichever you feel more comfortable with."

James noticed that Mr. Bachman was tall, like Nate, maybe close to six-one, with an athletic build. He had a full head of brown hair the same shade as Sally's, but with some gray around the temples, and the same pale blue eyes. He had a smile that lit up his face below gold wire-framed glasses. James was not skilled at guessing people's ages but didn't think Mr. Bachman looked old enough to be a grandfather.

"I'll go with Mr. Bachman," James told him. "My mom would never let me get away with calling a parent by their first name!"

Mr. Bachman laughed. "She taught you good manners," he said. "Your mother sounds like a good woman. I like her already."

Sally and James helped her father with getting dinner started while they waited for her mother to come home from work. James chopped vegetables for a salad, Sally stirred brownie ingredients together for dessert, and her father boiled water for spaghetti while they made small talk. The conversation warmed up when they started to talk about sports. They bonded over their memories of the Red Sox and lamented about the Curse of the Bambino.

"I know they'll win a World Series someday," Mr. Bachman said. "I just hope I'm still around to see it."

"That would be nice," James agreed. "I worry about that, too, and I'm only sixteen. We came so close in '75, but it'll take more than close to break the curse."

"And they were awful this year," Sally added. "I mean, they had a winning record, but they ended up in fourth place. Anyways, I like to go see the Red Sox on my birthday if they're playing at Fenway Park. Maybe we can all go together next summer. It's on a Thursday."

James laughed. "You already know what day your birthday is on next year?" he asked, wondering why he found this surprising.

"Sally loves birthdays," Mr. Bachman told him. "And not just her own. You'll be lucky if you have her around on yours. When's your birthday?"

"January twelfth," James answered.

"Don't you two laugh at me," Sally stated, "but it's on a Saturday."

"You've done your homework," Mr. Bachman said, smiling at her. "James, maybe you can come over and watch a Patriot's game with us sometime. It's usually just me and Sally, but I'm sure we can make room for you."

"I'd like that," James responded sincerely.

When Mrs. Bachman got home, she greeted them all in the kitchen, then informed them she was going to use the good dishes in the dining room. James and Sally put their schoolbooks away, helped her put down a white linen tablecloth, and set the table. "It's so nice to have everyone together on a Tuesday night," Mrs. Bachman said. "It really breaks up the week. Next time we'll need to invite Andie and the baby, too."

Sally called her brother down for dinner, and they all shared a nice meal. Nate created some awkward moments by talking about his recent dissections in the biology lab and relating extensive details about his exploits in the world of role-playing games. Sally realized since James was meeting Nate for the first time, he actually found some of what he talked about interesting and asked questions. Sally was relieved she did not have to intervene.

"Boys Do Fall in Love"/Robin Gibb

After dinner, Nate went upstairs. James and Sally helped clear the table and load the dishwasher and then excused themselves to go for a walk.

They bundled up in their jackets and gloves, and Mrs. Bachman loaned James one of her husband's hats and a scarf. She handed Sally a flashlight for safety. They walked down the street three blocks, then two more blocks to the right toward Lincoln Elementary, this time entering at the front end. The streetlights illuminated some areas of the playground. They walked to the swing set and chose two swings next to each other. They swayed gently back and forth, enjoying the quiet after the noisy dinner, and the silence was not broken until James got the nerve to speak.

"Sally," he said.

"Yeah, Jamie?"

"I need to tell you something."

"What is it?" Sally asked, pulling her scarf down from her mouth, where the condensation from her breath was making it damp.

"I . . . well, Sally, I think I love you."

"You think you love me?" she asked sweetly, grinning above her scarf. "How will you know when you do love me?"

James nodded. "I love you, Sally," he affirmed.

Sally nodded back. "I love you, too, Jamie."

James felt the relief wash through him. "I wanted to tell you days ago," he revealed, "but I didn't want you to think, you know, that it was just about our night at the motel. I mean, that's a part of it, but it's definitely not all of it. There are so many things I love about you, Sally." He stopped for a moment and thought then looked into her eyes. "Your sense of humor, the fact that you get all excited about little things, and how you're always willing to try new things . . . and I love the way you smile at me when you walk in the door at school every day. You know, I'm actually gonna miss that now that I'll be picking you up every morning. But picking you up will be even better."

Sally felt her blush warming her chilly cheeks. "Wow, Jamie," she said, her voice cracking. She had been looking into his eyes as he spoke, and now she felt a warm tear rolling down her face. "There are so many things I love about you, too," she said softly, "but I think if I try to tell you right now, I'll get all choked up and then my tears will freeze to my face!"

They spent several minutes sitting quietly on their swings with their new-found knowledge of how they felt about each other. Then they clasped glove-covered hands and started back to Sally's house. They decided to spend some time alone in James's car, out of the wind, to reacquaint themselves with each other's lips.

"Jamie?" Sally asked.

"Yeah?" James answered, his lips near Sally's earlobe.

"What do we, like, call what we did the other night? Like, when we refer to it?"

James sat back and contemplated. "Well, 'going all the way' sounds like something you only say before you actually ever do it, and 'doing it' sounds kind of vulgar."

"'Having sex' and 'intercourse' sound like something you'd hear in biology or sex education class," Sally added. "And I definitely wouldn't like using the f-word."

"Yeah, me neither," James agreed. "Although from now on, when I hear the f-word, it's gonna have a whole new meaning to me. Hitting a homerun doesn't sound right. Well, this might sound corny," he said with a grin, "but my brother likes to watch *General Hospital*, and sometimes I come home and he's there and I watch the last part of it with him. When they have sex on the show, they say 'making love.'"

"Making love," Sally said thoughtfully. "The physical manifestation of love. I kind of like it."

James raised his eyebrows and looked at her, impressed. "You make it sound both smart and sexy," he told her, going back to concentrating his lips on the spot below her ear.

"Okay, that settles it," Sally said, her head back and her eyes closed. "I can't wait until the next time we make love, Jamie."

"Me, too, Sally," James responded, wishing the next time was right then. "I really love making love with you."

Sally giggled. "Maybe we should only say that to each other," she said. "I'm guessing we would get teased mercilessly if any of our friends ever heard us say it!"

James laughed into her neck, tickling her and causing her to giggle harder.

Soon they went inside so James could bid the Bachmans a good night. "I was serious about coming over for football," Mr. Bachman said. "Maybe the weekend after Thanksgiving? The Patriots are playing on Thanksgiving for once, but it'll be too hectic here that day to enjoy it."

"And I can make some nachos and dips for the game," Mrs. Bachman added, looking to entice James back into their den.

"Yeah, I'd like that," James responded. "I'll ask my boss if I can switch shifts that week. But I'm pretty sure he'll say yes. Thank you so much for dinner, Mr. and Mrs. Bachman. I had a really good time."

Mr. Bachman shook James's hand, and Mrs. Bachman gave him a hug. Sally walked him to the door and gave him a quick peck on the lips. "Thanks for being so great with my parents and my brother," she said gratefully. "I think my dad really likes you."

"It was no chore," James assured her, pulling her into a hug. "I liked him, too." He kissed her one more time and said goodbye.

"I love you, Sally," James said softly as he stepped out the door.

"I love you, too, Jamie," Sally responded.

She closed the door, then leaned up against it, trying not to squeal with delight. She wanted to tell everyone they were in love, but she also wanted to keep it just between the two of them. She would decide what she wanted to do when she saw Michelle the next day. She wondered if James would tell anyone but decided he probably wouldn't, at least not yet.

Sally went back to the den where her parents were watching *Remington Steele* on TV. She sat on the couch next to her mother, who put her arm around her shoulders. "Dad and I were just saying we really like James," she said. "He's a good guest, and you two seem to get along well."

"We really do," Sally agreed, resting her head on her mother's shoulder. Her mother kissed the top of her head.

"I'm glad you're feeling better," she whispered in her ear. Sally tensed a bit and her mother felt it. "I know, I know, you were feeling fine," she corrected herself. "You are a strong and independent young woman, and you have good skills. But I'm still glad you're feeling better." She turned back to the television, and they watched the rest of the show in silence.

"A Sort of Homecoming"/U2
November 14, 1984

On Wednesday after school, James was surprised to see Howie at the house yet again. He was sitting on the couch, folding his laundry and watching the last scenes of *General Hospital*.

James sat down next to him and helped roll socks while they watched.

"So, Jimmy, I have some news," Howie told him after the final credits started. "And I didn't want to upstage your big night the other night."

"What's up?" James asked, experiencing an instant feeling of dread. He had been talking favorably about Howie recently, and now he was expecting the other shoe to drop, as it often did with his brother.

"Mom and Dad and I had a long talk on Saturday night," Howie started, "while you were out getting all freaky with your girlfriend. They decided to let me move back in, in January. They're gonna clean out Erin's room after she comes home for Christmas since she's not planning on moving back after graduation, and they're gonna let me stay there under a couple of conditions."

"Really?" James asked in disbelief. "What kind of conditions?"

"Well, one is that I see a drug and alcohol counselor, and the other is that I take some classes at the community college. As long as I take classes, they'll let me stay here."

"You're really gonna start seeing a counselor?" James asked, not wanting to get his hopes up too high.

"Already been seeing one," Howie told him.

James sat with this information for a few seconds, thinking about his positive interactions with Howie over the past few weeks. "Wait a minute," he said cautiously. "You've stopped using, haven't you?"

Howie beamed. "Seven weeks and two days, man. Fifty-one days, September twenty-fifth. No pot, no coke, no pills, not one single beer. It's all or nothing. Remember when I didn't come by for a while at the end of September and October?"

James nodded.

"I went into detox. I'd had enough, so I checked myself in. I was there for seven days, and while I was there, I made an appointment for outpatient treatment, and I've been going since then. I had been trying to quit on my own a few times before that, but it was just too hard. The coke only takes like a week or so to get out of your system, but my therapist told me it takes four to six weeks for the pot, longer for someone like me who's been using it for so long. But I'm feeling pretty good now. I had some bad cravings a couple of weeks ago, and I still think about it every day, but with the help of my therapist and the groups and meetings I'm going to, I'm doing okay."

"Wow, Howie, that must have been really hard to do," James empathized. "I'm really proud of you. I was saying to Sally the other day that it seemed like you've been, you know, like, better lately. Like you're really here when you're here, you know?"

"Hey, don't get all mushy, bro," Howie said. "I mean, yeah, I am learning to express myself better and stuff, but my therapist says it can take a good six months or more of sobriety for the true me to start coming out, and it might seem like I'm stuck emotionally at the age I started using. So be patient with me, okay, because I started using when I was twelve. So you're pretty much the emotionally older brother for now. Mom and Dad said I have to stay clean to stay here, and if I mess up, I'm out. I don't wanna mess this up. I'm ready for things to change, and to come home."

"I'll do everything I can to help," James stated sincerely.

"I know you will, Jimmy, but this is basically up to me. I have to take responsibility for my own behavior. So, if I mess up, it's all on me."

"You're starting to sound like a therapist," James told him.

"Hey, better than sounding like a dopehead, though, right?"

James nodded. "That's for sure." He stood. "Uh, would it be okay if I, like, gave you a hug or something?" he asked.

Howie shrugged but stood. "If you feel you have to, bro."

The two brothers approached each other and put their arms out awkwardly. James was the first to close his arms around his brother in an embrace. He could feel the stiffness in Howie's shoulders, but then it started to relax. Howie grasped him for several seconds then clapped him on the back and pulled away.

James felt like he needed to bring them back to their regular banter, to make things more comfortable for both of them. "I hope Erin doesn't suddenly decide to move back in," he said. "I like having my own room. I don't want to have to share it with you and your smelly feet again."

Howie smiled. "It's gonna be good to be back, James," he said. "I've missed having the chance to insult you to your face on a daily basis. I might be out of practice, though, so don't hold it against me."

"I won't," James promised, finally allowing himself to feel hopeful.

"Don't Ever Leave Me Again"/Patsy Cline
November 22-25, 1984

James and his family drove up to Maine on the Wednesday before Thanksgiving to stay with his mother's parents, Nonna Marie and Nonno Angelo Romano, for the holiday weekend. Sally's extended family came to the Bachman house on Thursday for dinner. There were twelve adults and four small children. The only person anywhere near Sally's own age was Nate, and she could only take small doses of him.

She did her best not to get overwhelmed by the noise and stimulus of the afternoon. She wasn't able to differentiate conversations she had with the adults who all asked her the same questions:

"So, Sally, how is school?"

"What grade are you in now?

"What are your favorite classes?"

"So, I hear you have a boyfriend?"

"Is he Jewish?"

"He's not Jewish? Don't you like Jewish boys? I know Mrs. Cohen has a nice Jewish grandson about your age."

"What do you want to be when you grow up?"

"You look like you've lost some weight, have you been eating enough? You don't have anorexia, do you?"

The day was easier for Andie, who could hand the baby to the relatives and then walk away. "Once you have a baby," she confided in Sally, "no one really cares about you anymore."

Sally made her way to the den to watch the Patriots game, but most of her grandparents and aunts and uncles were already seated on the couch and chairs, and the TV was off. She found her father and protested having to miss even one game, especially the special Thanksgiving one.

"Sally," he said, "I know you're frustrated, but it's only one day. Try to make an effort to talk to everyone. We'll see the highlights later, and we'll watch the game together next week when James comes over."

Sally had no intention of trying to make an effort. She didn't have to. Family members kept coming to her. The last straw was when her Great-Aunt Millie approached her, glancing at her chest. "So, Sally," she said. "You've grown a lot this year. What cup size do you wear now? You look like you're about a C."

Sally felt pressure building up inside her head. She didn't know how to respond, but she knew whatever she said, it wouldn't be good. Luckily, Andie had seen the whole interaction and made her way over to rescue Sally.

"Aunt Millie," she said, holding out Josie. "I don't think you've had a chance to visit with Josie yet today."

"Oh, look how sweet she is in that little dress," Aunt Millie cooed, taking the baby from Andie. Andie gestured for Sally to make her escape. She ran up the stairs to her room. She spent the next half hour on her bed with her exiled cats, reading her book with her door closed.

There was a knock on the door, and her mother let herself in. "Sally," she said, "it's time for dessert. Do you think you can come join us?"

Sally sighed. "Will they all leave after dessert?" she asked her mother.

Mrs. Backman sat down heavily on the bed and sighed. "Sweetie, I sure hope so!"

James brought his guitar to Maine to help him stay calm and deal with the stress of being with his massive extended family. He played it in the guest room he shared with Howie after dinner, when the howling voices of his younger cousins drove him out of the dining room. Nonna Marie heard him playing through the closed door, knocked, and let herself in.

"James," she said, "you play so beautifully. Can you come out and play for everyone? I'm sure they would all be impressed by your talent."

James froze. He wanted to comply with Nonna Marie, but he also didn't want to give a recital for the extended family. He only saw his aunts, uncles, and cousins once a year at Thanksgiving and didn't feel he knew them well enough to perform for them. Before he had a chance to tell her he was not comfortable with the idea, his mother joined them in the guest room.

"Mamma," she said. "Let's just let James play in his room, okay? He's shy about his music, and it would make him uncomfortable to play in front of so many people. Maybe he can play for you and Pappa later."

"Are you sure?" Nonna Marie asked, looking at him. "James, I don't want to make you uncomfortable. I want everyone to see how wonderful you are, like I can see."

Mrs. Newell took her mother's arm and started to lead her out of the room. "Let's go get dessert ready, Ma, okay?"

James sighed audibly and closed the door. He loved his grandmother and didn't want to hurt her feelings, but he was relieved he was getting out of her request.

After all the local family left, James approached his grandmother in the kitchen while she was finishing her cleaning. "Hey, Nonna," he said, "I'm gonna get another piece of pumpkin pie before bed. Do you want one, too? I can get the Cool Whip out for us."

Nonna Marie put the dish she was holding into the dishwasher and looked up at him gratefully. "I'd like that, James." She poured soap into the door of the dishwasher and then closed and locked it.

They sat at the table, eating pie and telling each other stories from their lives. James especially liked his grandmother's stories about her childhood. She had been born in Maine to immigrant parents, and her first language was Italian. She had only learned English when she started school. She grew up in a large, noisy extended family in Portland, Maine, during the depression, when everything was a struggle and there was rarely any excess. Her parents, aunts, and uncles doted on the children, and life always seemed happy, but she and her family were greatly affected by the Second World War.

"Nonno Angelo and I got married right before he shipped out to France," she told James. "It was hard, waiting for his letters, waiting to hear if he was okay. We would hear about the boys who didn't make it home. I was so lucky. I didn't lose anyone I loved to the war. Nonno Angelo was safe. I remember the night he got home. It was the first time I was able to breathe normally again. After the war, it felt so wonderful.

All the boys came home, and there were parties every night. We went dancing and stayed out until all hours of the night. It felt like the world was returning to normal again. Nonno and I decided to start our family, and not long after that, your mother was born, then Angelo Jr. and Gianni. Then much later we had Cecelia, who was a surprise package!"

James laughed. "Oh, so that's why she's not much older than Erin," he said. "I bet Nonno was so happy to be back from the war."

Nonna Marie nodded. "It was a horrible war. He saw a lot of very bad things. It took him some time to get back to some sort of normal. I know he still thinks about it every day, even forty years later, but he doesn't like to talk about it."

James shook his head. "War is horrible," he agreed. "I hope I never have to be in one."

"James," Nonna Marie started, changing the subject, "your mother tells me you have a lovely new girlfriend. Tell me about her."

James smiled. He liked this topic. "Her name is Sally. We used to be just friends, but this year, things changed. She's pretty. She has blue eyes and brown hair. Sometimes she talks a lot, but other times she really listens. She's funny, but I don't think she realizes it. She makes me laugh a lot. She loves to read. Mom and Dad like her. Howie thinks she's great. I think you would like her too."

Nonna Marie smiled at him. "You like her a lot, don't you?"

"I do," James admitted.

"Then I like her already," she said. "She sounds a bit familiar, kind of like your mother. She has her talkative times, and her quiet times. She and your father play off each other with their sense of humor, and they laugh a lot. And you are so much like your father. You're sweet and kind, and funny and clever. But sometimes, you can be introspective and thoughtful. It sounds like you and Sally are a good pair."

James smiled and nodded. "I think so. I hope you get to meet her sometime."

Nonna Marie patted his hand. "I would like that. But for now, I think I'm going to turn in. It's been a long day." She stood and gave James a kiss on the cheek. "Why don't you call Sally and wish her a happy Thanksgiving before bed. And if you could, please switch on the dishwasher when you're done."

"I will, Nonna. Thanks."

"Ti amo, Giacomo Filippino. Sleep well."

"Love you, too, Nonna."

After she left, James picked up the phone and called Sally. He would have to limit how long they spoke due to long distance rates, but he needed to hear her voice before he could go to sleep. She answered the phone from her room, and they talked about all their confounding family encounters.

"I don't think I like people that much," Sally told him. "I mean, I like individual people, but not people as a whole. It's like they're all the same. They all ask stupid questions."

"I know," James agreed. "It's so annoying. I had to tell three people what grade I'm in now before I even sat down at the dinner table. It's like, I'm sixteen. Do the math. And poor Howie. People kept asking him if he's keeping himself out of trouble these days. He's not handling it too well. I'm letting him chill out in our room right now. But I think he'll be okay. Promise me, if you ever see me get this way, you'll shoot me!"

"Jamie, it's inevitable," Sally warned him. "We'll become our parents someday, and then our grandparents. We need to enjoy our youth while we can."

"I guess," James agreed reluctantly.

"Jamie. There will be a time when I start yelling at small children to not cut through the dining room. I don't like it any more than you do, but it's totally out of my hands!"

James laughed. "Oh my God, I can totally picture it!" he said. "Maybe that's a good argument for getting a house with hardwood floors."

Sally paused. "I never thought of that. Good point." She sighed. "Jamie, when are you coming home?"

"Sally, you know I'm coming home on Sunday. I promise that hasn't changed."

"Can't you come home sooner?" Sally encouraged him. "I miss you so much."

"I miss you, too, Sally," James reassured her.

Mrs. Newell came into the kitchen and gave James a signal to wrap up. "Hey Sally, my mom says I need to hang up now," he said. "But I'll call you again tomorrow, about the same time."

"Okay, Jamie, I'll be here, thinking about you," she responded. "I love you." It was still new and felt strange but wonderful to say.

"I love you, too, Sally," James replied softly. "Good night." He hung the phone up on the wall receiver. His mother looked at him and beamed.

He stood up from the table, stepped over to the dishwasher, and switched it on. "What?" he asked his mother, who was still smiling.

"James, I didn't know you and Sally loved each other now. I'm so happy for you!"

"Mom!" James said, only letting her embrace him briefly. "Don't eavesdrop." But inside, he was smiling, too.

When Sunday evening came, James arrived home with his family. He left for Sally's house as soon as he could call her to let her know he was on his way. It took far too long to warm up the Vista Cruiser's freezing cold engine, but eventually he was able to head in her direction. She was sitting outside on the concrete steps when he got there and rushed to his car when he pulled in the driveway.

"Don't ever leave me again," she said as he wrapped his arms around her from the driver's seat. "I was miserable."

"That makes two of us," James responded, nuzzling up against her shoulder. "Next year, if we go back to Maine, you're coming with us. Actually, if we go anywhere, you're coming with us!"

It was late, so they drove to their Lincoln Elementary hideaway right away and made up for lost time. James could feel her cold hands on his body, but he helped her warm them up quickly. He covered her with kisses and caresses, and they showed their love as much as they could without words. Soon they had to head back for Sally's ten p.m. school night curfew. In her driveway, they held each other for several minutes before having to say goodbye again.

"I'll pick you up in the morning," James promised as he walked her to the door of her house. "Early. Be ready by eight." That would give them half an hour together until the first bell.

"I'll be ready," she assured him.

December

"I Am a Patriot"/Little Steven and the Disciples of Soul, December 2, 1984

James had been able to switch his work shift so he could go to the Bachman's house to watch the Patriots play the St. Louis Cardinals. James and Sally sat on the shag rug–covered floor of the den, leaning up against the couch, while Mr. Bachman sat on the couch. Mrs. Bachman kept to her word and had appetizers ready before the game. At halftime, Sally and James made chocolate chip cookies together, sampling generous amounts of the cookie dough.

James was surprised to hear Sally and Mr. Bachman yelling passionately at the TV when they saw a bad play or call.

"Oh, come on, he was out of bounds!"

"That wasn't a touchdown, he didn't get both feet down in the endzone!"

"Take him out of there if he's not gonna catch any passes!"

By the second half, James felt confident in making his own comments. "What kind of call was that? There's no way that was offensive pass interference!"

Sally looked at him and smiled. She was pleased to hear him getting into the spirit. James was impressed by Sally's advanced knowledge of football. And Mr. Bachman enjoyed the chocolate chip cookies.

In the end, the Patriots lost the game. It was their third loss in a row, and Sally and Mr. Bachman were indignant. James thought they were acting as if the Patriots had all conspired together just to ruin their day. But they eventually bounced back, and they all settled in to watch *Superman II* on *Sunday Night at the Movies*. Mrs. Bachman joined Mr. Bachman on the couch, and Sally and James sat on pillows on the floor. James felt like they were on a double date. Each couple sat close, with James's arm around Sally's shoulder, and Mr. Bachman's around his wife's. They ate TV dinners in front of the TV and finished the cookies. It was a relaxing evening, the Patriot's loss long forgotten.

The movie ended at eleven, and James got up to head home. Mr. Bachman stood up to say goodbye while Mrs. Bachman switched the TV to her favorite local news station.

"James," Mr. Bachman said, "thanks for coming over. It was fun. You're always welcome to come join us for a game, or just to visit."

"Thanks, Mr. Bachman," James replied. "And thanks for dinner, Mrs. Bachman."

Sally walked him to the door. "If you keep making such a good impression on them," Sally told him, "pretty soon they might ask you to move in!"

James held her close. "Only if I get the other twin bed in your room," he suggested.

Sally laughed. "Only if we can push them together," she whispered.

After a goodnight kiss, James was on his way home.

"Keep the Fire Burning"/REO Speedwagon
December 22, 1984

The holidays were approaching fast, and Sally fretted over what to get James for Christmas. She went shopping at the mall with her friends and finally settled on an official fitted wool Red Sox cap; a capo, a bag of assorted picks, and a set of strings for his guitar; and a U2 songbook for guitar.

James spent the first evening of Chanukah at the Bachman's house, and he learned all about potato latkes with applesauce and sour cream, as well as chocolate candy gelt. They played dreidel and lit the menorah. He was surprised to hear Sally say the blessings over the candles in perfect Hebrew along with her parents.

After the traditional festivities and meal, they all sat on the floor in front of the fireplace to open gifts, as the Bachman family had done since the kids were small. Sally had gotten fuzzy slippers for her mother and a navy-blue tie with a Red Sox emblem for her father. Mr. Bachman gave Mrs. Bachman a pair of turquoise earrings, and she gave him a fresh bottle of Old Spice After Shave, a scent both she and Sally loved. James gave the Bachmans a giant box of quality chocolates, which Sally had recommended and that he secretly thought might have been self-serving for her. Mr. and Mrs. Bachman gave Sally a cassette converter for the ancient eight-track player on her stereo and a gift certificate to buy some tapes to play in her room. James and Sally had decided to exchange their gifts on Christmas day when they would be together at the Newell's house. James found it hard to believe Jewish people exchanged gifts like this for eight nights. Sally assured him that most of the nights, the gifts were small, and the gifts from her grandparents counted as one night each. In the end, it was about the same as what most people got for Christmas.

It appeared all the packages had been opened when Sally's father handed James a long white envelope. "We didn't forget about you, James," Mr. Bachman told him. "This is for you and Sally. I think it's something you both might like."

James opened the envelope and pulled out two tickets to see U2 in concert in April. He was speechless.

"Mom! Dad! This is amazing! Thank you!" Sally yelled, jumping up to hug them both at once.

"Wow," James finally said when his words returned. "Thanks so much, Mr. and Mrs. Bachman. I love U2. I mean, the band!"

"We know what you meant, James!" Mrs. Bachman said, laughing.

"But how did you get these?" James asked. "Tickets haven't even gone on sale yet!"

"One of my clients is an advertising agency that does billboards for the local arenas, including the Centrum," Mr. Bachman explained, "and was able to get a bunch of tickets in advance. It's pretty common. They offered these to me, but I'm more of a Frank Sinatra fan, so I thought you and Sally might like them better!"

"I hear they're amazing in concert!" Sally exclaimed. "Bono is so cool! I can't wait to see them!"

James smiled at her excitement, and he felt it, too. He felt very lucky to be included in the Bachmans' holiday celebration, and in Sally's life in general.

Her mother had one more gift for Sally. "The concert's on a Thursday night, so we've decided to let you skip school that Friday. The Monday before is Patriot's Day, so you'll have a short week. Your grades were so much better this term, and we feel you've earned a day off."

She turned to face James. "I can't speak for your parents. Sorry."

"That's okay," James said, knowing his parents would probably let him skip one day that year since his grades had also improved. "I'll talk to them. Or I'll have Sally do it. They love her."

Mrs. Bachman broke open the box of chocolates and started to pass them around the group.

"Make sure to save me the ones with the coconut inside," she told them.

When it was time for James to leave, Sally walked him to his car. James was smiling. "I'm so glad your parents like me," he said. "Could you imagine if they didn't? We'd have to sneak around all the time, and we'd have to try to get U2 tickets on our own!"

Sally laughed. "My parents are pretty okay most of the time," she admitted.

James put his arms around her. "Don't forget to ask your parents if you can come stay over my house on Christmas Eve," he said softly into her ear.

Sally pulled slightly away. "I really want to, Jamie," she told him, "but I'm just a little worried about having to sleep in Erin's room with her. I haven't even met her yet. I just hope it's not weird. I mean, what if she doesn't like me?"

"She'll love you," James assured her. "You don't need to worry about that. She's really not that scary. She just looks like a regular person, you know? Even if she's wicked smart. I think you'll like her, too."

Sally shrugged. "I guess it's one of those sacrifices I'm willing to make for you," she said. "I'll ask my parents tonight, while they're still in a good mood!"

"Baby's Got Blue Eyes"/Elton John
December 24, 1984

With permission from her parents, Sally spent the night over at the Newells' on Christmas Eve. They traditionally had their big dinner on Christmas Eve, as they liked to reserve their Christmas Day for opening presents and relaxing with the family. Sally enjoyed a meal of turkey, stuffing, butternut squash, and green bean casserole. She experienced sipping on sparkling apple cider from a champagne flute for the first time. Mrs. Newell had also made a cranberry Jell-O mold and a pound cake with strawberries for dessert. She opened a box of Russell Stover chocolates, and everyone picked at it as the night went on. Mrs. Newell was able to convince James to bring out his guitar and play Christmas songs. All of the Newells sang along. Sally knew most of the words after hearing the songs on the radio and in shopping malls her whole life, but she mostly just listened to the Newells while petting and playing with Ringo, who had found a new pull toy under the tree. Soon, it was late, and everyone was getting drowsy. They all decided to turn in for the night.

James pulled Sally aside in the kitchen to say good night. "There's mistletoe on the doorway out there," he told her, brushing her hair out of her face and behind her ear, "but I didn't think you would want the kind of kiss I was planning on giving you in front of my whole family." Sally smiled and reached up for her kiss.

"Now it feels like Christmas," James said, putting his hands on Sally's shoulders. "It's amazing to have you here tonight," he said. "I wish we could find a way to sneak out to be alone, but with everyone here, it's just not gonna happen." He kissed her again softly.

Sally opened her eyes after the kiss. "I know, it would be nice to be alone," she agreed. "But I'm having a great time, Jamie. I love being with your family. We can be alone when you bring me home tomorrow."

"Do I have to bring you home tomorrow?" he asked, and then kissed her on the neck below her ear, on a spot he knew gave her goosebumps.

Sally held her head back, inviting more neck kisses. "What?" she said distractedly. "Oh. I know. I wish I could stay longer. But the good news is every time we say goodbye, we end up seeing each other the next day, anyway. I love that."

"I do, too," James agreed. "I love you, Sally."

"I love you too, Jamie. Merry Christmas."

Howie slept in his old bed in James's room, and Sally and Erin slept in Erin's room. It was Sally's first time meeting Erin. She was stunned that Erin was a part of the Newell family. She had blond hair like James, but she had bright green eyes, unlike her parents or brothers. She was petite, and prior to changing into her pajamas, she was dressed in a hot pink Izod shirt, pleated tan pants, and penny loafers. She wore minimal makeup, no jewelry, and kept her long straight hair in a neat ponytail. She wore large-framed glasses that flattered her face. Sally would never have thought to describe any of the Newells as preppy, but that was the first word that came to mind when looking at Erin. She looked like she knew things. Lots of things.

They chatted as they got ready for bed. "How long have you and James been dating?" Erin asked.

"Let's see." Sally counted in her head. "About three and a half months."

Erin raised her eyebrows. "Is that all? You guys already seem like an old married couple. And Mom and Dad seem like they've known you for years. They're always talking about you and James. 'Sally and James went to homecoming, Sally and James went to Fishmongers.' You've certainly made some sort of positive impression on them. They really like you. It's much better now when I call them. All I used to hear was how frustrated they were with Howie!"

"Really?" Sally said as she pulled on her pajama pants.

Erin finished brushing her teeth in the Jack-and-Jill bathroom between the two smaller bedrooms and took a drink of water. "Yeah," she continued. "And to be honest, James is like a different person now. Last year he was a wreck with everything going on with Howie. It hit him much harder than everyone else. He idolized Howie from the time he was a baby until he started using drugs in junior high. When Mom and Dad made Howie move out last year, James was angry at them for making him leave, but also at Howie for everything he did that led them to do it. It's like he stopped trusting people, and kind of checked out of the family. But now, he seems, I don't know, like he's back. He's much calmer now. And happier. And I think it's also rubbing off on the rest of them. And with Howie getting clean, it's kind of like everything's, well, I'd like to say back to normal, but I don't know if you could ever have called us normal!" Erin chuckled at the thought.

"Wow, Erin, I didn't know all of that," Sally told her. She realized since Erin had been away at school, she had a unique perspective about what was going on at home. Things had changed dramatically since she'd left on Labor Day weekend. "I mean, Jamie told me what happened with Howie, but we didn't go to school together last year, so I didn't see how it affected him at the time. I'm so glad things have gotten better."

"Yeah," Erin continued. "Me too. And Mom says James got pretty decent grades this term. I'm guessing that's got something to do with you, too."

"Well, I don't know about that," Sally said self-consciously. "I think we help each other."

"Nothing wrong with that," Erin said, pulling the sheets back on her bed and climbing in. "It's good to see him taking school seriously. Maybe he'll get into a good college. It would be nice to see him make a commitment to something."

Sally thought it would be nice for James to make a commitment, too, but she was thinking more in terms of herself.

"What about you, Sally?" Erin asked. "What colleges are you planning to apply to?"

Sally thought about it for a minute. "Well, I've still got a lot of time to decide, so I'm not entirely sure. And it depends on how I do on the SATs. I'll probably apply to Clark, Boston University, and UMass.

Possibly one of the schools in Providence. I haven't started doing any real research on any of it yet."

"Have you thought about Brown?" Erin asked hopefully.

Sally laughed. "I wish," she answered. "I could never get in there. But maybe Providence College or University of Rhode Island."

"You don't want to get out of New England, like New York or DC? They have some good schools. You could go to Hawaii or California. College is a good time to explore new places. There are good schools everywhere, and you could go to the beach every day if you wanted to."

Sally's mind immediately went to the thought that Erin wanted to Sally to go away for college so she wouldn't be near James anymore. "I had thought about that before," she admitted. "But now I'm thinking of staying closer to home. I mean, it would be nice to be somewhat close to Jamie."

"I love how you call him Jamie," Erin said fondly. "We used to call him that when he was small, and Dad was still going by James. It makes me think of little Jamie toddling around in a diaper and an oversized Bruins shirt. He was adorable."

Sally smiled. That was not the response she had been expecting. She could imagine the tiny Jamie from the pictures in the hallway with his platinum blond hair and giant blue eyes, trying to keep up with his older brother and sister. "He must have been so cute," she said, getting under the sheets and blankets on the portable cot that had been set up for her in Erin's room.

"Tomorrow, I'll show you some Christmas pictures we have of the three of us with Santa over the years. My favorite was the one from when James was two and wouldn't stop crying. I was seven and wearing these huge, awful glasses. James whacked me in the face while having a tantrum and knocked my glasses off. I put them back on, but then they snapped the picture, and it turned out with James screaming so hard you could see his tonsils, and my glasses slouching down low over one cheek! Santa looks horrified, like he wants to take the next sleigh to the North Pole to get away from us! Howie is the only one smiling at the camera, and it's a big goofy smile with missing teeth in the front!!"

Sally laughed. She couldn't wait to see the photos.

"Well, good night, Sally," Erin said, reaching up to turn out the light. "We might not be little kids anymore, but I can guarantee everyone will be up early tomorrow morning to open presents. Try to get some sleep."

"I will. Thanks, Erin, for telling me about little Jamie. Good night."

Sally rolled over to face the wall and thought about what Erin had told her. James had suffered when his brother was using drugs and stealing from his family and when his parents had to enforce the consequences by making him leave the house. James had been hurt by the people he loved the most. She thought it must be nearly impossible to learn to trust again after something like that happened. She remembered when they had their misunderstanding about Chad in October and how James had told her he trusted her when they had talked it out. She had never given him any reason to question that trust, and he let her know he would do whatever he could to keep her trust, too. Knowing that his trust had been violated in the past, she felt honored now, understanding how much that really meant to James. She promised herself right then and there that she would never, ever do anything to deliberately betray that trust.

"Do They Know it's Christmas"/Band Aid
December 25, 1984

The Newells opened gifts in their pajamas, and Sally got to see James in a red plaid set he had gotten from his grandparents the previous year. James opened his gifts from Sally and really liked them. He put on his cap and vowed to try the guitar accessories the next time he played. He flipped through the songbook to get some ideas for where to start. James had dipped deeply into his car savings to get Sally a new pair of black leather boots he knew she wanted, as well as some new earrings and a book in the new series she was reading. She thanked him with an excited hug and put the boots on over her socks and pajama pants. His parents gave her an oversized Patriots T-shirt and another book in her series. Howie gave her a card with a sweet message written inside. Sally gave the Newell family the movie *Against All Odds* on VHS. James gave his parents a cribbage board he had made in woodshop at school along with pegs and a new deck of cards. They took turns playing in front of the Christmas tree while they listened to a Bing Crosby Christmas album on the stereo. Erin made pancakes and bacon for everyone for breakfast and served it with tiny glasses of orange juice.

"Thank you so much for letting me stay and for my gifts," Sally later told Mrs. Newell when they were in the kitchen together making hot chocolate for everyone. "It was nice to be with you all for the holidays. This is my first real Christmas."

Mrs. Newell smiled. "You're very welcome, dear," she said as she dropped several mini marshmallows into each steaming mug and then threw one to the dog. "We're so happy to have you. And it was so nice of your parents to invite James to your Hanukkah celebration. I must tell you," she confided, "I have never seen James so happy, and so full of purpose. You have done wonders for him. I'm rooting for you two."

Sally felt herself grin broadly. These words coming from Jamie's mother, along with what Erin had told her the night before, were the best gifts she had gotten, even better than the box of chocolates she had hijacked from her mother during Chanukah.

In the afternoon, Mr. Newell went to pick up his mother from her assisted living facility and brought her back to the house for a visit. Sally had not met Grandma Grace before, but James had told her she was in the early stages of dementia. Sally liked her immediately. She told stories of her childhood in Northern Maine, of snowy Christmases she and her family had endured and enjoyed. She seemed to have an excellent memory of the past. Sally knew this was the woman who had once had to take her children and escape from her abusive husband. She admired her strength. She didn't seem to comprehend who Sally was, and she called all the males in the room James. Luckily, two out of three of them were named James, but it was clear she was referring to her son. But she seemed happy and appeared to thoroughly enjoy all the attention she was given.

Since it was a Saturday, and winter break, Sally stayed at the Newells' house all day. She enjoyed a late lunch of turkey salad sandwiches as well as other leftovers from the night before. Everyone gathered together on the couch, recliners, beanbag, and floor to watch *Against All Odds*. Sally had tears running down her face during the final scene and while the Phil Collins title song played over the ending credits. James pulled her closer and kissed the side of her head. She leaned on him heavily and wiped her eyes with the back of her hand. When James looked up, he saw his mother and Howie also wiping their eyes. He made eye contact with Erin, and they shared an amused eye roll. But James secretly found himself moved by the movie, too.

Finally, it was time for Mr. Newell to drive Grandma Grace back to her facility and for Sally to go home. She said goodbye and hugged all the Newells before she and James climbed into the chilly Cruiser.

"I had such a great time," Sally told James. "I can't believe the holidays are pretty much over."

"I had a great time, too," James agreed. "And the holidays aren't over yet. We still have New Year's. Do you think we should go to First Night?" First Night was Eastboro's public celebration, where buying an admission pin would get a person into all the events and attractions through the night.

"I'd be up for that," Sally said. "I went once with my parents, and last year I went with a girl from school. It was fun. Lots of people. It's like the whole city pretty much heads downtown."

"I haven't been yet, but I've heard good things," James admitted. "Will your parents let you stay out after midnight?"

"I can ask," Sally told him. "I'm pretty sure they would agree, but probably just for like a half hour or hour."

"That would be enough time to get you home after the fireworks, I think," James said. He pulled over behind Lincoln Elementary. "I'm thinking it's way too cold for making love out here tonight," he said. "But that doesn't have to stop us from, like, everything."

Sally smiled and reached over for a kiss.

January

"New Year's Day"/U2
January 1, 1985

On New Year's Eve, Sally and James wished their parents a Happy New Year and headed out to attend the First Night Festival downtown with Michelle and her date, Joey Cafaro. There was entertainment in the form of live music, street performers, and theatrical events indoors and out, as well as souvenirs and food to purchase. The night was frigid, and they were glad when they were able to go to the indoor venues. Right before midnight, everything stopped for the countdown, and Sally and James shared a long kiss as fireworks erupted above their heads. Sally was happy to see Michelle and Joey were also kissing their New Year's wishes.

"Happy New Year, Sally," James said as they embraced with their foreheads touching. "I want to spend the whole year with you. I love you."

"I love you, too, Jamie," Sally said back.

"So, it's 1985," Joey said when they were all done with their midnight kisses. "I am so glad 1984 is over. I never want to hear another joke about George Orwell or Big Brother again."

"Me, too," Michelle said, still pink-cheeked from her kiss and the cold. "I hope this is a good year. We'll be seniors this year!"

"Oh my God," Sally responded. "I don't want to think about being a senior. I mean, taking SATs, filling out college applications, going on campus tours, writing essays . . ."

"What are you talking about, Sally?" Michelle protested. "You love writing. You take a creative writing class just for fun instead of study hall! You're always writing stories about everything, and I know you keep journals. You'll probably blow colleges away with your writing."

Sally smiled half-heartedly. "Thanks, Michelle. But I don't know what kind of job I'd be able to do with writing. I mean, you have to be pretty good to get a book published, and I don't think I want to be a newspaper reporter. I haven't thought about what I want to be when I grow up since I was ten and wanted to be a rodeo clown."

James laughed. "I know. How are we supposed to know what we want to do forever when we haven't done anything yet?"

"I always wanted to join the Merchant Marines like my uncle," Joey announced. "But my mom told me she'd kill me if I did that. I mean, I don't want to upset her. I'll probably end up joining the regular Marines."

"I've thought about being a nurse," Michelle admitted. "But I don't know if I can handle all that science."

"Science is a big part of nursing," Sally agreed. "But you'd be a great nurse, Michelle. You have so much compassion."

"I've been thinking about going to culinary school," James said cautiously, glancing sideways at Sally.

"Really?" Sally said, turning to face him. "I didn't know that! That's so cool!"

James smiled, having half expected Sally would ask him why he didn't want to go to a regular four-year college instead. "Yeah, I mean, it's just something I've considered. It's a good skill to have. I've watched Lou managing his restaurant, and it seems like it could be a good business to get into. I haven't looked into what it would take yet. I hope if I decide to do it, my parents won't have any issues with me not going to a regular college."

"Jamie, from what I know about your parents," Sally said, "they want you to be happy and to not do drugs. You can do both of those things at culinary school. They already have Erin, who'll probably get her PhD by the time she's twenty-three. I think your parents would be happy to call you Chef James, especially if they see you in one of those cool white hats and chef pants!"

James knew she was right. He might face some initial resistance, but in the end, his parents would support whatever he decided to do if it led to his independence and happiness. He made up his mind to get more information about culinary school, so he would be able to answer all their questions if he decided it was what he wanted to pursue.

They had been walking toward James's car as they talked. The parking lot they were in was clearing out now that midnight had passed. They all piled into the Cruiser, and James set off to bring Joey and Michelle to Michelle's house, where Joey had parked. Sally secretly hoped Michelle would get to spend some time in Joey's parked car after they were dropped off, because Michelle had told her that was what she wanted. It was their third official date.

Heading back to Sally's house a while later, she and James held hands across the front seat. "Thanks so much for driving us all tonight, Jamie, and being so great with Michelle and Joey coming with us. I wish my parents would let me stay out later."

"I don't mind, Sally," James told her. "It really is a bad night to be on the roads late. I'll feel better knowing you're home safe."

"So, you'll call me, like, right when you get home, then, to let me know you made it okay?" Sally responded with concern.

"Of course."

Sally smiled. "Jamie," she said, squeezing his hand. "I am so proud of you. You've really been thinking about what you want to do with your life. You seem like you're starting to figure things out."

"Thanks, Sally," James answered, "but I don't feel that way all the time. I don't really know much, but one thing I know for sure is that I want you in my life. And I know I want to do something I like, not just something to make money. I hope whatever we both decide to do, we get to do it near each other."

Sally nodded. "I didn't say anything in front of Michelle," she said, "but I've been seriously thinking of only applying to colleges near home. I mean, not living with my parents or anything, but there are some good schools in Massachusetts, and in Rhode Island or Connecticut. I used to think I would want to get as far away from Eastboro as possible, but now, that's not what matters to me anymore. Now I want to make sure I get a good education and I'm close enough to you that we can at least see each other on the weekends."

James felt a warmth flow through him despite the cold outside. "The good news is we have more than another year before we have to make any decisions," he stated. "We can just enjoy being teenagers in love for a bit longer before we have to get all responsible and stop saying 'like' every other word."

"That is true," Sally agreed, laughing. "I like the part about being teenagers in love. Isn't there a song about us?" She tried to remember. "'The guy's wondering why he has to be a teenager in love," she recalled.

James laughed. "Yeah, that's the one! I would say that's our song, but I'm happy to be a teenager in love. Could you imagine us being middle-aged people in love?"

"Yes," Sally admitted thoughtfully. "Actually, I kind of can."

"Edge of Seventeen"/Stevie Nicks
January 12, 1985

For James's seventeenth birthday, his parents took him, Sally, and Howie, who had moved back into the house the previous week, out to dinner at Clifford's Steak House. James announced over dinner that Lou was promoting him to waiter at Luigi's now that he was seventeen. He would be working Monday, Wednesday, and Friday nights, with weekends free, much to Sally's delight. He would have to wear a uniform and would be making a lot more money in tips. He would also have the option of picking up shifts if one of the other servers was out. Since Luigi's was a family business, and Lou's family was quite large, the schedule could be fairly flexible. He had already assigned his fifteen-year-old son, Trey, to take over James's kitchen duties.

James opened his presents and was happy to see Sally had gotten him the new U2 album, *Unforgettable Fire*. He had been hinting he wanted it since Christmas. She also got him a U2 poster for his wall, a small stuffed black Scottie dog holding a plush red heart that said "Love," and a tin full of chocolate chip cookies she had baked. After dinner and dessert, they returned to the Newells' house, and James and Sally went out for a drive.

They parked in their favorite place, both of them long over their aversion to making love in the Cruiser. James kept a stack of blankets and a pillow in a bag in the back precisely for this purpose. He had laid the back and rear seats down flat and lined them with old sleeping bags he and his siblings had used at summer camp when they were small. Normally both he and Sally kept some of their clothes on in the freezing cold weather, but as this was a special occasion, they lay bare skinned, curled up with each other under all of the blankets on the vast backseat.

They looked up at the starry sky through the skylight, the car's one true redeeming quality.

"Sally," James said.

"Yeah, Jamie?"

"Will you go to the prom with me?"

Sally sighed happily. "Yes, Jamie, I will definitely go to the prom with you. But it's still too early. You're gonna have to ask me again later, at least after the prom date is announced!"

"Okay," James said, stroking her hair. She had been letting it grow out, and he loved to run his fingers through the strands and inhale the strawberry aroma that permeated the air.

Sally smiled. "Happy birthday, Jamie," she said and then kissed him. "I can't believe you're seventeen. You're only a year away from being officially legal, whatever that means!"

"I know," James responded. "It means I can vote, for one thing. And win the lottery. But what I really can't believe is that you can get your license in a few weeks." He tucked her bangs gently behind her ear, as was his habit. "Promise me, Sally, that when you get it, you won't drive away into the sunset and leave me behind in this two-bit town."

Sally placed her hand on his cheek. "Jamie, I can promise you right now," she said softly but seriously. "No matter where I go, I will never leave you behind."

"Bringing On the Heartbreak"/Def Leppard
January 21, 1985

Ronald Reagan took his second oath of the presidential office on Sunday, January 20. The inauguration had not been in the public square due to record low temperatures in Washington, DC, and the whole eastern half of the United States was experiencing unusually cold weather. Massachusetts, which usually had temperatures in the freezing range during the month of January, was also experiencing a deep and prolonged freeze, leaving students feeling chilled and unmotivated in school. On Monday, all the history teachers in all the grades at McKinney High showed their classes special educational videos about inaugurations and presidential celebrations. The students loved to watch movies in class. It meant the lights were turned out, and more mischief happened in the dark.

Movie day was all the talk in the cafeteria during lunch. "Seth Lamont actually fell asleep during my class," Kim told her group of friends as they scraped up the remains of their sweet and sour sauce from their trays with their chicken nuggets. Carl was munching on his peanut butter and jelly sandwich. "He actually started snoring. Mr. Jansen just let him sleep. I don't think he wanted to deal with it."

"I heard Richie Thomas and Maureen King were kissing in the back of their history class," Michelle offered.

"That doesn't sound right," Kim said. "Isn't Richie a senior?"

"Yeah, but he failed history last year, so he had to retake the class."

Sally and James ate their food in silence, listening to their friends gossip, and turning their heads from friend to friend like they would with players at a tennis match. It was like this during most lunch periods now since the girls' table and the boys' table had merged. Sally and James didn't engage in gossip, but they did find watching their friends at it more entertaining than most television shows.

"Did you guys hear about Rick Allen, the drummer from Def Leppard?" Chris asked the group.

"No," Darlene said. "Did he overdose on drugs?" This was a common occurrence among 1980s rock stars.

"No," Chris said, all eyes on him as he spoke. Chris was not usually one to gossip. "I was watching *MTV News* last night, and they said he was in a bad car accident on New Year's Eve and his arm was completely severed! They sewed it back on, but then they had to remove it again later because he got an infection."

"Oh my God," James said. "That's horrible! Could you imagine being a drummer and losing your arm? That's so tragic! What's gonna happen to the band?"

Chris shrugged. "They didn't say. They're taking a break for now. But I mean, they're either gonna have to break up or get a new drummer, I would guess."

"Yikes," Michelle said. "Your life can really change in a split second. One day you're a rock star, and the next, you only have one arm, and then what?"

"I hope he put some money away in savings," Sally said. "Can you imagine if he can't be a rock star anymore, and then he's broke? That happens to pro athletes all the time. They spend all their money on cars and houses, and then they get injured, and they lose everything."

"I was gonna be a rock star," Carl told them, "but now I'm not so sure that's such a good idea."

Chris laughed. "Carl, you don't even play an instrument. And I've heard you sing. Learn a trade, man."

Lunch period was almost over, and James and Sally excused themselves to go to their lockers. After discarding their trays, they held hands as they walked down the hall.

"That's totally messed up about Rick Allen," Sally said. "I mean, we both saw Def Leppard just last year. They're at the height of their career. It's really not fair."

"No, it's not fair," James agreed. "I always feel like nothing bad can happen to me. But like Michelle said, you never know, huh?" They stopped at James's locker, and he opened his combination lock. "It's supposed to snow again tonight," he said, his mind inadvertently drifting off to other thoughts.

"Crap," Sally responded, making James smile. He was always surprised to hear Sally say a curse word, even one as innocuous as crap. "I hope they don't cancel school again. We've had enough snow days in the last couple of weeks."

James laughed. "Sally, listen to yourself," he told her. "You've really changed. You don't want school to be canceled? Is that something you would have ever imagined yourself saying any other year?"

Sally smiled slyly. "No," she said, "but back then, I didn't have a smokin' hot boyfriend waiting for me by my locker every day to carry my books!"

"Okay, I get it," James said, taking out his books and shutting his locker door. "I can totally relate. I'll tell you what. If the world tries to keep us apart again with snow, I will walk to your house. I'll wear my boots and put Wonder Bread bags on my feet to keep them dry."

Now it was Sally's turn to laugh. "Jamie, that's like a ten-mile walk! Maybe if you had snowshoes." She thought for a minute. "But in all seriousness." They had arrived at her locker, and she turned the dial on her lock. "I guess it's safer to stay home. Especially after hearing about the drummer with one arm."

"Good point," James agreed, taking her books from her as she closed the locker door. "It's not worth it. We have too much to lose, even if we aren't rock stars. We can talk on the phone all day if school is canceled."

"Yes," Sally said emphatically. "All day. And if one of us has to use the bathroom, we can just leave the phone for a few minutes and come back. And if anyone else needs to use the phone, too bad for them." They walked up the stairs toward their fifth-period classes. "I just hope so much that there's no snow or ice on the day I take my road test."

February

"Drive"/Cars
February 1, 1985

Sally took her road test on the day she turned sixteen and a half, as was the law in Massachusetts. Her mother took her to the Registry of Motor Vehicles in the morning for her appointment and brought her to school after. The roads were clear and dry, and the sun was shining. Although she feared she would fail, she passed on her first try.

She and James decided to go for a drive in the Cruiser that afternoon after school, and James handed Sally the keys. She drove through her area of town, and she pointed out where her friends from elementary school lived, and her favorite playgrounds and parks. Then she drove by Randall Junior High and parked by Carson Lake, just blocks away. It was unbearably cold outside, and even their layers of clothing, jackets, and the blankets wrapped around them didn't keep them warm. They sat quietly looking at the water, which was covered with a thick sheet of ice. They could see the Randall students walking across the ice as a shortcut to get home from afterschool activities, and this brought back memories of their time in junior high.

"What's your favorite memory of Randall?" James asked Sally.

She thought for a moment. "Leaving at the end of the day," she said. James laughed. "No, really, I think it was the day Mr. Quinn challenged me to a Rubik's Cube race in math class. He had announced to the class that he was going to teach everyone how to solve it, and I raised my hand and told him I already knew how, because my sister's friend had taught me. We did it a different way, and he wanted to see which way was faster. I had a tiny little keychain cube, and he had a full-sized one. I was beating him, and then all the sudden, my whole cube exploded into pieces and fell on the floor!" James burst out laughing again. "Weren't you in that class, Jamie? That's the one where Mr. Quinn gave me a D at the end of first term, and I cried to you and your friends, and you all tried to get me to laugh."

"I remember that day," Jamie said, "but I must have been out sick or in the principal's office the day of the Rubik's Cube explosion!"

"Yeah, Mr. Quinn tried to say he won, but I knew the truth. I would have beaten him fair and square if the cube hadn't burst on me."

James still couldn't help laughing. "I wish I had been there to see the look on your face when it happened."

"Oh, I was pissed!" Sally admitted. "The whole class was laughing, and Mr. Quinn was boasting. I can be quite pissy if I want to be, and I think I probably mouthed off to him a bit. I'm surprised I didn't end up in the principal's office!"

"But you said it was your favorite memory," James reminded her.

"Yeah, well, it's probably because the class all took my side after. They knew I would've won. I was better than Mr. Quinn and they knew it. He just got lucky!"

"I guess that's a good way to remember it," James agreed. He could tell she was still passionate about this story, even two years later. He wished he had been there to see it.

"What's your favorite memory?" Sally asked him.

James thought for a moment. "I'm sure I could come up with one of the funny things that happened with me and my friends, but to be honest, it was probably when I got a B+ on my book report in eighth grade. It was a book about Les Paul. My dad got it for me because he knew I was into playing the guitar, and he thought I would like it. I chose to do the book report on it because I wanted him to see I appreciated it. I wanted to do a good job, to show him I could. When I showed him the report with the B+ written across the top, he told me he was proud of me."

He stopped for a minute to think. "Y'know, being the youngest kid, having a sister who's a genius and then having a brother who's a druggie kind of puts you in a weird place. I never really knew where I fit in with my family. I mean, they've always wanted me to be smart like my sister, but not a drug addict like my brother, but those aren't things I think about when I think of who I am. I want to be myself, but it's taking me some time to figure out who that is, you know? I mean, I know I'm basically a good person, but what does that even mean?" He turned to face Sally. "And I know who I want to be when I'm with you. I don't even have to think about it at all. That's easy." He realized he had been talking for a long time and stopped.

Sally considered what James had said. "Jamie," she said softly, "I know how your parents felt about Howie and drugs, but I don't think I have ever heard them making a big deal of Erin's intelligence. I mean, I know they're proud of her, but do they really compare you guys?"

James shrugged. "Well, I guess not so much anymore," he admitted. "It was more of a big deal in elementary school, when my teachers would tell them at conferences that I was goofing off and not paying attention. It was just hard for me. I wouldn't do it on purpose. But they would use Erin as an example and tell me to be more like her. She was always studying or going to the library. But after Howie started getting in trouble, I guess they stopped with the school stuff so much and were more worried about the drug issue. And then, you know, they got worried about me using pot in junior high and ending up like Howie."

Sally maintained eye contact with him in silence. Finally, she said, "I like your favorite memory, Jamie. You did well for your dad, and not to show him you were as smart as your sister, but to show him how much you appreciated him thinking of you by giving you that book and trying to make a connection with you. Jamie, your parents are really proud of you, I can tell. Your mom is always so interested in what's going on with you. Your dad, well, you told me what he said to you on our motel night in November. He wants to be there for you. And now that Howie's doing better, they don't have to worry so much about him. And now that we're together, they don't have to worry as much about you. It feels like the story is changing."

James heard her words and listened to them closely. He knew she was right. If Howie was getting better, then he wouldn't be able to use that excuse anymore. He would have to rethink for himself where he was going, and none of it depended on what his brother and sister did.

He reached out and took Sally's gloved hand. "That makes a lot of sense," he said. "I'm gonna have to think about it some more, but I think you're right. How did you get so wise?" he asked her.

"I was an owl in my last life," she told him without missing a beat.

"I bet you were one of those tiny owls with the fluffy feathers," he said softly. "We were talking about junior high memories, and then we went so deep. Just think if I had asked you about your worst memory!"

"Yeah, we'll save those nightmares for another day, thank you very much." Sally leaned toward James and touched her icy lips to his. "We should head back to your house," she told him, "before we accidentally freeze our mouths together."

"Sally?" James said.

"Yeah, Jamie?"

"Thanks. For getting me."

"I do get you, Jamie, and I get to keep you!" Sally replied with a smile. She shifted the Cruiser into drive and slowly edged back into traffic toward Greenhill Road.

"Sally?" Jamie said.

"Yeah, Jamie?"

"Happy half birthday. I hope we get to go to a Red Sox game on your real birthday." He shivered. "And I hope it's hot outside."

"Scenes From an Italian Restaurant"/Billy Joel
February 14, 1985

The McKinney High School student council took orders for single, long-stemmed red roses in advance of Valentine's Day for a fundraiser. Members of the council would go to each classroom throughout the day on the holiday, calling names and handing out the prized roses. James decided to have a single rose delivered to Sally during each of her classes, and later, he would give her five more he had purchased for a dozen in all. He was getting a quick education in how expensive it was to have a serious girlfriend, but he found the benefits more than outweighed the cost. He was rethinking buying a new car.

He picked her up for school at eight that morning, and when she got in the car, he handed her the gift he knew she would enjoy the most, a Whitman's Chocolate sampler. She had told James once that she always wanted a box for herself that she didn't have to share with her family so she could try all the different kinds of candy. She opened the box right away, studied the candy map, and chose two pieces. She offered the box to James, but he knew she was just being polite and declined. Those were her personal chocolates. She gave him a decorated Valentine's shoe box, like the ones they used to make in elementary school to collect cards. Inside was a giant Hersey's Kiss, a framed picture of the two of them from Christmas, and a soft black, gray, and blue cashmere scarf she said would bring out the blue in his eyes. He immediately removed his scratchy brown hand-me-down wool scarf and put on the new one. It was warm, cozy, and felt good on his neck. Sally told him he looked fashionable in it. She held the scarf by both ends and pulled him closer. Her kiss tasted like chocolate and caramel.

They arrived at school and stowed their winter outdoor gear in their lockers. James noticed Sally was wearing a fuzzy red crew neck sweater over a white turtleneck with tiny multicolored hearts all over it and a denim miniskirt with tights. He loved that she got so enthusiastic about special occasions. He was going to do everything he could to make this her best Valentine's Day ever.

Although he hated to leave her for first period, James was looking forward to seeing the look on Sally's face when she realized he was flooding her with student council roses. He could hardly wait until English class.

James got to English class as fast as he could after third period ended. When he entered the room, Sally was already sitting at her desk with her first three roses lying in front of her. When she saw him, she stood up and walked toward the door to meet him.

"James Phillip Newell, what have you been up to?" she asked with a smile, holding out her flowers to show him.

Just then, a student council member entered the room and called out names for that period's rose delivery. Sally heard her name called, grinned at James, and stepped up front to get her fourth rose. Then she came back over to James, and before he knew what was happening, she gave him a kiss. It wasn't a small thank you peck on the lips. It was a full-on kiss with her arms around his neck and their bodies touching. Some of their classmates made "Oooooh" sounds, but neither of them cared.

When she pulled away, she said, "Jamie. Thank you so much for my flowers. I'm guessing there are more to come?" James nodded. "Thank you for making me feel so special. I feel so loved. Not just today, but every day. I love you."

Jamie smiled at her. "I love you, too, Sally. And yes, there is more to come, not just roses."

They sat down when Mrs. Clark entered the room, and the rest of the class settled down. Several of the girls had roses on their desks. Mrs. Clark admired them then asked them to stow them away for class. Then she passed around a bowl of Valentine's Day candy. It was a good day so far.

At lunch, the girls in the cafeteria were showing their roses and other Valentine's gifts to each other. Sally laid her four roses on the table next to her tray, and her friends admired them.

"Nice job, James," Darlene told him. "Some guys don't quite get how important Valentine's Day is to their girlfriends." She glanced over at Charlie, who was sitting at another table talking animatedly to his friends.

"Hey," Sally told her, "that's kind of not fair, Darlene. Not everyone can have a boyfriend as perfect as mine!"

James laughed. "You make it easy, Sally. You've been reminding me that Valentine's Day was coming every day for the last two weeks!"

Now Sally laughed. They finished their lunch and returned their trays. "So, what's the plan for tonight?" she asked him as they walked toward the lockers. "Did you make a reservation at Luigi's?"

"No," James answered. "Tonight, we're going to Casa de Newell, and I'm making you dinner."

"Really?" Sally asked excitedly. "That's awesome! I can't wait! What are you making?"

"Hey, I have to have a few surprises left, don't I?" he teased. "You'll see. And I promise it's not from a can."

At the end of the school day, James walked Sally and her seven roses to his car. He got there first and told her to wait. He opened the back door, pulled out the five roses he had been storing there in a vase all day, and shook off the water droplets. They still looked perky from being out in the cold car. He came around to her side of the car with them behind his back and held them out to Sally. "To make it a dozen," he told her.

"Oh my God, Jamie, this is incredible! Thank you!" She added the five roses to her bunch, and they were a handful.

"Oh, wait," James said, going around to the driver's side of the car. "I have a vase for them. Don't poke yourself with any thorns." He brought her the vase, and she carefully arranged the stems inside. "Happy Valentine's Day, Sally."

Sally wedged the vase and flowers into the space in front of her seat then came out of the car and threw her arms around James's neck. "Happy Valentine's Day, Jamie," she said and then whispered in his ear, "the first of many."

They did their homework as soon as they got to the house, and then James started dinner while Sally sat in the den with his parents, chatting. They were going out for dinner, but it wasn't yet time for their reservation. Sally wasn't sure if this was their Valentine's Day tradition, or if they were simply clearing out to give James exclusive use of the kitchen. Either way, she was grateful to them for giving up the space.

Soon, Mr. and Mrs. Newell left for dinner, and Howie came out of his room to watch reruns of *M*A*S*H* on TV with Sally while she waited. They talked about the final episode of the popular sitcom that had aired the previous year, and they both agreed they weren't too fond of it. "I don't get how they could make Hawkeye go crazy like that," Sally said. "I mean, the show was all about how being crazy is what got them through the war."

"Yeah, you're right," Howie agreed. "Exactly. A weird thing about that show is that it was on for like nine years, and the Korean War only lasted for like three. I guess good ratings lead to longer wars."

Sally laughed. "That is weird. Y'know, *M*A*S*H* is my dad's favorite show, and his dad loves *Hogan's Heroes*. I wonder what war show we'll end up watching in thirty years."

"Probably still *M*A*S*H*," Howie said. "There were enough episodes so we can watch all of them tons of times and still not get sick of them. And I can't imagine them making a funny show about Vietnam."

James came out of the kitchen. The aroma of simmering tomato sauce followed him. "Okay, dinner will be ready in about ten minutes, so Howie, prepare to take a hike. Sally, I'll call you in when it's done."

"Can I do anything to help?" Sally offered. "Set the table or something?"

"Nope!" James told her. "I have it all under control. You just wait here." He went back into the kitchen.

Howie looked at Sally. "Has he ever cooked for you before?" he asked.

"No," she answered.

"Me neither," Howie answered. "But it smells good. Alright, I have to go do my homework anyway, so you two crazy kids have fun. I'll catch you later." He stood up and bounded toward his room.

"Bye, Howie. Happy Valentine's Day!" Sally called after him.

She turned her attention to the TV, and a few minutes later, James came back and announced, "Dinner's ready."

Sally turned off the TV and followed him back through the kitchen to the table. He closed the door tightly so the dog, and Howie, wouldn't disturb them. There were two candlesticks flickering in the middle of the white tablecloth–covered table, and the overhead lights were dimmed. There were two full place settings in front of their chairs and wine glasses filled with what Sally assumed was sparkling cider. James escorted her to her seat and pulled out the chair.

"My name is James, and I'll be your server this evening," he told her as she sat. "I'll be right back with the first course of your meal. And just so you know, no tip is required for this service. But the server does reserve the right to take the diner out in his Vista Cruiser later and have his way with her, if she is agreeable to his terms."

Sally laughed. "Yes, garcon, I think that sounds pretty reasonable, as long as you don't make this offer to all your customers!"

James came back with a plate of dinner rolls and a bowl of salad. He served Sally first, then himself, and then sat down. "Don't fill up on these," he warned her. "There's still plenty coming. And you'll need room for dessert."

"Wow, this is a fancy restaurant," Sally said. "I might not be properly dressed."

James smiled. "In my restaurant, you can come as you are. You look beautiful."

Sally bit into a roll and hoped she didn't look like she was blushing by candlelight.

After the salad and rolls were cleared away, James took Sally's plate and scooped up food from pots and pans and a baking dish on top of the stove. He carried the full plate to her. She could see it was pasta with something cheesy on top. He watched her as she cut it with her fork and knife. It was eggplant parmesan, her favorite Italian dish. "Wow, Jamie," she exclaimed. "This looks great! I didn't know you knew how to make this!"

James beamed. "I've been picking up some cooking tips from Lou. He's been letting me do some more advanced stuff in the kitchen before my shifts start to see if culinary school is really something I wanna do. I told him my girlfriend loves his eggplant parm, and he taught me the recipe. I had to shrink it down significantly for only two people, but I think it's pretty spot on."

Sally blew on her fork then put the bite in her mouth and chewed. She smiled. "This is delicious. It does taste like Luigi's!" She quickly cut herself another bite.

They ate and talked until they had their fill. James took their plates and stacked them in the sink. They sat for a while digesting their food and sipping on more cider. After a while, James went to get dessert. He came back with a flat chocolate cake with sliced strawberries on top and a tub of vanilla ice cream.

He put it down on the table, got a knife from the drawer, and cut it into eight even pieces. He took two small plates from the cabinet and put one piece on each. Then he scooped them each some vanilla ice cream to put on top. Finally, he drizzled Hershey's Chocolate Syrup over the ice cream and placed a plate in front of each of them.

"Voici," he told her. "C'est une tourte sans farine aux fraises. I made it last night, because I figured I wouldn't have enough time to do everything today."

"Jamie," Sally said, astonished. "You take Spanish class. How did you know how to say 'flourless torte with strawberries' in French?"

James grinned slyly. "Sally," he said matter-of-factly, "when you have a girlfriend who knows French, you find ways of impressing her by also learning words in French for the perfect moments."

She gave him a look intended to tell him he was hopeless, but in the best possible way. Then she took a bite of the torte and closed her eyes as she chewed. "Jamie, this is incredible. If I wasn't already planning to go off in the Cruiser with you later, this cake would have been what convinced me!!"

James laughed, thanked her, and took a bite. She was right. It was good.

When they were done and the dishes were cleared, they stayed seated at the table by the glowing candlelight, holding hands and listening to soft blues music coming from Mrs. Newell's kitchen radio. "Jamie," Sally finally said, "this has been a fantastic Valentine's Day. Honestly, I could not ask to have a better boyfriend than you. You are perfect for me."

"So are you, Sally, for me," James answered. "I have one more gift for you." He reached into his back pocket and handed Sally two tickets to the prom.

"Sally," he said, "will you go to the McKinney High School junior prom with me?"

"Yes!" Sally answered excitedly. "I will go to prom with you, Jamie!"

James waited but she said nothing else. "So I got it right this time?" he asked. "I don't have to ask you again later?"

"Yes, Jamie, you got it right." She jumped out of her chair, kissed him, and hugged him tight where he sat. Then she looked at him. "But if you want to, you can ask me as many times as you like! Okay, so, my dress will be pink if the one I like is still at the store. What do you think about wearing a black tux with a white shirt, and a pink bowtie and cummerbund to match my dress?"

"I think that sounds great," James agreed, although he didn't much care about the details. He pictured himself and Sally dancing around the gym in each other's arms and kissing in the middle of the basketball court, like they did at homecoming. He would wear a gorilla suit to the prom if she asked him to, but luckily, she just wanted him to wear a conventional tux.

"Jamie," she said, as he stood and put his arms around her. "I didn't think you could possibly be any more perfect. But I was wrong."

March

"Adult Education"/Hall and Oates
Week of March 4, 1985

Spring break was coming the third week of March. The snowpack started to melt as the days got longer, and the sun warmed the wet sidewalks. Purple crocuses burst out of the ground, some displacing loose slushy residue. Spring rain made everything smell fresh and new. Buds started to appear at the ends of branches, and the sound of birdsong returned each morning. The nighttime nip was no longer in the air each morning. It was a time to be outside, to breathe the fresh air and feel reborn.

March also brought midterm exams. Sally had exams scheduled every day the week before the break in all her classes except her art and creative writing electives. James was also anticipating exams in everything but music and wood shop. They both felt the stress exams brought with them, and the knowledge that they didn't always have the skills to get through them as well as they would like. They had to work harder than most of their friends to retain the information and then to be able to reproduce it in the exams. They both had done better than usual with their fall and winter exams, but exams were cumulative. They would need to study their notes and books from the whole year.

"It doesn't seem fair," Sally told James over lunch. "I mean, we already took tests on this stuff, and they know we know it. Why do we have to memorize so much? I can't imagine we're gonna have to do that in the real world after school."

James shook his head. He had not previously been seriously considering going to a four-year college and had assumed he would take classes at the community college for a couple of years until he decided what he was going to do with his life. Now, he was seriously thinking about going to school for culinary arts, and the stakes were higher. He knew there would be more competition, and he had to try to show he was worth admitting. He knew his restaurant job would help him, but it wouldn't be enough. And now he was motivated more than ever to have a purpose, because of Sally.

"We can study together," he offered, not knowing which one of them would benefit more from the support but assuming it might be him. "We did pretty well with that before, and we didn't get too distracted."

Sally nodded. "I mean, I think that's a great idea," she agreed, "but we only have one class together. We have the same textbooks for our other classes, but our teachers teach it differently and give different kinds of exams. We need to study with people from our other classes, too."

James was not too thrilled with that idea. He knew he could focus with Sally, but the thought of being in a room with and having to pay attention to other people whose styles he wasn't familiar with wasn't a pleasant one. He knew Sally wouldn't like it much either. But he thought of a compromise. "What if we ask Michelle to study with us?" he suggested. "You have three finals with her, I have one, and she has Mrs. Clark for English seventh period, and we have it together. I could handle studying with her, I think. And she's pretty smart and does well on exams. And if we have to, we can figure something out for our other classes."

"Okay," Sally replied. "I can ask her. That might work. I'm pretty stressed about memorizing French vocabulary, so maybe she and I can help each other with that another time. And we can all do history together, too, because it's basically just dates and battles. Maybe an essay or two. You'll have to find someone else for Spanish. And maybe having someone else there would help us stay more focused. You and I do end up kissing a lot when we're alone. I need all the help I can get."

When Sally asked Michelle in class later, she agreed to study with them, and they decided to go to her house Wednesday after school. James asked Lou for Wednesday off to study, and Lou, who valued a good education, agreed.

James drove himself, Sally, and Michelle to the Gormans' house, which was right on the other side of Twin Bridges Park. Her mother was home along with her ten-year-old twin brothers, who were watching cartoons in the den. The teenagers went upstairs after greeting Mrs. Gorman and closed themselves in Michelle's room. Her room was much less adorned than Sally's, although she did have Duran Duran and Flock of Seagulls posters on her wall. She had a small record player and a pile of albums, and a bookshelf half filled with paperbacks and the other half with stacks of teen magazines. Her room was clean, but Sally, having been there many times before, suspected that many of Michelle's belongings had been stuffed into her closet to prepare for their visit. Michelle had previously shared her room with her older sister who had moved out, so she, too, had matching twin beds. Michelle sat cross-legged on her own bed, and James and Sally did the same on the other. They dumped their books and notebooks on the beds and tried to organize them by subject.

"Okay, what should we do first?" Michelle asked. They chose history and found their appropriate textbooks and notes.

One hour and two subjects later, Mrs. Gorman knocked on the door and came in with a plate of steaming hot pizza rolls and a two-liter bottle of Slice soda.

"You guys have been hard at work up here," she said, placing the plate of hot food on top of Michelle's dresser. "I haven't heard a peep from you from downstairs. Why don't you take a break and have a snack. I brought you some pudding pies, too." She took the individually wrapped pies out of the oversized pockets of her sweatshirt and laid them next to the plate. "I'll go get you some glasses with ice for the soda."

"I'll help you, Mom," Michelle offered, jumping from her bed and heading to the stairs with her mother.

James put down his dog-eared copy of *Lord of the Flies*, got up, and walked over to the plate of pizza rolls. He picked one up and popped it in his mouth. "Hot," he said immediately after chewing and waved his hand in front of his open mouth. Sally laughed. He carried the plate over to her, and she grabbed one in each hand. She took care to bite into them gingerly at first to let the steam escape.

"Are you doing okay?" she asked James when he came back to sit on the bed carrying two chocolate pudding pies. "We still have a lot to study."

"I'm good," he responded, ripping one of the pies open and taking a bite. "I could go for another hour at least. How about you?"

"I'm okay for now," she replied. She sighed. "I can't wait for spring break!" she declared, letting herself fall back on the bed on top of their books. "I really need a vacation. We need to do something fun during break."

"Like what?" James asked.

"I don't know, we live in this great place so close to everything. We can go to Boston and go to Quincy Market. Or we can go to Newport and tour a mansion. Or both. I wish we could go to a Red Sox game, but the regular season doesn't start until we're back in school."

"We could take a day trip up to the Maine coast," James suggested. "It's a long drive, so we would have to leave early. It would be too cold to swim, but we could still go to the beach and walk around. We could go to Ogunquit. It's only like twenty minutes from my grandparents. Maybe we could meet them for lunch or something. I know my Nonna wants to meet you, and I would love for you to meet them, too."

"Yes!" Sally exclaimed. "I love that idea! I want to meet your Nonno and Nonna, too. We both have some days off from work, so we can figure out times to go, and then just go. It will be so fun! But first," she said, gesturing to their books, "we have to slog through all of this stuff."

"Bummer," James said.

"Major bummer," Sally agreed.

James leaned over and kissed her. "My grandparents are going to love you," he whispered. "My whole family loves you. But not as much as I love you." He kissed her again.

Sally relaxed into the kiss. James tasted like chocolate pudding. Then she straightened up. "I love you, too, Jamie," she said. "I can't wait to meet your grandparents."

"It will be nice to meet yours sometime, too," James said, rubbing his hands up and down her arms. "Don't they all live nearby?"

Sally's smile was thin, and James could feel her shoulders tense. "Oh, yeah," she said. "They do. Yeah, maybe you can meet them sometime, I guess." She picked up one of her books and started leafing through it without looking at the pages then closed it and put it down. She looked up at James. "Yeah, I think you'll like my Grandma Naomi. She's my deaf grandma. She's really great." She picked up another book and opened it to a random page.

James looked at Sally. She looked back up at him and smiled. He had never seen her react like that before. He wondered what the deal was with her grandparents.

Michelle and Mrs. Gorman returned with the glasses and poured out soda for the three of them. They sat and chatted for a few more minutes while finishing their snacks, and then they resumed their discussion of *Lord of the Flies*.

On Thursday, James went to Chris's house to study Spanish and math, and Sally would be studying French vocabulary and biology with Michelle. The day was too nice to miss time outside, so Sally and Michelle walked to the Bachmans' house after school and headed out to the picnic table on the screened-in porch.

"Do you think you'll get a car now that you have your license?" Michelle asked as she unpacked her French notebook.

"I doubt it," Sally responded. "Even used cars are so expensive. I mean, we live so close to school, and most colleges don't let you keep a car on campus if you live in the dorms anyway. What about you? Do you think your parents would get you a car?"

"Nah," Michelle responded. "Same as you. Too rich for our blood. My parents would never get me one. But at least you have James to drive you around."

Sally smiled. "That is nice," she agreed, sitting on the wooden bench, "but do you have any idea how cold that car got over the winter? I never complained, but man, it was freezing! It was actually warmer to roll down the windows!"

Michelle laughed. "You'll probably go to the prom in that car, too," she said. She sighed loudly. "I wish Joey would ask me to prom already. I mean, we only have like six weeks left."

"He will," Sally assured her. "I'm sure he's just waiting until the right moment. Do you think he wants you to ask him because it's not his prom?" she wondered. Joey was a junior at Murphy High.

"No, he knows I want to be asked," Michelle said. "He doesn't know that my mom won't let me buy a dress until I get asked, and I really want to buy a dress!"

"I'll wait for you, and we'll go together," Sally promised. "We still have time. I'm sure it will be soon." They sat in silence, both lost in their own thoughts about prom. "I wish that Jamie and I could spend prom night together," Sally finally said. "It would be so romantic, being together all night and waking up together in the morning. I know Jamie would like that, too. But I can't see any way for us to make that happen." She shrugged. "But it will still be an amazing night."

"It will be," Michelle agreed, opening her French book. "Let's start on the nouns for things in the park. What's la balançoire?"

Sally laughed. "That one's easy. One of my favorite places to go with Jamie. Swing. Maybe I won't get a zero on my French exam after all!"

"Stay the Night"/Chicago
March 31, 1985

Midterm exams ended, and spring break began. Sally and James took trips to Boston to shop, snack, and explore at Faneuil Hall and Quincy Market, and Newport to tour The Breakers and Elms mansions and hike on the cliff walks. Then they took the long drive to the beach in Ogunquit, Maine. They had lunch with James's grandparents at a seafood restaurant, dipped their feet in the ocean, hiked along the beach, laid in the sun, and built sandcastles. Sally bought herself a T-shirt or pullover hooded sweatshirt at each stop. On the other days, they worked and met up between shifts for lunch or dinner or a drive through Sally's neighborhood to their favorite spot. The days passed quickly, and it was nearly time to go back to school.

On Sunday, the day before the end of break and less than one month before prom, Mrs. Newell announced to James that she and her husband would be going to Florida on the weekend of prom to attend her niece's Disney World destination wedding.

"James, I'm so sorry, I didn't realize when I bought the plane tickets that it was prom weekend," Mrs. Newell told him. "I really wanted to be here to get pictures of you and Sally all dressed up. It's your first big formal event!"

James could recognize an opportunity when he saw one. "Mom," he assured her using his best faithful son voice, "you have to go to Tanya's wedding. We'll have Mrs. Bachman take pictures. Don't worry about it. It's okay. I'm just sorry you won't be here." His mother gave him an understanding hug. James thought maybe she might feel bad enough to leave him money to use toward dinner on prom night.

"I'll make arrangements for Ringo to go to the Coopers' for the weekend," she told him, "so you and Howie won't need to worry about having to be home to let him out. And Ringo loves Peter." She patted James on the back. "And I'll definitely leave you with some money for food for the weekend."

James was no sooner done with talking to his mother than he was on the phone in his room calling Sally to tell her the good news.

"Oh my God, I can't believe it!" Sally said. "Seriously? Disney World? This is like fate!" She paused for a moment then lowered her voice, "But my parents will never let me stay over at your house after prom, especially with your parents gone."

"Well . . ." James thought for a moment. "I guess we could come up with some sort of cover story."

"You mean like lie to my parents?" Sally whispered into the phone.

"Well, you can't exactly tell them the truth!"

"Oh, okay. I haven't ever really done that before, but I guess there's always a first time. I mean, as far as lies go, there could be far worse, but it will still feel weird."

"I don't make a habit out of lying to mine, either," James stated. Then he added, "At least not anymore. But we have to look at what's important. Sally, we *get to spend the whole night together*!"

"Yes!" Sally replied excitedly. "We've waited for this for a long time. We will make it happen. No matter what!"

"That's the spirit!" James exclaimed. He paused. "I'm gonna need to do something about Howie, too," he realized. "I wonder if I can talk Erin into inviting him to Brown for the weekend."

April

"Little By Little"/Robert Plant
April 15, 1984

Sally had informed Michelle of her plans with James for prom, and she was trying to help her come up with a story for her parents. Soon, the story began to take care of itself.

"So, Traci is going to the prom with Doug O'Leary," Michelle told Sally on the phone on Patriot's Day when they were home from school for the Massachusetts-specific holiday. "And Doug's gonna rent a hotel room for the night so everyone can hang out there, and crash if they get too wrecked, which I'm guessing they probably will."

"Doug O'Leary?" Sally asked. "Dougo? How does Traci know Dougo? He went to Randall. Isn't he a senior? And goes to Murphy?"

"Yeah," Michelle gossiped. "Traci's brother Bobby goes to Murphy and is friends with him, and Traci's always had a crush on him. She finally got up the nerve to ask him to go to prom when he was at her house and her brother had left the room. He said yes, and she's totally stoked! And he's over eighteen so he's legal to rent the room."

"That's great!" Sally agreed. "So, we can go to the hotel after prom."

"Yeah," Michelle replied. "And maybe your parents would be okay if you told them you were gonna crash there. I already asked my mom, and she said yes, believe it or not!"

"She did? But your mom is so strict!"

"I know," Michelle agreed, "but this is prom! And remember, my mom and dad went to both McKinney proms together, so she had to agree that it was special."

"I don't know," Sally worried. "Maybe I can try. I hate lying to my parents. But I mean, I guess it wouldn't really be lying if we were actually going to the hotel. I don't know what they would think about the hotel, even."

"Well, it won't hurt to ask them anyway," Michelle urged. "They won't say yes if you don't ask. Traci also invited us all to go in a stretch limo she booked from her cousin Ray's rental lot. She told Ray if she got a date, she would totally want to get one, and he promised her he would let her have it if she got a date, which she did."

"But Jamie and I are gonna go to his house after," Sally reminded her. "We'll need to have his car. If we go in a limo, we'll be stuck at the hotel. Plus, we aren't gonna drink, so Jamie can drive."

"Oh, yeah, that makes sense," Michelle admitted. "I wasn't thinking. I already forgot the hotel is a cover story for you guys. See? It's pretty convincing! But I want to go in a limo! I've seen those things driving kids around every year and I want to see what it's like to be on the inside of one. It will be such a rush! Maybe we can all meet up and take pictures at one of our houses, then whoever wants to go in the limo can go. We can meet at the restaurant and go to the school separately."

"Okay, that works for me," Sally said, relieved. The idea of going in on a stretch with five or more other couples felt like a nightmare to her. She would rather walk to the prom in high heels. "Jamie's working a long shift for the holiday tonight, so I'll talk it over with him at school tomorrow, and you and I can talk later with the final plans. Has Joey rented his tux yet?"

"Yes!" Michelle said dreamily. "He's getting a charcoal gray tux with a royal blue bowtie and cummerbund to match my dress. He's gonna look so great. I think he'll look kind of like Don Johnson on *Miami Vice*! I can't wait!"

"Yeah, that works for me, too," James agreed over their weekly lunch together in the cafeteria the next day. "And I was able to talk Erin into inviting Howie down for a couple of nights to Brown. She has ulterior motives anyway. Now that he's sober and in school, she wants him to see what it's like on a real college campus, as if Howie would ever be able to get into Brown. Hell, most people couldn't. But she's really proud of him and wants him to know she supports him."

"She should be proud of him," Sally said, pausing her soup spoon on the way to her mouth. "He's doing great. So now the only thing I have to do is talk, or lie, to my parents about the hotel. What do we do if they say no?" She put the uneaten soup back into the bowl and frowned sadly.

"Hey, if they say no, they say no. We'll find another time. I promise. I want this, too, so we will make it happen. Now eat your soup," he commanded. "It's good for you."

Sally looked forlornly at the bowl. "It's good for something," she said, "like grouting a tub, maybe."

James laughed and dribbled a drop of minestrone down his chin. He quickly grabbed a napkin and wiped it away. Sally snickered.

"Sally," James reminded her, "we have other things to think about. The U2 concert's on Thursday. That's two days from now. Let's put the prom stuff aside for now and get excited for the concert!"

"It's gonna be so cool," Sally said. "I can't wait to see them! I've been listening to them so often, I think I might know every word to every song. I can't believe I'll be in the same room as Bono Vox!"

James smiled. He liked that Sally could flip switches so quickly, from worrying about being untruthful to her parents to excitement about their upcoming concert date. She even started to eat her soup while naming the U2 songs she hoped to hear at the show.

"We Belong"/Pat Benatar
April 19, 1985

James picked up Sally the afternoon following the U2 concert. They had gotten home late and decided to let each other sleep in before going out and enjoying their condoned day off.

Sally was all smiles as she got into the Cruiser. "I'm still buzzing from the concert," she told James. "I still can't believe how great it was. I almost cried! It was so emotional. I can still hear Bono singing the last line of '40' in my head!"

James nodded in agreement. "It was so good. I've been to tons of concerts, and that has to be the best one I've seen. The best part was the encore. I mean, the band walking off stage one by one while the crowd was singing, and then the lights coming up. It was intense!" James was wearing the black U2 T-shirt he had purchased at the show with the money Mr. Bachman had slipped to Sally as she got out of the car at the Centrum. Sally had bought a baseball-style concert shirt for herself but was saving it for school on Monday.

They continued to talk about their concert experience as James drove them to the movie theater to see *The Breakfast Club*. They parked and went inside to buy tickets. They felt alternately like free-wheeling adults and kids playing hooky because it was a school day. No one questioned them being there. They both enjoyed the movie.

"I think movies are getting better," Sally said as they walked through the parking lot to the car. "At least for teenagers. It's like they finally figured out that we have brains. *Breakfast Club* totally deals with real-life types of situations, even if the characters were exaggerated to make their points more clearly. It was more real than most movies I've seen in the past couple of years."

"Yeah, it was definitely more real than *Police Academy 2*," James responded, citing the movie that he and his friends had seen the previous week. "I mean, it's funny, but really dopey."

"I like funny," Sally told him. "But sometimes I like some substance, too. I like to think about things. I hope someday I can write stories and books that make people think. Maybe I can write movies, too."

"That'd be great," James said, opening the car door for her. "You can make movies and make lots of money, and we can live in a mansion, and I can stay home with the kids. Maybe we'll get a nanny. Or if we're rich, two nannies."

Sally always got goosebumps when James talked about them being together in the future, especially fantasy scenarios where they were married, even if he was just being silly. "Two nannies?" she asked him when he got in the driver's side. "How many kids are we talking about here?"

James shrugged. "I don't know. Four, I guess. Two boys and two girls. The girls will look exactly like you, and I'll spoil them rotten. And the boys will look like me and they'll be rotten, but you'll love them anyway because they're just like me!"

Sally laughed. "This sounds a lot like the end of *Lady and the Tramp*, when they have a litter of puppies!" she quipped.

"I don't think I would want all the babies at the same time like puppies, though," James deadpanned. "One at a time would be good."

"Yeah, that sounds better to me, too," Sally agreed, smiling. She sat back in her seat and thought about what their kids would look like. One thing she knew was they would likely have blue eyes. She had learned this in the genetics section of her biology class.

It was nearly dinner time, and they headed to Sally's house to eat. James felt at home at the Bachmans' and no longer felt like he had to be formal or impress anyone. Sally's parents didn't treat him like a guest, and he was expected to clean up after himself and help with whatever Sally was expected to do. He sometimes almost called them Mom and Dad by mistake since he was expected to follow the same rules as he did at home.

Mrs. Bachman was making Sally's favorite stir-fry with steak, water chestnuts, bamboo shoots, and cling peaches. She was sautéing the food in an electric frying pan that sat on the counter.

"Can I help?" James asked Mrs. Bachman.

"No, thanks, James," she replied, stirring in soy sauce. "Why don't you help Sally with the dessert?"

Sally showed him the recipe she used to make her favorite dessert, chocolate pudding cake, and he helped her gather the ingredients.

When the batter was in the cakepan, she asked James to put the tea kettle on.

"Now watch this dessert-making magic," she told him. She sprinkled a mixture of dry cocoa, sugar, and brown sugar over the top of the batter. When the kettle steamed, she measured out one cup of boiling water. "Now pour the water over the top," she instructed. James looked at her doubtfully. "No, really!" Sally insisted. "That's what you're supposed to do!"

"Okay," James said skeptically. Then he poured the steaming water, which appeared to drown the batter. "I'm trusting you."

Sally laughed and then put the whole thing in the oven.

While the cake was baking, they sat in front of the TV watching music videos on MTV and playing *Boggle*. When the timer rang, Sally got up to take out the cake, and James was surprised to see all the water was gone.

It was just James, Sally, and her parents for dinner that Friday night, and Mrs. Bachman lit two candlesticks in fancy silver holders for Shabbat. It was the Jewish day of rest. She and Sally shaded their eyes and then said the blessings, just like they had at Chanukah. James knew Sally was not religious and had not gone to Sunday School since she had her bat mitzvah at age thirteen, but she really seemed to relish these special moments with her mother.

Dinner was delicious, and the conversation was casual. Then Mr. Bachman informed Sally he would be leaving for Pennsylvania on Monday for a couple of nights for a printing job.

"Dad, I wish you didn't have to travel so much," Sally said sadly. "I mean, I know you like your work, but you always seem so tired when you get home. Can't you get someone else to take your place sometimes?"

Mr. Bachman shook his head. "Sally, there isn't anyone else who does what I do. It's nice to have a skill that makes you indispensable. When I retire, they're probably going to have to get three people to do my job!"

"That just means you're doing the job of three people, Dad," Sally said with a sigh. "I hope they appreciate you."

Her father reached out his hand and put it on top of hers. "Hey, Sal Gal, I'm the parent here. Don't start getting all wise on me."

James cleared the dinner dishes while Sally put out the dessert plates. Mrs. Bachman got the cake.

"James, I hope you're coming over on Sunday for Josie's birthday party," she said as she spooned cake onto his plate. "We'll have a lunch spread and cake. And Sally's grandparents will all be here."

"I wouldn't miss it," James replied, reminding himself he needed to pick up a present. He looked at Sally. She was looking at her plate with a blank expression. He reached over and took her hand. She looked up and smiled.

James could tell that Sally was nervous about him meeting her grandparents, but he didn't know why. He considered that it might be because he wasn't Jewish. But there was nothing he could do about that. He just hoped the birthday party wouldn't be too stressful.

They ate their pudding cake with vanilla ice cream. James was amazed that the pudding had sunk to the bottom. "You're right, Sally, it is magic cake," he marveled, and they all laughed. He leaned in closer to her. "Someday," he said, "when I'm a famous chef, I'll make you cakes every week. And I promise, they'll all be magic."

"Anxiety/Get Nervous"/Pat Benatar
April 21, 1985, prom countdown 6 days

When Sunday arrived, James took care in dressing, as he wanted to make a good impression on Sally's grandparents. He put on a relatively new unfaded pair of jeans and a sky blue short-sleeved polo shirt. There wouldn't be any other babies at Josie's party, just family. James hadn't met any of the older generation yet, but Sally had implied they were not keen on his lack of being Jewish. He was hoping no one would say anything about that at the party. Maybe they would be too busy noticing his shirt was the same shade of blue as his eyes.

James went to the toy store and bought Josie a stacking ring toy and a book about kittens. He drove himself and the gifts to the Bachmans' house, and Andie let him in. Josie, who still had not mastered the skill of walking, crawled into the front hall behind her mother and approached James. She grabbed the leg of his jeans and pulled herself up. They were becoming friends now as they spent more time together. James handed Andie the gifts, picked up Josie, and gave her a kiss on the top of her head. Andie turned back to the door to greet another guest. James carried Josie into the dining room and hoped this would not be construed as a cutting-through infraction. He stopped at the table. There was a tray of deli meats, breads, and cheeses on the table. An older woman with a short cinnamon-colored wig, wearing a housecoat and owl glasses, was standing alone by a salad bowl, stirring in dressing. She didn't notice James coming in or look up when Josie babbled. He quickly realized this was Sally's deaf grandmother.

She glanced up and noticed him standing there. "Hello," she said to him. Her voice was so clear he wouldn't have ever guessed she was deaf.

"Hello," he responded, annunciating the letters clearly. "I'm James."

"Hi James," she answered. "I'm Naomi Bachman, Sally's grandmother. I think Sally has told you I'm deaf, and when you talk to me, you need to speak slowly so I can read your lips."

"Yes, she did," he said slowly. "It's nice to meet you."

She turned toward Josie, waved her fingers at her, and smiled. Then she turned her attention to James. "You, too, James. Sally tells me you're in English class together and have been reading modern classics. I also like to read a lot. Sometimes it's the only way I get information since people forget to tell me things. Oh, but I'm going on. Tell me how you met Sally."

James slowly recounted the story of their relationship. She asked him questions and nodded her understanding. Every once and a while, she would ask him to repeat a word she didn't catch.

James liked Grandma Naomi immediately and understood why Sally spoke so fondly about her. When they were done talking, he waved to her and moved on to find Sally.

Sally was sitting on a blanket on the floor in the den where Josie's toys were laid out and had seen the whole interaction between James and her grandmother. She felt touched that James had remembered her grandmother's limitations and still made an effort to connect with her. Sally loved all of her grandparents equally, but if pressed, she would have to say Grandma Naomi was her favorite. She missed most of the gossip and backbiting that went on in her extended family because she couldn't hear it. She took things at face value. She loved Sally and "listened" to her closely. That was the kind of listening Sally usually needed.

James came in and put Josie down on the floor with her toys. He sat on the floor and Josie immediately climbed right back up on his lap before he could reach over to give Sally a kiss. Josie picked up a rattle and put it in her mouth. She was teething and needed to be constantly chewing on something.

"Look over there," Sally told James as she gestured to the dining room. Grandma Naomi was talking animatedly to Mrs. Bachman, and Sally could tell she was saying nice things about her interaction with

James. "It looks like four generations of women in my family like you now, and of course I love you."

"Not too bad," James responded, smiling. "I love you, too, Sally." She smiled back.

He reached over to kiss her, but she put up her hand to stop him and pointed to the couch. There were two gray-haired men wearing casual slacks and short-sleeved button-down shirts sitting behind the coffee table engaged in conversation. They were watching a Red Sox–Yankees game and talking animatedly about winter weather patterns. It was obvious they had known each other for many years and attended many birthday parties for their mutual grandchildren. They both smiled when Sally came over and sat on the cushion between them.

"What's new, pumpkin?" Grandpa Irving asked, putting his arm around her shoulder and kissing her cheek.

"Grandpa Irving and Grandpa Harold, this is my boyfriend James," she said, gesturing to the spot on the floor where Josie was still pinning him to his seat. "James, these are my grandfathers!"

"Hi," James said, turning his head as much as he could to face them. "Nice to meet you."

Grandpa Harold turned to Sally. "So, this is the gentile boy you're involved with?" he asked, not unkindly.

"Grandpa, don't say that," Sally scolded. "Yes, okay, James isn't Jewish, but you're all gonna have to learn to deal with it."

"Fine," Grandpa Harold said with a sigh. He stood up, walked over to where James was sitting, and put out his hand. James took it and they shook. "James, nice to meet you. What's your last name?"

"Newell, sir," James said, feeling like the *sir* was necessary and expected in this situation.

"Newell. Is that a German name?"

"No, sir, it's English."

"What's your mother's maiden name?"

"Um, Romano?"

"That's Italian, right?"

"Yes, it is."

"Is she from Italy?"

"No, but her grandparents were."

"Were your grandfathers in the war?"

"Which war?"

"The Second World War."

"My Nonno Angelo was in the army in France."

"The Italian grandfather? Which side?"

"Uh, American side."

"Okay, good," Grandpa Harold said and then turned around and went back to his seat. He was done talking.

Now it was Grandpa Irving's turn. He stayed in his seat. "So, James," he asked, "where do you live?" Which then led to an interview:

"Where do you work?"

"What do your parents do?"

"Are you and Sally in classes together?"

"What are you studying?"

"Where do you plan to go to college?"

James was holding his own with both interrogations, but when the college question came up, Sally knew it was time to rescue him. "Grandpa, excuse me a minute, but James, I heard Andie asking where Josie is. Would you mind bringing her over to her?"

"No problem," James said, relieved. He didn't want to open the college can of worms with Sally's grandfather. He had enough to worry about with his own family. Maybe the grandfathers were the reason that Sally was feeling so uptight about him meeting her grandparents. If so, he thought he may have passed their test. It would all be okay. He stood and carried Josie through the dining room. He found Andie in the living room, sitting with a woman wearing a long floral dress, with short, cropped brown and gray hair. She saw Josie and smiled.

"Josephine! Come see Grandma Joanie," the lady cooed at Josie. Josie, who would basically go to anyone, reached out her tiny arms and was accepted onto her grandmother's lap.

"James," Andie started, "this is my mother-in-law, Joan Fischer. Joan, James is Sally's boyfriend."

"Pleased to meet you," Mrs. Fischer said while waving a small toy in front of Josie's face.

"You too," James responded.

Andie made sure Josie was settled with Joan then grasped James's arm lightly and led him into the hallway. "So, who have you met so far on our little Magical Mystery Tour?" she asked.

"Well," he told her, "there's Grandpa Harold, who wants my family pedigree so he can check if I come from a long line of Nazis, Grandpa Irving, who now knows enough about me to write my biography, and Grandma Naomi, who is one of the nicest people I have ever met."

"She is a gem," Andie agreed. "Deafness pretty much saved her from all the nastiness in the world. She's so grateful when people take the time to talk to her, she'll probably rave about you for weeks." She clapped her hands together and rubbed her palms. "So, three down, one to go. James, I think it's time you met Grandma Fran. Has Sally told you anything about her?"

"No, I've only ever heard her talk about Grandma Naomi," he told her, now realizing how strange that was. Andie led him though the dining room. He was pretty sure by now that no one followed the cutting-through rule when Mrs. Bachman wasn't paying attention. Mrs. Bachman was in the kitchen, putting the final touches on Josie's birthday cake over the stove. Another woman sat hovering over the kitchen table, jiggling both legs and engaged in a monologue. She had long gray hair pulled back in a neat braid that fell down her back. The skin on her hands and face was leathery and wrinkled, and she wore heavy, bright makeup on her eyes and cheeks. Her eyes were a deep chocolate brown, like Sally's mother. James listened to her speak but couldn't figure out what she was talking about. She was going from subject to subject with no stops. She sounded like she was rushing to get the whole conversation done in record time. Andie approached the petite woman and put her hand on her shoulder. The woman stopped talking abruptly and turned to face Andie.

"Hey, Grandma," she said. "I want you to meet Sally's boyfriend, James. James, this is Grandma Fran."

"James!" Grandma Fran exclaimed, jumping up and giving him a tight hug. She was so short, she only came up to his chest. She smelled of stale tobacco and onions. She was dressed in an oversized long-sleeved lavender smock and a blue flowered floor-length peasant skirt. Her feet were bare, and her toes nails dotted with chipped orange polish. "James and the Giant Peach!" she went on. "James, James, James. Are you related to Etta James? No wait, that was her last name. There's also Jesse James and Jesse Jackson. Oh, and Jackson Brown! My daughter

Rhona likes to listen to his records. Rhona lives in Canada. They get much more snow than we do. I've been told never to eat yellow snow. There's a song about that! Phyllis, did you put garlic powder in this onion dip? I don't taste garlic. I always put garlic in my dip. Can you give me my cigarette now? I'm sure it's been over an hour."

She had turned and redirected her conversation to Mrs. Bachman. Mrs. Bachman was still smearing icing on the cake. She stopped, gently placed the spatula in the mixing bowl, and wordlessly grabbed a cigarette out of a pack of Newport Menthols she removed from her apron pocket. She started to walk to the back door with her mother in tow to take her outside for her smoke.

James stood staring at Grandma Fran as she walked away, still talking animatedly. "What just happened here?" James asked Andie. "I mean, what the hell. Sorry, Andie, I don't mean to be rude, but seriously. What was that all about?"

Andie gave him a sympathetic look. "No, I'm sorry, James," she said, "but that was kind of a set up. You really get the full experience when you meet Grandma Fran. She has bipolar disorder. You might have heard it called manic depression. Her psychiatrist is making changes to her medications because her blood pressure has been too high. She's hypomanic, which means manic but not serious enough to have to go to the hospital. She's also hyperverbal, and you can probably figure out what that means. You can't break into her stream of consciousness sometimes to make her stop talking, but you can give her projects to do to keep her calm, like sorting change, or coloring in a book. The biggest problem is that she gets up every hour during the night to smoke, and drink coffee."

"And Grandpa Irving can handle all this?"

"Sort of. He's put up with it for years. It's possible he's losing his hearing now, which probably helps him cope, but he never complains. He loves her. There are caregivers that come to help a few times a week, to clean and sort her medication, and Grandpa takes her to the psychiatric clinic once every two weeks, but otherwise he's on his own with her. My mom tries to help when she can, but she works full time, and gets easily overwhelmed. Her sister lives in Canada, so she gets no help from her. So Grandpa's pretty much on his own most days. We've all tried to talk him into making a move, like to an assisted living facility, so they can still live together but have more help, but he's not ready for that yet. I really think they would be happier if they gave up their apartment and had people taking care of them."

"Yeah, well, I get that," James agreed. "My grandma lives in assisted living, and it's been great for her. And for my dad." He paused in thought. "Andie," he said. "Sally talks a lot, I mean not anywhere near as much as your grandma, but sometimes she can be all over the place."

"James," Andie said with a kind smile. "Don't worry. Sally doesn't have what Grandma Fran has. She just gets excited about things and can't contain herself. She's always been that way. Mom and Dad brought her to the pediatrician when she was in third grade to see if she had attention deficit disorder because she had such problems paying attention in school and getting her homework done. The doctor didn't even bother doing any testing. He said it's not often found in girls, and since she wasn't getting out of her seat in classes and disrupting the other students, they should be patient and wait for her to mature. What a quack. I still think Sally has ADD, but over the years, she's had to find some ways to adjust and get by on her own. I think she's doing really well with it." Andie glanced at her watch. "Hey, I'd love to talk to you more about this sometime, but it's getting to be time for cake. James, can you go get Josie from Joan while I light the candle?"

James went to get Josie while wondering if maybe he had attention deficit disorder, too, since he also had always struggled with paying attention and getting his work done. He found Joan now sitting on the floor in the living room with Mr. Bachman, playing with the baby. He told them it was time for cake, and he took Josie back to Andie.

James found Sally in the hall and finally gave her a hello kiss. The entire group filtered into the small dining room and sang "Happy Birthday" to Josie as Mrs. Bachman brought the cake in from the kitchen. Then Andie blew out the one candle for her. Mrs. Bachman had made a special cake in the shape of a cat for her granddaughter. She cut Josie a piece of the ear dend put it in front of her on the highchair. Everyone watched as Josie grabbed the cake in her tiny fist and shoved it in her mouth, smearing it on her face. They all laughed. Mrs. Bachman snapped pictures. The cake was served to everyone else, and the volume rose in the dining room as everyone ate and talked to each other at once.

Mrs. Bachman poured coffee from a pot into ceramic cups. When he finished his piece of cake, James caught Sally's eye, and she signaled him toward the door. They both put their empty cake plates on the table and made a hasty retreat out the front door.

"Love's Been a Little Bit Hard on Me"/Juice Newton

They walked in silence for a while, the only sounds being those of passing cars and their own footsteps. There was a warm spring breeze, and Sally caught the aroma of blooming flowers in the air. She inhaled deeply and reached for James's hand.

"So, what do you think?" she asked him after some time.

"Your grandparents are great," James responded carefully.

Sally laughed. "You're being too kind," she said. "My family's a lot to take. They're not so bad one at a time, but when you get them all together, it's like some bad scary circus."

"What's the deal with Grandpa Harold and the twenty questions about my family and World War Two?" he asked her.

"He was in the army overseas during the war," Sally told him, "but he never saw any action. He was assigned to the motor pool as a mechanic because that was what he did before the war. I think he feels guilty about that, even though it wasn't his fault and it kept him alive. He's really involved with the Veterans Administration and does a lot of volunteering at the hospital and VFW. But don't worry, now that he's grilled you and realizes you're an ally, he'll be fine with you." She paused. "So, you met Grandma Fran, too, huh?"

"Yeah," James said. "She kind of caught me off guard. Why haven't you ever told me about her?"

"I'm sorry, I wasn't trying to keep her a secret or anything," Sally explained. "It's just hard to talk about her. Jamie, she totally exhausts me. My mom, too. Sometimes when my mom and her sister were kids, she would disappear for a couple days at a time, and sometimes get brought home by the cops. It must have been so scary. She's not as bad now, but she's still hard to be around. And with her medication changes, it's worse. I feel so bad for my grandpa. He's pretty much been a single parent to my mom and aunt for their whole lives, while still taking care of Grandma. He's such a nice guy. And he never complains."

"Andie told me he's pretty much on his own," James told her. "That must be so hard. I wish there was something we could do to help,"

"Well," Sally said, "what would be nice is if you could come with me some time so I can go visit my grandpa at their apartment. I mean, some people find my grandma to not be that bad sometimes. Maybe you can chat with her while Grandpa and I talk, or maybe even he and I could go out and get an ice cream or something. Really, Jamie, she's much better when her medication isn't messed up, like it is right now."

James nodded. "I think I could do that," he told her. "I mean, since I know what's going on now, I wouldn't get freaked out when she starts talking a blue streak. I could take it for an hour or so, once in a while."

"Yeah, you just smile and nod at her," Sally said. She smiled warmly at James. "Thank you so much for offering, Jamie. Maybe we can try it out in a few weeks and see how it works out. And you'll get to see the house we lived in until I was four."

"Wait," James said. "Grandpa Irving and Grandma Fran were the grandparents you lived with when you were little? For some reason, I assumed it was your other grandparents."

"No," Sally explained, "it was my mom's parents. They actually own the house. They rented out the bottom floor, and we lived together on the top two floors. After we moved out, they moved into the middle floor, and rented out the top one. They did so well with the rental, they ended up buying a few more triple deckers in the neighborhood. That's how Grandpa was able to stop working and take care of Grandma Fran." She paused. "Now you can see why my parents were so motivated to save money and buy their own house!"

They had reached the school playground and sat down on the swings. They swung for a few minutes, enjoying the feel of the air against their faces, and then sat and swayed back and forth. Sally didn't seem to want to talk about her grandmother anymore, so James let it go.

"Have you asked your parents about prom yet?" he finally asked, trying to sound like this wasn't the foremost thought on his mind.

"No, I would have told you," Sally reassured him. "But I'm planning to soon. I'll let you know immediately after I talk to them."

"Good," James said, jumping from his swing and offering Sally his hand to help her up. "No matter what happens," he said, taking her in his arms, "we'll have a great time, I know it."

"I know," Sally said, resting her head on his chest and inhaling his scent deeply. "But it would be even better than great if we can pull this off." She looked up at his face. "Jamie, thank you so much for coming to meet my crazy family. It's good that you've met them all now and know all of our deep dark family secrets. And you're still here!" She smiled at him.

He smiled back. "Sally, they're your family," he told her. "You've met my family. It's not like we're the Waltons or anything. I mean, remember what Howie was like the day you met him? And you still stuck around. Everyone has stuff in their families they'd rather not have to deal with. But it would take much more than that to make me walk away from you. And by that, I mean, nothing would make me walk away from you." He wrapped his arms tightly around her, rested his chin on her head, and said softly, "I'm not going anywhere."

"I'd Do Anything For You"/Oliver!
April 23, 1985, prom countdown 4 days

Sally caught her mother on an evening after dinner when she was reading in the den while Andie and Josie were watching a video on the Bachmans' new VCR. Mr. Bachman was in Pennsylvania on his work trip. Sally knew her mother was in her most pliable mood when the baby was in the house. Also, since her father was gone, they could not outnumber her.

"Hey, Mom," she said sweetly as she walked in the room through the kitchen.

Mrs. Bachman looked up from her book. "That's your 'hey Mom I want something' voice," she said suspiciously.

"Well, I do," Sally said honestly. "I want to talk to you about prom." Andie's head popped up and she shot Sally a look. Sally gave her a "don't worry, I've got it" look back.

"What's the plan?" her mother asked.

"Well," Sally started, "as you know, the prom is Saturday night," she said, sliding on to the couch between her mother and Andie, "and it's gonna be a late night. So, Traci and some of the other girls are renting a room at the Marriott with their dates so we can have a safe place to go after the prom, and I was wondering if maybe I can spend the night there with them? That way you don't have to worry about me coming home really late, and I don't need to worry about having to come home really early."

Her mother looked at her with concern. "Spend the night in a hotel? Is there going to be drinking going on?"

"I don't know, Mom," Sally said, "but to be honest with you, there might be some. But Jamie and I aren't gonna drink anything. You know about his brother and his grandfather. We've been making smart choices, Mom, I promise. I think we'd be safer in a hotel with our friends than we would be on the roads late at night."

"Mom," Andie interjected, "not to try to give you any parenting advice, but you've met these kids. They're good kids. And you know James will look out for Sally. He wouldn't put her in any situation that would make her uncomfortable. And besides, you let me stay over with friends for my junior prom."

"But that's different," Mrs. Bachman said. "You were older. . . ."

"No, I wasn't," Andie reminded her. "I had just turned sixteen in October, and Sally's gonna be seventeen in like four months."

"Three and a half months," Sally corrected.

"Quiet, Salamander, I'm trying to help you here," Andie said as the baby curled up sleepily in her lap, sucking her thumb. "I went to the prom with Richard, and you trusted me with him. Sally deserves to have a great time at her prom, too."

"I don't know . . ."

"How about you have her call you when she gets there?" Andie suggested.

"Yeah," Sally agreed. "I can call you when we get there, and then I can call you in the morning, too. Jamie and I might want to do something in the morning, like go out for breakfast, or hang out."

Mrs. Bachman pursed her lips and looked down at her closed book. "Well," she finally said, "if you call me when you get there. And you call me if for some reason something doesn't feel right. I'll come and pick you up, no questions asked."

Sally smiled widely and jumped up to her feet. "Oh, thank you, Mommy!" she said. She threw her arms around her mother's neck and kissed her cheek. "Thank you so much! It's gonna be the best night!" She started to skip toward the dining room so she could go upstairs to call James from her room.

"Wait a second, young lady!" Mrs. Bachman said sternly. "Go through the kitchen, not the dining room. You know better. And this is all depending on what Dad says when I talk to him tonight." She smiled with some resignation and looked at Andie, since Sally had already gone through the kitchen and into the hallway. "But I'll make sure he says yes."

"You're a good mom," Andie told her mother.

"So are you," Mrs. Bachman answered. "But please, look after your sister. I worry about her growing up so fast. Don't let me regret this."

"You totally won't regret this!" Sally yelled from the stairs. "I'll get all A's for the rest of the year and next year and I'll clean the cat box every night!"

"No, she won't," Andie said.

A few seconds passed, and Sally yelled back down the stairs. "By the way, who the heck is Richard?"

"I Can't Wait"/Stevie Nicks
April 24, 1985, prom countdown 3 days

"I can't believe the prom is only three days away!" Michelle squealed when they sat down for history class the next morning.

"I know!" Sally said excitedly. "Three excruciatingly long days!"

"They'll go fast," Michelle assured her. "And then you'll feel like you need more time!"

They laughed. "So you tried on your dress again to make sure the alterations were good?" Sally asked her friend.

"Yeah, and it's perfect! I just need to get some new makeup. Then I'll be ready."

"And Joey picked up his tux?" Sally asked.

"Yes," Michelle answered. "Did James?"

"Yes! I can't wait to see him in it!" All around the room, the talk was about the prom. The juniors were making last-minute plans, and one girl was crying to her friend because her boyfriend had broken up with her just days before the prom. Sally couldn't imagine how bad that must feel.

"So I can't believe you and James are having a sleepover Saturday night!" Michelle said in a hushed voice. "It's like you're living together for a night! It's so exciting!"

"I know!" Sally responded. "Sometimes I can't believe it's real! Sometimes I can't believe any of it is real!"

"Can you imagine what it would have been like if you had stayed at Gearhart?" Michelle asked, her eyes wide.

"Bite your tongue!" Sally said. "But y'know, the weird thing is, if I had never gone to Gearhart in the first place, none of this would have happened, so in a way, I guess everything happens for a reason."

"I have no idea what things would be like for me, either," Michelle agreed.

The second bell rang, and conversations trailed off.

Mr. Gregg looked up from the newspaper on his desk. "What?" he said. "Nothing left to say about the prom?" The students laughed lightly. "Okay, let's get started. And just to let you know, I will not be assigning any homework this weekend, as I understand many of you probably won't be doing it anyway." Now the class applauded, and there was some chatter. Mr. Gregg raised a hand. The chatter stopped. "Okay," he said, "It's not prom yet. Open your books to chapter 14."

Sally felt like dancing through the halls between classes but restrained herself. She couldn't stop thinking about how things had turned out. And she thought about her classmate and her unfortunate breakup. She thought she would just die if anything ever happened to her and James. She couldn't imagine her life without him now. And she could never imagine herself with anyone else. She knew statistically the deck was stacked against people spending the rest of their lives with their high school sweetheart, but she also couldn't discount the connection she had with James. It was more than love, more than sex. They were best friends and soulmates. They deserved to be together. She didn't think any of their friends felt like she and James did about each other, not even Chris and Rhonda. She didn't see that kind of connection when they looked at each other. She hoped her friends would find their soulmates. She wished they could all be as ecstatically in love as she was with James.

Right on cue, she saw James walking toward her. His expressionless face broke into a huge grin when he saw her, and it felt like they were approaching each other in slow motion. She had a brief fantasy of running into his arms, and him lifting her and twirling her around, like a princess in a Disney movie. She laughed to herself and thought, *This is what it must feel like to be on drugs!*

They walked the last few feet to English class together, holding hands. Mrs. Clark looked up, caught Sally's eye, and smiled. *Even Mrs. Clark can see I'm happy,* she thought.

After lunch, they said goodbye for the day. Sally and Michelle were going to Filene's after school to shop for makeup. Since Luigi's was closed for the day for kitchen repairs, James was going home on his own.

"You Dropped a Bomb on Me"/Gap Band

When James walked into the den from the front door, he found Howie sitting on the couch, staring at the TV, but the set was turned off. He barely looked up when James walked in. James's mind went to the worst-case scenario, as he had seen Howie zoned out on the couch before, many times.

"You okay, Howie?" he asked cautiously.

"What?" Howie asked, looking up as if he had just realized James was there. "Oh, hey James, yeah, I'm good."

James sat on the other end of the couch and faced his brother. "You don't look like you're good, Howie. And you barely ever call me James. What's going on?" he asked.

"Oh," Howie responded, looking at his hands. "Well, I just came from therapy. Just some stuff." He looked up at James, a determined look appearing on his face. "Jimmy, I was actually waiting for you to get home so we could talk." He paused and took a deep breath, then exhaled. "Remember when I first got clean, I told you my therapist told me it might take like six months or so to, like, figure things out?"

"Yeah?" James said.

"Well, I'm starting to talk some of that stuff out with her now, and it's pretty hard to deal with. My therapist thinks it's a good idea to share some things with mom and dad and you and Erin, because you're, like, my support system, and I'm kind of worried that once some stuff comes out, things won't ever be the same again. Kind of like opening Pandora's Box, you know?"

"Howie," James started, "how bad could it be? I mean, we all knew you'd been using drugs, and we knew about the trouble you got in when you were in school, and when you stole our stuff. How much worse could it be?"

Howie looked down again. "Worse, bro, much worse."

James shook his head. "I mean, the only things I can think of that could be worse is you telling me you committed some horrible violent crime, or that you're gay or something."

Howie looked at him and chuckled. "Well, Jimmy, I can tell you this much," he said. "I have never committed any horrible violent crime."

James felt his skin grow cold as he began to understand what his brother was saying. "What?" he asked. "Oh my God, Howie! How long have you known?"

Howie pretended to count on his fingers. "Well," he said, "let's see. I started using when I was twelve. So, when I was twelve."

"Twelve?" James exclaimed. "Howie, that's a long time! How come you never told me?"

"James, I was a twelve-year-old boy who started having sexual fantasies about his best friend, another boy, getting naked with him," Howie admitted. "I didn't know what was going on. It was 1977. There wasn't much information out there for seventh graders. I thought there was something really wrong with me. And I was scared. And you were only nine, bro. I couldn't talk to you about it. And then one day a ninth grader offered me a hit off his joint on the playground, and suddenly, none of that stuff mattered any more. The problem was, every time the pot wore off, the fear came back. After some time, I think the pot is what caused the fear, but it was way too late by then. I barely remembered why I started. So, I moved on to the harder stuff, and the rest is history."

"Howie," James said softly. "I'm so sorry. I wish I had known. I wish I'd been older. I could have been there for you, so you could have known it was okay with me. I mean, you're my brother. I love you, no matter what. I mean, I don't really get having feelings like that, but I guess I'm not really supposed to."

Howie laughed bitterly. "Yeah," he said. "That would totally complicate things with your super serious girlfriend."

James laughed tentatively. "Howie," he said, "I know this is really hard for you to talk about, but I don't have any problem with it. This guy I knew at DeMarco is gay. He told me about it, but he never told anyone else. I never told anyone either. He goes to Murphy now, so I don't know if anyone there knows. Sometimes the kids at school can be really awful about people being different, so I'm guessing there are a lot of other people at school who are gay. But I don't care about who people like to go out with. Sally won't care, either. She doesn't care about things like that, and she already really likes you, no matter what."

Howie looked at James seriously, traces of fear in his eyes. "No, dude," he said, "you can't tell her. Okay? You can't tell anyone. Not Sally, not anyone. Especially Mom and Dad."

"Howie," James insisted, "you're gonna have to tell them at some point. Otherwise, you'll be living a lie all the time, and that's not fair."

Howie shook his head. "I know. I've been living the lie for like eight years. But I can't tell them now. I'm not ready. I'm not strong enough yet. I don't know when I will be. But until then, this'll be our little secret, okay?"

"Okay," James promised. "Not a word to anyone. I swear. I'll totally leave it up to you when you're ready to tell them. Are you gonna tell Erin?"

"I don't know," Howie said, falling back on the couch. "I mean, I might. I'm taking the bus down to Providence on Friday for the weekend. Did you know that?"

"I might have heard something about that," James answered. "You know, Erin's in college. She would probably be cool to talk to about this. She won't judge you."

"No," Howie agreed. "The only thing she judges me for is my lack of academic success."

James nodded. "Yeah," he said, "same here. But that's changing for both of us." He paused to gather his thoughts. "Howie," he said, "please make sure to be careful, okay? I mean, it's just not safe out there with, y'know, AIDS going around and everything. They talk about it on the news all the time. It's horrible. You know, you gave me some condoms that one time because you wanted me to be safe, and now I want to make sure you're all right, too, okay?"

"Hey, little bro, I got it covered," Howie reassured him. "I'm not involved with anyone, if you must know, and they say that it's not a good idea to start a relationship this early in recovery. I haven't always made the smartest choices, though, so I've been to get tested just to be sure. Twice. I'm all good."

James felt a wave of relief. "Good," he said. Then he added, "Howie, I'm so sorry I've given you such a hard time for so long about not having a girlfriend. I didn't mean anything by it. I was just teasing you."

Now Howie's laugh was genuine. "Dude, it's okay," he said. "There was no way you could've known. And you were just getting back at me when I was teasing you mercilessly. Remember the sixteen-year-old virgin jokes? Brothers do that stuff. And I have been with a lot of girls over the years. Sort of like a ruse, you know, to fool myself and other people that I was, well, not different. I could do that when I was using drugs with no problem. But not anymore. I'm done with that now."

"Good," James said. "I don't want you to have to be someone you're not, Howie. I really like you a lot better since you've been clean. You've been like a real big brother. You're not a bad guy under all that straggly hair."

"Hey, I'm gonna have Mom give me a haircut tonight, actually," Howie said. "And for what it's worth, James, you're turning out to be kind of a good guy, too. And thanks for not getting all, like, weird on me and stuff about this. I wasn't sure which way it would go. But I'm glad we talked."

James smiled at him. "Me too. You're welcome."

"Hey, let's watch TV now, okay?" Howie requested. "I've had enough serious talk for one day. And I want things to look normal when Mom gets home."

"Okay," James agreed, and he stood up to turn on the set.

"Hold Me Now"/Thompson Twins
April 25, 1985, prom countdown 2 days

James picked Sally up at home at eight on Thursday morning. He was relieved to see her. It made the heavy conversation from the afternoon before seem like a distant blip on his radar screen. He wanted to talk to her about Howie, to process how he was feeling, to tell her about his fears for his brother, and to figure out how he could help him, but he had sworn to keep it to himself.

And this was prom week. Sally had to be his first priority. She was the most enthusiastic prom-goer he could have imagined, and her spirit was contagious. He wanted to take notes on every little thing she did and said when she was this happy, so he could replicate it later. If he was going to take a class on Sally, he wanted to get an A+. Thinking about Howie's revelation would have to wait until after prom.

James had known Michelle, Darlene, and Kim since he was five. He had never seen them get excited about much of anything that didn't involve partying or getting out of school early. But spending time with Sally had turned them all into prom monsters who spent all their time talking about their dresses and makeup, and especially their dates. Traci was also looking content all the time, thinking about going to the prom with Dougo. The girls as a whole reminded him of Marsha Brady on *The Brady Bunch* episode where she was fixated on Davy Jones from the Monkees. He had yet to hear any of the girls say "he's so dreamy" about their dates, but he wouldn't be surprised if they were saying such things when the boys weren't around. It made him grin to think of his lifetime friends in this way.

Sally came out of her house and then bounced into the car like she was on a trampoline. James couldn't help but laugh, and she joined him as if they were in on a joke together. James wanted to hold her, but she didn't look like she could be contained at that moment. He waited until they got to school. When she got out of the car, he walked around to her side and caught her. He wrapped his arms around her waist and held her. She stopped vibrating from prom excitement and put her arms around his neck. He held her as they leaned against the car, every now and then tightening his grip to hold her closer.

She pulled her head away slightly, still smiling. "Is everything okay?" she asked.

"Yeah, everything's good," he answered. "I just wanted to hold you for a bit. I missed you last night."

"I missed you too." She let him hold her some more, and he breathed in the aroma of her hair.

"Tes cheveux sentent la fraise," James said into her ear with a perfect accent.

Sally pulled away. He could see the wheels turning in her brain. "Strawberry. Hair. I'm not sure what the verb is . . . wait a minute. 'Your hair smells like strawberry!' Jamie! Where are you learning all this French?" She looked at him in astonishment. "Are you taking some sort of class outside of school or something? You can't be! I would know!"

"Sally," James replied with an impish look in his eyes, "a magician never reveals his secrets!"

Sally shook her head and smiled contentedly, coming back into his embrace. "You do have some sort of weird magic effect on me," she admitted.

"Sally," he said into her neck, "I am so excited for Saturday night. For the prom, I mean."

Sally laughed. "Jamie, I know you're excited about prom. But I think you're more excited about Saturday night. Don't worry, I am, too!"

James stroked her hair quietly. Then he told her, "The best part, well, besides the obvious, will be waking up with you in the morning after sleeping with you all night. I can't imagine what it will be like to sleep together. Like will we curl up together all night, and will your feet feel cold if they touch mine?"

Sally giggled. "Or your feet," she said. "We can wear socks if we need to."

"And when we wake up, will we lie in bed together talking, or will we want to make love, or will one of us get up . . ."

"The answer to all of these questions and more will be revealed on Sunday morning," Sally promised. She looked up to kiss him and he looked down. They kissed like that until it was time to go in.

As they walked to the entrance, Sally turned to James. "Jamie, it's always going to be like this for us, right?" she asked. "I mean, we're always going to be learning new things about each other, trying new things together, stuff like that?"

"Yes, it will always be like this," James promised, clutching her hand.

Sally nodded. "Good. That's what I thought."

"Sally, you should come over my house after school today," James told her. "I mean, I have to work tomorrow night, and the next time I see you will be when I pick you up for prom. Come over and hang out with me."

"I can do that," she agreed. "We can finish up our homework, so we don't have to worry about it over the weekend, and then chill out for a bit. I've been so hyper about the prom for the last few days, I could use a bit of Jamie distraction!"

"You Got Lucky"/Tom Petty and the Heartbreakers

They got through their classes, and after school, headed to the Newells'. When they went inside, there was someone in the den. A man with short, neat brown hair, wearing a blue long-sleeved button-down shirt and crisp new blue jeans. He had a slim waist and a build like James's. He picked a denim jacket up from the couch and turned toward them, and Sally was surprised to realize it was Howie.

"Howie!" she said, going to give him a hug. "You got your hair cut and new clothes! I didn't even recognize you. You look great!"

Howie beamed. "Hey, Sal. Thanks! I got my mom to give me the Jimmy Junior cut last night. Then she took me out to get new clothes that actually fit me. If you haven't noticed, I may have put on a few pounds now that I'm, like, eating every day and stuff like that."

Sally did notice that Howie's jeans now fit him well, and his ribs no longer poked through his shirt. His skin had cleared up and his eyes looked bright under his long, dark lashes. He had been home for almost four months, and he was starting to show the healing effects of his mother's love and home cooking.

"You guys," Sally said, looking back and forth between them, "I can actually see now that the two of you look like brothers. Jamie, you're pretty much Howie with blond hair. If one of you dyed your hair, people might think you were identical twins!"

James looked at Howie critically. "Yeah, I guess I can see it somewhat," he agreed. "We do kind of look alike, Howie. I'm so sorry about that, man." They all laughed.

"Well, I have to take off for my English class, and then I'm going to an AA meeting," Howie said, "so I'll most likely be out late. Sally, I'm leaving tomorrow afternoon to go to Brown, so I won't be able to see you two all ready for prom. Take lots of pictures for Mom and Dad. Stay out of trouble. And have a great time. I'll see you Sunday afternoon, okay?"

"Bye, Howie," Sally said. "Have a great time in Providence. Tell Erin I said hi."

"Dude, come walk me out," Howie told James as he flipped his backpack with his schoolbooks onto his shoulder. James followed Howie out the door and to the sidewalk in front of the street.

"What's up?" James asked.

"Nothing much," Howie told him. "But I'm pretty sure I know why Erin suddenly invited me to visit her this particular weekend. And I'm pretty sure Mom and Dad are smart enough to figure it out, too. Just make sure you don't give them any reason to catch you guys when they get back. Mom knows every inch of that house. She'll know if something doesn't look right."

James grinned. "It's a risk I'm willing to take," he admitted. "But thanks for the advice." He looked Howie in the eyes. "And thanks for everything else, Howie. You know, for trusting me, and having my back all the time."

Howie nodded. "You know how it is, brothers for life, Jimm . . . James."

They clasped each other in an embrace. Hugs were feeling much less awkward now. Howie pulled away, still grasping James's forearms. "You've got something special with Sally," he told him softly. "You hold on to her. She makes you an even better person."

James nodded. "I'm planning on it."

Howie shifted his backpack to the center of his back and stepped away. "So, you guys need anything for Prom? Some money? Condoms? New dance moves?"

James laughed. "Nah, we're good," he said. "Thanks, though, Howie. I hope you have a good time in Providence. You deserve it."

Howie snickered, "I'm guessing not as much a good time as you guys will have here! I'll see you Sunday night." With that, he started toward the city bus stop to go to school.

James went inside and closed the door. "What was that all about?" Sally asked.

"Oh, just some brother stuff," James told her. "Happens more now that he's back home and sober."

Sally smiled. "Yeah, it's so great that you finally got your big brother back," she agreed. "Maybe he'll meet someone out in Providence."

"That would be nice," James replied. "I hope Howie meets just the right person when he's ready." He wanted so badly to tell her about Howie, but he knew it still wasn't his decision.

James and Sally sat at the dining room table and finished their homework, including anything due on Monday. With their work behind them, they could stretch prom out until at least Sunday afternoon.

Mr. and Mrs. Newell had rented the video *Vision Quest* the previous night and hadn't returned it yet, so James and Sally decided to watch it. James laid on the couch facing the TV, and Sally laid in the crook of his arm. Mrs. Newell came home and found them on the couch but told them not to get up. She was going to the kitchen to start dinner. And Sally must stay and eat with them. And no, she didn't need any help, thank you, it was just Manwiches. So James continued to hold Sally while the movie went on. It was a coming-of-age film about a teen wrestler. Sally laughed when one wrestling opponent told another with a bloody nose that he couldn't hold his mud.

"No one talks like that," she objected.

When the movie ended, Sally stood and stretched. James admired her from his position on the couch, then he followed her lead. They went to the kitchen and offered to make a salad for dinner. While rinsing and cutting vegetables, James and Sally talked about the movie. They agreed the story was decent, but there wasn't enough development of the plot. James thought the characters and acting were good, especially the supporting cast. Sally agreed but still felt she didn't care much about what happened to everyone in the end. Mrs. Newell, who had also seen the movie, listened as she cooked. After the discussion ended and there were a few moments of silence, she turned to them.

"It's fascinating to watch the two of you interact," she told them. "You both have opinions, and sometimes they're not the same, but you take time to listen to each other. I've seen you do this before, too, like when you're working on a homework problem and get different answers or debating what you want to do on a Saturday night. I enjoy watching the two of you work things out. You have a way of communicating that's unlike a lot of married people I know. You really impress me. You are wonderful together and it's a privilege to be a witness to your relationship as it keeps growing."

While Mrs. Newell spoke, both James and Sally had stopped what they were doing to listen. Sally was speechless. She put down her paring knife, walked to the stove, and gave Mrs. Newell a hug. She could feel tears rising but tried to stifle them.

"Thank you so much for saying that, Mrs. Newell," she said after releasing her from the embrace. "It just, well, it means everything to me to hear you say that."

She could see Mrs. Newell also had some dampness in the corners of her eyes. "Sally," she said, "I'd like you to call me Julia from now on. That's what my friends call me."

One of Sally's tears escaped and rolled down her cheek. "Okay, Julia," she said.

James watched this exchange in silence. His mother was not an overly emotional woman. She'd had to deal with many difficult things in her adult life and often had to hide her true feelings to support and console others. But here she was, sharing her feelings and her thoughts with the girl James loved. It was a true endorsement that he had the right mother, and the right girlfriend. Once he knew they were done talking, he stepped over and gave his mother a hug.

He whispered one word into her ear: "Thanks." That one word from a seventeen-year-old boy to his mother said it all.

As this scene was unfolding, Mr. Newell had let himself into the house and found them in the kitchen. "Mmm, Manwiches," he said, looking at the stove. "When's dinner?"

"In about fifteen minutes, dear," Mrs. Newell responded, still looking at her son.

Mr. Newell read the room. "Did something just happen in here right before I came in? Jules, you sound like you're about to cry, and Sally has tears on her face. Junior here looks like he's in a trance. What's going on?"

"Mom says Sally can call her Julia," James told him.

"Oh, well, that's nice. Well, Sally, I've always been okay with the idea of you calling me J.D. Mr. Newell was what they called my sorry excuse for a father."

Sally smiled and another tear ran down her face. "Thanks, J.D."

Mr. Newell opened the refrigerator and took out a bottle of orange juice. "Hey," he said, grabbing a tiny glass out of the cabinet, "have any of you tried the New Coke yet? I had one at work today. It's not good, not good at all."

After dinner, James drove Sally home. She was quiet and studied her fingernails for some time. "Jamie," she finally said. "Do you feel like we're at some kind of crossroad or something? It's like all the sudden, people are noticing us as a couple, and they have nice things to say about it. It feels like we might be coming to the end of something, and the beginning of something else, but I don't know what. We're juniors in high school. We can't really do anything drastic. I mean, if we're gonna stay together, we're gonna have to be patient for a long time before we get to the next step in our relationship."

James contemplated her words. "Yeah, you're right," he said. "I mean, it's not like we're gonna get engaged or married anytime soon. We're still kids, and we still want to be kids. So, what's next? Years of waiting until we can do those things? Or do we figure out some other plan, so we don't go crazy until we get there?"

Sally smiled, relieved James caught on to exactly what she was trying to say. "Well, at least we have another homecoming, and then senior prom, then graduation next year. Graduation will be new."

"And when we're in college, we can spend the night together any time we want in our dorm rooms." James said.

"And then after we're done with college, we can do whatever we want."

"We can buy a house."

"We can get a couple of cats."

"But we would also have to get a dog."

"So, we would need a house with a big fenced-in yard."

"We can stay out all night."

"Or we can stay in all night."

"Even better."

"We can build a treehouse for our four kids."

"Our two girls and two boys."

"It'll have to be a big treehouse because I'll want to go in it, too."

"We'll need lots of lumber."

"I can write a book."

"I can cook us dinner every night."

"Everyone will come to our house for the holidays because of your amazing cooking."

"But we can go to a playground if it all gets to be too much."

"We'll have our own swing set in the backyard, so we won't have to go too far."

"And we will never ever have to make love in a car again."

"Amen to that."

"The Most Beautiful Girl"/Charlie Rich
April 26, 1985, prom countdown 1 day

On Friday, the area by the junior lockers was buzzing. Boys were talking to their friends about their grand plans with their dates for prom, and girls were talking about the same thing but also about their dresses and shoes. Sally was torn between wanting to spend every minute with James and wanting to talk about prom with her friends. She decided to compromise by doing both.

"It's tomorrow!" Michelle exclaimed as she slid into her seat next to Sally in history class. "And it's still happening! Even Joey's getting excited, and it's not even his prom!"

"That's totally awesome!" Sally agreed. "I hope everything goes as planned for all of us."

"I wish I had alone time with Joey like you have with James," Michelle lamented. "I mean, I don't know if I want prom night to be, you know, the big night for us, but it would be nice to have the choice."

"I don't know," Sally warned, lowering her voice. "That seems like it would be a lot of pressure for your first time. Maybe you shouldn't even think about that so you're not, like, preoccupied all night."

"You're probably right," Michelle agreed. "Plus, I don't think I would want anything to happen in front of Dougo O'Leary and a bunch of gawkers. Gross."

Sally laughed. "Yeah, no better way to get yourself a great reputation around both schools."

Class started and Sally's brain was missing in action. She tried to focus her brain on Mr. Gregg's voice and follow his pattern of words, but it was hopeless. She hoped she at least looked attentive.

English class was worse. James's breath seemed unusually seductive on her neck, like he was deliberately trying to distract her with his sexy air. The skin on the nape of her neck was tingling below her ponytail, and the electricity was traveling down her spine. After class ended and he touched her lower back as they walked out of the room, she felt she might swoon.

They ate lunch with their friends and solidified plans for picture taking and dinner before prom. Sally and James made eyes at each other while the others talked about their limo ride and crashing at the hotel. James's parents were flying out that afternoon and would be gone by the time he got home. And Howie was getting on the bus around the same time to go to Providence. James had the time after work and the next morning to clean his room and prepare for Sally's stay. He wanted everything to be just right for her.

They kissed at the door to the school before Sally left for the bus to go to Michelle's house so they could practice their prom makeup. "The next time I see you," Sally whispered in James's ear, "you'll be looking amazing in your tux, and I won't be able to keep my hands off you."

"And you'll be wearing your dress and looking more beautiful than any other girl in the school," James told her. "Maybe the world."

"More beautiful than Cindy Crawford?" she teased.

"Well . . . actually, she's not really my type," he assured her. "Too tall. Too much forehead. You have exactly the right amount of forehead."

Sally smiled. "Forehead. Jamie, you always know just the right thing to say."

"I Just Can't Wait"/The J. Geils Band
April 27, 1985, prom day

Sally felt like she popped right from being asleep to being wide awake. She didn't remember having fallen asleep the night before. She never thought she would fall asleep, but sleep was merciful. She opened her eyes and looked at the ceiling for a few minutes before it occurred to her it was prom day. She jerked her head toward her nightstand to check the time on her clock radio. It was 10:54 a.m. She had a lot of time, but it would go fast. She had to paint her nails, shave, take a shower, do her hair and makeup, and finally, put on her prom dress. She couldn't imagine getting married was any more stressful than prom, and brides had attendants to help them. She jumped out of bed, used the bathroom, and ran down the stairs to make herself some breakfast. She knew she needed nutrients to get through this day. There was a note on the table saying her parents had gone out to buy groceries. Sally was relieved to be home alone.

Next on the agenda was a call to Michelle. "How did you decide to do your hair?" she asked her.

"Blowing it out and curling the bangs back, lots of hairspray," Michelle told her. "What've you decided?"

"I don't know yet!" Sally admitted. "I kind of want to do a French braid, but I'm worried if it doesn't come out well, I'll have to take it out, and then my hair will be ruined!"

"Well," Michelle said, "then you'll just have to wet it down again."

"But I'll already have put gel in it!"

"So you'll wash it again! It will be okay! Can't your mom help you?"

"No! She doesn't know how to French braid! I should have arranged to have Andie come over to help me get ready, but now she has other plans." Sally sighed. "I don't know if I've ever been so stressed out!"

Michelle sighed, too. "You're telling me!"

They hung up the phone agreeing to check back again later for moral support.

Sally went up to the bathroom she shared with her parents and turned on the tub to shave. She used a generous amount of her father's foamy shaving cream. She was extra careful not to cut herself, because she didn't want to have to wear a Band-Aid under her nylons. She had thought to buy two pairs of nylons in case she got a run in one while putting them on, but she didn't have an alternate plan for Band-Aids.

When she got out of the shower, she could hear her parents moving around in the kitchen, putting away groceries. The sound of their banter traveled up the stairs, sounding so normal and everyday that Sally found it irritating. She felt like they couldn't possibly understand the stress she was under. She tried to remind herself they were teenagers once, too, but the thought of her mother getting ready for prom was too hard to imagine. She pictured her mother as she was now in a prom dress and laughed aloud.

James vacuumed the entire house, except for Howie and his parents' bedrooms and the kitchen. He drew the line on mopping the kitchen floor, but he did clean the bathroom. He cleaned his room and dusted his desk and dresser. He pushed the two twin beds together and put on clean king-sized sheets. He gathered pillows for Sally to use. Instead of shoving his dirty clothes and sheets in the hamper, he washed, dried, and put them away in his drawers, only afterward thinking this might make his mother suspicious when she got back. He wanted to make his room look warm and inviting, so he searched the house for candles. He found some under the kitchen sink in his father's emergency kit, but they didn't speak to the mood he was looking for. He pulled on sweatpants and drove to CVS to buy some votives. He picked up a lighter at the cash register. He threw in a pack of spearmint gum for good measure. Then he drove to the bank and withdrew a large sum from his car savings account and ran an important errand before heading home.

When he got home, it was only noon. He had woken up way too early, and now he wasn't sure what to do with himself. He took his tux out of his closet and draped it over his bed. He decided to iron his shirt, although it didn't really look like it needed it. The smell of the steam from the iron was reassuring. When he finished, he hung it on the hanger and back in the closet. He sat on his bed and thought about what to do next. He couldn't think of anything. So he turned on the TV and watched cartoons. After a bit, he turned it off and went to the kitchen to make himself a turkey sandwich. He noticed his right leg was jiggling in what he knew was a sign of impatience and anticipation. Finally, he couldn't stand the sound of silence in his house for one more second. He picked up his phone to call Pete to invite himself over to play video games. Murphy High's junior prom wasn't until the next weekend, and it was early enough for Pete to have just gotten out of bed for the day. James grabbed his keys and headed out the door toward some welcome distraction.

Sally was still getting annoyed with her parents' voices, and she didn't know why. She chalked it up to being a sixteen-year-old girl with hormones and then had a moment of panic that maybe that meant she was about to get her period on prom night. She quickly remembered she was taking birth control pills, and she no longer got unexpected periods. But that didn't ease her nerves.

"Sally, would you like me to make you a salad for lunch?" her mother yelled up the stairs to her. "I'm making one for myself, and I could put some aside for you."

"I'm not hungry," Sally grumbled down to her. She wasn't hungry, but it was a nice gesture, so she forced herself to say, "but thanks."

She had a towel wrapped around her head, and another around her torso, and she still wasn't sure what to do with her hair. She finally decided to try the French braid. She shook her hair loose from the towel and combed it straight. She put some gel in her palms and rubbed them together. She flipped her hair, and worked the gel into every strand, blew it dry, then combed again. Then she combed off three sections in the front, stood in front of her mirror, and braided. She pulled it out and started again twice. Finally, she was finished, and looked at herself critically in the mirror. It looked good in the front. She used a hand mirror to see the back. It looked perfect. She pulled a few strands out on either side of her face and planned to curl them with her curling iron and spray the whole thing with hairspray after she got dressed. She decided to give the back a spray now so she wouldn't mess it all up.

She looked at her dress hanging up on her closet door. It was a beautiful pastel pink taffeta with a sweetheart neckline, and small, off-the-shoulder sleeves that lay flat against the top of her arms. She had opted out of the puffy look for prom: puffy hair and puffy sleeves. She knew that most of the girls at the prom would have both, but it was high maintenance, and she didn't want to have to think about how she looked during the actual prom. Her dress had a tapered waist and flared to below her knees. She had been told by several people that she had attractive legs, so she had decided against a floor-length gown. She had bought high-heeled white pumps with straps around the ankles to round off the outfit.

She wasn't ready to put her dress on yet. She had about an hour before Jamie would pick her up and her mother would take them out to the yard to take pictures. Then they would drive to Kim's house and take group pictures before the limo picked up the others to go to dinner. After dinner, they would all go to the school, and after that, the hotel. And after that . . . she shivered with glee at the thought.

She put on her bathrobe, painted her nails with frosty pink polish, then walked carefully down the stairs so as not to snag a toe on the carpet. She approached her mother in the kitchen and asked her to clip her pink bow onto her braid in the back. Mrs. Bachman was impressed by Sally's braiding skills. To reward her mother's assistance, Sally agreed to a small bowl of salad with chicken and mandarin oranges. She ate gingerly, constantly aware of her drying nails.

Finally, she was ready to get dressed. She brushed her teeth, gargled with mouthwash, and went to her room to start to apply her makeup. She put pink and purple shadow on her eyelids after circling her eyes with black eyeliner. She then added a thick coat of black mascara and curled her lashes with her curling contraption, which reminded her of a medieval torture device. Remembering how much Jamie enjoyed it on their first date, she smudged a bit of sparkle gel over both temples. She brushed on blush but waited to put her lipstick on until Jamie arrived. It would be the one item of makeup she would bring to the prom. Next, she took her heated curling iron and pressed spirals on to the tendrils of hair on the sides of her face. She covered her face and doused her head with Mink hairspray. She loved the way it smelled but didn't want to entirely mask the smell of her strawberry conditioner.

She put on the pair of sexy underwear she had bought at Victoria's Secret especially for prom, along with her strapless bra. She looked in the mirror and smiled at her profile. Then she took the dress from the hanger. Checking first to make sure there was no makeup residue on her hands, she held the dress at the shoulders and stepped through the top. She pulled it up and over her chest, then put her arms through the small sleeves. She reached back to pull up the zipper, and it got stuck about three inches from the top. She had to hold the whole thing up and trudge down the stairs to ask for help.

Her father saw her coming through the dining room and smiled. "You look beautiful, honey," he said. "Even with bare feet."

"Thanks, Dad," she said, smiling. "But my zipper's stuck. Can you help?"

She turned around and he pulled the zipper down an inch then back up to the top. It fit nice and snug. She turned to her father then did a model twirl.

"James won't know what hit him," Mr. Bachman promised.

Sally thanked him for his help, then ran through the dining room before her mother could see. It was prom day. Some rules just didn't apply.

It was time to put on her nylons, and she worried over any sharp edges on her fingernails. She carefully pulled up one side, then the other. No runs so far. She got a bottle of clear nail polish to put with her lipstick to stop any runs later. Then she grabbed her second pair of nylons and put them in her tiny purse, too.

She gently slipped her pumps on her feet and fastened the straps. She put small gold hoop earrings in her first piercings then her peridots in the second. She thought of wearing her peridot necklace too but decided against it. She wanted to keep it simple. She clasped on her plain gold chain. Now she was done.

The last thing she did was pack her overnight bag. She put in a change of clothes, her toothbrush, makeup remover, pill pack, and eyeliner. She didn't think she would need pajamas for bed, but at the last minute, she added a nightshirt for the morning. She also packed a warm pair of socks, in case of cold feet. She giggled to herself remembering that conversation with Jamie.

She took her bag and her purse and started downstairs. James would be there soon. She grabbed the white crocheted shawl she bought to put over her shoulders if it got chilly and then went to find her parents in the kitchen.

"Mom, are you sure you have enough film in your camera?" she asked. She grabbed her camera from the table and remembered she needed to bring the camera and extra film with her, too, so she could have Kim's mother take pictures for her. All the girls were bringing theirs.

Mrs. Bachman looked up from her newspaper at Sally. "Oh sweetie," she said. "Look at you! Jake, come look at Sally."

Sally rolled her eyes as her parents gushed about how she looked. "Thanks, you two," she said, "but Mom, the camera!"

Mrs. Bachman held up an extra package of film she had bought for the occasion. "I think I've got it covered, sweetie."

"Here Comes My Girl"/Tom Petty

The doorbell rang, startling Sally. She was ready, but she wasn't quite ready for James to be there. "Dad," she said, "can you get the door?"

"Sure thing, honey," he said, walking through the dining room. Sally could see her mother about to say something, but she stopped her with a look. Sally could hear her father and James greeting each other at the door, and her father complimenting James's tux. Now she couldn't wait any longer. She walked across the dining room and into the front hall, and they were face to face at last.

They stared at each other for several seconds without speaking. "Wow, Sally," James finally said, reaching for both of her hands with both of his. "I said you'd be the most beautiful girl in the world, but I'm gonna have to change that to the universe."

Sally smiled brightly. "Jamie, you look absolutely amazing."

They had both forgotten Mr. Bachman was there. He cleared his throat. "Well, I'll go get Phyllis for pictures," he said, stepping back into the dining room.

As soon as he left, James went in for a kiss. He kissed her gently and tenderly, adjusting for her high heels, which made her two inches taller but still two inches shorter than him. They finished their kiss as Mrs. Bachman arrived with the cameras.

"Oh, James," she said. "You look wonderful! Just look at the two of you, with your matching outfits! I'll get copies of the pictures I take for your parents."

"Thanks, Mrs. Bachman," James replied, still sporting a dumbfounded grin, still looking at Sally and holding her hands.

"Let's go outside in front of the rhododendron bushes, and we'll start there."

"Jamie, would you mind putting my things in the car first?" Sally asked, and she handed him an overstuffed small purse, her shawl, and an overnight bag. He started to get a fluttering in his stomach, thinking about the overnight bag.

While James was gone, Sally doubled back to the kitchen to get his boutonniere from the refrigerator. She met him out on the stoop. He was carrying a plastic box containing a wrist corsage with pink and purple flowers. Sally could smell the aroma of a summer bouquet. She ceremoniously pinned the boutonniere to his lapel, and he slipped the corsage onto her left wrist. Then they kissed to seal the transaction.

Finally, they were taking pictures, some with them beside each other, some with James in back with his arms around Sally, some in front of the bushes, and some under the blooming crabapple tree. Some cars driving by beeped their horns at them when their drivers saw them in their prom attire. When they were satisfied with the shots, they went inside to say goodbye to Mr. Bachman. Sally gave her mother a hug and promised again that she would call when they got to the hotel.

Then, they were off to Kim's house to meet up with their friends and take more pictures. They felt like movie stars headed for the red carpet.

They arrived at Kim's house, the last couple to get there. Michelle and Joey, Traci and Doug, Chris and Rhonda, Darlene and Charlie, and Kim and Carl, who had made a prom pact the previous year if neither had a date lined up, were all milling around the yard, chatting, when they arrived. The girls all gathered in a group and raved about each other's dresses and hair, and the boys made fun of each other's tuxes, but good naturedly. Finally, Kim's mother was ready to take pictures. She took all their cameras, then lined them up by couples, then the girls, then the boys, then the whole group together. Everyone had smile fatigue by the time they were done.

The limo pulled up at five, and the couples all gathered their belongings and made their way to their vehicles to head for the restaurant. Darlene and Charlie also took their own car, so James and Sally didn't feel so conspicuous not going in the limo.

They had a reservation for dinner at Tony's Italian Cucina at five thirty. James and Sally got in the Cruiser and followed the crowd in the limo. The restaurant was packed, and there were several long tables filled with their prom-going classmates. The volume level was loud, and the air was warm with the heat of young bodies congregating. The waitstaff rushed busily from floor to kitchen and back. James kept a tight arm around Sally as they made their way to their table. He was glad he wasn't working at Luigi's with their prom crowd that night. All the work and probably half the tips from high school students, if they remembered to tip at all.

They were both quiet during dinner but still enjoyed listening to the conversation and responding when they had something to say. The food was good. Just as good as Luigi's but not better. James got a tiramisu for dessert, and Sally got a creme chocolate. She let him have a taste, which reinforced for James that it was truly a special night.

When the bill was paid, James reminded his friends of what he did for work, and everyone chipped in several dollars for the tip. Then they were ready to go, and they headed for the parking lot. The group found their limo among several and piled in. James and Sally went to the Cruiser and settled into their seats.

"Ah, quiet at last!" James exclaimed. They sat and listened to the silence a few moments before starting for the school. When they parked in the side parking lot, Sally turned to face James.

"Are you ready for this?" she asked him.

"I think so," he said and smiled at her.

"Only two more things to do before we get to go home," Sally sighed.

James liked the way she said "go home." They got to go home together that night, and although he looked forward to their night of dancing, he could hardly wait.

"Hold Me, Touch Me"/Kiss

When they entered the gym, hand in hand, they were amazed to see prom was nothing like homecoming. The prom committee had gone all out to make the gym into a magical ballroom. The class had voted on the prom theme, and much to Sally's delight, they had chosen Prince's "Purple Rain," rather than the popular Journey "Faithfully" or Styx "The Best of Times" themes that many schools had gone with for the past two years. There were purple and silver balloons littering the floor and others floating in bunches and tied to the backs of chairs. The chairs were surrounding small tables covered with silver tablecloths and sprinkled with purple and silver glitter. At the center of each table was a large jelly jar filled with strings of purple lights, casting a warm glow on the students sitting there. There were empty champagne flutes circling the top of each table with the words "Purple Rain, McKinney High Junior Prom, 1985" applied to the front as favors. Strobe lights, purple and white, crossed the room and shone on the walls, while the disco balls from homecoming spun from the ceilings.

There were students on the dance floor, groups talking among themselves on the periphery, and others sitting at tables with finger foods. There was a table set up for voting for prom king and queen, with other fun categories such as Most Likely to Make a Fool of Themselves on the Dance Floor, Most Outrageous Outfit, and others. James and Sally agreed to take a good look around before casting their votes to see who best fit each category. Since they had just come from dinner and didn't want to snack yet, their only other choice was the dance floor. They stood to the side, listening to the music for a while, and when "One More Night" by Phil Collins came on, Sally pulled James out to the floor.

They held each other close, the strobe lights crossing purple and white light above, below, and across their formally clad bodies. James could feel Sally's head leaning heavily against his chest as they danced. Toward the end of the song, she looked up at him and mouthed the words to the bridge, as Phil Collins sang of following his love if she went away. James kissed her then held her tight until the song ended.

It went this way for most of the dance. One of them would hear a song they liked and bring the other out to dance. Other times, they would dance in a group with their friends to something that was particularly popular or easy to dance to. The DJ played "Thriller," and a few boys attempted to moonwalk. Some tried some other breakdancing moves, but they weren't very skilled. Sally got some good ideas about who to vote for in the category of making a fool of oneself on the dance floor. James mostly enjoyed the slow dances. He had learned over time that Sally took music seriously and could get emotional while listening to songs she really liked or could relate to. He liked to hold her close during these songs or watch her face as she felt the music.

After a while, they stopped to rest and get some punch. They got their ballots to vote for their classmates and filled them out. Sally voted for the most popular couple in their class for prom king and queen because everyone else would and she knew they would win. She voted for Chris and Rhonda for the cutest couple. She and James compared their votes, laughed over some of the funnier categories, then folded their ballots and put them in the box.

They grabbed some food from the small buffet. Sally found an empty table, and they sat down to eat. Soon, Michelle and Joey came to join them. "Having fun?" Sally asked Michelle.

"Yes!" Michelle exclaimed "I can't believe they made this place look so amazing! I almost feel like Prince might walk through the door any minute playing his guitar!"

"I know!" Sally responded. "It's perfect!" She leaned closer to her friend. "But I think my bra is starting to fall down," she said more quietly. "Come to the bathroom with me?" Michelle nodded, they made their excuses, and walked toward the hallway.

James was left sitting with Joey. Joey grinned at him. "Sally looks hot tonight," he said.

James smiled slightly, nodded, and responded, "Michelle does, too."

"Yeah, she's cute, huh? I think she got contact lenses just for tonight. I mean, I think she still looks hot in glasses, but it's nice to be able to see her eyes up close." He checked the room for chaperones then discretely took a flask out from the inside pocket of his tux jacket. "Want some?" he asked James.

James shook his head. "No, thanks, I'm driving."

"Glad I'm not," Joey responded and tipped the flask into his punch cup. James was glad to see he didn't add any to Michelle's cup without asking her before slipping the flask back into his jacket.

Sally fixed her bra, and Michelle made use of the facilities. Then they stood in front of the mirror touching up their makeup. They talked about how much fun they were having dancing with their friends and boyfriends, especially the slow dances. Then they heard a flush in one of the stalls, and the door opened. Kathy Marie D'Angelo stepped out and walked to the sinks. She looked up at Sally.

"Sally," she spat out.

Sally looked at her with no expression. "Hi, Kathy Marie," she responded coolly.

Kathy Marie turned on the taps. "I see you're here with James," she said. "So you're still together?"

Sally exhaled hard. "Of course we're still together," she said. "Are you here with Chad?"

Kathy Marie nodded. "Yeah," she answered. She paused. "He told me that he invited you to Amanda's birthday party last fall," she said. She squinted. "I don't want you getting any ideas about him wanting to go out with you, or even hanging around with you anymore. He's not interested in you at all."

Sally shook her head and snickered. "Kathy Marie," she said, "Chad asked me out, not the other way around. And if he didn't tell you, I'm the one who turned him down. I wasn't at all interested. I'm with Jamie, and it's gonna stay that way. You have nothing to worry about. Well, maybe you need to worry about Chad asking other girls out to parties without you knowing it, but you have nothing to worry about from me."

Kathy Marie sneered. "I'd better not," she said. She grabbed at the paper towel dispenser then dried her hands. She turned on her heels and walked out of the bathroom.

Sally and Michelle looked at each other for a moment, and then they both started to laugh. "I'm scared," Michelle teased. "How about you?"

Sally shrugged. "I wonder if she had been waiting all night to run into me so she could set me straight," she said. "Good thing she did, too. I can't believe she would think I was even interested in that jerk!"

Michelle nodded. "I actually think it's not you she doesn't trust," she said, "It's Chad. But it makes her feel better to turn it all around on you so she doesn't have to be mad at him. C'mon, let's head back." They went out the door and headed back to their table.

Sally walked up to James and gave him a kiss then sat down beside him. "Michelle said everyone is talking about leaving in about a half hour to go to the Marriott," she told him. "Does that sound okay to you?" James nodded his approval. They had already been there for close to two hours, and he felt they might be getting close to the maximum of the fun they were going to have at the prom.

When the first notes of "Purple Rain" came on, everyone got up to dance. It was slow even for a slow song, and James held Sally tight, only pulling away to kiss her. She rested her head contentedly on his chest. As soon as the song ended, the DJ put on Madonna's "Crazy for You." James knew Sally loved the song. He continued to move her around the floor, dodging other couples, as they clasped their arms around each other. Their friends were also dancing in couples around them. Kim had her head resting on Carl's chest, and Carl was smiling his biggest, cheesiest smile. James felt it was the perfect prom moment.

When the song ended, the junior class president, Rob Novak, got the microphone from the DJ. He tapped it twice, causing feedback to come loudly over the PA system. Everyone reached for their ears simultaneously. "Sorry guys," he said. "Alright, we've tallied your votes, and we're about to get started with our award ceremony, so if you could all move away from the dance floor, we can get this show on the road!" The juniors applauded and moved to the side and toward the tables.

"Okay, first category, Most Likely to End Their Night in the Back of a Police Car . . ."

As Rob called out people's names, the recipients came forward to get their trophies. Each one was fashioned to match the category it was awarded for. Rich Franklin got a toy police car, and Sam Johnson got a Michael Jackson action figure for his breakdancing skills, or lack thereof. The crowd cheered, clapped, and laughed along.

"Okay," Rob said as he got toward the end of the list, "we'll get to our prom king and queen soon. But first, everyone's favorite category, the coveted McKinney High Junior Class Cutest Couple, or in the case of these two, 'The Couple Most Likely to be Married with Three Kids by the Time of Our Tenth Reunion.' Let's hear it for Sally Bachman and James Newell!"

Sally and James looked at each other in astonishment. They heard the crowd applaud and cheer, and their friends urged them to go get their trophy. They clasped hands and self-consciously walked toward Rob and the microphone as the DJ played the chorus to the Spandau Ballet song "True."

When they got there, Rob looked at James and said, "Go on, give 'er a kiss!" The crowd cheered, and James reached over and gave Sally a quick kiss on the lips as a camera flashed. Then Rob handed Sally their trophy, which was a ceramic wedding cake topper with smiling bride and groom figures. They posed for the yearbook photographer while holding up the trophy then started to make their way back to their friends.

"Oh, my God," Sally said to James as they crossed the floor. "Us? I mean, of course I think we're the cutest couple, but the whole junior class? I didn't even know they knew my name!"

"Mine either," James admitted. "But we are pretty cute, though. I guess people noticed!"

Sally laughed. Their friends congratulated them, and the boys slapped James on the back. The king and queen of the prom were announced, but Sally didn't hear it. They weren't her friends, anyway. She looked at the cake topper and shook her head in disbelief. Most likely to be married with three kids by their tenth reunion? Okay, she would be okay with that.

As they drove to the hotel, James reached for Sally's hand and asked, "Was it everything you hoped it would be?"

Sally smiled at him. "It was!" she said. "It was great! I loved that they played so many slow songs!"

James smiled back. "I liked that part, too."

"Did you have fun?" Sally asked.

"I really did," James responded. He thought he could probably have fun in a mosquito infested swamp if Sally was with him. But the fact that there were no biting flies in the school gym was an added bonus.

"So, do you think we should have told them they got it wrong?" Sally teased. "It should have been four kids, not three!"

James laughed. "By our tenth reunion?" he asked her. "That would make us twenty-eight. We might need a few more years than that. Maybe the fifteenth reunion?"

"True," Sally agreed. "But it would be fun to try!"

They met up with their friends in the lobby of the Marriott. Dougo checked in, and they headed toward the elevator to go to the third floor. Some of the boys were carrying gym bags or backpacks James assumed were filled with beer or other alcohol. He worried security was going to stop them to check their bags. He felt they all stuck out like sore thumbs in their tuxedos and prom dresses, but there were a lot of prom-goers moving around beside their group. They were left alone. He held on tightly to Sally's hand so they wouldn't lose sight of each other in the group. When they entered the room and all settled down on beds, chairs, and the floor, he felt more at ease. As soon as Sally found the phone, she called her mother to let her know they had arrived safely.

Charlie and Darlene had stopped on the way to the hotel to buy several big bags of ice, and now Charlie poured them into the bathtub. Chris and Joey unloaded bottles of cheap champagne and beer from their bags and placed them in the ice. Kim finished off by adding three four-packs of wine coolers. Some of the group had been drinking spiked punch at the prom, and now they were laughing and talking loudly about how much fun they'd had. They made comments about James and Sally's award. None of their friends had won any of the awards, so they knew they would be the brunt of the fun.

"Hey James," Carl called out from across the room where he was sitting next to Kim on the bed, "are you two gonna get started on those three kids tonight? You don't have much time!!"

"James, I always thought you were cute," Kim told him, "but now you just look like a giant teddy bear to me!"

"Oh my God," Traci added. "You need to get one of those posters with the adorable kittens with the huge eyes, and you guys can use it for your yearbook picture!"

"Sally," Darlene started, giggling, "I need to get some cuteness tips from you so I can win next year. I hope you saved the cake topper!"

Sally had wisely left their cake topper in the car. She and James were good sports and laughed along with their friends.

They held out for about an hour before reaching their capacity for making small talk with drunk people. They were both anxious to start their overnight adventure. As soon as their eyes met, James stood.

"Okay, well, we're gonna hit the road," he announced, and Sally rose beside him.

"The old married couple's gonna turn in early?" Chris joked.

"Yup, that's what we're doing," James said, stretching his arms over his head in a fake yawn. "Way past my bedtime." Sally tried and failed to suppress an amused giggle.

"Let me walk you guys to the door," Michelle offered, jumping up.

They said goodbye to their friends, and Michelle accompanied them to the hall. "Jamie, I'll meet you at the elevator," Sally said, and he nodded, said goodbye to Michelle, and headed down the long hallway.

Michelle giggled. "I can't believe you two," she said, putting an arm around Sally's shoulder. "You really are the cutest couple. I voted for you!"

"You did?" Sally asked, still feeling disbelief. "Thanks! I had no idea anyone was voting for us. That was so unreal!" She caught a whiff of champagne coming from Michelle's breath. "Are you gonna be okay?" she asked with concern. "I know you're not much of a drinker."

"Oh, I'm good," Michelle replied. "I really haven't had too much to drink. I wanna keep my wits about me. I don't want to forget anything about tonight! But you're right. I'm such a lightweight, I'm kind of tipsy, but it feels good!" She giggled again.

Sally smiled at her friend. "I'm glad you're having a good time," she told her.

"You have a good time, too," Michelle told her sincerely. "I'm so happy for you. I want what you guys have."

Sally gave her a hug. "I want that for you, too. Hey, if you get any pressure to drink more than you want, take the drink, and then pretend you need to go to the bathroom and pour it down the drain. Then talk really loudly and laugh a lot and no one will know the difference!"

"Good advice!" Michelle said. "I might just do that. Hey," she said more quietly, leaning in toward Sally. "So, what do you think? Do you think Kim and Carl will hook up tonight? They looked like they were getting cozy at the prom. And they're sitting right up against each other on the bed. It's so weird! They've known each other since kindergarten!"

Sally smiled. "I hope so," she replied. "I never really considered them together, but Carl looked so happy when they were dancing. And Kim looked so relaxed. Maybe it's not such a bad idea, ending up with an old friend."

"If anyone would know about that," Michelle said with a grin, "it would be you, Sally. Call me when you get home tomorrow, okay? I wanna hear all the details, and if I have any details, I can fill you in!" They said goodnight, and Michelle rejoined the party.

Sally hurried to the elevator, giggling to herself giddily. James was waiting for her there, and he grinned at her conspiratorially. "Ready to go home?" he asked.

She put her arms around his neck, looked deep in his vast blue eyes, and said, "I have never been more ready," and then kissed him with all her heart.

"Be My Girl-Sally"/The Police

James opened the door into a dark house. He flipped on the light in the front hall and dropped Sally's bag on the floor next to his bookbag out of habit. They stood on the threshold and looked at each other, feeling nearly as shy as they had at the motel room in November. They stepped inside and walked through the den. Sally felt butterflies in her stomach. "I think I want to go wash my face and brush my teeth if that's okay with you," she said.

"Okay," James said, and he doubled back to get her bag. "Here," he said, handing it to her. "I'm gonna go into my room and start getting out of the monkey suit. Just come in when you're done."

While Sally got ready, James went into his room, removed his tux jacket, and lit the candles he had placed on different pieces of furniture around his room. He put Phil Collins, YES, and U2 albums in a stack on his turntable and flicked the start switch. He turned the volume low. He started to loosen his bowtie. Sally walked into the room slowly, looking around. She had taken off her jewelry, shoes, and nylons and had taken her hair out of her braid. Her usually straight hair hung in front of her shoulders and down her back in crooked waves. The candles cast shadows on her face, giving her a look of alluring movement while she was standing still, looking at him. He walked over to her, gently lifted her chin with his fingers, and softly kissed her on the lips. She kissed him back, and quickly their shyness fell away. James pushed the door closed on impulse, although no one was home, not even the dog.

Soon they were at each other's clothes, letting them fall to the floor by their feet. James paused to admire Sally's new black lace underwear and show his appreciation. Soon they were part of the clothes pile. They made their way to the bed and fell upon it gratefully. James held her hair in his fist, and he pushed her head closer to his, hungrily tasting her mouth.

The candles continued to flicker as they moved on the bed, and James began to kiss her neck then her body. He was determined to repay her for what she was willing to experiment with on him in November, the last time they had access to a real bed, and to show her there was no part of her body that was off limits to his kisses. She voiced her surprise and approval, and even giggled a bit as she helped him locate just the right places. Now she held his hair in her fist and guided him along. At one point she made a noise James couldn't interpret. He lifted his head slightly and said, "Do you want me to stop?"

"Oh, no," she replied, "please. Don't stop. That's good. Keep doing that. Please. Jamie."

He resumed what he was doing, and soon, he felt her hips rise and she pushed his head closer to her. "Right there," she said. "Keep doing that. Don't move." And soon, she was throwing her head back and making all the sounds he knew meant she was very satisfied.

"Why don't you get on top of me?" she finally asked, and he complied. They moved slowly and faster, and she continued to make those contented noises. Soon he was joining her in feeling contented and fulfilled, and eventually they slumped onto the bed together, breathless.

A little later, they were lying still and breathing hard. They both felt all the tension and anxiety of the past few days leading to prom run out of their fingers and toes as they lay together, limbs tangled under the sheets. They didn't say a word, they just breathed, listened to the soft music, and watched the flickering of the candles. James touched his fingertips to Sally's fingertips, and their hands lingered in the air as they watched them cast shadows on the wall.

"Jamie," Sally said softly. "I think you're gonna have to do what you did there every time from now on. I have never felt that way before. It was absolutely amazing. Like earth-moving amazing."

"I will," he promised. "I'll do anything you want me to." James noted to himself that when Sally had an orgasm first, the rest of their time together was incredibly intense. He vowed to himself to always attend to her needs first.

The Phil Collins album ended, and the YES album dropped down. James finally broke the silence. "Sally?" he said softly.

"Yeah, Jamie?"

"I love you."

"I love you, too, Jamie."

"I have a present for you."

Sally looked at him. "You do?" she asked. "What for? It's prom, not my birthday."

James smiled. "Do you want to see it, or do you want me to make up a reason?" he teased.

Sally propped herself up higher on her pillows. "See it!" she insisted.

James slipped out of bed, reached into his top dresser drawer, and withdrew a medium-sized jewelry box. He handed it to Sally and then crawled back into bed next to her. She looked at him quizzically. Then she opened the top.

"Oh my gosh," she said, looking inside. She pulled out a thin gold-linked chain. Attached at the center of the chain were three small solid gold hearts in a row. In the middle of the left heart was a small peridot, and in the right, a reddish orange stone. The heart in the middle displayed a tiny diamond.

"The green one is your birthstone, and the other one is topaz, my birthstone," James explained. "That one's on the right side because when you put it on, it'll be on the left, over your heart. And the diamond is a promise."

"A promise?" Sally asked, staring at the light reflected on the beautiful charm.

"Yeah. Not too long ago, we were talking about how because we're still in high school, we have such a long time before we can, you know, get to the next level in our relationship. But I don't want to wait. I know how I feel about you, and I know how you feel about me, and I think that means we can make a promise to each other. A commitment. Like, that we will stay together. And that someday, we will get to the next step. This isn't just a fling, Sally, this is the real thing. And I promise you, as we get older, things will only get better. And that one day, we can go to bed together every night, and wake up together every morning. Every day. Even if you have cold feet when you sleep."

He waited to see tears, and he wasn't disappointed. One rolled down her cheek, passed over her chin, and landed on her bare chest. He wiped it away. "Jamie, you had this made for me? I don't know what to say," she said. She handed him the chain, turned away from him, and lifted her hair so he could clasp it around her neck. She turned around and kissed him hard then held him to her for a long time. Finally, she pulled away and looked in his eyes. "I love you so much, Jamie. This, this is everything."

They lay on the bed wide awake, cradled in each other's arms, listening to the music for a long time, until finally the last album dropped. It was U2, and the song was "A Sort of Homecoming." Sally and James looked at each other, smiled knowingly, and soon, by silent consent, they were kissing, and they made love again, skipping no steps and making sure each of them was thoroughly satiated. Finally tired, they lay still.

"Sally?" James said.

"Yeah, Jamie?"

He faced her, propping his head on his hand. "So, my parents usually rent a cabin at Webster Lake for two weeks in the summer, but this year, my dad's got access to the Aries company's beach house in Newport because he's a manager now, and we're going in early July."

Sally felt her stomach flip. "So, you'll be gone for two weeks this summer?" she asked.

"Well, I'll probably just go for one week because of work, but the thing is Sally, I want you to come, too. My parents said it's okay. You would have to bunk with Erin, and I would have to bunk with Howie, and when I say bunk, it might actually be bunk beds. It's probably pretty rustic. I was thinking, if you can come, we can go look at the colleges in Rhode Island together. There's the University of Rhode Island. They have a journalism program. And Providence College is a good school. They have a good basketball team, which I know you'd like. It's a Catholic school, but you don't have to be Catholic to go there, I checked. And then we can also go check out Johnson and Wales College. They have a great culinary program, and if you do the four-year program, you can actually get an MBA the second two years. That might be a good place for me to start looking."

"Wait, hold on," Sally said, now propping her head on her hand so she could look in his eyes. "So, you're inviting me to go on vacation with you and your family?"

"Yes," James said. "I promised after last Thanksgiving that if I went away again, I would take you with me, remember? I'm sorry, I'm getting way ahead of myself talking about what we'll do when we're in Rhode Island, and you'll need to ask your parents first."

"Yeah," Sally agreed, excitedly. "But I think they'll say yes. It's not like we'll be sharing a room or anything. And they trust you, too. Well, maybe they wouldn't if they knew what we were doing tonight, but still. They would probably love that we were going to look at colleges and that you've already been looking at some. Parents love that stuff. Y'know, though, my mom will probably ask to meet your parents first. That's just something she would do."

"I'm okay with that," James told her. "I mean, they're gonna have to meet at some point, right?"

"I didn't think about that," Sally admitted, yawning. "But yeah, if we're gonna be doing all this staying together forever stuff, they're gonna have to meet eventually. So, I guess we could try to set something up." She lowered herself onto the mattress and rested her head on the pillows.

James laid back contentedly and put his hands behind his head. "See," he said, "we can figure all this stuff out. And if we both stay in the area, we can see each other on weekends, maybe even more. Even if you decide to go to college in the Eastboro area and we're two hours away from each other."

"If the Vista Cruiser doesn't fall to pieces on the highway," Sally said sleepily, "just like my old Rubik's cube."

James looked at her out of the corner of his eye. She had her eyes closed. He got out of bed quickly and blew out the candles. Then he got back in and held her to him in spoon fashion, and soon he heard her breath become slow and even. He watched her sleep by the light coming in the window from the streetlights, until he, too, started to drift off. His last thought on prom night was that Sally's feet were toasty warm against his.

"Somebody's Watching Me"/Rockwell
April 28, 1985

The phone rang in the den, and James's eyes sprang open. He glanced at his clock. It was 10:28 a.m. He turned to Sally. At some point during the night, they had rolled away from each other, but their legs were still touching. Again he watched her sleep, the softness of her face, the relaxation of lines on her forehead. She must have felt him looking, because soon her eyelids were fluttering, and she opened them and caught his eye. She smiled. James had never understood the phrase "bedroom eyes" until that exact moment.

"Good morning," Sally said, her voice slightly raspy.

"Good morning," James said back. He pulled her to him in an embrace.

"Oh, wow, James, are you always, um, this, uh, excited in the morning?" she asked him, her eyes widening as she blushed.

"Actually, yeah, pretty much," he admitted. "But, you know, I just woke up with a hot girl in my bed, so that doesn't hurt. So," he teased, "what do you want to do now?"

"Uh, I think I want to stay right here and make the most of this, don't you?" she said, grinning and running her hands down his body.

James leaned into her and they began to kiss. They started to make love for the third time since they got back from the prom, this time forgoing foreplay in their desire to unite. Even so, they both found their morning connection to be one of their best and most satisfying encounters yet, both feeling the thrill of having woken up together and experiencing their first ever morning sex. Afterward, they stayed in bed, cuddled together, not wanting the whole experience to end. But soon, both could feel their stomachs rumbling, and they realized they could not get by on love alone. They needed food. James pulled on his boxers, and Sally found her nightshirt and underwear, and they walked through the den and toward the kitchen, making quick stops in the bathroom.

"I'm gonna make pancakes," James announced.

"You know how to make pancakes?" Sally asked.

"I know how to get the Bisquick out of the cabinet and add water and an egg," James said. "And my mom always gets the good maple syrup, like the kind she grew up with in Maine, so it will be extra special."

Sally found the orange juice in the refrigerator and got two large glasses out of the cabinet. "Why do you think they always serve orange juice in tiny glasses?" she asked. "I mean, is it literally made of gold or something? I mean, when I want orange juice, I want to have a lot of orange juice!"

James laughed. "That's a really good question, but one we may never know the answer to. But it's still worth asking." He turned on the burner and added oil to the frying pan. "Have you ever had banana pancakes?" he asked.

"Actually, yes," Sally answered. "Grandma Naomi makes me banana pancakes when I stay over there. I love them."

"I knew there was something I liked about Grandma Naomi," James said. "I will make you some banana pancakes. They may not be as good as Grandma Naomi's, but they'll be as good as Chef Jamie's!"

Sally laughed. "I can't wait!" she said. "But I will."

James poured the batter into the pan, and Sally could hear the pancakes sizzle as they cooked. After some time, James flipped them over. He got two plates from the cabinet and soon flipped the finished pancakes onto the plates. He got the real maple syrup out of the refrigerator and put the container in the microwave for twenty seconds to take the cold edge off. Then, he placed the plates on the table, sat, and they began to eat.

"Wow, Jamie, these are good!" Sally said while chewing on a bite. "I always seem to forget how ravenously hungry one gets when one spends the whole night making love!"

Jamie smiled. "I'm glad you like them. It was my plan to wear you out with sex, so you'd be hungry and love my pancakes. And it worked!"

"Yeah, it did," Sally said, smiling back. She dipped her finger in a pool of maple syrup on her plate and then smeared it on the tip of James's nose. "Oh no," she teased. "Now you're all sticky!" She grinned mischievously. "I guess we're gonna have to go right to the shower once we're done to get you all cleaned up!"

James laughed, then looked at her, all his feelings right at the surface. "Sally?" he said.

"Yeah, Jamie?"

"Will you go to senior prom with me?"

Sally laughed. "Oh, Jamie, of course I'll go to Senior Prom with you," she assured him. "But it's way too early to ask. You're gonna have to ask me again later!"

May, 1990

"Here Comes the Rain Again"/Eurythmics
May 24, 1990

It was the day of Sally's graduation from Providence College, and everyone attended the ceremony: her parents and James's parents; Andie, Derrek, and their three young children; Nate and his wife, Terry, and their infant son; Erin with her husband, Ted, and twin toddler daughters; and Howie, fresh out of his first full-time year in the pre-law program at Boston University, with his boyfriend, Dominic. It was a rainy day, and the graduates, dignitaries, and speakers sat under a canopy, but the guests had to fend for themselves against the elements.

Sally looked for James and the rest of her group in the crowd. She saw him and waved. James tilted his umbrella toward his mother and waved back. James had completed culinary school with an associate's degree two years before and now was working nights as a sous chef at a large hotel in downtown Providence while finishing his MBA program at Johnson and Wales. He would graduate after the summer term. They had both lived in their school dorms for the first two years of college, but once James had secured a decent paying job, they moved in together in a small parent-subsidized one-bedroom apartment close to Sally's campus. Sally had completed her degree in journalism with a minor in creative writing. She hadn't found a job yet, but she was applying for every writing position she could find and was feeling optimistic she would find something in her field. She was writing every day. And every day, she and James went to bed at night and woke up in the morning together.

The ceremony seemed to take forever, but eventually the speakers ended, and the handing out of diplomas began. When Sally heard her name, near the beginning of the alphabet, she walked across the stage and accepted the certificate, which was mounted on a hard-backed folded cover, sporting the university's colors of black, white, and silver. She could hear her family and friends yelling out whoops and applauding as she walked the length of the stage. The ceremony ended a half hour later after the final remarks, and she joined her and James's families out in the rain for congratulatory hugs and kisses.

James and Sally went to their apartment to change out of their wet clothing and shoes while their families went back to their hotels, with the promise everyone would meet at Oregano's, which was Sally's favorite local Italian restaurant, at six. They had reserved a whole room just for their group.

James came into the bedroom after Sally had showered and dressed and was applying gel to her long spiral-permed hair.

"Jamie," she said to him without turning around, "have you seen my promise necklace? I can't find it anywhere. I wanted to wear it tonight."

"I haven't seen it," James responded. "Where is the last place you saw it?"

"In my jewelry box," she replied, flipping her hair over her head. "I took it off before finals and put it in there. I've looked there like ten times. It's not there."

"I'll help you look after I take my shower," James said. "In the meantime, here." He handed her two envelopes, one blue and one white. "These are from our parents. They wanted us to open them together before dinner."

"Okay," Sally said, sitting on the bed and taking the envelopes. "That's weird. I wonder why they didn't want to give these to me at dinner."

James shrugged. "I have no idea," he said, sitting down beside her.

Sally opened the blue envelope first. She pulled out a card with a sappy graduation message and watercolor flowers in a field on the front. She was sure it was chosen by Jamie's mother, who liked sappy cards. She opened the card and a check fell out onto the floor. James picked it up. "Oh my God," he exclaimed.

"What?" Sally replied, grabbing the check. When she saw it, she could not believe her eyes. "Five thousand dollars??" she gasped. She looked at the card and read the written note aloud. "To Sally and to James, this gift is to be used toward a down payment on a house. Sally, congratulations on your graduation. We are so proud of you!!! With all our love, J.D. and Julia."

"No way!" Sally said. "How can they afford this? I mean, we aren't even married. What are they thinking?"

"Open the other one," James prompted her.

Sally ripped open the white envelope, which contained a card that had a cartoon cat in a graduation cap on the front. Only her father could have picked this one out. Again, a check fell out, but Sally caught it this time. "Another five thousand dollars!" she exclaimed, shaking her head. She read the card. "To our wonderful daughter on her graduation. Please use this toward a down payment on a house. We love you so much." It was signed separately by each parent, Mom and Dad.

"Jamie, we can't accept these!" Sally protested. "I mean, it just doesn't seem to be right. I mean, I was expecting maybe a new journal, or a Cross Pen set or something for graduation. This is way over the top. And both of our parents?!"

"Well," James said, "I know my parents have been putting aside money since we were kids to help us get started as adults. They helped Erin with her down payment, and I know they've been helping Howie over the years. It looks like our parents were conspiring together to get us to buy a house. Maybe they want us to make some kind of commitment or something." He smiled at her.

She smiled at him like she would at a small child who didn't know any better. "Jamie, of course we're gonna make a commitment or something," she responded. "You know that. We've talked about it for years! But you know you're gonna have to find the right moment. You're gonna have to ask me formally."

"I know," James said. "Do me a favor, Sally? Don't say anything to our parents about their gifts until after dinner, okay? I just don't want to make anything, you know, awkward."

"Okay, I promise," Sally agreed.

James reached over and embraced her tightly. He kissed her and felt her respond in a positive way. He started to lift her dress and she didn't stop him. God, he loved her so much. He hadn't lost any of his passion for her through the six years they had been together, and he poured it out for her, taking his time, knowing they had limited time, but not wanting it to end . . . but when it finally did, they held each other in a desperate embrace, not wanting to let go, even though they shared space now every day and would be together again, that night, in each other's arms. Finally, James checked the time. It was almost time to go meet their families. He reluctantly got up to go into the bathroom to shower and shave.

"No More Lonely Nights"/Paul McCartney

Things at Oregano's were chaotic. Fourteen adults and six children took up an entire room and required two waitstaff to take orders. They feasted on bread, then salad, and then delicious Italian entrees that met everyone's dietary needs. After the plates were cleared away and dessert and coffee ordered, James turned to Sally.

"Sally?" he said.

"Yeah, Jamie?"

"You know, I had an interesting conversation with your parents recently."

"Really?" Sally asked. "Without me? That's weird. When was that?"

"Last week," James answered, "while you were taking finals and I went to visit my parents, remember? So anyway, I asked them what they thought about us as a couple, you know, and if we had what it took to make it, you know, long term."

"What did they say?" Sally asked, already knowing what they would have said. Her parents adored James. Then she suddenly realized that James had started saying "you know" more often, which was something he did when he was feeling nervous. She quickly looked around the table. Everyone else had gone quiet when James had started talking, and she saw Andie and Erin shushing their children. They were all looking at James and Sally. Her heart started to pound.

"Of course, they said they thought we were great together," James answered. "They said they already think of me as family. And you know my parents already think of you as family, too. So I thought, you know, there was only one thing left for me to do to make us all officially family."

He stood up from his chair, sank down on one knee in front of her, and took both of Sally's hands in his. She gasped involuntarily.

"Sally Ann Bachman," he started, "I have loved you since the first day I saw you looking lost and confused in the hallway of McKinney High School. It only took me about three days to realize I wanted to be with you forever."

He looked at Howie, who took a small jeweler's box from his pocket and handed it to him with a look of brotherly pride. James snapped open the top and held it out to her.

"Sally, will you marry me? And please, don't say I will have to ask you again later!"

Sally's hands went up to her mouth in shock. "Oh my God," she whispered. "Yes, Jamie, yes, I will marry you. I was always going to marry you!"

James smiled widely, took the ring out of the box, and slipped it onto her procured finger. She gasped again as she got a closer look at the three-quarter-carat diamond ring in a white gold setting with two tiny diamonds, one on either side of the larger stone.

"See the little diamond right here?" James said, pointing to the one to the right. "That's your promise diamond."

Tears welled up in Sally's eyes. "My necklace," she said, reaching instinctively to her chest where it usually would lay.

"Yes, I borrowed your necklace," James confessed. "I was hoping you wouldn't notice it was missing until after tonight. But I promise I will give it back, with a new stone in the middle. I always planned to use that diamond for your engagement ring. Even when I was seventeen, I knew someday I would propose to you. Now you see why it was a promise. And I always keep my promises."

The ring fit Sally perfectly. She helped James to his feet and then kissed him hard on the mouth, ending in a joyful embrace with a bit of hopping up and down. There were "aww"s around the table, and then their family members applauded and began to congratulate them.

She faced her parents when they came to give her and James hugs. "You knew about this," she said. "You knew, you and James's parents knew he was going to propose, and you gave us down payments toward a house to start our lives together. As engagement gifts." She turned to the Newells. "You knew, too."

"Yes, we all knew," her mother answered. "James didn't ask our permission, but he wanted to let us know his intentions. And of course we gave him our blessing. And we all wanted to be part of this night."

Julia took Sally's hand and admired her ring. "I always knew you were the one for James," she told her fondly. "The two of you are a team. You can accomplish anything you set out to do together. When James told us he was planning to propose, I was so pleased he decided to include us all."

"I knew about it, too!!" six-year-old Josie yelled out, not wanting to be left out. Everyone laughed.

"So, I was the only one who didn't know," Sally said. "Jamie, I don't know how you pulled this off! You've never been able to keep a thing from me to save your life the whole time I've known you!"

James smiled. "I know," he responded. "But some things are just too important to screw up." He hugged her again and whispered in her ear, "And don't worry, Sally. Even though you didn't say it this time, I promise, I will ask you to be my wife again later, and then every day for the rest of my life."

January 2003

"Grow Old With Me"/John Lennon
January 19, 2003

"So, wait a minute," Jessica said to her father with disbelief on her face. "That's really how you proposed to Mom?"

"Yup," James answered proudly. "It was perfect. I didn't mess up at all. And your mom was happy, and everyone there was really happy for us."

"That sounds like a movie," James and Sally's middle daughter, Naomi, said dreamily. At seven, she was a big fan of happy endings.

"Yeah," answered Jessie, who was more cynical at age ten. "A really bad and sappy chick flick. Those type of things don't happen in real life." She rolled her eyes.

"Oh, yes, they do," Sally stated, balancing their two-and-half-year-old son on her hip as she walked down the stairs to join the rest of the family in the den. James Daniel, named after his grandfather, was the third generation of Newell sons to be named James, so they had nicknamed him Trey. Sally set Trey down on the floor in front of his toy shelf. "I was there," Sally continued. "I can vouch for everything Daddy said."

"Then what happened?" Naomi prompted.

"Well," Sally continued, "we got married the next April on a beautiful spring day. . . . You've seen the pictures."

"Yes," Naomi said happily. "At the barn. And Josie was the flower girl. Uncle Howie was the best man, but Aunt Andie was pregnant with Samantha, so Michelle was your maid of honor. But who was Dominic?"

"Dominic was Uncle Howie's boyfriend at the time. It was way before he went to law school and met Uncle Kevin," James explained.

"And all of our grandparents were still alive back then," Jessie said sadly.

"Yes," James agreed. "It was a long time before Grandpa J.D. died, and he had such a good time dancing with Nonna Julia at the wedding. Everyone had a good time."

"Then," Sally continued, sitting on the couch and putting a comforting arm around Jessie, "we bought this house because we loved it, and it was big enough to fill with lots of kids and it was halfway between our families and the hotel Daddy worked at. Daddy worked his way up to head chef, and then manager, and as you know, eventually we opened our own restaurant."

"Milo and Ginger's!" the girls said together, and Sally laughed.

"Yup, we named it after my childhood cats! And I started working as a writer for a magazine, then I went back to school and got my master's degree in writing. And then I wrote my first novel."

"Which we're not old enough to read yet, I know," Jessie said.

"And then we had you three," James said, "and we knew we had the best possible life."

"Did you have three kids by your tenth reunion?" Naomi asked.

"Oh, you told them about all that, huh?" Sally teased him.

"I told them everything but edited out the parts that are only suitable for adults," James promised, winking at her. "So we skipped a lot!"

"No, sweetie," Sally explained to Naomi while giving James a knowing grin. "By our tenth reunion, we had already had Jessica, and you were almost done growing in my tummy. Trey was still only a glint in his daddy's eye."

"We didn't go to our tenth reunion anyway," James said.

"Why not?" Jessie wanted to know.

"Well, Mommy was very pregnant and uncomfortable for one thing, and also because we didn't feel we needed to. We had stayed in touch with all the people we wanted to stay in touch with over the years, Darlene, Michelle, Chris, Carl, and Kim, and everyone else, well, we didn't really need to see."

"And," Sally continued, "we would rather stay at home than go to crazy crowded parties. We learned over the years that we don't need to keep trying to make big groups of friends. It makes us uncomfortable. We like spending time at home with each other, and we do better having two or three close friends nearby, kind of like you, Jessie."

Jessie nodded. She had heard this part before. "Yeah, I know. And you both figured out you have ADHD, like I have, even though you didn't take medicine when you were kids, like I do."

"I'm not like that," Naomi stated. "I like being around lots of people. It makes me feel happy. And I don't have ABCD."

Sally and James exchanged smiles at Naomi's mispronunciation. "And that works perfectly for you, sweetie," Sally told her. "Just like Grandpa Jake and Josie. Everyone has to figure out what feels right for them as they grow up."

"What happened to the Vista Cruiser?" Jessie asked.

"I don't know where it is now," James admitted. "It's probably a pile of rusted rubble in a car junkyard somewhere. But it wasn't exactly the best and most reliable car, so when I got my first cooking job, I traded it in for a new used car that had a working heater so Mommy wouldn't have to freeze her butt off every time we went for a drive in the cold weather! And we've gotten two other new cars since then."

"They have a Vista Cruiser on *That 70s Show*," Naomi said. "It's a funny name. I thought they made it up."

Sally shot a look at James. "Jamie, how does our seven-year-old know about *That 70s Show*?"

Trey, who had been quietly playing with his toys, suddenly looked up and said, "Mommy, I'm hungry. I wanna cookie and choco milk. Peas?"

Sally glanced at her watch. Close to seven p.m., snack time. "Okay, Trey. Why don't you all go to the kitchen and get your snack, and Daddy and I will be there in a few minutes. Jessie, can you please help your brother and sister?"

"Okay, Mom," Jessie replied as she jumped from the couch and scooped her little brother up into her arms. He threw his arms around her neck and held on tight.

"Saved by snack time," James mumbled.

The kids filed out of the den and through the swinging door into the kitchen. Sally got up from her spot on the couch and repositioned herself across James's lap, putting her arms around his neck. James marveled at how much Trey resembled his mother in his looks and mannerisms, while the girls looked and acted more like him. He thought all four of them were perfect.

"So how did it happen that you were telling the girls all about our great high school romance?" Sally asked him.

James smiled. "One of them, I think Naomi, finally asked me why everyone else calls me James but you call me Jamie."

"Ah," Sally responded. "Well, it's a good story, with a happy ending."

"It's not over yet," James corrected her. "You took the test without me, didn't you?"

"I did!" Sally exclaimed. "I'm so sorry, but you know me. Trey was on the little potty in the bathroom, and the box was right there. I couldn't help myself. How did you know?"

"You are literally vibrating, Sally. You can never keep secrets from me. It was positive, wasn't it?"

"Yes, Jamie, it was positive. I told you it would be positive! I know these things by now. Oh my God, Jamie, I knew it, but I still can't believe it. We're having another baby! Our fourth baby! But we have got to finish potty training Trey. I really need to have some time off from changing diapers!"

James laughed. "Oh, how our priorities have changed," he said. "Remember when we took the first test for Jessica? All we could think about was decorating the nursery and buying tiny clothes! And finding some clever way to tell our families." He held her tighter. "Are you happy about the baby?" he asked her.

"Jamie, I am so incredibly happy to be having another baby with you!" Sally exclaimed. Then she lowered her voice. "I mean, a bit freaked out, but happy. Are you?"

James smiled. "I am. Both happy and freaked out. Four babies. Even though we didn't really plan for it. It'll be our surprise package, like my Nonna had with Aunt Cecelia. Even if it wasn't by our tenth, or even fifteenth reunion."

They kissed then held each other for some time. Sally finally pulled away and faced James.

"So, Jamie," she asked, "do I have to put a parent guard on the TV for when I'm not around?"

"No," James answered sheepishly. "I have no idea how Naomi knows about *That 70s Show*. She must have been watching it at your mom's or Andie's house. They let them get away with murder when they're there. I saw Trey cut through your mother's dining room last week, and she didn't even bat an eyelash. You know, Sally, it is fun to watch that show and see the characters in the Vista Cruiser. Sometimes I miss my old monster car. You and I got a lot of mileage out of that thing for two blissful years in high school."

Sally smiled contentedly at the happy memory. Then she frowned. "Jamie, we're gonna have to get a minivan," she said, making a disgusted face.

Jamie laughed. "I can't wait to drive all around town in our snazzy new minivan!" he announced.

Sally laughed, too, and her hand automatically went to the necklace on her chest. "Oh no!" she exclaimed. "I don't have room for any more birthstones on my charm! What do you think the chances are that this baby will come on a month I already have?"

James counted on his fingers. "Pretty good, actually, if I'm doing my math right," he said. "I mean, Trey started coming into our bed right after Thanksgiving, and it took us until after New Years to get him back into his own room, so it most likely happened before that, right? So that would probably make us due sometime near the end of August or early September? We lucked out with Jessie being born in January like me, and Trey and Naomi both being born in April, so I could get you a new diamond. Maybe we'll get lucky again, and the baby will be a peridot. But if I need to, I'll get you whatever the stone is for September, and a second chain to put it on, I promise."

"And you always keep your promises, I know." Sally replied affectionately. Suddenly, she started to laugh.

James looked at her in confusion. "What's so funny?" he asked.

Sally took a deep breath. "All of the talk about the past had me thinking about what happened the day after prom at your house, when your parents walked in . . ."

". . . and we were just coming out of the shower," James finished for her. "We were both wrapped in towels and walking back to the bedroom with our hair dripping wet. My mom looked like she had walked in on a burglary! Yeah, I didn't tell that part to the girls. But it is definitely a moment I'll never forget. And then my mom went in my room and saw the beds pushed together, the candles all around, and the clincher, your prom dress lying on the floor. . . . I think I was grounded for two weeks after that."

"I was just so happy that they didn't ever tell my parents," Sally admitted. "And then they acted like you were the one who corrupted me, and actually let me come over while you were grounded, because they didn't think it was fair to punish me!"

James smiled. "Yeah, they still adored you even after they found you in a compromising position with their baby. I'll tell you, Sally, that night together was worth it. It still would have been worth it even if they had grounded me for a month. I would do it again in a second."

Sally threw her arms back around James's neck and put her forehead against his. "James Phillip Newell," she said, looking him right in the eyes, "You are the absolute perfect boyfriend for me. Will you marry me?"

"Of course I will marry you, Sally Ann Newell," he answered. "But," he whispered into her ear, "you're gonna have to ask me again later."

Fred MacMurray's Chocolate Fudge Upside Down Cake

(In my family, we called this Chocolate Pudding Cake. It's been passed down through three generations. –DMQ)

1 1/4 cups white sugar (divided use)
1 tablespoon butter
1 cup flour
1/4 teaspoon salt
1 teaspoon baking powder
1/2 cup milk
5 & 1/2 tablespoons cocoa (divided)
1/2 cup walnuts, chopped
1/2 cup brown sugar
1 & 1/4 cups boiling water

Cream 3/4 cup of the white sugar and butter. Sift together flour, salt, baking powder, and 1 & 1/2 tablespoons of cocoa. Add to first mixture alternately with milk and put into a 9-inch buttered cake pan. Sprinkle with nuts. In another bowl, mix brown sugar with 1/2 cup white sugar and 4 tablespoons cocoa. When blended, spread in pan on top of nuts. Pour boiling water on top. Bake 30 minutes at 350°F / 175°C. Turn upside down. (We left it upright in pan. –DMQ) Serves 8 to 10.

Acknowledgments

Biggest thanks to Jonathan Meltzer, my brother, marketing manager, alpha reader, and biggest believer that the McKinney High Class of '86 needed to be presented to the public. Thank you to my friend Tim Lea for being my first reader (FTR) and teaching me everything I needed to know about culinary school and other important stuff to make the story authentic.

Thanks to Adam Najberg, Eleanor Schnur Kohlsaat, Abby Meltzer, Tanya Banderet, Sandy Meltzer, and Clint Chico, for reading my book and giving me wicked awesome feedback.

To my writing group, Charlotte Redway, Liz Murvihill, Amanda Martin, Jane Savage, Melanii Lambert, Kristi Torto, and Eliza, for giving me the nudge I needed to start writing again. I cherish you all.

Most of all, I thank my husband, Al, for sitting quietly and supportively on the couch while I wrote nonstop in front of the TV, day after day after day; and my daughter, Tory, who will be happy when all of this book stuff is over and she never has to hear about any of it, ever again. I love you both.

Debby Meltzer Quick is a full-time social worker in Portland, Oregon. She has been writing for fun since age twelve. *May I Have Your Attention Please* is her first foray into the publishing world. Growing up in Massachusetts, she became a huge fan of Boston sports, especially the Red Sox and Patriots, and she aspired to be a sports reporter. She is an avid reader of fiction. She lives with her husband, daughter, two cats, and one rabbit. She plans to release at least three more books in the McKinney High Class of 1986 series.

Don't miss the next installment in the McKinney High Class of 1986 series:

I Just Can't Say I Love You

Coming in September 2023

Please enjoy the following excerpt

Chapter 1: Let's Make a Pact
SOPHOMORE YEAR, APRIL 1984

"I think the prom is stupid," Kim Drake lamented out of nowhere.

Carl Bishop was picking a tiny fleck of dried out Frosted Flake off the hem of his Black Sabbath T-shirt. "What?" he responded, looking up to find the source of the comment. Kim was sitting next to him in English class, like always. She was frowning. "What did you say?" he asked her.

"I said the prom is stupid," Kim repeated, turning in her seat to face him. She was hoping Carl would respond. She didn't want to be observed talking to herself before class. It was just weird. "I mean, I think it's stupid. It's so fake. Kids dressing up like they're going to a royal ball or something. I don't even want to go to the prom."

"Maybe you won't," Carl said, instantly regretting his choice of words.

Kim glared at him. "Why would you even say something like that, moron?" she demanded. "You don't think anyone will ask me to the prom? Why? Do you think something's wrong with me?"

Carl almost reached up to shield his face with his hands in defense. He was no stranger to being shoved hard by Kim when he said something dumb. When they were seven, she had shoved him down in the sandbox when he made a comment about her hair looking like a rat's nest, and he spent the next two days finding sand in his body crevices. She was much stronger than her petite frame let on. This time, she let him off the hook. "I didn't say no one would ask you," he said. "I just mean maybe you'll decide not to go. Maybe you'll turn down like eight guys or something."

"Yeah, right," Kim said, pouting. "That's another thing I hate. So if no one asks you to prom, you just don't get to go? That's just not fair."

Carl agreed. He had been on the receiving end of rejection a time or two, and it was no fun. And now his best friend and cousin, Chris Mahoney, had a serious girlfriend. Rhonda Jenkins. They were so happy and touchy, and it made Carl feel creeped out. Or envious. He hadn't decided yet. If he had a girlfriend, too, he wouldn't even have to think about prom next year. He would just go with her. "Maybe we can start a petition or something," he suggested to Kim. "So that anyone can go to the prom, even without a date."

"I don't think there's actually a rule against going without a date, moron," Kim said. "But I mean, who would want to even be the person to try to find that out by doing it? That would be pretty lame."

Carl thought about it. Yeah, it would be lame to go by yourself. He could see himself standing against the wall of the gym, his hands in his tuxedo pants pockets, one formally clad foot perched up against the wall, watching all his friends slow dancing with girls. No, he wouldn't go if he didn't have a date. "Yeah, maybe I won't go to the prom either."

Kim looked at him with a touch of sympathy. That was unusual. Usually, she looked at him with contempt. Carl didn't like when Kim acted unusually.

"Carl, why don't we make a pact?" she asked him.

"A pact? What kind of pact?"

"Well," she started, grasping her hands together and grinning at him maniacally. "Why don't we say that, next year, if it's getting close to prom, and we both don't have dates, we go to prom together, you know, as friends?" She seemed very pleased with coming up with this idea on her own. "That way, we both get to go, and we don't have to stress out all year about whether we'll be able to find dates."

Carl considered this. "But what if one of us gets a date, and the other doesn't? Won't that be weird?"

Kim nodded. "Yeah, but I'll try to find a friend to go with you if that happens." She laughed.

Carl glared at her. "So you're saying I'm probably gonna be the dateless one. Thanks," He scratched the back of his head, then glanced at his fingernails. "I don't know. Maybe. Yeah, okay, let's do that. Let's make a pact. I could do that. But we also have to promise that if one of us does get a date, they'll do everything they can to help find a date for the other one."

"Okay, moron," Kim agreed. "We can do that." She spit a little into her palm and held it out to Carl.

Carl didn't hesitate. He spit in his palm, and they shook hands firmly.

"Don't even think of falling in love with me or anything," Kim warned. "If we go to the prom together, it'll only be as friends."

Carl grunted. "Don't *you* go falling in love with *me*," he responded.

Kim guffawed. "I don't think we have anything to worry about, Carl," she told him. "I've known you all my life. You're okay, but you're still a moron. I could never see us as anything more than friends. Gross."

"Yeah, gross," Carl agreed. Well. Maybe not gross. But at least weird. He was pretty sure he didn't want a girlfriend whose nickname for him was "moron."

Chapter 2: Impact of the Pact
JUNIOR YEAR MARCH 1985

"So I need to invoke the pact," Kim said as she slipped into the desk next to Carl's in biology class.

"Say what?" Carl responded.

"The pact, moron, the prom pact," Kim said in an irritated tone. "I need you to go to prom with me. I don't have a date. And it's next month. It's getting too late to find anyone else."

"Why do you still want to go to the prom with me if I annoy you so much?" Carl asked.

Kim sighed. "Sorry, okay? I didn't mean to offend you. But we made a pact. Do you have a prom date? If you do, you need to find me a date, remember?"

Carl shook his head. "No, I don't have a date yet," he admitted. "I don't know if I'll find one at this point. And yes, I remember the pact. I'll respect the pact. We can go to the prom together since we don't have dates."

"How romantic," Kim mumbled sarcastically. "I can hardly wait."

"Wait," Carl objected. "Now I'm confused. You specifically told me that if we went, it would be as friends. Do friends have to be romantic with each other? Or do you want to go to the prom as actual dates?"

Kim rolled her eyes dramatically. "Friends, of course," she responded. "Okay. So, we'll go to prom together. It's settled."

"Just one rule," Carl told her. "You can't call me moron at the prom."

"Fair enough," Kim agreed. "You get a moron reprieve for one night."

"So what do we do now?" Carl asked. "Do we have to buy tickets?"

"Yeah," Kim told him. "We get tickets. We each pay for our own. And then I get a dress. And then you get a tux that matches my dress. And then right before prom, you have to get me a wrist corsage, and I have to get you a boutonniere. And we have to make plans to go out to dinner with our friends. It's all traditional. Oh, and Traci's getting a limo, so we can all go in the limo. And Dougo, her date, is renting a hotel room for after, so we can go there after and have sort of a party and sleepover, so no one has to drive home after drinking."

"Uh," Carl said, "I think you might need to write some of this down for me. That's a lot to remember. How much is all this gonna cost?"

"I don't know!" Kim told him. "You can ask Chris or James. They're going, too, so they might know. I just need to go find a dress and stuff. But you know, I think it will be fun. Going as friends."

"Yeah," Carl responded cautiously. "Fun. But it also sounds like a lot of work for one night. But all our friends will be there, so yeah, it'll be fun. But yeah, maybe still write it all down for me."

"Moron," Kim whispered under her breath. "I seriously don't know how you make it through each day."

Chapter 3: Prom Greetings

Carl straightened his maroon bow tie and smoothed out his cummerbund. He brushed a speck of dust off the lapel of his black tux jacket. He reminded himself how grateful he was that Kim had not decided to wear some bizarre or obscure color, like prune or aqua marine. His brown eyes and tan complexion looked good with maroon. At least that's what his mother told him when he'd put it on earlier. Now, she was dropping him and an overnight bag off at Kim's house before prom so they could fulfill the pact they had made sophomore year. Carl had asked one girl, Debbi Fields, to the prom, but she had politely declined. At least she hadn't laughed at him. Maybe there was a hint of pity in her eyes. He was kind of glad he was going with Kim. He didn't have to act a certain way to impress her or worry all night about her regretting her choice of dates. Carl and Kim knew each other, and well. They had been in school together since kindergarten and pretty much friends since the first time they had met at age five. He just had to ignore the fact that she found him dumb as dirt. He knew pretty clearly he was not dumb as dirt.

His cousin Chris had arrived already with his girlfriend, Rhonda. Carl joined them on the lawn, carrying Kim's wrist corsage. Darlene and Charlie, Michelle and Joey, and Traci and Dougo all wandered over to them. They had all already exchanged corsages and boutonnieres before he had arrived. Kim was nowhere in sight. They were still waiting for one last couple, James and Sally, to arrive in James's ancient Vista Cruiser station wagon. Everyone else, except Darlene and Charlie, would be traveling by limo to dinner and the prom.

The front door of the house opened, and Kim stepped out. Carl barely recognized her. She was a sight in her maroon dress with off-the-shoulder puffy sleeves. Her dark brown bangs were feathered back high off of her head, and she had curled spirals into the long back of her hair.

Her makeup and fancy accessories made her look older and more mature than she even looked yesterday at school. Her high-heeled maroon shoes gave her some height, but at a petite five-foot-two, they didn't work miracles. Carl sometimes forgot that Kim was pretty. To him, she was always just Kim.

Carl stared at her along with the rest of his friends as she walked toward them, making an entrance, but suddenly he remembered that he was her date, and he was supposed to be doing something now, too. He stepped forward and greeted her. She had his boutonniere, and she fastened it on his lapel. Then he slipped her corsage onto her wrist. They smiled at each other.

"Looking good, you two," Chris said proudly, as if he were responsible for their appearance.

James and Sally pulled up, parked, and then joined them, and they broke up into groups of girls and boys to chat as they waited.

Mrs. Drake came out to take pictures. When it was time to take couples shots, Carl slipped his arm around Kim's back gingerly, worried that he might break something on her fancy outfit. The part of her back that he touched, near her waist, was bare with a fabric cut-out, and her skin was smooth and warm. He expected her to pull away at his touch, but she stood still and smiled for her mother behind the camera.

The limo arrived, and they all left for dinner. They dined at Tony's Italian Cucina, which was crowded and hot, but still good and fun. Carl was prepared to pay Kim's bill, but she declined.

"We're here as friends, moron," she reminded him. "You're not obligated to pay for me."

Carl shrugged and did not object. He knew that once Kim decided that something was a rule, it was written in stone. Plus, he had offered. He came close to reminding her about her promise to refrain from calling him a moron, but he decided to let it go, for now.

Finally, they left for the school to attend the main event. Kim gasped as they walked into the gym and were quickly inundated by the Prince "Purple Rain" theme. The gym had been transformed by the purple, gray, and white decorations, and Carl could hear his friends making impressed noises. He milled around the gym with Kim and their friends, and when they all went out to dance, he followed. He knew dancing wasn't one of his strong points, but his group of friends didn't care, and there were others there who were far worse than him.

They danced, ate, and socialized for about two hours. Michelle's date, Joey, poured shots of vodka for everyone who wanted from a flask he had carried into the building in his inner tux pocket. Later, Chris produced a flask from his pocket and shared. Carl wondered when everyone had suddenly gotten flasks. He felt himself getting a slight buzz and decided to pace himself. There would be beer and champagne at the hotel after. He didn't want to be the guy who vomited in the limo.

Soon, they all started to discuss heading out to the hotel. But first "Purple Rain" came on, and everyone went out to the floor to dance to the prom theme. Carl took Kim's hand and led her to the floor, and they danced close in the crowd. Carl could smell her perfume. It smelled flowery. Next, the DJ played "Crazy for You," and Carl felt Kim relax in his arms. She pressed her head up against his chest. He felt the taffeta of her dress and the warmth of her skin, and he smiled. He liked the feeling of dancing close, and Kim was just the right height to nuzzle below his neck. He couldn't see her face, buried in his tux, but he felt she was enjoying the dance. He let his body move freely to the music.

Before they left the dance, the class president, Rob Novak, announced class awards, leading up to the announcement of the prom king and queen. To no one's surprise except the recipients, their friends James and Sally won the Cutest Couple award. Carl had never seen anyone look so horrified to win anything, but James and Sally were both very private people. He envied their closeness and their sureness about their feelings for each other. They never had any doubts that they were right for each other. Carl hoped that someday he would feel so sure that something was just right.

When the awards ended, they all headed for the exits. They were going to the Marriott for the night. The limo dropped them off in the loading and unloading zone, and Charlie and James parked their cars in the parking garage. Doug O'Leary, who everyone called Dougo, checked in. He was over eighteen and was legally allowed to rent a hotel room. Carl guessed that any of them probably would have been able to get away with renting a room, but Dougo gave them a sense of legitimacy, especially with their parents.

The room was crowded with the six couples and only two full-sized beds. They all found places to sit. Carl and Kim were able to find space on one of the beds and sat next to each other, shoulder to shoulder. Soon, Carl went into the bathroom to get himself beer and a wine cooler for Kim from the stash on ice in the bathtub.

Everyone was in a good mood, and no one was too drunk at that point of the night to participate in conversation. They drank and joked around for about an hour. Everyone teased James and Sally for winning their award, and everyone, including the lucky couple, laughed along. When James and Sally got up to leave for James's house, the tone of the party changed. Everyone got up for more drinks. Michelle and Joey found their way into a corner and started to make out. There was more room on the bed now, but Kim still sat pressed against Carl. He was watching her, making sure she was okay. She was pacing herself with her drinks, and Carl was glad. He wanted to be able to have fun without having to worry about peeling Kim off the floor the next morning.

Kim was smiling. He could tell she was having a good time. He was, too. Kim was being nice; she had danced with him to all the slow songs and had been willing to touch him without starting to gag. He had enjoyed touching her, as well, and remembered the smoothness of the skin on her back. He wondered what it would feel like to touch it again. He resisted as long as he could, and when their drinks were nearing empty, he reached out lightly and brushed his fingers against her. "I'm gonna go get us another drink, okay?" he said. He felt slight bumps rising on her skin. She didn't pull away.

"Okay," she said.

He rubbed his fingers together on the way to the bathtub. He hadn't realized how erotic back skin could be. He shook his head back and forth. He had to shake out these thoughts. This was Kim. She felt more like a sibling to him than his own brother. He could not allow himself the luxury of thinking of her in any other way. Even if he could think of her that way, she would never allow those thoughts to become reality. He needed another drink.

When he came out of the bathroom, he could see Kim still sitting on the bed, laughing at something that Traci had just said. Her laugh caressed his ears, and he blinked his eyes slowly. Kim looked beautiful tonight. There was no denying it. She was hot. And he was touching her back skin just minutes ago. He thought of how he might be able to do that again.